FAMILY SHADOWS

Further Titles by Rowena Summers from Severn House

ANGEL OF THE EVENING
BARGAIN BRIDE
ELLIE'S ISLAND
FAMILY SHADOWS
HIDDEN CURRENTS
HIGHLAND HERITAGE
KILLIGREW CLAY
SAVAGE MOON
THE SWEET RED EARTH
VELVET DAWN
A WOMAN OF PROPERTY

Writing as Jean Saunders

GOLDEN DESTINY
THE KISSING TIME
PARTNERS IN LOVE
TO LOVE AND HONOUR
WITH THIS RING

FAMILY SHADOWS

Rowena Summers

This first world edition published in Great Britain 1995 by
SEVERN HOUSE PUBLISHERS LTD of
9–15 High Street, Sutton, Surrey SM1 1DF.
First published in the USA 1995 by
SEVERN HOUSE PUBLISHERS INC., of
595 Madison Avenue, New York, NY 10022.

British Library Cataloguing in Publication Data

Summers, Rowena
  Family Shadows
  I. Title
  823.914 [F]

  ISBN 0-7278-4830-5

All situations in this publication are fictitious and
any resemblance to living persons is purely coincidental.

Typeset by Palimpsest Book Production Limited,
Polmont, Stirlingshire
Printed and bound in Great Britain by
Hartnolls Ltd, Bodmin, Cornwall.

For Geoff,
as always

Chapter One

There was a glorious sense of serenity over the whole countryside that spring evening. It was as if the entire county was ready to embrace the new season with welcoming, open arms. The air was perfumed with wild flowers; and in the sky above, there was only the glitter of the myriad stars to disturb the heavens. It was a night to make even the most staid of married women feel like a young girl again.

Morwen Killigrew Wainwright was nowhere near to fitting the former description yet. To her, it was just a romantic, perfect night for loving . . . but even as the thought danced through her head, she knew there was something that had to be discussed and aired with her husband before considering such delights. She glanced at him across the splendour of the drawing room and spoke determinedly.

"What are we going to do about Bradley?" she said.

Even as she said it, she felt an odd sense of unease. It was as though she was hearing the words drop like pebbles in a pool, whose ripples would spread out and linger long after the moment.

She knew she was being over fanciful, but she also knew that the question had been left too long unsaid. She sipped her glass of hot gingered chocolate, seeing the heavy frown darken her husband's handsome face.

He barely looked up from studying his newspaper, the flickering gaslight in the room accentuating his strong features. And for a moment, Morwen marvelled that while she had thought this night so magical, here was a man who saw nothing but the black and white print of a miserable newspaper.

1

"The children's behaviour is supposed to be your responsibility, honey," he drawled, using the term that Morwen had once found so charming, and which now seemed to be spoken more with sarcasm than anything else.

If there was anything guaranteed to rile her lately, that was it. And he knew it. It was as though he took great enjoyment out of seeing her fume. She had never been one to suffer fools lightly, and Ran was nobody's fool.

She put down her glass on the side table with a clatter. Sometimes, Ran frustrated her beyond words. There were even times when she felt she didn't know him at all. Times when, remembering how the stubbornness of her first husband's last years had tormented her so, it seemed, eerily, than Ran was turned out of the very same mould. It was hard to credit. Ben Killigrew and Randall Wainwright had seemed so different from one another, and yet . . .

And those times when Ran's irritability ate away at her, were times when she longed so guiltily for Ben's very Cornishness, instead of the hard business brain of the American she had later married. It had seemed wonderful beyond belief to have found such love twice in a lifetime, but maybe such good fortune was more than any one person deserved, and there was bound to be a reckoning . . . The unease of such a thought made her bite the inside of her cheek until she winced with the self-inflicted pain.

But a sudden surge of nostalgia for those far-off days took her unawares. They had been so alike, she and Ben; born into different classes, but still born of the same hardy stock and the same background. They belonged. Cornwall was in their blood, as it had never been in Ran's, and never would be, as she had discovered too late.

The impatient rustle of the newspaper jerked her thoughts back to the man seated opposite her now on the elegant sofa. When had he changed from the vital and dynamic man she had married, she thought, in some amazement. Or was it Morwen herself who had changed, sitting back and letting her man take over the running of the clay works that had once been her life, and simply failing to acknowledge how single-minded was the cancer of ambition in him?

2

"All right, let's have it." He practically snapped out the words. "You want me to thrash Bradley's hide for some petty misdemeanour, is that it? He's nine-years-old, for God's sake, Morwen. He's feeling his feet and growing robust. You should know about treating boys differently from girls, and giving them some leeway when they start growing up. He'll not thank you for turning him into a mummy's boy."

"I would never do that! I didn't do it with Walter or Albert, did I? Nor with Justin. I won't have you accusing me of being soft with the boys, Ran!"

To her fury, he dismissed the names as carelessly as if he was swotting flies on the wall.

"Walter and Albert were never your boys in the true sense of the word. You raised them, but you never gave birth to them, did you? Nor to Primmy, who's turning into a precocious little madam, if you want my opinion. They were never yours, Morwen, so you can't take the credit for the way they turned out. And as for your own pair, Justin and Charlotte—"

"I certainly think I can!"

She bridled at once. She'd heard enough, but for now, she could ignore his scathing reference to her natural son and daughter. But she felt sharply defensive at this dismissal of her surrogate motherhood of the other three.

"Ben and I took them in and brought them up as our own, and they wanted for nothing. Ben saw to that. He was the best father they could ever have wanted. You know that!"

She didn't miss the derision that came into Ran's eyes at this. He'd had little time for her first husband, and Morwen didn't need telling that it had been a mistake to throw up his good points at this moment. It usually had the effect of coarsening Ran's tongue, and this time was no exception.

"It's a pity the bastard died so young, then. If he hadn't, I wouldn't have had to listen to these constant references to the saintly Ben Killigrew!"

"He was no saint, and I don't pretend that he was. But he was my husband, and he cared for my brother's children as much as I did, and I won't have you belittling his name."

3

She leapt up from her chair, angered by his cursing, and swept out of the room with her head held high, knowing that nothing was resolved about Bradley's latest escapade of stealing apples from one of the local farmers. It wasn't a terrible crime, and it was one that the tolerant farmers would probably overlook from one of the popular young Wainwright children, but it was still something that had to be stopped before it got out of hand . . .

She walked swiftly, still with the easy, sensual grace that had so seduced Ben Killigrew into wanting her when she was no more than a lowly bal maiden in the great china clay works called Killigrew Clay that his father owned.

Her eyes were salty as Ran's raucous voice followed her. She tried not to listen to the final snide remark that it was a pity she couldn't resurrect Ben Killigrew from his grave in St Austell churchyard, since Ran was bloody sure he was the one she still hungered for in her bed, alive or dead.

"I can't stand much more of this," she muttered beneath her breath, as she went stiffly upstairs in the house Ran had named New World in deference to his American roots.

It had enchanted her so much then; it did nothing to enchant her now. She closed her eyes for a moment, as if to shut out the bad temper that seemed to be the only emotion Ran could give to anyone lately.

For a second, she remembered how it had been with Ben, when he was told he had a heart defect that could kill him at any moment. The shock of it had changed his personality totally . . . and perhaps to react so badly against such a death sentence was forgivable . . . but she was certain Ran didn't have the excuse of being told that a fatal illness was shadowing his every movement.

If he had, she would surely sense it. She had always had the uncanny Cornish intuition for such things, and she knew that in Ran's case, it was just sheer bloody-mindedness that made him the way he was. That, and the undoubted sense of anxiety that was becoming more and more evident about the china clay fortunes lately. The threat of strikes and the demands for more pay when profits were low made this hardly the best of times. But he didn't have to take out his

4

business worries on her and the children, and she hardened her heart against him.

A whiff of herbs and wild flowers teased her nostrils from the landing above. It came from the arrangements of aromatic blooms that the old housekeeper kept in the great jardinières on the landing. No matter how costly the container, Mrs Enders had declared for as long as Morwen could remember that nothing filled them more splendidly than the fragrance and healing properties of nature's own garden. It was a sentiment that earned Morwen's full approval. She was of this land, and she understood.

Morwen stood quite still, breathing in the scents of the Cornish waysides and moorlands, lost in a world of misery for present fortunes, and a frustrated longing for the past. It did nothing to settle her jangled nerves, and she knew full well that it was a futile, foolish thing for a mature woman to spend so much time dreaming, especially one who was now mother to eight, for pity's sake!

They didn't all live with Ran and herself at New World. After Morwen's second marriage, Albert and Primmy had chosen to live at Killigrew House with their grandparents, and had now set up an establishment of their own in Truro. Albert had proved to be a talented artist, and held exhibitions in the town. The two of them mixed with artists and potters, and with what Ran scornfully referred to as the more poncey fringes of society, while Primmy's musical entertainments on their Bohemian evenings, belied her childish frustration with the pianoforte.

Morwen openly admired their independence, and was always happy to see them and hear about their different world. But when all the children and relatives came visiting together, it seemed that this house, however spacious, was about to burst at the seams.

And ever more frequently these days, Morwen felt a great and guilty need to be out of a house that could be as confining to the senses as a prison cell, to run free and wild on the open moors, as if she was a young girl again. She knew very well she should quench such feelings, but she no longer bothered to deny them. Days that could never come again were sometimes the best of all days. And maybe it took a mature mind to recognize that fact, and even more so, to accept it, she thought.

But far too often now, she seemed to stand outside herself and her family duties, no longer the woman in her forties with three grown-up adopted children who had been the fruit of her brother Sam and his wife Dora; mother of Justin and Charlotte, who had been born to her and Ben; and the young ones that were hers and Ran's: Bradley, Luke and Emma. She stood outside of all of them, and just became herself.

This was just such a moment, when the sweet imagery of the past filled her mind. When it seemed that she was no longer Morwen Killigrew Wainwright, respected wife and mother, but Morwen Tremayne, as fey and spirited as the wind. And trying not to be overawed at being summoned with all her family to the big house in St Austell town on old Charles Killigrew's whim of an invitation.

It had been her seventeenth birthday, but she had been of no more importance than any other of his bal maidens working in the linhays and stacking clay blocks up on the moors at Killigrew Clay. She had been gauche and young and nervous at the invitation; and then the son of the house had looked at her and been charmed by her, and told her she was beautiful . . .

"Oh Ben, why did you have to die?" she mourned in silent accusation into the scents and creakings of New World. "Why did everything have to change?"

Sometimes she tried to imagine how things would have been for them now, if the awful accident when Ben's ship had foundered taking the clay blocks to France, hadn't accelerated the heart attack that took him from her . . . and the memories wouldn't go away, even though she knew she was being totally disloyal to the man downstairs, with whom she had found love a second time.

Suddenly, all her nerves jumped as she heard two things simultaneously. The clink of bottles and glasses from the drawing room below told her that Ran had begun his nightly

6

heavy drinking again, which was also ironic, since Ben too, had succumbed to the drink.

And six-year-old Emma cried out in her sleep for her "Mammie". Contrary to the way that finer folk than she was, insisted on their children saying "Mother", Morwen had stubbornly let hers choose their own name for her, and she had gloried in the fact that they chose to call her "Mammie", as she still called her own mother.

Emma called out fretfully again, and Morwen pushed the memories out of her mind, and hurried along the landing to the child's bedroom. But even as she did so, her daddy's wise old words seemed to swirl around in her head with an inevitable and somehow warning ring to them:

"We can't ever go back, Morwen love. You know that. All we can do is go on the best we can. 'Tis all any of us can ever do."

She went swiftly into the small bedroom that was painted in light colours for her youngest daughter, and put a bright smile on her face as she saw Emma's hot little figure sitting up in her bed, her blue-black hair tumbling about her shoulders.

"What's wrong, my lamb? Did you have a bad dream?"

Emma shook her head. Her voice was squeaky thin. "I woke up and there was shouting. I was afraid. Was it you and Daddy shouting, Mammie?"

"We were just talking, my love, and I daresay it was a bit loud for so late in the evening. It was nothing for you to worry about."

Morwen smoothed back the dark hair and tried to look reassuringly into the large, candid blue eyes that all the children had inherited from her family. In particular, this darling child had her mother's eyes. Always, they seemed able to see through the façade of story-telling, and to ferret out the truth like a dog worrying a bone . . .

It was another of her daddy's old sayings, and Morwen knew this was going to be a bad night for her too. When Hal Tremayne's words intruded so sharply into her senses, it always indicated that Morwen's peace of mind was disturbed. It boded a restless night, full of dreams and uncertainties . . . and with every likelihood of a migraine headache in the morning.

She folded the child securely in her arms and began a rocking motion with her. She had been born an optimist, but the bright and joyous future she had begun with Ben Killigrew all those years ago, walking to Penwithick church as a bride, with garlands of wild flowers perfuming her hair, seemed as elusive and far away as ever.

"Shall we go and see Grandma Bess tomorrow?" she murmured into the tangle of Emma's hair. "You'd like that, wouldn't you?"

As she heard the mumbling assent from her daughter, she relaxed a little. She pushed aside the thought that it was her own need that made her suggest a visit to the Killigrew House that she had handed over to her parents when she married Ran Wainwright and moved into New World with her children.

Killigrew House was where her association with the Killigrews had begun to change from that of lowly employee to wife and mother. And every time her troubled relationship with Ran flared up, it was the place where she wanted to return.

There must be something wrong within her, to want to cling so much to the past, Morwen thought uneasily. Some clever head doctor could possibly tell her what it was, but she had never had much truck with any doctors.

They could do all sorts of things to make folk well, but the old women on the moors could do as well, if not better, with their herbal remedies and potions and charms . . .

And Morwen too, was reputed to have healing, calming hands . . . hadn't they comforted old Charles Killigrew in his dying days?

"Mammie, you're hurting me," she heard Emma's wailing voice say now, and she realised she had unconsciously tightened her grip on the child with the memory of an old moorland witch-woman, whom she hadn't thought about in years.

But it was all entwined in the past that seemed intent on dogging her tonight. Old Zillah, and her evil-smelling

8

cottage, and the two young girls who had gone there begging for a potion to find their true love. Morwen and her best friend, Celia, who had eventually died a horrible death in the milky-white waters of a clay pool . . .

"I'm sorry, lamb," Morwen said quickly to Emma. "It's just that I love 'ee so much that sometimes I feel as if I could crush 'ee to death—"

"Why are you talking in that funny way?" Emma said at once, as Morwen unconsciously lapsed into the old patois of the moors. It was a soft and comfortable way of speaking that had been smoothed out and tidied up during her latter years as the respected wife of a businessman and landowner; and as the part-owner of Killigrew Clay.

"Was I?" she said woodenly.

"You were talking like those people at the clay works, the way Grandma Bess talks too. It fits Grandma Bess, so I don't mind when she does it," she added generously, "but Daddy doesn't like it, does he?"

Daddy didn't like a lot of things these days, Morwen thought with a sigh. She bent to kiss the flushed little cheek, and told her daughter to try to sleep now, because tomorrow they'd definitely go into St Austell town and visit Grandma Bess.

"Maybe we'll go up to Killigrew Clay one day soon too, if Walter will agree to it. You'd like that, wouldn't you?"

She listened to herself, and wondered uneasily just how dangerous it was to try to keep too tight a hold on a past that was gone. Not that Killigrew Clay itself would ever be gone from her heart or her pocket, Morwen thought, more prosaically. She was still part-owner, along with her husband and her father.

And to the outside world the clay works were still a prosperous and thriving business, high on the moors above the town. The physical evidence shone out over the countryside where the white spoil heaps, whose discarded quartz and mineral deposits glinted like diamonds in the sunlight, were an ever-present reminder of the fortunes gained by the Killigrews from china clay.

Killigrews and Tremaynes; and now Wainwrights, she

9

added silently, for their lives had become too intertwined to separate one from the other.

And Walter, her brother Sam's son who had always been her best-beloved, she thought unashamedly, no matter that it had been her sister-in-law Dora who had borne him, was now the fine and respected Works Manager of one of the biggest clay concerns in Cornwall.

She had such a fierce pride in Walter, such a damnable sense of pride that was hard to contain at times, but of all the older ones, he had turned out the best. And she wasn't so stupid as not to see it and to know it. And it was still incredible to her that he was a husband now, and soon to become a father himself. Life moved on . . .

Once Emma was settled, Morwen went silently back along the passage to her own room. Ran wouldn't come upstairs for hours yet, and when he did, he'd sprawl across the bed, practically insensible from the drink. It was too much like the curse that had caught up with Ben, and the comparison certainly didn't help her to deal with it.

It was surely a cruel twist of fate to have been blessed with two such passionate, virile husbands . . . and then for both of them to be dragged down by the same demon.

She was still tossing and turning in the big bed they shared, when she was aware of someone or something beside her bed. She felt her heart leap, wondering if she had conjured up some unearthly apparition through all her introspection.

Because just for one moment, for one spectacular, delirious moment, she thought it was Ben standing there . . . and then the tall, masculine figure moved slightly, and in the low light from the landing, she could see that it was Ben's son.

"Mammie, you'd best go and see what's wrong with your husband," she heard Justin urge.

He always used the formal term when he was disturbed by Ran's drinking, and at other times he rarely called him anything but "Father", which kept him at an emotional distance.

"I'll get up right away," Morwen said at once, hearing the

crashing about from the floor below. How she had missed the noise before, she couldn't think . . . unless she had simply shut Ran out of her mind.

"Shall I come with you?" Justin said.

"No. You go back to bed. I can handle him," she said quietly, knowing of old that Ran would turn on the boy at once with his sarcastic remarks.

Not that Justin was a boy any longer, she thought swiftly as she pulled on her dressing robe. He was a handsome young man now, and nearing his twenty-first birthday, which was an occasion they would all be celebrating in a few weeks' time. And she recognized that the very fact of Justin reaching his majority seemed to be bringing out the worst in Ran lately.

As if, with her son's coming-of-age, Ran was seeing a glimpse of his own mortality. It was ridiculous for a man in his virile years to think that way, but she couldn't apply Ran's resentment of Justin to any other reason.

Unless . . . it surely couldn't be because of the boy's education and sharp brain. Of all the children, Justin was the acknowledged clever one. He was the one who had gone to college in Truro and followed a legal career, was now working in Daniel Gorran's Accountancy and Legal Chambers, and was very likely to inherit the practice when the old man passed on.

It surely couldn't be jealousy on Ran's part, although he himself had once had a legal leaning, and had considered working with Daniel Gorran himself when he first came to Cornwall from New York. Loyally, Morwen wouldn't put Ran's feelings down to anything as petty as jealousy. Still, Justin could always hold his own in an argument with his stepfather, and usually won. Maybe that was what galled him so much.

Morwen tried to push the family squabbles out of her mind and hurried down the staircase to where Ran was muttering angrily to himself in the drawing room. She closed the door swiftly behind her, thankful for its solid oak construction that muffled any sounds.

It was an unwritten rule of the house that if doors were

11

left open, they invited anyone to come in, but the younger ones and servants alike knew better than to interrupt when doors were tight shut.

"What do you think you're doing?" Morwen said sharply. "Are you determined to waken the whole household?"

"And why should I not, if I feel so inclined? It is still my household, I believe, Ma'am?" he said, oozing a drunkard's elaborate sarcasm.

She sighed, moving across the soft carpet to him, and placing her hand on his arm. She spoke more pleadingly. "Please Ran, don't let's fight. Come to bed."

The moment the words left her lips, she knew she had chosen them badly. But then, she hadn't chosen them at all. It was the most natural thing in the world for Morwen to speak openly and frankly about anything and everything.

But when Justin had woken her, she had simply slipped a loose dressing robe over her night-gown without bothering to tie it at the waist, and she saw how Ran's dark eyes gleamed now at the realization.

His hand reached out to fondle the softness of her breast, and to her chagrin, she felt its ready reaction and her own quickening breath. But this wasn't the time or the place, and her earlier romantic mood had vanished. She was in no mood now to respond to a drink-sodden lover, or so she believed . . .

"Is that an invitation, honey?" he said in a softer, deeper voice, and, despite herself, she caught her breath at its sweet seduction. It seemed so long since he had been this way, that she felt herself weakening, despite herself.

"If you like," she said huskily. "Only please leave the bottles behind, Ran."

"Are you suggesting that if I have any more I shan't be able to perform?" he said, still with the mockery he seemed unable to resist these days.

"No, I didn't think that," she said, her beautiful eyes steady, and refusing to be provoked. "But I prefer to have my husband's undivided attention when he makes love to me, and not to be sharing him with a bottle."

For a few seconds he said nothing, and then he drew her

to him, his arms hard and powerful, and holding her so tightly she thought she would break. He buried his face in her neck, and then his kisses roamed over her closed eyelids and cheeks, to the tip of her nose, and finally sought her open, waiting lips.

"I'm a prize bastard to you sometimes, honey, and I know it," he muttered in a voice that was heavier with desire than with the effects of drink now. "But God preserve me from ever taking so much liquor that it blinds me to all that you mean to me."

"Then let's go to bed," she whispered again, aware of the hardness of that desire through the softness of her gown.

And he was still holding her in his arms, and still kissing her, as they left the room with the door wide open. They were hungry for love, and everything else was forgotten but their need for each other.

Chapter Two

Spring days in Cornwall could be as seductively warm as a summer's day in upcountry England. This was just such a morning, and a glorious burst of sunlight glinted on the whiteness of the towering spoil heaps above St Austell, exposing all the glittering fragments of quartz and mica and other minerals that mingled with the discarded earth before the china clay was extracted.

The boys had climbed part-way up the biggest mountain that was locally and quaintly known as a sky-tip, leaving their struggling small sister a long way behind as she vainly tried to keep up with them on her short, sturdy legs. The eldest boy turned to laugh at her, then wobbled, losing his balance and sliding down the length of the sky-tip, to crash in a heap at the bottom.

Emma squealed as he fell onto her, all the breath knocked out of her. And then it was Bradley who was yelping, as he was hauled up by the scruff of his neck by one of his brother Walter's pit captains.

"Now then, young feller-me-lad, you've been told a hundred times that it's dangerous to play on them heaps," the man said, scowling.

Bradley wriggled, none too pleased at being held this way by a man who might be a slice above most of the clayworkers who toiled for the family business of Killigrew Clay, but was still an employee. And it was well known that the man's sons were ne'er-do-wells, who hung about the waterfront at St Austell, while Bradley was about to be sent to one of the best schools in Truro, and could hardly ever stop bragging about it.

"You'd best leave me be, George Dodds," he yelled, in

14

his loudest voice. "Or I'll tell my brother you've been cuffing me."

The man let him go with a careless laugh, and Bradley fell sprawling back onto the spoil help. Clouds of white clay dust rose around him, covering him from head to foot, and he was furious to know he resembled a circus clown more than an owner's son.

"You can tell him what you like, you young bugger," Dodds said, with no more respect in his voice than if he spoke to a bal maiden. "'Tis certain sure that Mister Walter will believe me more'n he believes you, from what I've been hearing lately. I pity the likes of the teachers in this fine school you're going to. They won't know what's hit 'em."

The small girl was looking from one to the other of them in astonishment. Nobody ever spoke back to her brother like that, and she was still pondering on why Bradley didn't lash out at the pit captain, when, as if from nowhere, the middle one of the three came scrambling down the slopes of the spoil heap, and landed with a flailing of arms and legs at his brother's feet.

"Get up, Luke, you gorm," Bradley scowled at him, venting his anger on his younger brother now instead of the pit captain. "I'm going to Grandma's, and you two can follow or not as you please. I'm tired of this place, and I'll be glad to get away from it."

"And you mind and tell your mammie how you came to look so comical, young sir. She'll enjoy the sight of 'ee, I'm sure," George Dodds called after him mockingly, as Bradley tried to march through the soft white slurry that clogged his boots and hindered his proud progress.

"Bloody stupid oaf," Bradley muttered beneath his breath, but not quietly enough to stop the other two from hearing. Emma gasped, while Luke stopped in his tracks, so that she almost fell over him.

"Grandma Bess says you'll never go to heaven if you say those words," she stated.

Bradley scowled, glowering down at her from the superiority of his nine years.

"I hope I don't then. I'd rather go to the other place where

15

I'll be sure to meet up with some of the old Killigrews, and then I'll find out why they stayed in this miserable backwater for so long, instead of moving upcountry like any sane body should."

"Well, you're not a Killigrew," Luke said, always one for infuriatingly pointing out the obvious. "You're a Wainwright, same as us."

Bradley's handsome face darkened, and the blue eyes that were the hallmark of his mother's family glared at him. He gave Luke a swift punch in the gut that drew a howl of complaint from his brother, and strode away from him.

Luke didn't have to remind him of his name. He'd grown up with it, but he couldn't forget his rage when Grandma Bess had shown them all the names recorded in the big family bible at Killigrew House one Sunday. He'd been no more than knee-high to a flea then, as Grandad Hal had been forever saying, but that was the day he'd discovered that his mother had married for a second time and lost the proud name that was so respected in the county of Cornwall. He hadn't even known that his mother had once married into the Killigrews.

Bradley learned that day that he and his siblings had been born very soon after the second marriage to Randall E Wainwright. He'd never seen eye to eye with his father, and from that moment on, the name of Wainwright had seemed to him to be of far lesser importance than Killigrew, and still did.

Even his mother's maiden name of Tremayne had a fine Cornish ring to it. Some of his uncles and male cousins, of course, still continued it. And it was well known in the district, if not the world, Bradley thought expansively, that Killigrew Clay had become a flourishing china clay business once again, after a fluctuation in fortunes some years ago.

But at that point he was always forced to admit to the common knowledge that its new burst of success had been mainly thanks to the money and intervention of business skills brought to it by his own father, Randall Wainwright. All the same, none of it held the same charm for a boy

16

with too much pride, and a strong streak of snobbery, as the Cornish name of Killigrew.

Heads down against the moorland breezes now, the three children left the area of the spoil heaps on the high moors above St Austell town and the glittering sea beyond, and Bradley brooded on his lot. Why couldn't he have been his uncle Matt Tremayne's son, and been born in the golden land of America across the Atlantic Ocean like his cousin Cresswell? And like his father, Ran Wainwright himself, who was the cousin of Cresswell's mother.

There was such a mish-mash of them all, Bradley scowled, still smarting from George Dodds' taunting, and from the fuss in his father's study that morning. He'd been summoned there after breakfast.

He could see by his father's florid face and heavy eyes, and his mother's troubled ones, that something was up. Something was definitely up. It was his favourite expression of the moment. And he stood defiantly awaiting whatever censure was to come, displaying a mute insolence that irked Ran more by the minute.

"You've been stealing apples, I understand," he said at once, never one for wasting words.

"They were lying on the ground, no good to anybody, so I just helped Farmer Penwoody in clearing 'em up," he said, far too jauntily for Ran's mood. For his cheek, he got a cuff around the ear that sent his senses spinning.

"So you don't yet know the difference between asking for something, and stealing other peoples' property, is that it?" Ran said. "And is this the boy who wants to go to Justin's old school in Truro and carry on the family name?"

"What family name?" Bradley said, still on his private crusade. "Justin was a Killigrew, while I'm only a—"

He caught the sparkle from his mother's eyes, and paused. Maybe it was time to go back over his tracks, and he looked up at Ran with the blue eyes that could be so deceptively innocent when he chose.

"I'm sorry, Father," he said abjectly. "I know it was wrong, and I promise not to do it again."

17

"Good," Ran said, frowning, and never quite sure who was getting the better of whom where Bradley was concerned. "And I'm sure if you ask Farmer Penwoody, he'll let you take your pick of the fallers any time."

"All right," Bradley said, avoiding his mother's glance. But if his father was short-sighted enough to think that having free rein to the apple orchards was the same as the excitement of pinching them, he was quite sure his mother was not.

But the censure had been short-lived, and his father had more important things to worry about than apple pinching. There had been a disastrous clayworkers' strike early in the year, which had left many of them penniless. Yet now there was even more dissent among them, and rumblings of more ludicrous pay demands, and Ran Wainwright had called a meeting of his pit captains and all the other owners and pit captains in the area, to quell it quickly.

Ran was anxious to be gone into St Austell where the meeting was to be held. Too anxious to waste time on piddling childish misdemeanors. Business had to come first. There needed to be a solid front on this, and no more threats of wildcat strikes – or worse still, organized marches into St Austell to storm the Killigrew offices, as in times past.

Morwen had bundled Bradley out of the study before he could irritate his father further, and told him he could take the younger ones up to Killigrew Clay if he had a mind to it.

"Can't I go by myself?" the boy sulked. "Why do I have to take the babbies with me?"

"Because I want to see Grandma Bess on my own, and I promised Emma I'd take her there. So when you've had an hour or so at the clayworks, you can all come visiting at Killigrew House and then come home with me in the carriage."

"We can't walk all that way," Bradley protested. "And I don't aim to carry Emma!"

Morwen sighed. Was there ever a child so keen on objecting at every turn?

18

"I wouldn't expect you to. Gillings will take you in the cart. You can walk down to St Austell, but don't stray from the proper pathways. I don't want you three young ones to be wandering over the moors by yourselves."

"Why not?" Bradley said at once.

She glowered at him. Loving one's offspring could sometimes be stretched to the limits, she thought. But she'd never been one to evade an honest answer.

"Bad things can happen. Old mine workings can cause accidents, and there may be strangers about who would do you harm," she said vaguely.

"And witch-women?" Bradley said eagerly. "I heard tell of them at school, Mammie. Do you know of them?"

"Maybe I do, but this isn't the time for telling," she said briskly. "Go and remind the others to get ready, and I'll ask Gillings to bring the cart around to the front of the house. I'm going into town with your father."

She and Ran had driven silently towards St Austell, as distant as though the loving that had ended last night's quarrelling had never happened. She remembered the loving with a rush of pleasure. It been so tender and so beautiful . . . Morwen glanced at the profile of her husband and sighed. Why couldn't it always be like that?

For an hour or so, it had seemed as if the old Ran had come back to her, the strong, passionate man who had wanted her so badly, even while she was still married to Ben. The man who had shown her the glory of love in a small London hotel room, and banished all thoughts of guilt. For if Ben had no longer wanted her, then this man did, and she had felt loved and cherished, and a woman once more.

"How long do you think the meeting will take?" she said, softer and huskier than usual as the memories of those times filled her mind.

"God knows," he said in his clipped American accent. "When it ends for the day I'll be home, but don't be surprised if it's not until the early hours."

"Ran, it's eleven o'clock in the morning! It can't go on into the early hours of tomorrow!"

"You don't understand, honey. It's best for small groups to discuss things privately, as well as collectively. I mean to do all I can to nip this strike threat in the bud before it begins."

"It's really serious then?"

He looked at her witheringly.

"Where have you been these past months, woman? Of course it's bloody serious. If you haven't been listening to me, you've been reading it in the papers, I presume? Tom Askhew's been putting in a damn sight more than his two cents' worth in *The Informer*."

She flinched, hearing the dislike in Ran's voice. None of them liked the brash Yorkshireman who'd run the newspaper down here for a time, and then gone back up north with his family for a few years. Then he'd returned to Cornwall, better heeled and more powerful than before, and wielding ever more influence to get his radical views into print. But even worse than his frequently vindictive accounts in the newspaper, according to Ran he was a strikers' man, if ever he saw one.

And talk of the ominous threat of strikes among the clayworkers was very much on everyone's lips right now. If they came to fruition, it would be just up Tom Askhew's alley, Ran frequently said, to whip up the clayworkers into action. He'd do it, if only to get back at the business he despised, and more especially the family who overlorded it. He had no love for the Killigrews, nor anyone who married into them, which included Tremaynes and Wainwrights. The only exception was for the daughter that he doted on. And even there . . .

Morwen was perfectly sure that the sharpest thorn in Tom Askhew's side was the fact that his adored Cathy had never wavered from her determination to marry Walter Tremayne. And after several years of marriage now, she was to have a child. The couple were overjoyed, as were Morwen and Ran, but in the local kiddley-winks Askhew had been heard to say sourly that it would just be another little bugger with the Tremayne hallmark on it, and more working fodder for the clayworks.

"You'll sort it all out, dar, I know you will," Morwen said swiftly to Ran now, more confidently than she felt.

He gave a half-smile. "Your faith in me does you proud. But my name's Wainwright, not Tremayne, and it sure as hell ain't Killigrew. I daresay Ben might have known how to handle them, and your daddy would have had a fair chance of quelling any riots in the old days. But when it comes to a brash colonial, they suddenly go deaf."

"I wish you wouldn't call yourself that! After all these years, you're practically as Cornish as the rest of us."

"And you're talking moonshine, honey," Ran said drily.

They both knew it. It took more than ten years of marriage to a Cornishwoman to absorb what had been in the blood for generations. Morwen wondered if there was anywhere else in the world quite so insular as here. It was the first time she considered it with resentment.

"Is Daddy joining you for this meeting?" she asked, ignoring the jibe.

"Naturally. It's as much his concern as mine, wouldn't you say?"

"*I* would, yes, but the men—"

"The men will just see old Hal Tremayne getting his two pennyworth of interest out of Killigrew Clay's business, the same as he always did before he so-say retired. Don't worry. It would take more than a roomful of raucous clayworkers to make him forget himself and give away the true state of affairs."

Yes, thought Morwen. Even now, there would be some who still fiercely resented the fact that Hal Tremayne had come up in the world to be one of the bosses. And even more so to realize how much money Hal had put into it, when none of them knew he had any. It was a well-kept family secret, known only to the older ones, on Hal's own insistence. He was a simple man, who cared nothing for power and money, but he'd accepted what was offered to him with dignity, and was wise with his advice when it was needed.

"And what of Walter? I can't imagine he'd leave Cathy too long at this time."

Ran shrugged. "You never made much fuss when it came to your birthing time, and Cathy seems a sensible girl, for all that her father's such a hot-head."

"Ran, I wish you wouldn't always refer to Tom Askhew in that way," Morwen said wearily. "He's not a monster, for pity's sake—"

"You'd consider him more like a saviour in one respect, I daresay," Ran drawled, glancing sideways at his wife and seeing the swift colour stain her cheeks.

"Don't be ridiculous—"

"I'm not ridiculous, nor blind, nor forgetful. I know just how thankful you were when he came on the scene and lured your Miss 'finelady' Jane away from Ben. That *was* your name for her, I believe?"

"I was young and foolish then. And Ben and Jane were never more than friends," she snapped.

He laughed outright now. "And you were never jealous of them, were you, honey? You seem to forget I knew your brother before I knew you, and learned all about the family history before I came over here."

His reference to her brother Matt made her forget all about Tom and Jane Askhew. Matt had been the only one of her brothers to leave Cornwall, to prosper in the goldfields of California more successfully than any of them could ever have dreamed possible. And when he'd come home on a visit with a wife and son some years later, it was Matt who had been the real saviour of their dwindling family fortunes.

The prodigal son had returned, and in returning had been the catalyst for so many things. Not least, the fact that his wife was American and had a cousin in New York with a yen to see this south-west corner of the country that held itself so much apart from the rest of England. And the cousin's name was Randall E Wainwright.

"Don't worry about this meeting today, Morwen," Ran said. He was more gentle now, misunderstanding her look as she stared ahead without seeing any of the surrounding moorland.

"Then I won't," she said, turning on a bright smile for

him. "You, Daddy and Walter make a formidable team, and the clayworkers know that already."

He nodded, satisfied. They had reached the old Killigrew House, where her parents lived, and he leaned forward in the carriage to kiss her. Later, Gillings would meet the younger children at the foot of the moors and bring them to the house, eventually taking Morwen and the children home.

She clung to Ran for a moment, and as she did so she felt a small shiver run through her, like a premonition that something bad was about to happen. She wished she could ignore it, but such feelings were rarely wrong.

"Just take care," she said, knowing it was as much as she could say, for if she voiced her fears, he would dismiss it out of hand. Such fanciful Cornish forebodings had no place in a hard-headed businessman like her husband.

She alighted from the carriage and watched it trundle away towards the town centre and the meeting house where the bosses, pit captains and the clayworkers out of their shift would be gathering. She knew just how it would be. It would start out in a civilized manner, with everyone having their say . . . and by the end of it there would be jostling and pushing, cursing and fisticuffs.

There would be more than one bloodied nose, maybe a lot worse, and quite probably the constables would be called in to quell it all, and haul a dozen or more off to the cells to cool off for the night.

Those of them that were still in one piece would most likely crawl off to "Kitty's House", the bawdyhouse along the coast from St Austell, for the kind of comfort and pleasure that many sage wives turned a blind eye to, while their menfolk blithely imagined they knew nothing of their activities. It was always the same pattern after a rowdy meeting: the cells or the bawdyhouse or the Blue Boar kiddley-wink . . .

She gave up worrying about their doings. She was going to find out what the rest of the family had been doing lately. Her mammie was always a great source of news, Morwen thought with a smile. She hardly went anywhere these days, and she wasn't a gossip, but somehow the information

23

always came her way. And it would be good to hear how the rest of her large family fared.

Bess Tremayne had spent a lifetime caring for other folk. Firstly in the little clayworker's cottage high on the moors, where Hal and herself and the five children had lived, snug as bugs. And then, when the children had mostly grown and gone their own ways, in the larger place, halfway between the high moors and St Austell town, that Charles Killigrew had offered them when Hal's status in the clayworks had been raised.

Hal had argued and blustered about being given charity, but it had been herself and Morwen in particular, who had persuaded him that he'd be a fool to turn his back on where fate was leading him. And a true Cornishman had never been one to argue with fate.

And now, there was this. Bess looked around her with some satisfaction on that April day when the windows gleamed and sparkled from the maids' diligence, and everything was pristine clean from her own administering. For she'd been a worker for too long not to want to see to the furniture polishing herself, and she prided herself on the fresh smell of herbal creams and polishes that permeated Killigrew House.

Killigrew House! Even as she surveyed her domestic domain, a smile curved around Bess Tremayne's lips for a moment. Who'd ever thought she'd be mistress here, for pity's sake! Sometimes she still wondered if she was dreaming, and she'd wake up in the mean little cottage where they could see the stars through the rafters, where she'd spent her days working in the linhays at the clay pits, and her nights sewing dresses and underpinnings for finer folks than herself.

"Mammie, are you ailing?"

Bess jumped as she heard her daughter's anxious voice. She hadn't heard the Wainwright carriage arrive, and she gave Morwen a cheerful smile now.

"I'm as right as ninepence, my lamb. Just thinking, that's all."

Morwen bent to kiss her creased cheek, making little fuss about it. As a family they weren't given to too much kissing, and Bess wouldn't want anything made of the fact that it was rare for Morwen to find her mother just sitting and thinking. But Morwen was relieved to see that there was really nothing wrong, and that Bess rang for tea and biscuits to be brought in. It was still difficult for her to act the lady, and it had taken a long while before she'd finally got used to sending for refreshments instead of seeing to it all herself.

When they were both settled with cups of steaming tea in their hands, Bess turned to her daughter.

"As a matter of fact, there is summat I'm fretting over, but I didn't want to say it just yet."

Morwen put her cup down on her saucer and gave her mother her wide, unblinking blue stare.

"Well, now you've got this far, you'd better go on, hadn't you? You can't dangle half a story in front of me, or worse still, just the sniff of it!"

Bess sighed. "You know what they say. Once you put a thing into words, 'tis there for all eternity."

"I thought that was when you put it in writing," Morwen said drily, knowing there'd be no hurrying her mother until she was ready to speak. Bess nodded slowly.

"Well then, 'tis our Freddie and Venetia," she said.

Morwen looked at her in surprise. Freddie had turned out to be the least complicated of her brothers after all. She would have reserved that judgement for Matt, her beloved, dreamy Matt, but he was far away with his family in California, and had found his own level of contentment.

Sam – darling Sam – had died many years ago now in a tragic accident, but his memory could still stir her heart with sorrow. And Jack was a flourishing and well-respected boat-builder, away in Truro with his delicate wife Annie, who had blossomed so amazingly after the birth of the son that had defied all the doctor's advice.

But Freddie had seemed so happy with his Venetia – the Honourable Venetia Hocking Tremayne, Morwen reminded herself with a hidden smile. Surely, after all these years, there wasn't a problem there. There had been

25

such traumas for Freddie in the past that she didn't care to think about . . .

"What's wrong, Mammie?" she said, her voice a mite huskier, unable to forget the shock and horror on the young Freddie's face when he'd come across the dashing army captain and his music teacher locked in a forbidden embrace in the summerhouse. The sight of the two men had had far-reaching effects on the vulnerable young boy, almost threatening to emasculate him . . .

"Nothing exactly," Bess said uneasily. "'Tis just a feeling, from summat our Freddie said, that's all. I'm probably making mountains out of emmet-hills."

"And you're probably not. So why don't you share it with me, and then we'll both have summat to fret about?"

Morwen reflected that it was true what Emma had said. When she was with her mother, it was easy to slip back into the old comfortable way of speaking. But so what? Who was to hear, and who was to care?

"Well, 'twas just the way our Freddie spoke when they invited us to tea in that rambling great place of theirs. They took us round the stables as usual – you know how Venetia can't resist showing off her horses, and then our Freddie said summat about expanding, and mebbe goin' in for racing as well as breedin', see?"

"Well, what's wrong with that? Lord knows they can afford it with all the money her father left her—"

Bess went on as if she hadn't spoken. "And then he got quite cagey, the way he does when he's saying summat and meanin' summat else."

Morwen nodded, understanding her mother's own brand of logic, and knowing there was more to come.

"It was when he said so casually that the real place to be for breedin' and racin' was Ireland."

"I daresay he's right about that," Morwen said.

Bess's blue eyes were filled with a momentary pain. It was the way they had looked when she discovered her son Matthew had fled to America because of some wickedness he and his cousin Jude Pascoe had done. The way they'd looked after they'd come and told her that her first-born Sam

26

had died in Ben Killigrew's rail track accident on the moors. The way they always looked when she sensed instinctively that one of her brood was going to leave her.

Morwen drew in her breath. "You surely don't think they'd up stakes and move to Ireland, do you?"

"Mebbe they would and mebbe they wouldn't. I'm only saying what I heard, but I've got a bad feeling about it, Morwen. I don't want to lose another of my sons."

Sons! They were always so special, Morwen thought, but without more than a smidgin of resentment, since she knew she felt the very same way. All of hers were special too, from Walter down to little Luke.

Her girls were special too, she thought hastily. In many ways there was a sweet telepathy between mothers and daughters, a womanly sisterhood that could never be denied. But a boy would always hold the key to his mother's heart. And the look that passed between mother and daughter then made her almost wish she'd been born a boy too.

Chapter Three

Freddie Tremayne breathed in the pungent smells of horseflesh and fresh straw. While many folk might be repelled by them, he thought there was little to compare with the way they could tease and tantalize the senses.

Except, in a very different way, the musky scents of his wife, of course, the earthy, rumbustious woman he had married, and who was a constant source of delight to him. She had been a dainty little thing when he'd married her, but had quickly grown fleshy, and some might say a little coarse, in her countrywoman's pursuits. But these facts did nothing to lessen Freddie's pleasure in her. There was just more of her to love, as he frequently and generously told her.

Some, jealous of the contentment these two had found in one another, even hinted that the Honourable Venetia Hocking Tremayne was a sight more mannish than her more slightly-built husband, with her ever more strident voice, and her penchant for wearing riding breeches whenever she chose to do so, even in town where such behaviour often outraged decent society.

None of this disapproval, silent or otherwise, gave the slightest bother to either Freddie or Venetia, and merely caused them to chuckle gleefully at the scandalized looks they sometimes got. Theirs was a marriage into which they fitted like the best-made pair of soft leather gloves, and to blazes with what the rest of the world thought.

But the rest of the world didn't involve the close-knit Tremayne dynasty, and now there was the problem of telling the family what they were about to do. Despite their lack of inhibitions on a wider front, Freddie knew this was something that needed proper thinking about.

"We'll put it to our Morwen," he said suddenly, and with no preamble. "She was always the one who knew best how to handle things."

They were walking around the fertile land that had been left to Venetia by her father, the late Lord Hocking. They were hunched up in riding jackets and breeches in the cool of the April evening, their long boots matching stride for stride before they paused to lean on a fence and gaze with satisfaction at the fine riding stable they had created between them.

It took no more than a breath and an eye-blink for Venetia to follow where Freddie's thoughts had led him. She looked approvingly at him and she hugged his arm.

"Of course, that's the answer to it. We'll tell Morwen first off, and let her sort it out with your folks. She'll be just the one for smoothing things out."

He hugged her arm to his. "I daresay you're thinking me a great loon for not wantin' to tell 'em right off—"

"No, I don't! You're just thinking of their feelings, and not wanting to hurt them. You never want to hurt anybody, do you, my 'andsome?" she said, her voice slipping easily into an exaggerated accent to tease him.

He laughed. "Well, I'm not like Ran or Walter, always ready to let fly with words and fists if necessary. Our Jack was never backwards in coming forward if a fight was in the offing, neither. Now young Bradley is starting to taste his oats – and there's a hothead if I ever saw one."

He avoided her eyes. Ten years back, when Morwen was expecting Bradley, he and Venetia had been expecting a child too, both women falling soon after the honeymoon, and happily anticipating that there'd be another playmate for Jack and Annie's baby Sammie.

But Venetia had miscarried badly, tearing her insides, and they had learned to their anguish that there was never going to be another child. Morwen had encouraged them to spend long hours with her own baby son, wisely thinking it the best therapy. Despite Venetia's first resistence to the idea, she knew she couldn't close her eyes to other women's children forever, and she gave in.

To her own surprise, it had gone a long way towards healing the pain, and had forged a special bond between herself and Morwen's baby. In time, both Freddie and Venetia had not only grown fiercely attached to the boy, but were oblivious to his faults. And Bradley adored them too, seeing in their country estate the epitome of all that a gracious family life should be.

"How will he take it, do you think?" Venetia said now.

"I don't know," Freddie answered, knowing that Bradley would be uppermost on his wife's mind, as well as his. "It's summat I don't rightly care to think about too deeply."

Venetia leaned over and kissed her man's cheek. "Let's forget about it for now and just enjoy being with the horses. Then we'll go indoors and have a nightcap before bed."

The horses were their life, and could always be guaranteed to cheer them up. They smiled at one another in perfect harmony. And Freddie marvelled briefly at the memory of the sensitive young man he had once been, trying to find himself in the arms of a whore to prove that an early discovery of homosexuality in others hadn't blighted his whole life. And then the glorious realization that the loving and fumbling discovery of two people who truly loved one another was all the aphrodisiac that was needed.

He owed Venetia more than words could ever say. His only regret was that through no fault of their own, he couldn't give her the child she still craved. Not that she ever mentioned it now. She had her man and her beloved horses, but Freddie knew her too well, and there was still a longing inside her that hadn't been fulfilled. The way she glowed and came alive whenever young Bradley Wainwright came to visit them at Hocking Hall was proof enough of that.

The object of Freddie's thoughts was at that very moment being severely upbraided by his mother. Subdued and chastened, Luke and Emma stood by, heads down in disgrace, while Bradley brazened it out as usual.

"How dare you come to Grandma Bess's house in such a state!" Morwen raged. "You're a disgrace to the whole family, and what the townsfolk must have thought when they saw you traipsing down the hillside, I can't think. You look like clowns, the lot of you."

She paused for breath, and Bradley howled in protest as she shook him, sending more clay dust flying around the pristine drawing room, where it caught the sunlight and hung about in sparkling dust motes.

"You said we could go to Killigrew Clay," he yelled. "We were only having fun on the sky tips. There's nothing else to do up there, 'cept listen to the boring clayworkers talking. And Walter's always too busy to talk to us."

Morwen avoided her mother's eyes. They'd all been clayworkers once, her entire family, beholden to the Killigrews for pennies and their very existence, including every bit of food they put in their bellies. And this — this pompous, spoiled, *precocious* little brat considered the clayworkers *boring*. She was tempted to slap him soundly, and only Bess's hand on her arm stopped her. He didn't know, she reminded herself. He couldn't know how it had been all those years ago . . .

She snapped at the trio of children. "The three of you can go upstairs this minute and into the bath. Sophie will see to you."

Bradley howled again. "No! I hate Sophie. She scrubs me raw, and anyway, I'm too old to be bathed by a servant!"

This time, Morwen couldn't stop herself, and she cuffed him around the ear, making matters worse by scattering the white powdery dust from his hair over the tea tray, and causing Bess to mutter beneath her breath.

"You'll do as you're damn well told," she said, and then she paused as she glimpsed the real misery in the boy's eyes, and knew it would be a bad thing to humiliate him so when he was on the brink of growing up.

He may be only nine years old, but he had a remarkably mature head on those young shoulders, for all his rebellious nature. And he was a well-built boy, who would hate the attentions of a woman servant. For a moment, she remembered how she had once had the same feeling with

31

her brother Freddie, when he was just leaving boyhood behind, and knew that she couldn't shame Bradley.

"All right," she conceded. "Sophie will fill the bath with hot water, and you will wash yourself while she brushes the dust out of these disgusting clothes. Luke and Emma will wait until you're finished. But be quick, or I shall scrub you myself, and I'll be no less gentle than Sophie."

"Will you bath us, Mammie?" Emma said, her voice quavering. "I don't like Sophie, either."

"This is meant to be a punishment, not a pleasure—"

"I'll do it, my lamb," Bess said quickly. "'Tis a long while since I've had the enjoyment of bathing young 'uns, and then 'twas only in a tin tub. I promise your Grandma will be gentle with 'ee."

"You spoil them," Morwen said, when Sophie had taken the three children off to the splendid bathroom in Killigrew House, with firm instructions that her only duties were to run the baths and take their clothes away, and brush them clean enough for wearing home again.

Morwen let out her breath in a long sigh. Life with Bradley always seemed to be verging on a battlefield nowadays, but she had to admit that he was definitely feeling his feet in an adult world. He took after Ran for height and breadth. And at least this little battle had now been dealt with, and her mother had already sent for someone to take the tea tray away and to bring some more. Bess made little fuss over the incident, and Morwen knew that she'd smother the children with indulgence given half a chance. And such spoiling wasn't altogether good for them.

"You stay here and have some more tea, lamb, and I'll go up and see to them," Bess said comfortably, when the fresh brew had arrived. "Charlotte will be coming for a visit in a little while, and I know you'll be wanting to hear how she's doing in her grand new place."

Morwen gave a small shrug of acceptance as her mother went out of the room. In her own way, Bess was still in control of them all, and still adept in organizing her family. She was stiffer than of old, and the once luxuriant hair was iron-grey now. But she still carried herself with the same dignity that belied a woman who'd toiled all her life as a former bal maiden in the clayworks, and with her seamstress's fingers pricked and hardened from long hours of tedious work done by candlelight.

Bess and the little ones were still upstairs when Morwen heard a light voice calling out hello, and then her daughter Charlotte came into the room, bringing with her a breath of springtime.

At seventeen, Charlotte was like a mirror image of what Morwen had been when Ben Killigrew first set eyes on her. There were the same vivid blue eyes, the same glorious blue-black hair, the same blossoming sensuality in the walk and the full, red lips . . . the sight of Charlotte in one of the dainty, flower-sprigged gowns she always favoured, could always startle Morwen for a few seconds. It was as if she truly looked at her daughter and saw the reflection of her younger self.

And she fervently wished for Ben's girl all the love she herself had known, and none of the heartache. But she knew that such a hope of Charlotte following a similar pattern to her own, or an infinitely better one, was futile. Everyone had to go wherever destiny led them.

So it had been no surprise to Morwen when her daughter announced that she wanted to be a children's nursemaid, even if Ran had protested that it was hardly dignified for a well-to-do young lady to be cleaning up after other peoples' infants. But Charlotte had turned her far-seeing blue eyes on him and stated exactly what Morwen had expected her to say.

"It's no less dignified than my mother caring for her father-in-law and being such a comfort to him. And I'm said to have the same calming hands as she had, so providing she doesn't object, I shan't be dissuaded."

Ran had shrugged and capitulated, knowing that the two of them were a formidable force when they wanted something badly enough. In any case, Charlotte was hardly going to look after roughnecks. There were plenty of genteel families wanting a similarly brought-up young lady to care for their children. The Pollards, who were one of the oldest and most influential families in St Austell, had welcomed Charlotte Killigrew to care for their children with open arms.

"So how are your little charges today?" Morwen asked, when they had made their greetings, and Charlotte had helped herself to tea and biscuits.

"They're both well," Charlotte said. "I took them to Par Sands this morning, made sand pies with them, and they enjoyed it enormously. They're really well-behaved children, and not such a trial to me as I hear Bradley is being to you, Mother," she finished with a grin.

At the noisy sounds emanating from upstairs, Morwen laughed, dismissing the small slight to her own son, and simply accepting the truth of it.

"That's so, but your Grandma is dealing with him at this minute. The three of them have been up to Killigrew Clay and got covered in clay dust."

"Really?" Charlotte said carelessly.

The clayworks were no longer of any interest to her, and her whole world now revolved around the little Pollard children. She had been given rooms of her own in the mansion and was happier than she had ever thought she could be. And there was also a certain young male relative of the family who now came more frequently to the house since Charlotte moved in, who was also filling her days with sunshine. But she wasn't ready to confide in her mother about Vincent just yet.

Morwen noted the faraway look in the girl's eyes and mistook it. Charlotte's apparent disinterest in the family fortunes suddenly irked her. It was the one thing on which they disagreed, however mutely. Charlotte had no more than a superficial interest in the past, and all her thoughts were concentrated on the present and her new life.

It was as it should be . . . but Killigrew Clay had been so much a part of Morwen's own life, and it had shaped the fate of her whole family. She was always defensive of it and its workers, from Works Manager down to the lowliest kiddley-boys who ran barefoot when their parents couldn't

34

afford to buy shoes, fetching and carrying, and making tea for the rest.

"There could be real hardships ahead if the clayers don't see sense," Morwen said now. Charlotte blinked, her thoughts elsewhere. Rarely for Morwen, her intuition didn't alert her to the real cause, and she merely thought Charlotte was becoming too uppity to care about her own family's doings.

"You *do* know what I'm talking about, I suppose? Or are you so immersed in nappies and nursery diets for these other folks that you forget your attachment to your own family?"

They were both startled by the vehemence in Morwen's voice. She hadn't meant to sound as snappy or as downright petty as the words implied, and Charlotte's eyes widened now as she took in how edgy her mother seemed to be today.

"I don't know what you mean, Mother," she said resentfully. "I'm here, aren't I? I always come to see Grandma on this day of the week, and I was more than happy to see you here too. But I can't divide myself in dozens of little pieces in order to satisfy everybody!"

"I didn't mean any such thing—" Morwen began, but it seemed her daughter didn't want to listen to apologies either.

"Where's Grandad Hal? He always has a chuckle with me when I come visiting. I didn't see him in the garden."

If she meant to imply that there wasn't much chuckling going on between the two women in the drawing room now, Morwen chose to ignore it.

"He's gone to the meeting house in town," she said quietly. "Ran, Walter and Grandad Hal are having discussions today with the other bosses and pit captains, and with some of the clayworkers, trying to avert this strike threat. But we'll leave such talk to the men and not bother our heads with it. Have you spoken to Justin about any plans for his birthday celebrations?"

She turned the conversation quickly, and saw that Charlotte relaxed. The air had become decidedly prickly

35

between them, and it was something Morwen didn't care to prolong. Life was too short for such tiresomeness, but that was also something you had to learn by experience.

"He didn't want to do anything, but I told him you'd insist on having a big family party. You will, won't you, Mother? And allow us to bring some of our own friends to it?"

Morwen didn't miss the anxiety in her voice, nor the sudden sparkle in the expressive blue eyes, or the warm glow in her cheeks. And her intuition didn't desert her a second time. There was only one reason for a beautiful young lady of seventeen summers to get that special look on her face. And right now, Charlotte looked ready and ripe for falling in love . . . the knowledge filled Morwen with a mixture of shock and tenderness.

It was bound to happen, of course, but when it happened to one of your own chicks, it always made you aware of your own mortality, she thought. Her feelings now were comparable with the way she felt about Walter and Cathy being so soon to become parents, and moving her into another generation. She spoke quickly, to cover the momentary shadow that passed through her mind.

"Of course. And do you have a special guest you want to invite?" she said, with a teasing smile.

She thought Charlotte was not going to respond. Then she became animated, almost childlike in her wish to speak her beloved's name as often as possible, and bring him near by doing so. Morwen recognized that need so well.

"I just know you're going to like him. Everybody does, Mother! His name's Vincent Pollard, and Justin's already met him on one occasion when he had to go to Daniel Gorran's Chambers on family business. Justin thought Vincent was a fine young man, so I know he'd have no objection if I invited him to the party—"

Morwen laughed as she rattled on, but far from becoming noisy in her excitement, Charlotte's voice was becoming softer and more melodic by the minute. As soft as if she caressed her beloved's skin . . . Morwen caught herself up short with a little start. But she knew all the signs. Her girl was head-over-heels in love with this unknown Vincent, and

36

she just prayed that the young man would not only love her in return, but respect her too.

"Well, I assume that if Justin approves of him, and you believe him to be an honourable young man—" she began, with heavy-handed caution, at which Charlotte burst out laughing.

"Oh, Mother, you're so transparent! This is 1877, not the Dark Ages! I don't need to be told how to behave myself, not with you and Grandma Bess always trying so hard to keep me on the straight and narrow path of righteousness!"

"Resorting to the scriptures doesn't make you a saint my girl," Morwen said tartly. "And you know full well what I mean. I wasn't talking about you, in any case. Young men have different urges to young women and don't always know how to control them."

She felt her face go hot as she spoke, seeing the humour on Charlotte's face. Why, if her mother had ever spoken to her so frankly, Morwen would have died with embarrassment. Not that Bess would, or ever could have done so. Such intimate things were never discussed when Morwen was a girl, and only those with a more worldly attitude seemed able to discuss them freely now.

The thought gave her an anxious moment, and Charlotte didn't miss the little frown between her mother's eyes. As they heard the chatter of the children coming back downstairs with Bess, Charlotte gave her mother an unexpected hug and whispered quickly in her ear.

"Don't fret, Mammie dear. I haven't had carnal knowledge of Vincent, and nor has he suggested it. He's far too upright and honourable a young man for that!"

But her eyes were dancing with wickedly teasing laughter as she said it. She turned to hold out her arms to her three half-siblings who ran towards her now, clean and wholesome again, and joyful as ever to see her. Charlotte was a terrible tease, Morwen thought, but there was no doubting the affection she had for children, nor how they responded, and even Bradley was pleased to see her.

She'd be a perfect mother herself one day . . . but Morwen hoped fervently that day wasn't too soon in coming.

37

There was a wonderful springtime between adolescence and maturity that was so quickly gone, and which should be savoured to the full. It was only the participant in that springtime who so rarely realized it. Right now Charlotte was like a bright golden flower, and it was all too soon that the petals began to fall.

Amid the children's noisy chatter and Charlotte's laughing rejoinders, Bess saw her daughter shudder.

"What goose has just walked over your grave, my lamb?" Bess said quietly.

"None, I hope," Morwen said, unable, for the life of her, to give a light reply.

She told herself she was too old to put any store in premonitions. She was nearing her mid-forties, and the old, delicious times when she and Celia Penry dared to believe in the words of witchwomen and love-potions and seeing the face of your future lover through the hole in a Cornish standing-stone, were long past. But she shuddered again.

"We've been talking about Justin's birthday party," she said quickly. "Charlotte wants to invite a new friend, and I daresay Albert and Primmy will be bringing along some of their arty friends as well."

Charlotte pulled a face. "Must they? Some of those people are so odd, Mother."

Bradley piped up. "They wear bright clothes and paint their faces, and people turn to stare at them in the streets."

"Well, I hope people don't turn to stare at Albert and Primmy in the streets," Morwen said, taken aback at this knowledge. "Where on earth did you hear such things, Bradley?"

"Aunt Venetia told me so, the last time I saw her," he said nonchalently. "And she didn't seem to mind."

"Oh, well, she wouldn't," Charlotte said, grinning. "She's a sketch herself wherever she goes—"

"Well, I like her!" Bradley said, scowling at Charlotte now. "She takes me riding, lets me stay up as late as I like, gives me sticky buns for tea, and never cares if I wash my hands first or not!"

By now, Charlotte was chortling loudly, and the two

older women hardly knew whether to laugh or scold him. The younger children stared open-mouthed at these reckless indiscretions, while Morwen said that if that was the way he was permitted to behave in his Aunt Venetia's company, she wasn't sure if he'd ever be allowed to visit her again.

It had been said mildly enough, and without any seriousness, knowing how Venetia doted on the boy, but she wasn't prepared for the little whirlwind that Bradley became. He threw himself at her, almost knocking her off-balance, and she hadn't realized what strength he had. He pummelled at her chest, while she held him off as best she could.

"You won't stop me going there!" he raged. "I'll run away from home if you do, and I won't even care if I never see you again."

"For heaven's sake, Bradley, control yourself!" Morwen said, aghast at this show of temper. "There's no need for all this. You're shaming me in front of everyone. Stop it, now!"

He gradually became chastened as he realized that everyone had quietened, wondering if he'd gone quite mad. For a moment, he'd felt in danger of it, knowing that if he was banished from Hocking Hall for good, he'd be only half-alive. He knew all about family love and loyalty, but when he was with Venetia and Freddie, there was a different kind of love. With them, and their free and easy way of living, he felt as if the whole world was his for the taking, and that he was capable of greater things than ever came out of a clay pit.

But he couldn't tell his mother that, and he'd certainly never confide in his father. Ran would merely scoff, saying he was getting above himself, and in serious danger of losing what little grey matter he had if he thought that riding about the countryside on horses was any better than being in control of a great company like Killigrew Clay.

But with a burst of mature insight he knew that since he couldn't even control his own temper, there was no hope of him controlling Killigrew Clay if he ever got the chance. Not that he'd want to. He'd far rather be with Freddie and Venetia and the horses. He wished he had the nerve to tell the lot of them so, but he wasn't quite brave enough for that.

"I think it's nearly time we went home," Morwen said meaningly, and Bradley knew there'd be more fuss when his mother got him on her own. "There's no use waiting for the men, since it could be hours before the meeting's over."

"As you like, dar," Bess said comfortably. "But we still haven't settled whether to have Justin's party here or at New World. Do you have any ideas on it, Charlotte?" she said, bringing the girl into the conversation.

"Justin won't care where it is," Charlotte said at once. "But I daresay we won't please everybody."

It was a veiled reference to the fact that Justin and their stepfather didn't get on either. Morwen was set to rise to the bait, but Bess spoke first.

"I say we hold it here then. Hal and me will be only too pleased to have all our young uns under the same roof once more, and the little uns can sleep upstairs. Lord knows there's room enough in this rattling great place for all of 'ee, and 'tis easier for Albert and Primmy and their friends to get to us from Truro, and for Jack and Annie's brood too."

She added the last names as she saw Charlotte's eyes flash at the mention of Albert and Primmy's Bohemian friends. Charlotte definitely didn't like them, Morwen thought, but there was no reason known to her, why she should not.

"It's for Justin to have the last word on it, of course," Morwen said. "But I'll put it to him, if you're sure it won't be too much for you, Mammie."

"When the day comes that 'tis too much trouble to cater for my own, you'll be the first to know, Morwen," Bess said drily. And there was no more to be said.

Chapter Four

The air in St Austell's meeting house was thick and cloying, blue with smoke from the mixture of many expensive cigars and humble hand-rolled cigarettes. But it was neither thicker nor bluer than the insults and blasphemies flying backwards and forwards across the room, in the ever-growing crush of clayworkers and bosses gathered there. The meeting had dragged on through the morning and afternoon, and was now into early evening, nothing sensible having yet come out of it. Nor was it helped by the Union men who objected to every suggestion put by the bosses, and scotched most of them.

" 'Tis madness," Hal Tremayne shouted above the din. "What bloody fool let all these buggers in? If we get many more coming off shift and trying to put in their two pen'orth, the floor will be fair near to collapse with all the weight."

"You were the one who said all and sundry should be allowed to come, man," Ran Wainwright snapped at him.

Hal glared at his son-in-law. He respected Ran, liked him well enough, but there were times when his sardonic American twang drove him wild. Bloody colonials, he thought viciously, coming over here and thinking they're God's gift to humanity . . . he caught the gleam in Ran's eye, and knew the American was following his every thought.

"They've every right to be here, Wainwright," one of Bult and Vine's bosses leaned forward and spoke. " 'Tis our way to let the workers have their say, and always has been, and we don't aim to change now."

And sure as hell not for the likes of you, said the unspoken words. Their eyes clashed, and Ran felt the same spark of animosity he had felt from Hal. It was he who who looked away first, but only when his stepson Walter cracked the

41

wooden mallet on the table, bellowing into the rowdy crowd, and making them all jump as if it was a pistol shot.

"Why don't you all shut up and let them that know what's what have their say?" he yelled, his words tripping over themselves in his effort to be heard. "We're gettin' nowhere with all this arguing, and I for one want to get home to my bed tonight."

"Yeah, and who wouldn't, with a pretty little wifey like yourn," one of the clayworkers at the back of the room heckled, sniggering suggestively. In the momentary silence Walter had created, the words were audible to all, causing more sniggers and obscene gestures, and his proud face flushed a dull, angry red.

And one man at the back of the room, dressed in clayworker's garb and with a slouch hat pulled well down over his face, made discreet comments in a notepad under cover of the crumpled newspaper he carried. He was careful not to be observed. If any of these roughnecks ever guessed that a disciple of Tom Askhew's newspaper, *The Informer*, was present at this closed-shop meeting, he'd be skinned alive before he could reach the door.

But he knew Askhew would be pleased with the ingenuity of his young protégé in gaining access to this meeting, and gleaning what information he could. And any gossipy snippet about young Walter Tremayne and the news editor's pretty daughter would be a bonus, especially when it was sent in anonymously to the letters page. Even more so when that same ambitious young reporter with an eye to the future knew how it would incense Tom Askhew and undermine his confidence as to where those damn letters were coming from.

Ellis White bent his head as a burly clayworker alongside him suddenly stared hard at him. Deftly and surreptitiously, Ellis managed to slide his notepad and pencil into his coat pocket.

"Who're you with, boy?" the older man said suspiciously. "I ain't seen you afore at Killigrew Clay and I know most of the men here from Bult and Vine's."

"I'm from over St Dennis way," Ellis said quickly,

evading the main question. "I'm a newcomer to the business, and I need to know what's in it for me, see?"

The other man laughed raucously amid the din that was already starting up again.

"You'm in the wrong trade then, boy. There ain't no money in china clay no more. Any fool can tell 'ee that. Why the devil d'you think we're all here?"

He turned away from the younger man, bored with an idiot without the gumption to see there were no fortunes to be made from an ailing industry. There never had been for the clayworkers, the man scowled. Even for the bosses, the glory days were past. And by all accounts, unless a miracle happened, those days that were left were fading fast.

The bosses were so busy filling the works with newfangled machinery that did the job no better than the old ways, in order to compete with one another, that there was no money left for those that toiled in the sodding wet clay in all weathers. All that happened was a glut of clay, with nowhere to sell it, except at rockbottom prices.

The man became incensed with his own thoughts, and the indignity of the clayworkers' lot. And this young fool was daft enough to come into it at what some saw as the worst of times . . . To the horror of Ellis White, he suddenly found himself grabbed by the scruff of the neck and almost pulled off his feet by a pair of huge hairy hands.

"Take a look at this young feller-me-lad," the man bawled out, while Ellis's heart thudded furiously, thinking his ruse had been found out. He'd have to bluster it out somehow, he thought wildly. He might be ambitious, but he wasn't a physical man, and nor was he prepared to take on these uncouth bastards for the sake of a newspaper story . . .

"What's to do wi' him, Herbie?" the man jostling him yelled back with some relish, sensing a fight.

The man called Herbie bawled out above the heads of the crowd, many of whom were turning their heads to look at the to-do at the back of the room now. Herbie's voice gathered pitch and momentum.

"This is what we'm here about, men. A young whippersnapper like this 'ere 'andsome lad, just making 'is way in

43

the world. What future is there for the likes of 'ee, when the bosses won't even consider givin' us the piddlin' extra two shillin' a week they promised us back a year and more. How's the likes of this un going to raise a family on such a pittance as is paid now, I'd like to know?"

The roars that accompanied Herbie's words drowned out the choking sounds from Ellis White's throat. He managed to point desperately at his throat, while he felt his eyes begin to bulge and his knees to buckle.

As if only just aware of what was happening, Herbie let him go. Whether or not he'd actually been suspended an inch or two above the floor, Ellis couldn't even tell. But it felt as if he had. He could barely swallow, and he wanted to crawl away and die from the fiery sensation in his throat. He'd be bruised tomorrow, he thought savagely, just when he'd arranged to meet a new friend, and now he'd be black and blue . . .

Well, if they wanted news of their doings put in print, they'd get it. An honest and fair report of their grievances by "our correspondent" would appear in *The Informer*, no matter how mysteriously they thought it had been obtained. And the anonymous and infamous letter writer who was causing such a stir whenever he put pen to paper, would take a sadistic pleasure in condemning the mentality of men as clodhopping as the clay beneath their feet, who conducted their meetings with all the finesse of wild animals tearing at each others' throats.

He felt his own throat tenderly for a moment, but his anger was being tempered now by knowing his own capabilities. He had few friends, and he was what folk termed a lone wolf. But if he didn't get along with people, at least words were his friends, and his education wasn't going to waste, he thought, preening himself. Words were powerful weapons, and although Tom Askhew himself was unaware of the letter writer's identity, Ellis got great satisfaction out of sniping away at all and sundry, especially his own editor, whenever he felt like it.

There was a sudden hush in the room, and the combined

raised voices of Walter and Hal Tremayne, Ran Wainwright, and Bult and Vine's representatives, dwindled away. Ellis swivelled his neck, wincing as he did so, and relishing the bloody tale he'd have to tell, of how he was manhandled in the company of these clayers . . .

Then, even his vicious thoughts were scattered as he saw what folk nearer to the door had seen.

A flash of scarlet satin startled him. Among this company of drab, dishevelled clayworkers, most of whom had lately come off their shifts, with grey-white, unwashed faces and filthy garb; and the bosses in their pressed suits and their high-polished boots and gaiters; the newcomer shone out like a glorious, glowing beacon.

Ellis's considerable command of words made his thoughts momentarily lyrical, and then the vision moved determinedly towards the platform where the bosses sat, and he closed his gaping mouth to try to think who the devil she was.

And a *woman*, for God's sake! What was a woman doing here, in this company, when no bal maiden would dare show her face, and not even Morwen Wainwright, with her rightful stake in Killigrew Clay, interfered with mens' business to this extent. His newspaperman's curiosity was aroused, overcoming his recent urgent need to get out of the cloying atmosphere and to breathe some clean salt air in his lungs.

"Who the devil is she?" he heard himself croak, and as the pathetic squeak came out he wondered for a frantic moment if his throat had been permanently damaged from the clay lout's rough handling.

But he didn't need to ask a second time. As the silver-haired woman with the feathered scarlet hat atop her curls, and the proud bearing in her slim, scarlet-clad shoulders, approached the platform with such assurance, the whispers of recognition were already rippling around the room.

" 'Tis Harriet Pendragon from over Bodmin way."

" 'Tis she who puts the fear o' God into her workers, but pays 'em shillin' for shilling' for a good week's work."

"Oh ah, wi' all the money old Pendragon left her, she can

45

do as she pleases, but 'tis dragon by name and dragon by nature, by all accounts."

"She be a fine creature, for all that, and one that a man 'ould be mighty eager to get his leg over, and her wi' no man to call her own no more—"

Ellis craned his neck, his interest quickening. He'd never seen the lady before, but he'd heard of her right enough. Who hadn't heard of Harriet Pendragon?

So this was the woman who had scandalized the county by taking over her husband's clayworks when he lay dying, and had continued to lord it over her workers ever since, behaving with all the ruthless power of a man. The woman with rumoured untold wealth at her disposal, who threatened to undercut the prices the other bosses got for their clay blocks, and was one of the prime suspects for already doing so, though nobody seemed able to prove it. And one who already paid her workers sixpence a day more than any other owner to keep them sweet.

If there hadn't been so much superstition attached to working for a woman, together with her reputed toughness, it was certain there were plenty of workers who'd desert their old employers and go to work at Pendragon Pits.

But, good God Almighty, Ellis thought anew, as he saw her mount the rostrum with voluptuous grace. This was no scarecrow bitch, ready to tear the eyes out of the first man to get in her way. This was a charmer of the first order . . . and one filled with staggering self-confidence to turn up in a whore's colour, and wear it so magnificently . . . he didn't dare get out his notepad again, but his memory was pin-sharp, and he mentally noted every iota of her appearance, and was ready to record inside his head every word she uttered.

He saw Hal Tremayne rise angrily to his feet. He knocked over his chair and left it where it fell, glowering at the woman with no quarter given in face or manner.

"Madam, you have no place here. This is a meeting called to order among men to discuss men's business, and I'll ask you to leave quietly."

Harriet Pendragon stood her ground and stared him

46

straight in the eyes. Hers were a strange silvery grey, almost matching the unnatural colour of her hair, as opposed to Hal Tremayne's hard blue eyes. If Ellis had been of a more regular inclination, he could have been stunned by such brittle beauty, but women held little interest for him.

He pushed such thoughts out of his mind for the present, and concentrated on what was happening on the platform. It was as if the whole roomful of men were doing the same, but for various reasons. Few of them had moved, and yet it seemed as if they all pressed forward, hanging on the drama being unfolded in front of them.

"None can dispute my right to own Pendragon Pits, and as a boss I've every right to have a say in the general mechanics of ownership. You've all shut me out for too long, Tremayne, and you're all fools if you take no notice of me, for I'll have the lot of you on your knees yet," she said, in a musical voice that belied the threat in her words.

"A woman can't control a couple of hundred men—" Hal snapped at her.

"Can you?" Harriet Pendragon countered. "I've seen no evidence of it here, and I understand this miserable meeting has already lasted most of the day with no conclusions drawn."

You had to admire her, thought Ellis White, as the mutters of assent ran round the room. She knew exactly how to pull the listening men to her side, while they waited for Hal's curt response. But it was Ran Wainwright who put a restraining hand on his father-in-law's arm and got slowly to his feet to face the woman.

"Mrs Pendragon, you have my sympathies," he said coolly. "A woman trying to walk in a man's shoes is always a pathetic creature."

She stared in disbelief at his gall, taking in every lithe line of him, infuriated yet intrigued by what she saw. A man to lean on was something Harriet had never had, nor ever wanted. But she could see that the Killigrew widow had got herself a man of some stature in all respects, despite the dislike she saw in his face towards herself.

47

"What?" she finally said, starting to laugh. "I don't think you know just who you're talking to, sir."

"Oh, but I do," Ran went on, his voice insulting and clipped, and at his New York best. "Just as I see exactly the effect you were trying to make in coming here tonight dressed like a streetwalker."

Harriet gasped in outrage, her hands clenched tight by her sides. Walter hid a chuckle, but she heard it, and rounded furiously on him.

"You think that's amusing, do you, young Killigrew? Well, perhaps you won't find it so funny when I take half your workers and give them decent jobs, and house them in cottages where the damp doesn't seep through the walls and give them all consumption by the time they're twenty-years-old!"

Some of the reps from Bult and Vine's had clearly had enough of this wrangling upstart, and had begun gathering up their papers, preparing to stalk out until another day. And the body of men in the room were alternately cheering and shushing their neighbours, in order to hear what was going on.

"I can see there's nothing to be gained here today," Harriet said, staring directly at Ran. "You're beneath bothering with, the lot of you. I came to offer the hand of friendship, but you'll never get any assistance from me now. I'll see you all rot in hell first."

She paused, and then spoke more coldly. "As for calling me a streetwalker, I'd look to the various amusements of your own adopted family if I were you, Ran Wainwright, before you start throwing insults at others."

She turned, and with her head held high, she walked through the throng of clayworkers, who parted their ranks at once, as if she was a ship in full red sail going through the parted waters of the sea. She was just as majestic, thought Ellis White admiringly, and his newspaper column was going to be full to the brim with today's events. He couldn't wait to get back to his digs and get started on it, and he was already composing the first paragraphs in his head by the time he slid out of the meeting house.

*   *   *

48

"It's high time we went home, my lovelies," Morwen told the children again, seeing how darkness was falling.

The younger ones were all but falling asleep on Bess's sofa now, and Bradley had stopped prowling about the house, his head now buried in some of the books in old Charles Killigrew's library.

By now, he had wheedled his grandmother into letting him stay the night, much to Morwen's annoyance. But she had eventually given in, knowing how much Bradley liked to jaw with his Grandpa Hal, though Lord knew what time he would be coming home tonight.

There would also be less friction in their own house without Bradley there, which left Morwen feeling guiltily that this was a fine way to regard her own son. But knowing it didn't alter her feelings. She glanced at her mother now, trying not to show her anxiety about the men's business.

"Do you suppose all is well in town?" she murmured, avoiding saying too much in front of Luke and Emma.

Bess shrugged. "Whether 'tis or not, there's nothing we can do about it, my dear, so we might just as well not fret over it."

"I knew you'd say that. You always do," Morwen said with a smile. It didn't help her at all, and she wasn't at all sure that her mother believed in her own wise words.

"The men know what they're doing. Strikes have been averted before, and there's no reason to think we'm heading for trouble yet," Bess said sagely.

"A strike wasn't averted earlier this year, was it? It lasted all of nine weeks then, and more than one family were made paupers by it," Morwen said.

She couldn't forget Tom Askhew's screamingly abusive newspaper headlines over a clayman who'd taken his own life rather than face utter destitution, and putting the blame for it squarely at the door of the clay bosses.

It wasn't as if Morwen hadn't sympathized, or agonized over the incident. She'd quietly visited the wife and children and taken them gifts of food and cast-off clothing. She wasn't one to broadcast her actions, but no matter what her

49

part in the ownership of Killigrew Clay, she couldn't forget her roots, nor how it felt to be without shoes or shame, or food in her belly, and the little family had been pathetically grateful.

Bess couldn't follow her thoughts, and commented sharply on Morwen's remark.

"Ah, and it all began through one young idiot being martyred after being let out of jail after one riot, and causing another. They all want their heads banged together if you ask me. 'Tis a pity women don't rule the world, then there'd be no talk of strikes and suchlike."

Morwen gave a half-smile, despite her worries. Her mother could always be relied upon to uphold the virtues and common-sense of womenfolk compared to their male counterparts, and she didn't altogether disagree with her.

"Anyway, I hope you're right about things being settled tonight," she said with a shiver. "Ran insisted that I keep well away from the town while the rioting went on in the new year, but I remember another time when the clayworkers marched right down to St Austell from Killigrew Clay. It terrified the whole town, and I hate to think our menfolk will have any hand in such a thing happening again."

"You can't dictate to claymen. It depends how much they want food in their bellies, and how strong their leadership is. If they think they've got a just cause to fight, there'll be no stoppin' 'em, Morwen. Never was, and never will be," Bess said.

Her mother was doing nothing to allay her fears, Morwen thought. She'd wanted Bess to say that of course the men wouldn't do anything so horrendous as marching on the town again and smashing up all that was in their way, and frightening decent folk to death . . . she wanted Bess to say that of course the bosses would see reason and go halfway to settling their demands . . . but she hadn't.

And as one of the bosses, Morwen knew just how bad the situation was. You couldn't just put your hand in your pocket and give extra dues when there wasn't the money to spare. Clay fortunes had fluctuated badly recently, and there was a glut of unsold clay in the whole industry going for dirt-cheap prices. You couldn't get gold out of a stone . . . and it was well known that there were some unscrupulous bosses ready to sell to any bidder in order to clear their stocks. Those who had unlimited resources of their own . . .

Emma yawned, and Morwen rang for the maid to alert Gillings to bring the carriage to the front of the house, and said they would be ready to leave for home in five minutes.

She caught sight of Bradley hovering by the door.

"You can come in, Bradley. I won't eat you," she said. "And since you persuaded your grandmother to indulge your wishes, I'm not insisting that you come home with us."

He came inside, relief on his face. And something else. He held an old book in his hands, and his usual ruddy complexion had become decidedly pasty.

"What have you found there?" Bess said at once.

"It's a strange tale about the town of St Dennis," Bradley said, his voice hoarse. "Did you know that three hundred years ago a shower of blood rained down on an acre of land thereabouts, and the stains stayed visible for about twenty years? And soon afterwards there was the great plague and the city of London burned, and all kinds of other ills occurred. You believe in such omens, don't you, Mother?"

Emma gave a little scream of fright, and the child rushed to her mother and hid her face in her skirts.

"He's horrid, Mammie, he knows I hate hearing about blood. It couldn't really rain blood, could it?"

"Of course it couldn't," Luke said loftily. "Bradley's making it all up."

"If you weren't such a dunce I'd tell you to read it for yourself," Bradley snapped. "It's all here, recorded in this book, and I bet the preacher could tell us something about it, too."

"Well, it was all so long ago I daresay it's got coloured a lot in the telling," Morwen said evasively. "I'd advise you to put that book away before you go to bed, Bradley, or you'll be having nightmares."

She was determined not to let his words upset her tonight,

when all her thoughts were on the threatened clay strike. She wanted no ancient omens to disturb her, nor would she acknowledge that of course she believed in omens. It was part of her nature to believe in all things being possible beneath the moon and stars, and even the fact that Bradley had discovered this ancient bit of folklore on this particular night could be construed as a bad sign.

She took a deep breath and ushered her children together as the sound of carriage wheels was heard outside. Thankfully, she bade her son and her mother good night, and let Gillings tuck the travelling blanket cosily around the younger ones before taking them home.

The night was starlit and still and very beautiful. A great yellow moon had risen in the sky, lighting the leafy lanes and byways almost as brightly as if the daytime hours still lingered. This was a good sign, Morwen thought determinedly. The moon and stars were guiding them safely home, and no bad things would happen to them between here and New World.

But she found that her fingers were crossed as she thought it, and superstitiously, she prayed that a hare wouldn't run across their path, for that would be a very bad omen indeed. If an old moorswoman was wandering abroad in the dark hours, begging for coins or food, this too would be bad, for she had nothing with her to give.

And everyone knew that a moorswoman who was refused sustenance could turn in a trice and curse the non-giver with all manner of ills. Morwen had been a child of the moors for too long to ignore such beliefs. So it was with enormous relief that she saw the solid structure of her home come into view, light beaming out from the windows, welcoming them home.

"We're here, children," she murmured, wondering why she had let herself become so gripped with terror and fancies that she had hardly been able to say a word to them on the journey. But it hadn't mattered, for both children were fast asleep now, and oblivious to anything other than their own sweet dreams.

52

"I'll call Mrs Enders to help 'ee in with 'em, Ma'am,"
Gillings said, as he called the horses to a halt at their
own front door. But as Morwen alighted thankfully, the
front door opened, spilling out more light into the night,
and the housekeeper bustled out to greet them without
being called.

"I was getting feared for 'ee, me dear," she said, with
the familiarity of one who had been in the same family's
service for many years. "Tis not a good time to be out of
doors with these babbies. And it seems that you've lost one
of 'em already."

Morwen smiled. "He's staying at his grandmother's house
tonight, Mrs Enders."

As the children stirred and fought against the housekeeper's embraces, Morwen spoke quickly. "Leave the
children to me, and just make us a hot drink, Mrs Enders.
I'll be down in ten minutes."

"As you wish, me dear. Will Mr Wainwright be following
on soon?"

"I don't know how long he'll be, but I'll be waiting up for
him, however late it gets. He'll be glad of a bit of company
when he gets home, so I'll keep the fire stoked."

Chapter Five

It was long past midnight when Ran Wainwright let himself quietly into the sleeping house. There were no lights left burning, and rightly so at this hour. There was only the orange glow from the dying embers in the drawing room fireplace to give a welcome bit of warmth to a man who had fought tooth and nail to make those blockheads see sense.

The crux of their worries was the fear that there might be a general lowering of wages until times improved, as had happened in the past. They wanted firm reassurances that it wouldn't happen again. The devil of it was, that no matter how adamant the bosses were in saying such a situation would be averted at all costs, the clay workers just didn't trust them. And Ran had to admit that their wording was ambiguous and full of loopholes.

Nobody could predict the future, and the present looked bleak enough. His nerves still raw, Ran wondered just what the hell it took to convince them.

And after an entire day and evening of trying to reason with fools, it wasn't only his nerves that suffered. His voice was hoarse, his throat sore and dry, his thoughts staccato-sharp, going over and over it all. If they would just hold on, things would improve. They'd done so before, and they'd do so again.

Ran was born an optimist, but he wasn't a blind one. And there were surely faint signs of better times ahead, if only these hotheads would exercise a bit of patience, and resist being sheep-led by rabble-rousers as usual, they'd all benefit by it.

He vented his feelings by muttering a colourful string of oaths into the silent room, wishing them all to Kingdom

54

Come. He strode across the drawing room to the drinks table and poured himself a large brandy. He felt the fiery liquid run slowly down his throat, soothing and stinging at the same time. God, he needed this.

A soft sigh from somewhere in the room made his heart stop and then race on madly for a moment. And then he saw a movement from the deep couch near the fire, and realized that he wasn't alone. But it was no ghostly spectre come to jeer at the upstart Yankee clay boss, who thought he could overturn the ingrained opinions of past generations of clay men by clever words.

"Morwen, what the devil are you doing there?"

The sudden shock of her presence would normally have produced an angry outburst. But the strain on his throat from this day's work made him huskier than he intended. And in the orange fireglow, he saw her give a tremulous smile and stretch out her hand towards him.

"I couldn't rest until I knew how things had gone, dar. Come and be warmed and tell me how you fared."

He stared down at her without speaking. She had undressed to be comfortable, and she lay there in her night-gown and dressing robe. Her glorious hair was unpinned and tangled about her shoulders, giving her a wanton, voluptuous air. She was still drowsy with sleep, and probably stiff with lying so long on the couch waiting for him. Waiting for him . . .

He sank down beside her as she shifted to the back of the couch that could easily accommodate two, making room for him. And as her arms reached out for him, and her soft lips touched his cheek, he was suddenly and unexpectedly intoxicated in a way that no amount of brandy could achieve.

"Well, dar?"

But she spoke in a whisper now, well aware that there was a time for discussing business matters, and a time for other things. And even more aware that Ran knew it too. She could sense it by his quickening breath, and feel it in the growing hardness of his body next to hers.

"Well, honey?" Ran echoed softly, his hands running

down the length of her in the soft, loose garments. She felt a shuddering pleasure at his touch, and a revival of all the sweet sensations that had seemed so lacking of late. Ran gently pushed aside the dressing robe, gently palming her breasts before bending his head to kiss the erect nipples through the soft fabric of her night-gown. Such an action was teasingly erotic, and Morwen felt her heart begin to hammer in her chest, knowing that this was only the beginning, and that the best was yet to come . . .

"If you really want to hear of today's happenings now, I'll tell you," he murmured. "Though there's nothing that can't wait to be told, and you and I have far more important things to attend to here."

"Then let's attend to them first," she whispered back.

All day she had fretted and worried over what was happening at the meeting house. But, in her daddy's own wise words, worrying over a thing didn't change it, and if there was nothing you could do about it, you might as well get on with something of more importance . . . and right now there was nothing more important for her husband and herself, than this renewal of love . . .

"I closed the door," Ran said, unnecessarily, for it was well past the middle of the night, and even if anyone would dare to abuse their unwritten law of privacy behind closed doors, no one else was awake at this hour. The whole house was sleeping, save for the two lovers intent on rediscovering each other in the firelight's glow.

"God, I love you, my darling girl," Ran groaned.

She was the one area of sanity in this crazy day. He clung to her, lifting her night-gown and finding her with his fingertips. She was warm and moist and ready for him, and he quickly shed his clothes and slid into her, glorying in the lush feel of her closing around him.

"Oh, I love you too, Ran," Morwen said, with a catch in her throat. "Always, no matter what. Don't ever doubt that, my dar."

"How could I, when you give me all that a man could ever want in his woman?" he said, his voice thicker now as the rhythmic movements of love claimed them both. His weight

56

was heavy on her, but she welcomed it, just as she welcomed the familiar pattern of his lovemaking. It was unquenchable, this love he felt for her, and her for him. It took them to the stars and dazzled them with its brilliance.

And when it was over and he had filled her with his loving, they still clung to each other, still a part of each other, as if each was reluctant to become half of two separate beings again.

They didn't speak for long moments, and merely lay caressing one another in the sweet afterglow of love. When the rapture had died down a little, Morwen spoke softly against her husband's cheek, as he nestled his face against her neck.

"How shameful we are, making love in the drawing room like two clandestine lovers, instead of two respectable middle-aged married people!" she said, a smile in her voice.

Ran twisted his head to kiss the soft mouth that was still swollen with passion. His voice was quietly arrogant with the memory of a man's pleasure in a woman.

"God forbid the day should come when we ever succumb to being no more than that, honey. You'll always be my lover, first and foremost – my sweet, seductive, beautiful lover – and don't you ever forget it!"

"No, Sir," she whispered back, secure in his love and revelling in the uninhibited words he uttered.

But she wasn't oblivious to the fact that times like these were far less frequent now than they once were. It was only natural, she supposed. Time moved on, and they moved on with it . . . but she wished she could hold on to these golden moments for ever, and never let them go.

It wasn't until the next morning over a late breakfast that she asked him how the meeting went. The children were already at their lessons in the nursery with their tutor, and Justin hadn't yet appeared downstairs. Last night had been too precious to spoil with mundane reports, since Ran had already implied that there was nothing of any great import to tell. But now she had to know, and the questions tumbled out.

"Were the men satisfied that it's impossible for any of us to improve their wages for the present, Ran? Did you make the position absolutely clear, and were you convinced there was no threat of any new strikes in the offing? And were Bult & Vine solid behind us?"

"For God's sake, one question at a time, Morwen! It all ended reasonably peaceably, given their natures, and Bult & Vine's were rock solid behind us – eventually," he said grimly. "God help them if they hadn't been, after all our efforts beforehand. We had to be solid, honey, or we'd surely have had a riot on our hands."

"But I can't believe there was no hint of trouble. Are you telling me everything?" she persisted, unable to imagine such a meeting being conducted quietly.

She knew the clayers too well. And she knew her own menfolk too well. There had been other times when shots were fired in the air to quell the noise . . . she saw Ran frown, and half-wished she'd never started this inquisition. But it was her right to know, and if he didn't tell her, her daddy would.

"There was the usual heckling and baiting, and a couple of irritating incidents," he said, more sharply.

"*Well*? Am I supposed to guess what they were?" she demanded as he paused.

"I suppose your father or your son will report it all, if I don't," he said shortly.

"Yes, they will. And I do have a right, Ran!"

"Oh yes, I was forgetting. You were a Killigrew before you were a Wainwright, weren't you?"

Morwen bit her lip, refusing to retort to this jibe. After last night, she simply didn't understand how he could be like this. As if the loving had never happened. As if the closeness between them had vanished like a moorland mist. His ability to switch from passion to coldness so successfully seemed to signify the difference between a man and a woman, she thought. For her, the magic still lingered . . .

"I'm sorry," he said now, as she remained silent. "That was an unnecessary remark, and I withdraw it."

You can't withdraw it, Morwen thought. *Once said, the words were there for all time.*

Justin came into the breakfast room at that moment, and she turned to him with some relief. He looked tired, and she said at once that Daniel Gorran was working him too hard.

"Don't mamby-pamby him, Morwen," Ran said at once, before Justin could answer. "He's a man, for God's sake, not a callow youth. At least, he'll be old enough to call himself a man in a couple of week's time."

"That bothers you, does it?" Justin said, staring him out with his cold blue eyes. Morwen had never realised how cold those eyes could be until they looked at her husband with such dislike. Since she loved them both, she mourned the fact that they would never get along, but she wasn't prepared to let it ruin her life.

"Why should it? You'll always be a boy while you're living under my roof," Ran snapped.

Justin turned to his mother, while he helped himself to kippers and toast from the side table.

"That's something I have to talk to you about, Mother," he said. "Daniel Gorran has offered me a partnership on my twenty-first birthday, and I can take over fully in six month's time when he retires to St Ives with his sister."

"Justin, that's wonderful news!" Morwen said.

"But I can move into the living accommodation above the Chambers as soon as I like. I thought I'd do so after my birthday, if you've got no objection."

Morwen stared at him. She hadn't expected him to live at home for ever, but nor had she expected this to happen so soon. But the small sneer in Ran's voice warned her that it was the most sensible thing to happen for all of them.

"Congratulations, Justin. A legal partnership at your age is quite a feather in your cap."

"Yes, it is. I'm grateful for all I've learned at Gorran's, and I mean to take this chance," he said quietly.

And oh yes, Morwen thought. Whatever Ran might think of Ben Killigrew's son, he was already a man. He was modest enough to know his worth, and strong enough to be unaffected by it. She went to her son and kissed him.

"Well done, my love. I shall miss you, though," she said softly.

His arm slid around her slim waist and hugged her. "It's not as if I'm going a million miles away, is it? And I'll still be involved in the fortunes of Killigrew Clay through my work."

Before Ran could comment further on every damn Killigrew and Tremayne having a finger in the pie, Morwen spoke quickly.

"Grandma Bess wants to throw a party for your birthday, Justin, and I've said we'll hold it at Killigrew House. You won't make a fuss now, will you? She wants to do it for 'ee so much."

"I can hardly refuse then, can I?" he grinned, hearing the way her voice softened and mellowed, and thinking that between the two of them, his mother and grandmother could twist most folk around their little fingers.

"I've work to do in the study so I'll leave you two to your discussions," Ran said, pushing his chair away from the dining-table, as if he couldn't bear to watch the intimacy that existed between them. Justin, of all her family, was the one he seemed to resent most. And Morwen didn't need telling that it was because he was so like Ben.

But when her son had left for St Austell she followed Ran into his study, knocking on the door first and being told coldly to enter. She stood with her back to the door, waiting until her husband finished fiddling with the sheaf of papers on his desk, and decided to look up and ask what she wanted.

"You can be so ungracious!" she burst out. "I sometimes think there are two people inside you, Ran! One that can be warm and loving, and everything I want, while the other one—"

"Well, if that's the case, then I'm afraid it's the bad guy that you see this morning," he drawled. "Now, what is it that you want? I'm very busy, as you can see."

Her eyes caught sight of the long envelope on his desk,

60

with the distinctive American postmark. She drew in her breath, and everything else was forgotten for the moment.

"Have you heard from Matt?" she exclaimed.

He shuffled the envelope and its contents into the folder in front of him.

"I haven't heard from your brother in months," he said. "These are business documents, and nothing more. Now, I must ask you again what you want, Morwen?"

Her swift excitement dwindled into disappointment. She hadn't heard from Matt in months either, and nor had her mother. And he'd been so good in writing in recent years, and telling them all about his life in California with Louisa and Cresswell. His own son would be twenty-one very soon too, she remembered, and wondered what kind of celebration they would be having for him.

"*Well?*" Ran snapped.

The frisson of annoyance she felt towards him, erupted into something much wilder. She marched forward and leaned on his desk with the flat of both hands, her eyes jewel-bright with anger.

"You are without doubt the most irritating and impatient man I know!" she snapped back. "I'm still waiting to hear about these two incidents at the meeting yesterday, and I demand that you tell me right now. Is that too much to ask? Or do I have to ride up to Killigrew Clay and get the news from Walter? A fine sight that will look, won't it!"

For a moment they glared at one another, and then a slow grin spread across Ran's face.

"It may be a tired old cliché for a man to tell a woman she looks magnificent when she's angry, but by God, Mrs Wainwright, you sure as hell do!"

She said nothing, but despite herself, her mouth began to twitch, and then she was grinning back at him, as daft as a Cheshire cat. But she sat down on the chair on her side of the desk and folded her arms, and had no intention of moving until she got an answer.

"There was a fellow at the meeting I hadn't seen before," he said abruptly. "There was something about him I didn't like. He could have been a county man or a spy from some

61

other works, for all I know. One of the men almost throttled him, by all accounts, but it happened so near the back of the room that the truth of it was garbled. It probably meant nothing, but for some reason it niggles away at me."

It didn't sound like much to Morwen, but she knew how the men guarded their precious meetings from prying eyes and ears. They hated the interference of the Union men, and not even the bal maidens were allowed to join in, no matter that many of those women had given all their working lives to one particular clay works.

"What was the other incident? You said there were two," Morwen said, thinking that if the second was no more interesting than the first, she was sorry she'd bothered to ask at all.

She saw Ran glance at her and then glance away, and at once her intuition was alerted. She didn't know the reason, but she knew Ran would prefer not to pass on this second piece of information. And she was just as determined to hear it. She stared at him without blinking, knowing how it would push him into speaking.

"You've heard of Harriet Pendragon, of course," he said shortly.

"Of course. Who hasn't?" she began, and then the farthing dropped. "You aren't going to tell me that woman turned up at the meeting, are you?"

"She said she had every right to be there. She's a clay boss—"

"So am I, if it comes to that! At least, I'm part owner, but I wasn't invited to attend—"

"God dammit, woman, neither was the Pendragon female! You know that well enough, so don't go making something out of it that don't exist."

"So did she just walk in and join you all on the platform then?"

She hadn't felt jealousy in years. There had never been any cause, and there probably wasn't any cause now. If the accounts that circulated about the Pendragon woman were anything to go by, she was probably an old hag. But the feelings of jealousy surging through

Morwen's veins right then were sharp and bloody and cancerous.

"She tried it," Ran said, unwittingly adding to the feelings. "But between us all, we soon sent her packing."

"So what did she want?" Morwen said, trying not to let the red rage take her over completely.

"To make some kind of a deal, I gather. We didn't listen long enough to find out. We just wanted to get her out of there before she undid all the good we'd done."

Morwen didn't say anything for a moment. But she had to know something more.

"What was she like? She's kept well away from this district for so long, I can't think why she would want to interfere with us."

"Maybe times are hard for her too, despite all her assets," he said, though without conviction. Any fool could see that wealth oozed out of the woman. Her self-assurance alone confirmed as much.

"Are you going to describe her to me, or do I have to ask Walter about that too?" Morwen demanded.

"Damn it, woman, why can't you leave things alone? She was no more than a bloody interfering nuisance, flouncing through the men, done up in scarlet satin and feathers that would have looked more at home in a whorehouse!"

Morwen felt as if she physically reeled backwards, even though she didn't move a muscle. The words were vicious and ugly, but even if he didn't realise it, Ran painted a vivid picture of a beautiful woman, not the hag that everyone had believed Harriet Pendragon to be.

"So," she said slowly, when the silence between them stretched into minutes. "This Pendragon woman is somebody to be reckoned with, is she?"

Ran looked at her in surprise.

"I didn't say so, and nor do I think so. She's one woman among a dozen clay bosses—"

"I'm a woman too, and I own a share in Killigrew Clay," she reminded him. He brushed her words aside as if they were of little consequence.

"But you've always agreed that the running of the

business is rightly left to men, Morwen. This damn woman is no more than a thorn in our sides, that's all."

But still somebody to be reckoned with, Morwen thought, *and not just in the business sense, either*.

But it would do no good to question Ran further. He was already busy with his papers, and shutting her out. It was as if she had nothing to do with Killigrew Clay at all. Well, she had a say in everything. The works belonged jointly to Hal Tremayne, Ran and herself, and she'd be damned if she was going to be pushed aside as a mere woman, especially when there was another one on the horizon who seemed to have control of everything she owned.

Morwen had never been covetous of the business before, and she wasn't now. But she could see that this Pendragon woman wielded a power that she herself didn't have, and there was nothing like the aphrodisiac of a powerful business rival, man or woman. She prayed that the woman wouldn't be a rival in another sense too.

"I'll leave you to your papers," she said quickly, wishing to God the thought had never entered her head.

"All right," Ran said, as carelessly as if he hardly heard her. "Enjoy your day, honey."

She went out, resisting the childish urge to slam the door behind her. *Enjoy your day* indeed! As if she was one of those females who spent their days idling in social chit chat, when she had always done an honest day's work . . .

She brought herself up short. She was thinking in the past again. It had been many years since she'd toiled in the clay with the other bal maidens in their bright dresses and bonnets, scraping the blocks in the linhay and being part of a close-knit world that was unlike any other.

Where men and women and young uns all worked together like an army of ants on the moors above St Austell, gouging out the earth's humble white substance that had such rich, far-reaching properties. Providing fine table-ware for dukes and princes. Settling a clayman's stomach after a night's drinking by scooping up a handful of slurry that they swore was God's own medicine.

Seeing through the production of the clay, the drying

and stacking, and sending off the twice-yearly careering wagonloads piled precariously high to the ports, down the steep hills to St Austell and beyond. Remembering the pleasures and pains of it all, the cheery young kiddley-boys, the bronzed young men stoking the fire-hole, stripped to the waist with their bodies gleaming with sweat . . .

She drew in her breath as a sudden sharp image of Ben Killigrew filled her senses; young and virile and determined not to let the men think he was too proud to do a man's work despite being the boss's son. And her own daddy, Hal Tremayne, pit captain of Clay One at that time, viewing the educated Killigrew boy with new respect as he never wavered all that long, hot day in the fire-hole.

Was it true that, after all, she still longed in her bones for the man she had once loved to distraction? Did love ever really die? Was Ran Wainwright more canny than she supposed, in suggesting that she still wanted Ben Killigrew in her bed, alive or dead?

Morwen jerked herself into action, knowing she was letting herself be overtaken by disturbing and distasteful thoughts. But the longing to be as she was, just once more, was too strong to resist. Without questioning it any further, she went upstairs to change into suitable clothes and then went to the stables, instructing Gillings to saddle her mare.

"'Tis a good day for a ride, Ma'am," he said, nodding. "You know what they say – rain afore seven, fine afore eleven. I reckon theym right an' all."

She hadn't even been aware that it had been raining earlier in the day, but now she could see that the moors above were shining in the April sunlight, as new and green and gold as if they had been specially painted by an artist's hand. And far above them, their tips just visible from here, were the towering sky-tips. She couldn't see them glinting from this distance, but she knew they would be diamond-bright. But the rain wouldn't have stopped any of the work at Killigrew Clay. The beam engines would be grinding away, the little trucks would be shifting slurry onto the ever-growing spoil heaps, the chatter would be never-ending . . .

She hadn't left any messages as to where she was going. The children would be busy at their lessons all day; Justin would have departed for Gorran's Chambers by now; and Ran wouldn't miss her.

The closer she got to Clay One, the more the sense of excitement seized her. This was where they had all worked, all her large, rumbustious family; her Mammie and Daddy, her brothers Sam, Jack, Matt and small Freddie; and herself. It had been their life, and as she breathed in the chalky dampness of the clay and nodded to one and another who recognized her, she felt a peculiar sense of coming home. Only when she passed the milky-green waters of the clay pool did she feel a twist in her heart, for this was where her friend Celia Penry had been found floating face down in the scum.

"Mother, is something amiss?"

She turned her head swiftly, thankful for a familiar voice, and smiled reassuringly at the tall figure of Walter Tremayne, as she slid down from the mare's back. The fact that the heels of her fine leather boots sank immediately into the slushy earth didn't bother her in the slightest.

"Of course not, Walter. Why should there be?" she said brightly.

"What are you doing here then?"

It occurred to her that he looked less than pleased to see her. She frowned, surprised by his businesslike manner.

"Can't I come to visit my own son when I choose? I hardly see you or Cathy these days, and I do have a personal interest in Killigrew Clay!"

Dear God, she was defending herself now, but she was starting to feel more unsettled by the minute. Walter took hold of the mare's reins, and walked with her.

"I know that, but these are sensitive times, Mother, and after yesterday's meeting—"

"What exactly went on, Walter?"

"Hasn't your husband told you?"

Oh, but there was no doubting the friction between them now. She could hear it in his voice. She recalled a sweet,

66

long ago moment when Ran had told her that her children had more sense than she did, when she was dithering about marrying him . . . the children had wanted her to marry him then, even the older ones, Walter and Albert and Primmy . . . but that eagerness had fizzled away over the years. Justin actively disliked his stepfather, and sometimes she sensed that Walter merely tolerated Ran Wainwright and his American ways.

"I know there were a couple of incidents," she said flatly. "And the appearance of a certain woman."

To her annoyance Walter began to laugh. His good humour was quickly restored, and he leaned forward and kissed her in full view of the curious clay workers thereabouts.

"Oh Mother, you've no need to be jealous of Harriet Pendragon! She and Ran were both in a battling mood, but I assure you he gave her as good as she gave him."

Which was just the kind of remark that didn't assure Ran's wife one bit.

Chapter Six

In retrospect, it hadn't been such a good idea to visit the clayworks. Although many folk had recognized her, it was quickly obvious that Morwen wasn't being viewed in the old familiar way. She was no longer one of them, and she didn't belong here any more. She knew it in her heart, and she should have accepted it years ago.

The women workers that she didn't know fell silent as she spoke to the others, and even they only answered when they were spoken to. She could have wept at their servile attitude, compared with the camaraderie of old. It wasn't what she wanted or what she had expected.

But she knew she was being completely naïve in feeling that way. Her daddy was right, as always. You could never go back, and it was a foolish person who tried to recapture a past that was gone. Even the row of cottages where they had all lived, was different now. The slate roofs were repaired and moderately tidy, the windows had been replaced and had a reasonable shine on the glass, and some of the tiny yards had flowers struggling to survive in them.

It wasn't all poverty then, Morwen thought, and the fierce pride of the clayworkers was obviously extending to their homes. She rode past the cottages, ignoring the sight of the one where her own family had once been crammed inside, and headed onwards to Penwithick Church.

She hadn't intended going there, but something drew her to the place where she and Ben had been married, and where they had brought him for his final long sleep. Where too, her brother Sam and his wife, and her best friend Celia, were all buried. She was spooked by memories, and unable to rid herself of them.

She tied up her mare and went inside the ancient grey church. It was cold and musty and hushed, and she sat down gingerly on one of the wooden pews near the door. She closed her eyes and said a little prayer for all of them, asking for help in their fortunes, and a return to constant happiness for herself and her husband. But maybe that was too much to ask for. Constant happiness could be as much of a burden as constant misery . . .

"Mrs Killigrew?"

She jumped at hearing herself addressed so, and all her nerves were on edge as she heard a man's scratchy voice alongside her.

"I beg your pardon, Ma'am," the voice continued. "I should say Mrs Wainwright. But it is you, isn't it?"

Morwen kept her eyes closed a moment longer. The last thing she wanted was the company of some pauper asking for help . . . and she was immediately ashamed at the thought, for her own family had been near enough to being paupers at one stage of their lives, and she mentally wondered what coins she had in her purse . . .

Then she saw that it was the elderly preacher of Penwithick Church, more bent and crumpled than of old, but still the same man. And she felt her face flood with colour.

"I'm sorry. I probably shouldn't be here at this hour of the day—" she said, scrambling to her feet, but the old man put a restraining hand on her arm.

"Where else should a troubled soul be, if not in God's House?" he said.

"Oh, but I'm not—" she stopped speaking as he looked at her sorrowfully.

"'Tis a sadness that folk often forget to praise God when things be going well, and only show their faces in His House in times of trouble."

It was a reproach, but it was said with resignation rather than malice, and Morwen knew guiltily that it was true enough. Not that her family was beholden to Penwithick Church, for they lived outside the parish now, but nor did they frequent any other.

"My troubles aren't worth mentioning, compared with

many others," she said quietly, noting the patched jacket and trousers that the man wore, compared with her best quality wool riding costume.

He patted her hand.

"God knows all about it," he said, with a comfortable vagueness, at which all Morwen's finer feelings vanished, and she felt a great irritation towards the smugness of the man. She shook off his hand and got to her feet.

"Well then, He'll forgive me for not stopping any longer," she said. "My children will be watching out for me."

He let her go without another word. He made her feel distinctly uncomfortable, as if she trespassed in a place where she had no right to be. But for once, she could find no comfort in a church, and she stepped out into the sunlight with a feeling of relief. The clumps of daffodils along the grassy churchyard paths nodded and danced their heads in the small breeze, and she swallowed hard, knowing that if she remained here it would be Celia she saw in their faces.

It was a bad omen, she thought, as she mounted the patiently waiting mare. All this clinging to the past, and the ghosts of those who were no longer with them . . . even coming here, where those she loved rested for all eternity . . . it was definitely a bad omen.

She dug her heels in the mare's sides, and raced the animal down the steep hillside all the way to New World. But despite the exertion involved, she was chilled by her own fey thoughts, and they wouldn't leave her. As if she stood and watched a play being enacted through a misty veil, she knew with certainty that death was hovering somewhere in the wings. And she couldn't stop it.

Two days later, Ran came storming home from St Austell, and threw a newspaper down on the drawing room couch where Morwen was reading to Emma. She told the child quickly to go upstairs and wash her hands ready for her tea, and to tell her brothers to do the same.

"I don't know where they are," Emma wailed. "I think Bradley was going to the beach to find shells—"

"He'd better damn well not have gone there without telling anybody, nor taken Luke with him," Ran snapped, diverted briefly. "Anyway, Miss, you go and do what your mother tells you and see if the boys are in the house."

He shooed her to the door, and closed it firmly behind her. Morwen didn't yet know what had happened, but it was obviously not good, and she sighed again, seeing that Ran was in such a black mood. Her recent visit to Penwithick Church had eventually calmed her nerves to a certain extent, but she should have known it wouldn't last.

"What's happened, dar?" she said quietly now.

He picked up the newspaper as if it stung him, and flicked through the pages until he found what he was seeking. The headline was bold and black, and Morwen took in the gist of it in one glance:

WOMAN CLAY BOSS DISRUPTS CLAYWORKERS' MEETING

The article beneath the headline was vicious and snide. It reported all the doings of the meeting in great detail, and it made hay of describing Harriet Pendragon's appearance in similar terms to the way Ran had done. It took special glee in the clash between the male and female bosses, and left the reader in no doubt that the clay industry was once again in a state of chaos.

When Morwen had skimmed through the offending article, she looked at Ran. Her mouth was dry, for however vicious the reporting, there were too many grains of truth in it to be ignored. But *how* . . .?

"You didn't know there was anyone there from the newspaper?" she said unnecessarily. Ran glowered at her.

"You know as well as I do that it's our rule to provide them with a statement on our affairs when we think fit, and not before. We don't invite newspaper scum to our meetings, when things can get out of hand, and anything can be twisted to suit their scandalmongering."

"Then either somebody from *The Informer* got in illegally, or you've got a spy among you," Morwen said flatly.

71

"I'd already come to that conclusion. Any one of the bastards could be willing to sell his grandmother for the sake of a few extra pennies."

"Is that fair?" Morwen said, defensive at once. "They need more dues, Ran, and we all know it. The fact that we're unable to pay them any more at present won't put shoes on the children's feet, or food in their bellies."

"What's bloody fair about disloyalty? They've all got work, which is more than they'll get if they go on strike again. This time, we won't hold their jobs for them. Once they strike, they go."

Morwen jumped up from the couch, staring down at her husband with tight-clenched hands.

"Ran, you can't do that! The Unions will be down on you faster than a flea on a dog's back. It's a man's right to strike if he has a genuine grievance, and unless he commits a crime against his employer in doing so, his job should remain open to him."

"I wish you'd keep your bloody head out of business affairs, and stick to your homemaking," he snapped, but she knew he was retaliating now because he also knew she was right. She sank down beside him, taking his hand tightly in hers and looking pleadingly at him.

"I know you're hurt by this newspaper article, dar, but we just have to weather the present circumstances. Things have got to improve. The clay blocks are due for shifting to the port any day now, and once the money for them comes in, maybe we can pay the men a small bonus, even if it's only a shilling a man. 'Tis very little for the work that they do. Believe me, I know."

"Your trust in human nature blinds you to hard facts, Morwen. What makes you think we'll get payment on time once we shift the blocks? Nobody wants to pay up these days, and with other firms undercutting us—"

"It's the Pendragon woman, isn't it?" Morwen said. "It has to be her. I'm not so blind that I can't see that, Ran."

"Maybe," he said, removing her hand and crushing the pages of the newspaper into an untidy mass.

*   *   *

Walter came to the house unannounced while they were still arguing. It was rare for him to leave the clayworks in the middle of the day, but one look at his face, and Morwen knew he'd seen the newspaper too.

"Who did it, I'd like to know?" he shouted at Ran. "What bastard sold us up for a miserable few pence?"

"Walter, I'm sure it wasn't one of our men—" Morwen put in nervously, hating to see him so incensed.

"I'm thinking the same," her son said, to her surprise. "In fact, I've been giving serious thought to it, Mother. But there was somebody else there who'd not be displeased at having our doings reported for all to see, wasn't there?"

"Harriet Pendragon," Morwen answered.

"Aye, the same," Walter said grimly. "'Twould be to her advantage to let folk know there was such trouble among us all, wouldn't it?"

"What would be the point, since she's a clay boss herself? And just what do you suppose was in it for her, apart from trying to wheedle her way into a man's world?" Ran said.

"You obviously haven't turned to the Letters Page. The phantom letter writer who declines to give his name seems to have a pretty fair knowledge of the lady's intentions."

Walter snatched up the crumpled newspaper and tore through the pages until he found what he was seeking. He jabbed a finger at the heading above the first letter:

LADY BOSS WANTS COMPLETE CONTROL

The letter went on to say that the writer had it on good authority that a certain fair-haired lady with a penchant for vivid dressing, and unlimited assets to her name, intended to buy up all the china clay businesses in the area. And how would the likes of the Killigrew bosses take to that?

Morwen felt total shock at the bald statement, though she wasn't prepared to take it seriously. Even so, there was something here that she didn't like.

"Why should the letter writer single us out?" she said quickly. "What has the man got against us?"

"If it is a man," Ran growled.

Walter scoffed at this. "I'd lay odds it's a man all right. But I'd say he also had a pretty good sniff at the way the Pendragon woman was eyeing up somebody on the platform."

Ran's face darkened to a dull red.

"Just what are you implying, Walter?" he snapped.

"I'm implying nothing. But if you've forgotten why a woman's eyes sparkle in a certain way, then you're older than I thought," he taunted.

"You're talking absolute rubbish, and I'd have thought there were more important things for you to think about than trying to make mischief between your mother and me."

Morwen listened in tight-lipped silence. It was so unlike Walter to act this way. He might roar like a lion at the works, but he was a peaceable man at home, and he'd never willingly upset her. But he was doing so now.

"There's nothing we can do about this, except to keep our eyes and ears open," Ran went on. "It's probably all down to an over-active imagination on some fool's part, and I refuse to issue a statement on such wild conjectures. If we ignore it, it will die a natural death."

"I disagree—" Walter began, but Ran broke in.

"Well, God knows you rarely agree with anything I say, so that's only to be expected."

"Ran, that's not fair," Morwen said uneasily, hating to see these two at loggerheads. "Anyway, can we please leave it for now? I want to hear how Cathy is, Walter."

"Well enough," he muttered. "These last weeks are a trial for her, and the baby's lying awkwardly. The doctor has warned us that it's a big child, and the birth might be difficult, and of course her father blames me for that, as well as everything else to do with his daughter!"

The sheer frustration on his face at that moment was too much for Morwen. She put her arm around him and hugged him close. Big as he was, he was still her son, adopted or not, and still her best beloved.

"Tom Askhew's an idiot," she said steadily. "Everybody knows that, just as everyone knows that a big child has a better start to life than a puny one."

74

Walter gave her a thin smile for the first time since coming into the house.

"I knew I could trust you to put things in perspective, Mother," he said, but without much conviction.

Ran gave an impatient sigh. "Well, if you two have finished putting the domestic world to rights, I suggest that Walter and I consult with Hal over this newspaper rag. I don't aim to do anything about it, but we need to consolidate on what to do if anything comes of this ridiculous suggestion regarding the Pendragon woman."

"Right," Walter said at once, and Morwen thought how little tact it took on Ran's part to make her son feel worthy again. Since Cathy became pregnant, he'd shown a vulnerability she hadn't suspected in him. It would be a good thing when the baby came, and he wasn't constantly living on his nerves.

Ran gave her a perfunctory kiss goodbye, but she wouldn't let him go like that. She wound her arms about his neck and held him to her for a longer moment than was necessary, seeing Walter turn quickly away. She spoke softly in Ran's ear.

"I love Killigrew Clay, dar, but I love you more, and I'd see it destroyed before I saw it destroy us."

He breathed in sharply at such an unexpected avowal, and she was surprised at herself. She hadn't intended saying any such thing, and nor had she known such a sentiment existed in her. But it did, and now it was said. Ran squeezed her waist hard and gave a small nod, before turning to leave for St Austell with Walter.

"There's somebody to see you, Ma'am," Mrs Enders said a while later, her voice high, and her face full of disapproval.

"Who is it?" Morwen said, taking the card from the silver salver as she spoke. Her heart leapt uncomfortably as she saw the name on the visiting card. The words *Harriet Pendragon* danced in front of her eyes. What did that woman want with her? And how *dare* she come here uninvited? Not that she would ever be invited to Morwen's home . . .

"Shall I tell her you're not at home, Ma'am?" Mrs Enders said, awaiting instructions.

It was so very tempting.

"No. I can't think what she wants with me, but I'll hear what she has to say. You may show her in here, Mrs Enders, and tell her I can give her ten minutes and no more."

And in stating her terms, Morwen underlined her position here. She sat up very straight, smoothing down her pale green afternoon gown, and priding herself on the tasteful ambience of the drawing room. Someone who had gone to a men's meeting dressed in scarlet satin should be effectively intimidated by the quiet grandeur of New World and the self-assurance of its mistress.

The next moment, Morwen had a job not to let her mouth drop open with shock. She had expected a vulgar, buxom streetwoman, newly rich with her elderly dead husband's money. What she saw was a woman in gaudy enough garb, the deep purple satin gown and bonnet shrieking with bad taste; yet it complemented the silver-blonde hair and the startlingly light eyes in a way no other colour could have done. And she wasn't old, or fat, or ugly . . .

Morwen rose stiffly, completely knocked off-balance by the aplomb of the woman walking gracefully towards her now, a half-smile on her rouged lips, her slender, gloved hand outstretched to greet her as if they were old friends.

"Mrs Wainwright, I do hope you'll forgive the informality of this visit, but since I was in the area, I wanted so much to meet you."

There was a trace of a Cockney accent in the voice. Morwen remembered hearing at the time that old Pendragon had met his wife while on a short outing to London, and had married her within weeks. Looking at the woman, it would seem likely. Those hard, silvery, calculating eyes were taking in everything about the room now, and Morwen wondered if she was mentally pricing it all up in her mind. She declined to take the proffered hand, and Harriet Pendragon withdrew it with an amused smile.

"I can only give you ten minutes," she reminded her. "I have other appointments today, so please say what you've come here to say."

She knew she was being ungracious, but she didn't care.

She was filled with a deep mistrust of this woman. There was an aura surrounding her that was as dark as the colour she wore. It was as crystal clear to Morwen as if she had painted it there herself. It was a devil's colour. She shook her head as if to clear her mind, and asked Harriet Pendragon abruptly to sit down. Not for the world was she going to offer her tea and turn this into a tête-à-tête, but she could hardly leave a visitor standing. Besides which, the dark aura was very strong, and while the woman was on her feet, it threatened to overpower Morwen.

Harriet sat down with a ripple of satin fabric, sitting with her hands folded perfectly in her lap. Morwen knew instinctively that she hadn't been born a lady, but she had learned and practised the etiquette of good manners. Morwen hadn't been born a lady either, but knowing it did nothing to endear her to this one.

"You'll have seen the current issue of the Truro newspaper, I daresay," Harriet said, with no attempt at the niceties of conversation.

"I don't believe there was anything in it of great importance to me," Morwen said coldly.

"Do you not? From all that I've heard about you, I wouldn't have taken you for a fool, Mrs Wainwright, and I thought that as two women clay bosses, we might have been able to reach a common goal."

Morwen could hardly believe her cheek. Coming into her house and implying that she was a fool, and then suggesting that they might work together, was more than outrageous. It was obscene. She got slowly to her feet.

"I don't think we have anything more to say, Mrs Pendragon. My position is totally different from yours, and I wouldn't dream of putting the two of us in the same category. Moreover, I don't deal with Killigrew Clay's business affairs. I leave all of that to the men, the way it has always been."

"That's where you have the advantage over me then, since I no longer have a man at the helm of my ship," Harriet said coolly. "But I can't believe you're of the opinion that a woman doesn't have a brain?"

"I didn't say that," Morwen said, irritated at how the woman seemed to be getting the upperhand. "Of course a woman has a brain, and can think for herself."

"Then why don't you?" Harriet said, with a sudden show of passion. "Why don't you tell these damn-fool male bosses that the only way to gain the clayworkers' confidence is to guarantee their wages for the year ahead?"

"How can anyone guarantee that with things the way they are?" Morwen said hotly. "Unless you have unlimited funds at your disposal, it would be madness to do so."

She paused, seeing the triumphant look in the woman's eyes. Harriet Pendragon seemed to be saying all too clearly that she had those funds, and would stop at nothing to be the most powerful businesswoman in Cornwall.

Morwen turned away from that voluptuous face, and looked deliberately at the clock on the mantelpiece.

"I believe your ten minutes is up," she said. "You've accomplished nothing in coming here, and I would appreciate it if you didn't come here again."

Harriet stood up. She was taller than Morwen, and her stance was so intimidating that Morwen felt as if she mentally stepped back a pace. It infuriated her to know that she was so affected by the woman, but she couldn't deny the feeling that there was an inexplicable sense of ill-will coming from her. Such instinctive feelings were rarely wrong.

"Oh, but you haven't seen or heard the last of me, Morwen Wainwright," Harriet said softly. "I aim to get what I want, and nothing stands in my way. I've tried one approach, and if that fails, there's always another."

Her eyes strayed to the portrait of Ran that stood on the piano, and Morwen caught her breath. There was a sexual threat in Harriet Pendragon's voice now that was almost tangible. But before Morwen could think of another word to say, there was a swish of purple satin, and she was alone.

She was still standing motionless with clenched hands when Mrs Enders came back into the room.

"What's happened, my dear?" she exclaimed at once. "Did that one upset you? I knew she was bad news, the minute I laid eyes on her. For all her airs and graces, she was more fitted to bein' with the sluts on the waterfront than in a decent woman's drawing room. Sit yourself down, my lamb, and I'll bring 'ee in a nice hot drink of tea."

Morwen let her prattle on, without taking any of it in, and then she spoke sharply, needing to bring everything back to a homely, familiar level.

"Has Bradley appeared yet? If so, I'll join the children in the nursery for tea, Mrs Enders."

The houskeeper looked at her uneasily.

"The two little uns are up there, Ma'am, but young Bradley's not returned yet. Gillings has gone to look for un, since we know Mr Wainwright don't like him bein' at the beach so late in the day, and he's been gone a fair time."

Dear God, this was all they needed, for Bradley to commit one of his misdemeanours today. Her nerves were scratchy enough now, without trying to act the peacemaker between her son and her husband. But if Gillings had gone to look for Bradley, there was nothing more she could do about it.

"Then I'll take tea with the other two," she said, praying that the normality of it would help to ease her mind and settle the growing fear that there were bad days ahead.

Morwen and the younger children were reading together in the nursery by the time her errant son came home, hauled up the stairs none too gently by Mrs Enders, and thrust into the nursery to present himself.

"Look at the state of un, Mrs Wainwright! He looks more like a ragamuffin than the son of a gentleman, wi' his clothes all torn and filthy, and wi' no explanation to say where 'e's been."

As she paused for breath, Bradley tore himself out of her clutching hands. He bawled at her furiously.

"Leave me be, you old witch! I don't have to answer to a servant, and there's some that don't consider damn Yankees to be gentlemen, anyway—"

He was stopped in mid-flow by a stinging slap across his cheek from his mother, sending him reeling backwards so fast that he staggered and fell. Emma screamed, and

79

Mrs Enders went to her at once. She held the child close, muttering that she wasn't to fret, but her own face was as red as a turkey cock's with mortification at Bradley's onslaught.

Morwen hauled the boy to his feet and slapped him again. She rarely hit her children, but this one was becoming impossibly arrogant.

"How dare you speak to Mrs Enders like that!" she raged. "You will apologize to her at once, and then you will go and bathe and take yourself off to bed."

"I haven't had any tea!" Bradley howled.

She shook him violently. "You'll get nothing to eat in this house until you can learn to behave like a civilized human being. And your first lesson is to make a proper apology to Mrs Enders. *Now*, Bradley!" she added, as he stood with his jaw sticking out mutinously.

"I won't," he scowled.

"*What*?" she said, her eyes flashing dangerously. The two younger children had fallen silent and scared at this outright defiance.

"Perhaps you should leave it for now, Ma'am, until he's had time to consider it," Mrs Enders said nervously.

"I will not leave it, and neither will he. He's becoming uncontrollable, and I won't have it. None of the other boys gave me this much trouble, and I won't be ruled by one of my own chicks. Bradley, you will do as I say, and you will do it *now*!"

For a minute longer he glared at her, their identical blue eyes matching in fury, and then he dropped his gaze and stared sullenly at the floor.

"I'm sorry for calling you a witch, Mrs Enders. But I'm not sorry for the other thing. There's plenty of folk who say my father's nothing but a damn Yankee, and I don't care to be called a damn Yankee's son, so there!"

He twisted away from his mother and hurtled out of the nursery, slamming the door behind him. Morwen took a step to follow him, and then resisted the temptation. In any case, her duty now was to calm the little ones, instead of continuing this verbal abuse with her obnoxious young sprat.

80

What was the use, anyway? She'd only hear more of the same, and she could well do without any more accusations against her husband. But she had a horrible suspicion that when Ran got his dander up with folk, Bradley's words were more cannily true than false. It took more than years of living in the community to become a Cornishman.

Chapter Seven

Ran's reaction was to declare savagely that if there was one more incident, then Bradley was to be sent away to an English boarding school. Despite his lofty attitude to everything that was Cornish, it was a prospect the boy loathed, but the more he railed against his father, the more Ran became adamant. The atmosphere in the house became ever more bitter, and the relationship between father and son ever more fragile.

Morwen could hardly bear to be around while the constant baiting continued between them, and she was more than thankful when the day of the fortnightly meeting of the Tremayne women arrived. They always met in Fielding's Tea Rooms in St Austell, and had done so for some years now.

Venetia rode in from her country mansion like a latterday Boadicea, scorning a chaperone; more sedately, Jack Tremayne brought Annie over from Truro. Being of an age that required no escort herself, Morwen always arrived in her own pony and trap, relishing the freedom of having no male company. Bess was always driven into town by her husband, and Hal enjoyed a brief greeting with his womenfolk before taking himself off to jaw with Jack for an hour or so.

There were many things to discuss today, not least of them being the preparations for Justin's twenty-first birthday party. But first, Annie wanted to hear the news about Cathy. Having gone through bad pregnancies herself, she had an interest in the slight young girl that Walter had married.

"She's well, by all accounts. Not that I've seen her lately," Morwen admitted, thinking guiltily that she should really make more of an effort to visit her daughter-in-law.

If it hadn't been for the fact that on the last two occasions, the girl's mother had been firmly ensconced in the house, she surely would have done . . . she quickly turned her thoughts away from Jane Askhew and asked Annie in return about her own children.

"They're well," Annie said, her smile lifting, and Morwen couldn't help thinking how self-centred and insular Annie had become in recent years. She dutifully asked about other family members, but most of the time all her energies were turned inwards towards her own. "The girls are going away to nursing college in London soon. Jack's arranged it all, and they're that excited—"

"You're not sending those babbies away to London on their own?" Bess almost exploded.

"Mother, they're sixteen-years-old, and they'll be boarding in the college. They'll come to no harm, and Jack's vetted it all very carefully," Annie said, amused at this old-fashioned attitude, and preening a little at her twin daughters' ambitions. "They're determined that in time they'll get good posts as private nurses for some of the best people."

Bess shook her head. "Time was when a family got together and discussed things of such importance, but not any more," she said.

"We did discuss it," Annie said deliberately. "Me and Jack and our girls."

And if that wasn't intended to shut her mother out of any such discussions, Morwen didn't know what was. Quickly, she asked after Sammie, and Annie's face cleared.

"He's a rascal at times, Morwen. Takes after your Bradley, I think, and sometimes I don't know what to do with him." But her indulgent voice told Morwen that Annie's ten-year-old would be having far more leeway than Bradley.

"And how go things with you, Venetia?" Bess said, turning to the sunnier of her daughters-in-law.

The other three women all looked towards Freddie's wife in some relief, expecting the usual titbits of information about horses and harnesses, and the rising cost of fodder, but wondering all the same how decently soon they could change the conversation to something of more interest to them all.

But it occurred to Morwen that instead of bubbling over with her usual enthusiasm, Venetia was hesitating. Dear Lord, surely there was nothing wrong there, she thought with a silent groan. As Venetia took a deep breath, she mentally braced herself.

"Freddie and me were going to tell you together. In fact, we were going to see Morwen first, and ask her advice on telling the rest of you. But, well, now that we're all here, this might be as good a time as any, I daresay, and Freddie won't mind if I'm the one to say it."

She stopped, and knowing it must be something of importance, her three listeners paused in drinking their afternoon tea, and biting into the spicy fruit buns for which the Tea Rooms were famous.

"Well, are you going to tell us or not?" Morwen said, putting her tea cup into her saucer with a clatter. "Don't give us half a story, Venetia."

"She hasn't given us anything at all yet," Annie said drily. "Not that I can imagine there can be anything so all-fired exciting in the horse world."

"No more than I can imagine being interested in glueing and hammering bits of wood together and seeing 'em float." Venetia flashed back.

"Come on now, my lambs," Bess intervened, seeing the antagonism between them. "There's no call for any of this. Freddie's a success at rearin' his horses, and our Jack's a fine boat builder, and there's none that'll say any different in my presence."

"I'm sure they didn't mean anything by it, Mammie," Morwen said impatiently. "But for pity's sake, put us out of our misery, Venetia, and tell us your news."

The girl looked at the others with apprehensive eyes. It must be something serious, Morwen thought. Surely it wasn't something to do with Freddie's traumatic experience all those years ago . . . it couldn't be having a disastrous

84

effect on their lives together now . . . but then she knew it couldn't be anything like that.

Venetia would hardly be likely to discuss their intimate lives in a public place, and certainly not with her mother-in-law, nor with Annie Tremayne, with whom she had never really got along.

"Freddie and me are selling up and moving to Ireland," she said, all in a rush.

She couldn't have caused more of a stir if she'd said they were flying to the moon. For once, Annie said nothing, Bess drew in her breath sharply, and Morwen spoke quickly.

"Why on earth would you think of doing such a thing? You're both nicely settled, and I thought that breeding horses was your life—"

Morwen saw her mother's face redden slightly, not missing the unintentional intimation that there was no other kind of breeding on their horizon.

"We're going to breed horses there," Venetia said steadily. "It's all been arranged, and we move out in a month's time."

Bess looked as if she'd been hit in the face with a hammer. All the colour drained from her face, and Morwen couldn't miss the fact that with her skin so parchment white, she looked suddenly old.

"So another of my sons is leaving me," she muttered. "Our Jack's near enough at hand as to make no difference, but I doubt that we'll see our Matt again. And Sam—"

She swallowed, and Morwen knew she was remembering her first-born with an ache in her heart that no amount of time could dispel. Seeing the shadow pass over Bess's face, Venetia spoke with real distress in her voice now.

"Please don't take it badly, Mrs Tremayne," – she had never quite been able to bring herself to call Bess by any other name – "and we really do want you to come and see our new place and stay there a while. It's not as if it's the other side of the world." But she bit her lip as she said it, knowing she was making matters worse, in reminding Bess that another son was already on the other side of the world, thousands of miles away in California.

85

"Well, since you and Freddie managed to decide on this move without family approval," Annie said, unable to resist the barb, "how did you find out about this place? You surely aren't going there without seeing the property?"

"Oh, I've seen it many times. It belonged to my uncle, and my parents used to take me there every year when I was a child. I fell in love with it then, and I've often told Freddie about it. And when we went to Ireland for my uncle's funeral two years ago, my cousin said then that he was thinking of selling up and coming to England to live. Freddie said if he ever decided to do so, to give us first refusal."

"And now it's happened," Annie stated. "Well, good for you," she went on, to everyone's surprise.

Though Morwen knew she shouldn't have been surprised, Annie's selfish streak, and her strange resentment of the family closeness over the years, made perfect sense of the fact that she saw Venetia and Freddie's decision to break free as a healthy one.

"I doubt that me and Hal will ever come to visit," Bess said woodenly. "We've never been much for travelling."

"Then we'll just have to come back to see you as often as we can, won't we?" Venetia said, determined not to let her lovely dream be deflated by Freddie's mother. It wasn't only *her* dream, she amended. Both of them wanted this, more than anything in the world, and nobody was going to spoil it.

"What will you do with Hocking Hall?" Morwen said, recalling the lovely mansion and the land that went with it.

"We haven't decided yet. We don't really want to sell it. My father loved it so. We'll maybe rent it to someone we know and trust, but we intend to keep the ownership of it for when we come home on visits."

But she smiled at Bess with genuine warmth as she said it, and was rewarded by seeing some of the colour come back to her face.

Even so, Morwen was more troubled than she admitted. When Bess had gone so white, saying she was losing another of her sons, it had seemed all too much like the premonitions Morwen had from time to time. As if she saw a glimpse of a future she didn't want to see. She refused to dwell on it, and got the discussion back to Justin's birthday party as quickly as she could.

"'Tis all going forward," Bess said in some relief. "You ask him who he wants to invite, and let me know how many there's likely to be, Morwen, and I'll see to the catering. I take it that Albert and Primmy will be bringing a few of their friends to liven things up?"

"I'm sure they will," Morwen said with a smile. "And Charlotte has a young man too, though I'm only supposed to refer to him as a friend at the present time."

The rest of the afternoon passed pleasantly enough, with one and another putting in their spoke about the whys and wherefores of Charlotte meeting a young man, while Morwen let the conversation drift through her head, trying not to think how everything was changing. She was almost glad when the sun went lower in the sky, turning moors and sea alike to a pastel world of pink and gold. And the women left the Tea Rooms and went their separate ways.

Albert and Primrose Tremayne were at that very moment relaxing on floor cushions in a fragrant smoke-filled studio, surrounded by a group of their Bohemian artist friends. They leisurely extolled the wonders of their beautiful universe, becoming more and more expansive with the effects of the forbidden substance they inhaled.

As one of the young men suggested a midnight picnic on the beach on a particular night at the end of the month, the date triggered a recollection in Primmy's mind.

"We can't. We have to go to our brother's party on that night. We'll have to leave it until another time," Primmy said drowsily, "but you're all invited to come to the party as our guests!"

"Not a good idea, Primmy," Albert said, his words terse as always as the smoking seemed to tighten his chest, even though he never took in as much as the rest of them, and was far more clear-headed than most. The anxiety he felt from the swirling shapes that the drug produced in his brain, and the sense of breathlessness that accompanied it, alarmed him far more than the desire to be transported into a magical world akin to that of the fabled *Thousand and One Nights* . . .

Not for worlds would he admit any of that to the rest of them, though. This was his studio, and he was Jack-the-lad here. So he smoked very little, and was thankful for the success of his own charade, even though he felt he was letting his friends down by his actions.

"Why is it not a good idea?" Primmy said to him. "Justin will want us there, and you can do his portrait as a birthday gift from us both, and I'll play the piano, and our friends can sing and entertain." She began to laugh shrilly. "We could introduce them as the entertainers, and nobody need know they're really our guests at all! What do you say?"

She blinked through her darkly dilated pupils at the wishy-washy outlines of the group seated all around her. She really was feeling rather ill, and it was becoming extremely urgent for her to go to the water closet . . . she retched suddenly, and a rainbow stream of vomit spattered those nearest to her. They all shrieked with hysterical laughter as if she had done something terribly funny.

Albert yanked her to her feet, where she swayed alarmingly. "Come on. You need to clean yourself up," he said.

Primmy shook him off. "Don't manhandle me, sir!" she said, in as pompous a manner as she could. The group erupted into more laughter, and then Primmy knew no more as all her bones seemed to turn to jelly and she sank down in an unceremonious heap over the nearest of them.

When she awoke, it was night. She was in her own bed, and Albert was sponging down her heated face with a cool cloth. There was no one else in the room, but the windows were open, and a cool breeze blew the curtains slightly inwards. She gave a low groan, feeling as if she was dying. She always did – afterwards. The tremendous burst of mind-expanding energy and excitement of it all was never worth the feeling that came later. She knew it, but still she did it.

"You're a fool, Primmy. It will kill you if you go on like this," Albert said quietly.

"And you're so noble," she said weakly. "You were

the one to try it first, and now you're going all pious on me."

"I never thought you'd get so addicted, and I don't want to lose you," he said.

"I'm not addicted! I can stop any time I want to," she said indignantly.

"Then you won't mind if I put the rest of the stuff down the water closet, will you?"

Her voice was full of panic. "No, don't, Albie – please don't. Just leave me a little. I promise it will be the last time."

"This *was* the last time," he said, seeing how the perspiration broke out on her forehead at the thought that he was taking away her supply. But he had to do it. Dear God, if she went on like this, she'd be a raving lunatic in no time at all. And if that happened, it would surely break his heart. She was his sister and he loved her, and he couldn't bear to see her already getting so out of control. The drug was already degrading her.

For a moment, he wondered how his upright family would react if they only knew. His blood ran cold at the thought. Morwen, and their grandparents, in particular, were so proud of the two of them setting up their own establishment in Truro; the talented artist and the accomplished concert pianist. It had all sounded so very grand – and it had all become so very sleazy.

Not the work, of course. The façade of respectability stood them in good stead. Fond mamas brought their daughters to have their portraits painted, as well as commissioning studies of their family groups; and Primmy played at the several concert halls in the surrounding towns, and was invited to the best soirées to perform. The high life they led was a glittering success, and their secret life was gutter low.

"Albie," Primmy said huskily now, breaking into his brooding thoughts. "I know you're right. I do know it, really I do. And I want to be over it. So be strong for me tonight. Don't give in to me, there's a love."

And he didn't, not all through that long night when she

begged him and cursed him and lashed out at him to give her what she craved. He had no idea if he was doing the right thing or not. He only knew he had to save her from the demons that plagued her while there was still time.

The man walking with his dog through the streets of Truro took a stroll along the lower banks of the Truro River where the more bohemian of the town's inhabitants lived and worked. He didn't normally come this way, nor this late, but the lurcher needed his exercise, and was strong enough to fend off any attackers who might be out and about after dark.

He paused suddenly, and his blood froze for a moment, recognizing the sounds of a woman shrieking and blaspheming. The sounds were coming from the upstairs windows of a house that stood apart from its neighbours, and he hesitated, wondering what to do. The last thing he felt like was putting up his knuckles to some unknown assailant. And if he'd been anyone else, he might have slunk away to the nearest Inn, and forgotten what was probably a normal domestic row between husband and wife. He disliked violence of any sort. And he disliked the entire female sex with their simpering ways and perfumed bodies.

But he wasn't anyone else, and there were other instincts that he'd been trained to follow. He wasn't a newspaperman for nothing, and this was an area that was reputed to harbour murky shades of life, as well as the successful arty set who were supposedly so respectable. There might be a story here.

Ellis White crept forward, his hand clutching his dog's collar, and straining his eyes and ears to hear words and voices. There wasn't much light coming from the upstairs room, and the moon was obscured by clouds, so he could creep right underneath the bedroom window and listen intently without fear of being discovered. The woman was still shrieking, her voice tortured.

"Albie, I'll never ask you for anything else. But for God's sake, if you love me, don't put me through this hell—"

Ellis caught his breath. He didn't know the woman's

voice, and he didn't immediately recognize the name, though it seemed vaguely familiar. He searched his memory, but he couldn't readily place it. The man was speaking in a low voice now, and he had to strain his ears to try to catch the words.

"You know I love you, and I always will, but it's wrong, my lovely girl. We've got to stop, and we both have to accept it."

"I don't want to stop, you bastard!" the woman screamed. "Don't you understand? I can't live without it—"

There was a sudden scuffle from above, and Ellis White scrambled back in the shelter of the bushes, snatching the lurcher back with him in the process. The dog gave a low growl, and he clamped his hand over the animal's mouth to keep it quiet. Ellis could barely breathe himself now, keeping all his senses alive and excited at what he might be on the brink of discovering here.

He didn't yet know what it was, but he sensed instinctively that it was something that should probably be kept secret. And therefore something that the anonymous letter writer in *The Informer* might be able to use to his advantage. Ellis took a perverted pleasure in being the unknown scandalmonger of the district. He had a power that no one suspected, not even Tom Askhew, his hated boss, and he took great delight in making those in authority squirm.

He jerked up his head as two shadowy shapes approached the dimly-lighted window of the bedroom. He couldn't see who they were, but he knew they were young. The man's tall, protective stance, together with the long, dark hair and sensual shape of the woman clinging to him, were proof enough of that.

They had seemed to be walking backwards and forwards around the room, but now, without warning, the woman thrust her head through the window and vomited. Ellis scrambled back further into the bushes, disinclined to be sprayed by the filthy stuff. Like many of his kind, he was fastidious about other peoples' unpleasant bodily functions.

He fell heavily over his dog, and the lurcher let out a

91

howl of rage. At the same time, the man pulled the woman inside, and within seconds he had thrust his head out of the window. He held a lantern aloft, while Ellis cowered unseen under cover of the bushes.

"Who's down there?" Albert shouted. "Clear off, whoever you are, or I'll set the constables after you."

Ellis had to decide quickly what to do. Whether to run, or to play dead. The dog was behaving itself, and before he could decide, the woman had appeared again, putting her arms around the man and pulling him inside. She seemed quieter now that her brief bout of sickness was over. And Ellis heard her voice quite clearly.

"Close the window, Albert, and let's go to bed. I promise I won't ask you for anything more tonight, darling. I'll be good, really I will."

And as the man complied, Ellis White's jaw dropped open in disbelief as the proverbial penny dropped. Dear God, this was a scoop and a half, he thought. The Killigrew sprogs were committing a crime he'd never have dreamed of, and he doubted that anybody else had either.

Incest. It was worse than bastardy in his eyes. It was obscene. And it was going to make a bit of very interesting information on the Letters Page . . .

He'd have to be careful, though. He was knowledgable enough to know he couldn't name names. Unless you actually caught the pair of 'em canoodling, you couldn't actually accuse them, or you'd be in court yourself with a libel suit against you. But innuendo was the next best thing. Better really, because you could keep it going as long as you liked . . . and it was easy enough to put the idea in folks' heads so clearly that there'd be no doubt who the culprits were . . . Never was there a truer phrase than the salacious pen being mightier than the sword, Ellis thought gleefully. But Albert and Primrose Killigrew sharing a bed as well as a kitchen . . . who the devil would have believed it?

"Don't do it," his lover advised him flatly, when he'd rushed home and related all that he'd seen.

"Why not?" Ellis was deflated at once. He rarely shared

his intentions with anyone, but he trusted Leonard, and he'd been all fired up to begin on his letter that night.

"It's not worth antagonizing the clay folk for your own sadistic pleasure," Leonard said, studying his polished fingernails with a satisfactory air. "Anyway, you can't really be sure of what you saw. The girl might have been ill, and her brother was just helping her to bed. If she was about to faint, he'd have had no option but to support her, would he, my dear?"

"I do know what I saw," Ellis said firmly. But he hesitated now. Leonard's judgement was usually sound. "Do you think I should wait for more evidence before proceeding then? Maybe go back another night to find out more?"

"If you must. Personally I think these clay folk are a terrible bore, and I don't know why you waste your time on them, Ellis." His pale eyes suddenly flashed. "Unless there's one of them that has a special interest for you?"

"You know there is not!" Ellis said quickly. He hadn't known Leonard long enough to want to lose him now. They were extremely compatible, and he had high hopes of it being a long-lasting relationship.

"Then forget all about them for tonight," Leonard said, more affectionately. "Come and warm yourself by the fire, my dear, and later on I'll cook us a nice supper."

And Ellis willingly gave himself up to delights of a very different nature from that of composing a letter about people he couldn't have cared less about in normal circumstances. But the images of the two he'd seen in the house by the river remained at the back of his mind, all the same. Once the glimmering of a story had been ferreted out, it was not his way to abandon it for ever.

But he was prepared to wait. After all, what was the hurry? If the two of them were truly cohabiting, it was unlikely they were going to stop. And he was probably the only other person to know it.

Chapter Eight

For once, supper time was calm in the New World household. Morwen had related some of the conversations with her sisters-in-law and her mother that day, and mention of their Uncle Jack had the children clamouring to know when they could go out in a boat.

"For goodness' sake," Morwen said, laughing, "your uncle builds them for rich folk to buy. He doesn't take children for pleasure rides."

"Why not?" Bradley said at once, always ready to argue. "I bet Sammy's been in one of his boats."

He didn't like his cousin, but that was nothing unusual, thought Morwen. At the moment, Bradley didn't like anyone. Without thinking, she dropped a bombshell into the conversation.

"Freddie and Venetia will be going on a boat soon," she said to Ran.

"Oh?" He looked up from his leek and veal pie at this unusual piece of information. "Don't tell me they're dipping into some of her daddy's money and taking a trip?"

Morwen looked at him mutely as all the children stopped eating and waited expectantly for her to continue. Why on earth had she mentioned it at all! It didn't take a genius to know that Bradley was going to throw an almighty fit once he learned that his favourites were shortly going to leave Cornwall for good.

"I'll tell you more about it later," she murmured.

"Tell me now," Ran said, adding to her annoyance. "It can't be such a secret, can it?"

"You seem to have secrets from *me*," she retaliated.

He stared at her. "Good God, what does that mean? I don't have any secrets from you!"

"Yes, you do," she said, thinking that at least she'd turned the conversation away from Freddie and Venetia. "You've had a letter from our Matt, and you're not going to tell me what's in it."

Ran gave a half-smile. "I have not had a letter from our Matt, though I have had a letter from California. All right then. You tell me your secret, and I'll tell you mine."

"Later, Ran," she said, trying to tell him with her eyes that her secret wasn't for the children's hearing. But she'd reckoned without their impatience.

"We want to hear it too, Mammie!" Emma shrieked, and Bradley howled in accord, while Luke banged his knife and fork on the table in unison with the chorus.

"Be quiet, the lot of you!" Morwen snapped. "You're a disgrace at the supper table."

"Tell me, Morwen," Ran ordered in a none too patient voice himself, and she sighed, knowing that the calm was over.

"Freddie and Venetia are planning to move to Ireland next month—"

As she had expected, she got no further before Bradley leapt to his feet, his eyes blazing.

"It's not true! You're a liar, and I hate you!" he shouted. "They wouldn't go and leave me behind—"

"For pity's sake, Bradley, stop behaving like an idiot, and sit down," Ran said irritably. "What your aunt and uncle do with their lives has nothing to do with you—"

"Yes, it does. They always said I was their special boy, and they wouldn't go and leave me."

"Well, you're our son, not theirs, and if they're going to Ireland to live, then you've got no choice," Ran snapped, as always losing patience very quickly with his volatile son.

They were so alike, Morwen thought. So damnably and vulnerably alike when it came to never being able to find the right words to say to one another.

"I'll run away," Bradley yelled. "I'll stow away on the boat taking them to Ireland and live with them. I'll help Uncle Freddie with the horses, and you won't stop me!"

Ran didn't believe in hitting children unless the circumstances were extremely deserving. He considered it a coward's way to behave. But as if she watched the scene being enacted in slow motion in front of her eyes, Morwen saw him rise from the table and walk slowly round to snatch Bradley up by his collar and yank him to his feet. He shook him like a rag doll, his voice low and tight.

"You will do no such thing, my boy, and I most certainly will stop you, if I have to tie you up in chains to do so."

Emma began to cry, and Morwen went to her at once. The atmosphere in the dining room had become appalling, and she couldn't bear it. She saw Ran let Bradley go, and the boy sank sullenly down in his seat again.

"We'll now resume our supper, and when we've all calmed down, I'll tell you all my secret," Ran went on, more coolly than Morwen would have believed. She hoped fervently that it was going to be a good one, and not something that would have Bradley sneering.

In the next ten minutes nobody spoke, but the children only picked at their food, and in the end Ran gave a sigh and pushed his own plate away.

"All right, I think we may say that supper is over for tonight, and pudding can wait until I've told you all something to put the smiles back on your faces."

From the look of Bradley's face, it would take a miracle, thought Morwen, but she felt her heart begin to quicken in anticipation. Ran must know it had to be something special . . .

"Please don't keep us in suspense any longer, dar," she said, her voice almost breathless.

"You were wrong in thinking I'd had a letter from your brother, honey," he said directly. "It was from Louisa."

"Oh. Well, that amounts to almost the same thing, I suppose," Morwen said, remembering Matt's American wife. She concurred it was reasonable to suppose that Louisa would write to Ran, being his cousin. But then another thought struck her, and she caught at her husband's arm. "There's nothing wrong, is there? Our Matt's not ill, is he—?"

Ran spoke quickly. "Don't you think I'd have told you before this if that was the case?"

The children were silent now, wondering what was to come, and Emma yawned, bored with all this talk of kinfolk she didn't know.

"Then what?"

"Can't you guess?" Ran said, but her intuition wasn't in evidence tonight, and she shook her head impatiently.

"I was trying to keep it as a surprise, but I see now that it's impossible. Louisa and Matt are giving Cresswell a trip to Europe for his birthday, which as you know is around the time of Justin's own twenty-first—"

Morwen leapt to her feet, her eyes glowing, her face flushed with colour, and for an instant Ran saw the beautiful girl he had married.

"And they're coming home!" she said joyfully, ignoring everything else. "Oh Ran, is our Matt *really* coming home? For how long? And – well, Europe isn't just Cornwall, is it?"

He held up his hand as she dithered. "Let me finish, honey, though you can read the letter for yourself now you know most of it. They'll all be here in time for Justin's celebrations, and the overall trip is for three months. But Louisa and Cress will go on to Europe, and Matt will stay here while they're gone. He'll want to see his family and to see what's happening with Killigrew Clay."

And whether Ran liked it or not, it had been Matt's money from the Californian goldfields that had put the clayworks back on its feet again after a disastrous slump ten years ago. Matt also had a family stake in Killigrew Clay that went back far beyond that. From kiddley-boy to clayworker, he knew the business as well as any of them.

Morwen's heart was thumping so much with excitement she could hardly breathe, and it was only when she had hugged and kissed her husband that she looked to see the effect the news was having on her children. The first and last time Matt had brought his family to England, these three

97

hadn't been born, and she had still been the widow of Ben Killigrew.

And Cresswell had unwittingly betrayed the secret she and Ben had kept so carefully for all those years. That Walter, Albert and Primmy weren't their own flesh and blood, but the children of Morwen's oldest brother Sam and his wife Dora. Sam had died in Ben Killigrew's railway accident, and Dora had died from the measles. And after Cresswell's unthinking remarks, Justin and Charlotte had considered themselves the rightful heirs of Killigrew Clay, causing powerful ructions within the family.

The ghosts of the past whispered through Morwen's mind now, as she looked at the three blank faces of the Wainwright children. They knew nothing of the intricate family history, except for what Bradley knew from Bess. But the younger ones were still innocent of how ugly the closest family unit could turn when its members fought for their rights.

"Will I like these people, Mammie?" Emma said finally, in a dubious voice. "Will Cresswell play with me?"

Bradley gave a hoot of laughter, breaking the spell.

"Of course he won't, you ninny, not if he's as old as Justin. They'll talk differently, as well." His eyes suddenly narrowed as a new thought struck him. "Perhaps they'll take me back to America with them, then I won't fret so over Uncle Freddie going to Ireland."

Ran threw up his hands in despair at this, and refused to discuss it any more as Mrs Enders oversaw the serving of the chocolate pudding and custard. But while Bradley wittered on about the possibilities of finding out more about America from his cousin Cresswell, and the other two muttered less excitedly about meeting new relatives, all Morwen could think about was that Matt was coming home.

Her mammie obviously didn't know yet, and Ran had intended keeping it to himself a while longer. Bess should be told immediately. Bess would be over the moon in gathering her ewe lamb back to her bosom. And Morwen would insist on telling the rest of the family too. Ran had to grant her that.

*   *   *

98

She told Justin the minute he came home late that evening. By then, the children were in bed, and she had seen the letter from Louisa. She liked Ran's cousin, though they had only seen her on the one visit that had ended so disastrously. But it wasn't Louisa's fault that Cresswell had been so obnoxious, and he hadn't been aware of any family secrets. She readily forgave him in her mind. Right now, she could forgive anybody anything, knowing that Matt was coming home . . .

Justin's reaction was totally unexpected.

"I don't want that idiot Cresswell at my party, Mother," he said flatly. "In any case, he won't know anyone but us, and he'll be totally out of place."

But as Justin spoke, it was *Walter's* anguished voice that Morwen could hear so uncannily in her mind right then. A gauche and youthful Walter, suddenly putting two and two together, and finding the truth more painful than he could ever have believed.

"He says we're not Killigrews. He says Sam Tremayne was our Daddy instead of our uncle. He says Killigrew Clay's not my inheritance, but Justin's—"

Cresswell had taken away all Walter's innocence at that moment. And Walter had wanted the clayworks so much. The clay was in his blood, as it had never been in Justin's . . .

She shook her head a little, pushing the memories out of her mind, and coming back to the present. Justin's face was angry, spoiling all her pleasure in Matt's homecoming.

"You can't be so ungenerous," she snapped. "Cresswell is your cousin, and whatever you may have thought about him in the past, he's a man now, the same as you."

"I always thought him a little shit-bag, the same as everyone else did," Justin said, using the careless language of the clayworkers, and not even noticing it. But Morwen did. She noticed it, and ignored it, for nothing could have told her more clearly that the rawness still simmered between her children and the American cousins.

"It's only for one night that you have to be sociable, darling," she said, more pleadingly. "And think how it will

99

upset your grandmother if you object to Cresswell. He's her grandson too."

Justin glowered darkly, but at his hesitation she felt relieved, knowing that she had won. Mention of Bess could usually twist the boys around. Bess loved all her boys, and her boys loved her.

"And I hope you've got that guest list prepared," Morwen said brightly. "I need to send out the invitations very soon, so let's get down to it."

"I don't want a fuss," Justin said at once. "Just the family and one or two others, that's all. And I definitely don't want any of Albert and Primmy's vacuous lot there."

"They'll be upset if you shun their friends—"

"No, they won't. Especially if they know the Americans are coming. They'll be happy enough with just the family – if they bother to come at all. And what about Walter? If Cathy's about to burst, they may not bother. You know I'm not keen on these things, anyway, Mother, so why can't we just forget it?"

"And what about Charlotte?" Morwen went on doggedly, knowing how upset her mother would be if it all fell through.

"She's anxious to show off her new friend. Vincent, isn't it?"

Justin relaxed a little, stretching out his long legs as he lounged on the drawing room couch, and he began to smile at last.

"Oh yes, I was forgetting about dear Charlotte being so taken up with Vince Pollard. You'll like him, and they make a nice couple."

Morwen wasn't prepared to couple them up quite so soon, but she let the comment pass.

"All right," Justin said, succumbing. "Let's agree that there's going to be a party. But I insist on keeping Albert and Primmy's lot out. It's my day, isn't it?"

Bess Tremayne gave a glad cry when Morwen told her the news. She wasn't one for great shows of emotion, but there was no disguising the tears over this. When she got over the initial excitement, she wiped her eyes and composed herself, and her voice was full of longing, dredging up fears she'd held inside for a long time.

"I sometimes wondered if we'd ever see our Matt again, Morwen. You young uns may have done so, but time's running out for your daddy and me—"

"Don't say such things, Mammie! You know I don't like to hear it."

Bess gave a wry smile. "There's no stopping time, Morwen. It goes on, whether we like it or not, and me and Hal ain't gettin' any younger, nor any livelier. We know it, and we've discussed it sensibly."

In Morwen's opinion, such morbid talk was simply inviting bad luck. You couldn't blithely go on pretending you were immortal, but nor did you need to keep looking over your shoulder for the first sighting of the grim reaper. And she didn't want to know what arrangements her mammie and daddy had been discussing.

"I've brought Justin's guest list, and he only wants a couple of people outside the family," she said quickly. "You know how he hates a fuss, Mammie."

"Oh well, 'tis his party, and now there'll be three extras," Bess said, her voice lifting with pleasure, for large family gatherings had never worried her. "I remember the other time Matt came home, and it was as if he'd never been away."

"He'll be older now, like all of us," Morwen reminded her, wondering how Bess could have forgotten the change in him then. She shivered, knowing she was doing exactly as her mother had done, and felt momentarily as if she donned her mother's mantle.

It was the way folk felt when the oldest person in a family died, and the next in line took on the role. She didn't like the feeling, and she concentrated on the party list, and tried not to think of this coming birthday as a special milestone in all of their lives.

Morwen checked through the names again, half-amazed at the way the family had grown so big. There had once been just Hal and Bess and the five Tremayne children crammed into the tiny cottage on the moors, and now . . .

"There's you and Daddy; Matt and Louisa and Cresswell; Ran and me, Walter and Cathy, Albert and Primmy, Justin and Charlotte – and Charlotte's friend Vincent – Bradley, Luke and Emma. Then there's Freddie and Venetia, Jack and Annie, and their girls, Sarah and Tessa, and young Sammie. Justin wants Daniel Gorran to come, but he's happy to leave it at that. I make that twenty-five in all, and I think that's quite enough for you to cope with, Mammie."

"You'll have to be sure and let Albert and Primmy know their friends won't be welcome, then, though I don't know what Justin's got against 'em."

"Neither do I," Morwen said thoughtfully. "But you know what a stickler he's become for correct behaviour, and I doubt that any of that Truro set would behave themselves according to his rules."

It shouldn't have surprised her, really. All the boys, especially the older ones, were very different. Walter's heart was in the clayworks, and Justin had set himself up in direct opposition to him from the moment he'd learned the truth about their backgrounds. While Walter had been desperate to dirty his hands in his beloved clay and learn the work from the inside out, Justin had only ever wanted to dress as a gentleman and do a gentleman's job.

And as for Albert . . . if Justin's business brain held no aesthetic feelings towards the arts, nor did he consider himself a prig. But in his opinion, Albert and Primmy had as good as sold themselves to the ways of the devil, in their style of dress and behaviour, and in the company they kept. Justin had serious doubts about that aspect of their lives too, but he knew better than to mention any of it to his mother.

"There's to be twenty-five of us then," Bess said now.

"Are you quite sure about having it here, Mammie? It won't be too much for you, will it?" Morwen said again.

"O' course it won't. You just do your part, and me and cook and Mrs Horn will do ours," Bess said keenly, and Morwen knew there was nothing more to be said.

"We'll have to think of a birthday gift for Cresswell, too," she said suddenly. Justin was receiving a horse and trap of his own, but they couldn't give Cresswell anything so fine. Besides, what did you give to a young man with gold dust literally at his feet?

"Why don't you ask Albert to do a portrait of un while he's here, and we'll pay for it? Albert commands a fine price in the town nowadays, I hear."

Bess's voice was a little incredulous, finding it difficult to imagine folk paying good money for such idling work. To Bess, it could never compare with scratching a living in the clay, or even working long hours by candlelight as she herself had once done, stitching fine seams for the gentry. But then, Albert had never had to do such menial jobs, and wouldn't know the half of it, she thought generously.

"That's a lovely idea, Mammie," Morwen exclaimed.

"I'll take a ride into Truro now and suggest it to him. It's a while since I've seen him and Primmy, and I can call in on Jack and Annie at the same time, to tell them about our Matt coming home."

Every time she said the words, she felt the same glow in her heart. *Matt was coming home . . .*

She didn't often go to the Truro studio. Truth to tell, she was a little uncomfortable herself about the people Albert and Primmy associated with. Not that her own two chicks looked any more proper, and never was a young woman less aptly named than Primmy, Morwen thought wryly.

And if Venetia Tremayne could shock folk by riding into town in her country gear, then how much more eyebrow raising were the young Killigrew set, in their arty clothes and their frankly unconventional appearance? If it wasn't for their undoubted talents, and the way influential folk were ready to receive them because of it . . .

It was best to put such thoughts out of her head. Besides, there was a time every year when the bal maidens from all the clayworks roundabout, were a sight to behold too, walking for miles in their bonnets and bright garbs to the annual fairs, and attracting curious onlookers. Morwen had once been one of them. Morwen, and her friend Celia Penry . . .

She drew up in her trap in the courtyard of the house where Albert had his studio, and where Primmy acted as his assistant-cum-chaperone when needed, as long as she wasn't performing herself. Morwen hoped she would see both of them, and she pushed open the studio door after a perfunctory knock. The whiff of something sweet and sickly met her nostrils, and she wrinkled her nose. It wasn't unpleasant, but she didn't like it all the same.

The next minute she forgot it all as Albert came through from a back room. He smelled of paint and turpentine, but he smiled broadly, calling out to Primmy at once.

"Mother, it's been an age since we saw you!" Albert said gaily. "What brings you to Truro?"

Morwen smiled back into his blue eyes. "The best news! Your uncle Matt and his family are coming home from America in time for Justin's party."

She saw the smile tighten a little, and remembered too late that Albert had smarted as much as all her adopted children when they had discovered the truth about their background. She wondered if it was one of the reasons why he and Primmy had fought so hard to be themselves, and to be independent of the family. They hadn't wanted to be clayworkers, nor Killigrews either. They had just wanted to be themselves.

"You won't be difficult about this, will you, Albert? You will come?" she persisted.

"If Primmy wants to," he said carelessly. "I hadn't really made up my mind."

"Albert, I've never liked a divided family, and what happened in the past should remain there."

Their glances clashed, and he shrugged. Truth to tell, he'd largely forgotten all those upsets, although Cresswell's name alone was enough to make him bristle for a moment. But his mother was right. The past was the past, and he was too busy struggling with the present situation with Primmy to waste his energies on it.

What the devil was the girl doing?, he thought suspiciously now. He'd rid the place of the narcotics, but so far he hadn't convinced their friends to stop bringing more, and the next step was to ban them from coming here altogether if they didn't agree. The prospect filled Albert with sorrow, but he knew his sister's life depended on it.

Primmy came through from the back room at last, and Morwen was shocked by the sight of the girl. Her face had an unhealthy pallor, even though her eyes were almost feverishly bright, and she was more painfully thin than the last time Morwen had seen her. Primmy kissed her on the cheek, and the sweet, sickly scent surrounded her.

"Mother, how lovely! I know we've been neglecting you of late, but you'll have some tea with us, won't you? I can't promise that it will be served from a silver teapot, but it'll taste just as good."

She laughed as if she had made a great joke, and Morwen followed the two of them through to their sitting room with a great ache in her heart. Something was terribly wrong here, and she had no idea what it was.

"So to what do we owe the pleasure?" Primmy said.

"The Americans are coming for a visit," Albert said abruptly before Morwen could reply.

Primmy gasped. Life had moved on, but she never forgot the last visit of her uncle and his family, and the way everything had seemed to drop out of her world when the odious Cresswell had betrayed the best-kept family secret to the unsuspecting children.

"I won't see them," she said at once.

"Don't be ridiculous, darling, you have to see them. They're our family, and it will distress me and your Grandma greatly if you were to shun them," Morwen said. "Besides which, we want you to do something for us, Albert," she turned away from her mutinous daughter.

"What is it?"

"If Cresswell will agree to it, Grandma Bess and I would like you to paint his portrait as his birthday gift, and we'll pay the proper price for it, naturally. It'll be Cresswell's coming-of-age around the same time as Justin's, and we thought it would be a nice thing to do."

She was furious at her own nervousness in saying it. It had seemed such a clever idea, but she could see the spark

105

of anger in Albert's face now, and the disbelief in Primmy's. And then Albert began to laugh.

"All right. Why not? It'd be good to let the insufferable little brat see that not all the family are content to be boring clayworkers."

Morwen let that pass, relieved enough that he had agreed. But Primmy wasn't so amenable.

"He's not coming here!" she spluttered. "This is our place, and I hate him."

"Primmy, please don't be difficult," Morwen said quietly, sensing that the girl was on a knife edge for some reason. "The Cresswell you knew was only a boy, and he had no idea at the time that he was going to hurt you so by his revelations about your real parents."

She looked at Primmy steadily, remembering that during that awful time, this girl that she loved had been so sneering of the bal maidens on their way to Truro Fair, yet Morwen knew the time had come to tell her that she and Bess had been bal maidens too. It was an honest job, but her girl had been shocked, and showed herself to be just as outright a little snob as Cresswell Tremayne had ever been.

They had hated one another so much, and she felt an uneasy sliver of apprehension now, at the wisdom of Bess's idea. But this was Albert's studio, not Primmy's, and if he agreed to it, then Primmy would just have to make herself scarce while Cresswell was sitting for his portrait.

Chapter Nine

By the end of the month the spring despatches had been variously sent to the port for loading, and onto the loaded waggons for trundling upcountry to the Staffordshire potteries. The orders had been completed, and there was still a mountain of clayblocks idling at the works.

As always, Hal Tremayne came to New World for the post-despatches discussions. Ran had long since moved the Killigrew Clay offices to his own home where everything was at hand. As the third partner, Morwen was also entitled to sift through the delivery orders and invoices, but she invariably declined, waiting for the outcome rather than add her voice to the inevitable wrangling.

After the two men had been locked in the study for several hours thrashing out the situation, and going through the disappointing figures and the dwindling orders, they joined Morwen in the drawing room.

"I'll ask Mrs Enders to bring in tea and coffee for us all," she said at once. "You're probably parched after all that talking."

"So we are, honey, but tea can come later. It's a stronger drink that we need now, wouldn't you say, Hal?"

"A brandy would do me fine," Hal agreed, to Morwen's surprise. Her daddy wasn't much of a drinking man, but the tautness of the two faces told her they'd been doing some serious talking, and her heart sank.

She so wanted everything on the horizon to be sunny, with Justin's birthday imminent, and Matt and his family due home a few days before it. And with the glorious idea that Freddie had put to them all, when he'd finally gone to Killigrew House himself to tell his parents of his plans.

"We want to offer Hocking Hall to Matt for the three months he'll be here," Freddie said. "They can move in wi' us right away to get the feel of the place, and 'twill give the land agent time to find a suitable person to rent it from us on a more permanent basis. But 'twill keep the property in the family for the time being, and also give us all some breathing space from one another."

It was a perfect plan, especially remembering how they had all begun to get on one anothers' nerves on Matt's last visit, incredible though it seemed. But even then, they realized how they had all changed in the intervening years, and now they had moved on another ten.

But it did no good to brood on something that couldn't be changed, and she thought instead that when Louisa and Cress had departed on their European tour, Matt would have the freedom of the lovely estate of Hocking Hall to himself. And she could visit him there as often as she chose, and hopefully recapture the special sibling friendship that had always existed between them.

She watched now as Ran poured the two large glasses of brandy for himself and his father-in-law, while she waited for the tea to be brought in. Only then did she burst out with what she was dying to know.

"Well, are you going to tell me or not? Is it bad news? Or will we survive another year?"

Her father snorted. "There's no foretelling the future, me dear, but I'd say we're keeping our heads above water – just."

"Your family were always optimists, honey," Ran drawled. "But Hal knows as well as I do that if prices fall even further we'll be heading for real trouble. And we'd have to think seriously of the options to put things right."

"But you wouldn't lower the men's wages? Daddy, we can't do that," she said passionately, turning to her father, and remembering only too well the bare feet of most of the kiddley-boys in wintertime. If she had her way, she'd fit them all with boots . . .

"No, I don't mean that," Hal said shortly. "I'd rather lay

a few of them off than cut the wages of all on 'em, though your husband don't see it in the same way."

"I do not. It makes more sense to me to cut the wages of all, as sparingly as possible, and still keep the lot of them in work," Ran said, just as curtly, and it was obvious that this had been a major clash between them, and that their meeting had gone far from smoothly.

"But for the time being, things can stay as they are?" she persisted quickly, sensing that nothing had been resolved.

"Well, providing that damn Pendragon woman don't come along wi' her offers of higher pay and better conditions," Hal grunted. "The clayers are loyal enough as long as they can feed their young uns, but when they can't, they'll be tempted right enough, and who can blame 'em?"

Now was the time, Morwen thought. She had never breathed a word of Harriet Pendragon's visit to Ran, believing now that she had merely been trying to alarm Morwen, since nothing more had been heard from her. She hadn't wanted to bring the woman's name into her consciousness, but it was here now, and perhaps it was just foolish to go on pretending the visit had never happened. She took a deep breath.

"Mrs Pendragon came to see me," she said flatly. "I never told you, Ran, but she was quite threatening – oh, not in a physical way – but she made it clear she was used to getting her own way, and that she wanted Killigrew Clay."

She avoided his eyes. It had been clear to her that she wanted all that went with it too, and that included Ran Wainwright. A thrill of jealousy ran through her, seeing the anger in Ran's eyes, and knowing that he too would be remembering the arrogant splendour of the Pendragon woman.

"Why the hell didn't you tell me this before? When did it happen?"

"A couple of weeks ago, soon after the meeting in St Austell," she muttered.

"You should have told us, Morwen," Hal said.

"What was the point? What could you have done about it? Gone to see her and told her to stop harassing me? A fine ninny I'd have looked then, needing my menfolk to look after me, when she – she—"

She stopped, but her thoughts finished all that she didn't want to say out loud. *When Harriet Pendragon was so all-fired self-assured, and could probably twist any man around her little finger as soon as look at him* . . .

Her eyes blurred, and then she felt Ran's arms go round her. She leaned against him, feeling his strength flow into her, and unembarrassed that her father was witnessing this show of affection.

"She'll not get it, nor anything that goes with it," he said, and there was a meaning in his voice that she knew and understood and accepted. "I know what Killigrew Clay means to you – to all of us, and I'll fight tooth and nail with the rest of you to see that it remains where it belongs."

Morwen looked up at him, her face flushed. Her daddy had moved tactfully away to look through the long windows at the spacious well-kept gardens of a gentleman's house, and she spoke softly to her husband.

"I already told you that Killigrew Clay means a great deal to me, dar, but you mean more. I meant it then, and I mean it now. I always will."

She touched his cheek with her lips, not daring to be any more demonstrative at this hour of the day, and with her father the width of a room away. But the promise of love was in her eyes, and all the loving strands of their lives that bound them together were as strong as steel once more.

Walter came bursting into the house a short while later, his eyes shining, and all three of them turned to him in relief. Any kind of good news from the clayworks would be just what was needed at this time, Morwen thought, but it wasn't clay business that he'd come about.

"Congratulate me, Grandad!" he said directly to Hal, but encompassing all of them. "I've just become the father of a fine young sprig, and he's the spit of his great-grandaddy!"

He was embraced by three pairs of arms then, and Morwen thought fleetingly how strong were the family ties too.

110

"But it wasn't due to happen for three weeks!" she gasped. "Is Cathy all right? And the baby?"

Walter laughed, and clearly nothing was going to cloud his pleasure today.

"They're both wonderful. It happened so fast that there was no time to let anybody know. She felt odd all evening, but assumed it was a just a bit of colic. Then in the middle of the night she thought we should send for the doctor and midwife to be on the safe side, and they only just arrived in time for the birthing."

"And there was no trouble?" Morwen persisted, seeing all this rush from a woman's point of view, and praying there hadn't been any tearing or undue bleeding.

"Not wi' my Cathy," Walter said, as proud as if no other woman had ever given birth before. "She were a real Tremayne, and Grandma Bess would have been proud of her."

Hal laughed, pleased at the compliment, and slapping him on the shoulder, while Ran pressed a glass of brandy in his hand to wet the baby's head.

In the midst of her delight, Morwen couldn't ignore the thought that another set of grandparents would also be pleased at hearing their daughter had come safely through the ordeal of childbirth. Tom Askhew and his wife, Miss "finelady" Jane . . . She tried to forget the ridiculous name she'd given the girl she'd thought so enamoured of Ben Killigrew all those years ago, and smiled at Walter, sharing in his joy.

"When can I come and see them?" she said eagerly. "And what are you calling him?"

Walter drank deeply before he answered, obviously enjoying Ran's good brandy, but intoxicated enough without it.

"Come as soon as you like, Mother. Cathy's longing to show him off. We thought we'd call him Theodore, but Theo for short, since 'tis such a mouthful for a tiddler."

"Theo Tremayne," Hal echoed. "'Tis a good name, Walter, and I'm glad you weren't persuaded to give un one o' they northern handles."

But no oblique reference to Tom Askhew was going to upset Walter today, and he merely laughed.

"You should know by now that nobody persuades me and Cathy to do anything we don't want to do," he said with a grin, and Morwen knew how true that was.

From the moment they met and fell in love, they had been determined to be together, no matter what the opposition. And it had been very bitter opposition at first, but love had weathered all the storms and separations, and been all the stronger for it.

She had a sweet glimmer of memory of the two of them, hiding from prying eyes in the secret, turreted room in this very house, just so they could be together. And then Freddie had come to the rescue of the young lovers, offering a sensible solution to all the opposition.

Morwen drew in her breath, as the glimmerings of another idea came to her mind. Perhaps it was impossible, but Freddie seemed destined to be the solver of so many things . . . but she wouldn't even let herself ponder on it yet. It was something to keep private until it was properly thought out.

She gave her best-beloved another hug, congratulating him again on his new role as father.

"I'll come to see Theo this very afternoon," she said.

"Good. Cathy will be pleased."

He was obviously finding it difficult to get his thoughts onto anything but his wife and son, but now he turned to Ran. "I'm forgetting everything but my own good news, but since I'm here, do you want me to make any comments on the despatches? I can't promise to keep my mind on it, though, since I was up all night."

"For goodness' sake, man, I wouldn't expect anything else. Get yourself off home to your wife and family," Ran said with a smile. "There are more important things in life than dull old books and figures, and there's no other day in the world to compare with the day your first-born arrives."

Sometimes, Morwen thought, Ran showed an insight that reminded her just why she had fallen so madly in love with him, and she felt a lift in her heart. Maybe Theo's arrival heralded a new beginning in many ways. A new baby in the family was always a good sign. It meant that life and hope in the future were being renewed, and life was good.

Morwen went into St Austell that afternoon, to the small house where Walter and Cathy lived. They had waited a long time for Theo, but now the family was complete.

Her face dropped a little as she saw the carriage standing outside the house. The Askhews were here, and for a moment she wondered if she should go away and come back later. She could always go and see her mother . . . but then she told herself not to be so spineless. They all shared a common stake in young Theo Tremayne's future, and she would have to come in contact with these people sometime or other, so it might as well be now. She knocked at the door, and Walter himself answered it.

"Cathy's parents have been here a while, Mother, but I'm sure they'll be leaving soon," he said, once he'd greeted her. She immediately felt awkward.

"Don't be silly, Walter. All the grandparents will be anxious to see the new baby, so I certainly don't want to push them out."

Dear Lord, she was a *grandparent*, thought Morwen. The excitement had carried her along all day, but now she had time to stop and think about the new status Walter had given her. Even while she knew she would love the baby, she didn't care too much for the title of grandmother.

She went upstairs to the bedroom Walter and Cathy shared, feeling her heart pound a little. There was excitement, yes. There was awe, of course, because every birth was a little miracle. And there was also the wish that she'd managed to come at some other time when she didn't have to meet the eyes of Miss "finelady" Jane Askhew . . .

She forgot all of that when she entered the bedroom. The two people sitting on one side of the bed meant nothing. The only thing that mattered was pretty Cathy Tremayne, sitting up in bed with the shawl-wrapped bundle in her arms.

Morwen moved quickly forward and bent to kiss her daughter-in-law. She smelled of soap, talcum powder and rose-water, and that indefinable scent of new motherhood that every woman's own baby recognized so miraculously.

"I'm so glad you came to meet your grandson," Cathy said, smiling. "He'd very much like you to hold him."

Morwen drew in her breath. Her arms were suddenly hungry for the baby. Having given birth to five of her own, and been surrogate mother to three more, she knew the God-given sense of belonging when you held a newborn child in your arms. And this one was part of her . . . she reached out for Theo, and as she did so, a little tremor ran through her, as keen as a knife.

This baby was no more part of her than any other child in the county. Walter wasn't her birth son, and therefore Theo wasn't her true grandson. These Askhews, that she had never been able to accept, were the true grandparents.

The momentary shock of realization passed, as Cathy pushed the baby into Morwen's arms. She gazed down mutely on the perfect little features, and as she felt the tiny fingers curl around her own, her throat thickened. And then when the baby's eyes opened and gazed unseeingly into hers, her world righted itself again. They were the bluest of blue Tremayne eyes, and the features were far more like Walter's than Cathy's, though she could see why Walter had said the baby's little wrinkled old man's face was the image of Hal's.

"Isn't he adorable, Morwen?" Jane Askhew said softly. "We're so lucky to have such a handsome grandson."

Morwen gave a half-smile. It was undoubtedly the offer of friendship, but then, Jane came from a more genteel family than a clayworker's daughter, and found such platitudes easy.

"He could hardly be otherwise," she replied, annoyed at her own thoughts, "with two such handsome parents."

Tom Askhew's nasal northern voice broke into the women's admiration of the baby.

"Aye, well, he's got a good solid background to live up to, I daresay. On the one side there's the clay doings of his father's family, and on t'other side there's the brains of the newspaper business."

Morwen refused to take the bait, and neither did Walter, even if Tom made it obvious which business he considered superior. He'd made it so obvious over the years, it hardly counted for anything now.

"It's time we went, Tom, and let Morwen have her time with the baby," Jane said at once, and her very understanding of her husband's sneers was enough to irk Morwen. But then, everything about Jane had always irked her, and probably always would.

She watched as Jane bent to kiss her daughter, and the old elegance hadn't deserted her one-time rival, even in her early forties. She had been a fair-haired beauty as a young girl, and she was a fair-haired beauty now. While Tom Askhew had become grossly fat, and more pig-like than ever.

Morwen wondered how the fastidious Jane could bear to have him near her, let alone paw her with those great fat fingers, and lust for her with that heavily asthmatic breathing. She felt her eyes glaze, wishing such thoughts didn't spring so imaginatively to her mind.

They revolted her one minute, and in the next they made her want to burst out laughing at the incongruous thought of Tom Askhew bouncing up and down on Miss "finelady" Jane and squeezing all the breath out of that so genteel body . . .

"You've gone all soft-eyed, Morwen," Jane was saying gently now. "Babies have that effect on a woman, don't they?"

"Yes," Morwen said, in an oddly choked voice, but it wasn't young Theo who was causing her to squirm with thoughts far too embarrassing to acknowledge. She bent to look into his wise young-old face, and let the Askhews make their private goodbyes.

Freddie and Venetia were going to Falmouth to meet Matt and his family, and bringing them to New World for the first family get-together. Hal and Bess had driven over during the afternoon, and they were all in a flurry of excitement by the time the carriage drew up outside the house.

The children were too excited to wait inside, especially

Bradley. Though his eagerness was more for his beloved Uncle Freddie and Aunt Venetia, rather than these strangers he didn't know.

Even the charm of their distant land had paled for him, now that Freddie's departure to Ireland was coming ever nearer. By now, Ran had declared that rebelling over it had turned an obnoxious child into a monster. It was something that had to be dealt with, and soon. But not today. Not on this day when Matt was coming home.

She followed the children out into the garden, her heart pounding. She had been devastated when Matt had gone to America all those years ago, with Ben's cousin, the hated Jude Pascoe. The two of them, in some disgrace over a suspected crime nobody could prove . . . and Morwen being the only person to know of the greater crime Jude Pascoe had committed – that of raping her friend and causing Celia to drown herself rather than face the shame Jude had brought on her. It had been a terrible burden for both girls to bear . . .

She shook herself, seeing the tall figure of her brother emerge from the carriage. So tall and so elegant, in his fine clothes, and still with those charming blue eyes of the dreamer she always associated with Matt. But older . . . with a shock she saw the creased lines in the Californian suntan, and the receding hairline . . . and then she saw nothing but the gladness with which he held out his arms to her, and she fell into them with a little cry of joy.

The rest of the family came out of the house, and hugs and tears and laughter mingled in fair measure. Hal and Bess hugged their boy, and they hugged Louisa too, making her just as welcome. And Cresswell . . .

He was the last to emerge from the carriage, and Morwen felt her heart leap as she saw him.

"Dear Lord, Matt," she breathed. "But that's a handsome boy you've got there, and no mistake."

"Does he remind you of someone, honey?" he said, in the American accent that sat so naturally on him now.

She frowned, but no, Cresswell didn't honestly remind her of any one person. He was a mixture of them all – of

116

Matt, and Sam, and Freddie and Jack . . . but above all, he was a true Tremayne, from the thick black hair and vivid blue eyes, to the proud set of his shoulders.

To her astonishment, he came straight to her, put his arms around her and kissed her. The last time he'd been here, she had shamefully hated him. But as she had so rightly said to Albert and Primmy, Cresswell had gone away a boy, and here was a man.

"I've so longed to see you again, Aunt Morwen," he said, with all the aplomb of the American college graduate.

"Have you?" she said in some surprise.

"Oh yes. We have many things to talk about, and above all I intend to make my peace with your family for what I did to them. It was totally unintentional, but it still weighs heavily on my conscience."

Dear God, but he had his father's artless charm, she thought, and the gift of conversing without embarrassment that was so lacking in many of his age. And she forgave him everything in an instant. She hugged his arm.

"The children are dying to see you, Cresswell—" she began as they all went indoors, at which he laughed.

"I doubt that, but I hope to make my peace with them. And it's Cress, by the way."

The younger children were in awe of him, but Matt and Louisa were soon at home, especially with Ran, since they spoke virtually the same language now.

There were *four* Americans here, Morwen reminded herself, not just three. Her brother had become completely colonized, as the more sneering of acquaintances would say. But it suited him. He'd flourished and grown rich in his adopted land, and he'd done it by his own efforts, and no Cornishman would begrudge him that.

When all the gifts they'd brought had been distributed and the hubbub of noise had died down a little, the children were sent upstairs for their tea to give the rest of them a bit of peace. And while the various plans were suggested and accepted, it was noticeable to Morwen that her parents were content to take a back seat and simply listen, preferring to move a little apart from these energetic folk.

"Justin's birthday party is taking place at Killigrew House, courtesy of Hal and Bess," Ran said, smiling. "And since it's Cress's birthday soon too, we'll be making it a joint celebration."

"Sounds good to me," Matt said.

"It sounds just wonderful, and you people are all so generous," Louisa murmured.

"We want to give Cress a portrait of himself for his birthday," Morwen said, before she let herself think there was anything condescending in Louisa's words. "Albert's a very fine artist now, with exhibitions in Truro twice a year, and the best people going to his studio. He's agreed to do the portrait for Mammie and me, if you'll sit for him, Cress."

She held her breath. The boy could refuse, since there had been so much bitterness between them. But the man smiled and said he'd be glad to do so.

"And we've already told Matt about our proposition for moving into Hocking Hall," Freddie put in. "He thinks 'tis a good idea, and has agreed to it."

"But we'll want to see plenty of you all before Louisa and Cress go off to Europe, and after their trip too," Matt said quickly. "The plan now is that they'll be gone a month, and spend the rest of the time back here. And I shall want to go up to Killigrew Clay, of course, but there'll be plenty of time for that."

Even so, Morwen could see the tiny sense of relief on Louisa's face that they didn't have to stay in the house of these quaint clayfolk who were Matt's parents, nor even here with her cousin Ran and his brood of children. But it was Cress who surprised her the most.

"I've told Mom and Dad that I intend to explore the neighbourhood by myself, and Uncle Freddie's putting a horse at my disposal, so I won't be a bother to anyone," he said enthusiastically. "I especially want to re-acquaint myself with all my cousins before we leave for Europe, and it will be fun to call on them informally."

It wasn't the English way, but Americans were obviously

118

different. Morwen found herself warming to the unconventional, refreshing attitude of this handsome young man, and gave him her full approval.

There was so much talking to be done that it was late in the evening by the time the American family finally left for Hocking Hall with their hosts. Hal and Bess had left much earlier, and it had occurred to Morwen that her Mammie and Daddy were a little intimidated by the impressive businessman Matt had become, and by his self-confident family. But they were still family, for all that, and she refused to be overawed by them.

Justin had come home before they left, and after an initial wariness had become surprisingly agreeable towards Cresswell. He found him an interesting, highly intelligent character, with the ability to converse about many things other than the endless talk about china clay.

Morwen was mightily relieved to see that at least one of her older brood had been able to put the ghosts of the past squarely where they belonged.

Chapter Ten

Cress Tremayne was not a young man to waste time. He had a quick and eager mind, and once this birthday trip to Europe was over, he'd be shortly entering into a law firm in Sacramento with a first-class honours degree from his college.

With their mutual legal interests, he and his cousin Justin had discovered they had much in common. It was good to know it, but he still had to make his peace with the others he'd upset so much in the past.

Cress had never forgotten the shock and pain he'd brought to their young lives, when he'd so innocently blurted out the truth of their parentage and background. He thought he'd have been able to put it behind him. But the older he got, the more the thought of it had weighed on his mind. And that troubled him.

He wanted to see them all, and to put the record straight. And his first call was going to be at Albert's studio in Truro, where he hoped to see Albert and Primmy at the same time. They were the most involved, after all, along with Walter.

His expensive riding boots rang on the cobbles as he tethered his horse to the hitching post outside the studio alongside the Truro River. The smells of the river were neither unpleasant nor unknown to him, for although their huge Californian mansion and estate was in the heart of the gold country, his expensive college had overlooked the wide river where his father's gold shipments were carried to all corners of the globe.

There were some aspects of his own background, and that of these clayfolk, that were not so very different, he thought.

And he hoped to God he wasn't being snobbish in thinking it, for it was the last thing he intended.

He rang the bell at the studio, and the door was opened by a young woman with long, carelessly combed black hair, and a fragile air about her that was almost otherworldly. Her eyes were very blue in her exquisitely beautiful face, despite the dark shadows beneath them. She was dressed in a loose bronze coloured gown that scorned the fashions of the day. There were brightly coloured ribbons braided around her waist and around her throat, and on her face, tiny star shapes glittered at the sides of those glorious eyes.

"Good morning, Ma'am," Cress said, stunned by this vision. "Is it possible to see Mr Albert Tremayne? I'm afraid I don't have an appointment."

Primmy's face filled with heat. She knew him immediately. She hadn't seen him in ten years, and he wasn't remotely like the idiot who had gone away, but his voice and his looks gave him away. He obviously didn't recognize her, and she knew it wasn't only the fact that she had grown into a woman that prevented that recognition. In her casual mode of dress, she knew she looked nothing like the daughter of a prosperous businessman, and the look was quite deliberate.

She struggled with the idea of turning the caller away and saying that Albie was unavailable, but what was the point? They were obliged to meet very soon at Justin's party, and they might as well get it over with. But she wasn't yet prepared to say who she was.

"I'm not sure if Mr Tremayne's available," she murmured instead. "I'll have to see if he's free. Will you please come inside?"

"Thank you," Cress said with a smile. "I apologize if it's an inconvenience, but perhaps you would tell him I've come on a personal matter."

He removed his hat and followed the girl inside. She had a trim, slender shape, and she walked with a natural and easy grace that reminded him of his Aunt Morwen. So did that glorious hair, and those fabulous eyes . . .

Cress caught his breath, knowing what he should have known straight away.

121

"Primmy," he said softly. "It *is* you, isn't it?"

She stopped walking towards the door leading to the inner sanctum, and stood quite still for a moment before she slowly turned around. Cress had the feeling she would much rather have got through that door before she had to face him again. When she did so, she looked as if she was about to say something, and then he saw her eyelids flicker, and she paused while she took in his appearance properly.

"Yes," she said at last, in a wobbly voice. "And I know who you are."

Cress didn't waste words. "You know who I *was*, Primmy. But I very much hope you'll want to know me as I *am*."

She wasn't used to this sort of talk. It was too frank, too embarrassing, too colonial, and too soon.

"I'll go and see if Albie's free," she said quickly, and fled.

Albert looked up quickly from cleaning his brushes as his sister slammed the door shut behind her and leaned with her back against it.

"What's wrong?" he said at once.

As always, his thoughts went to what he thought of obliquely as her "trouble". He'd finally felt obliged to banish their old friends from the place now, and they were openly resentful. At the back of Albert's mind was always the fear that they'd betray what had been going on here for some months, either to the wretched newspaper or the constables.

Primmy moved forward quickly, to put her arms around him. She knew his anxiety was for her, but this time it wasn't her trouble. Besides, she was over it. She knew she was. It had been madness, but it was over . . . and she hadn't been so sucked into its depths as Albie had feared.

"For God's sake, Primmy, who was at the door?" Albert said urgently, as she seemed to be struck dumb.

"It's him," she whispered. "Uncle Matt's son. He wants to see you."

"Cresswell, you mean? That's his name, isn't it?"

She hadn't even been able to say it. All the hurt had come flooding back, and she didn't want anything to do with Cresswell Tremayne. Yet she knew that the healing process and the exorcism could only truly begin by facing up to a problem. She had already proved that.

"Yes."

"He's got a damn nerve, coming here unannounced. All right, I'll see him, Primmy, but I don't have to be sociable. You stay here and I'll soon get rid of him."

"No." She spoke slowly. "Albie, I admit it was a shock when I realized who he was, but I think we do have to be reasonably sociable. He's our cousin, and besides, you've already agreed to do his portrait. He'll have to sit for you. And I think – well, I think it's best if we hear him out, for Mother's sake."

She avoided his eyes, hardly knowing why she was defending the American cousin. But the visitor in the reception room wasn't the little snot who had hurt her so. This was a handsome, well-adjusted young man, and the flamboyant Primmy Tremayne, who scorned all the things that other fond mamas wanted their daughters to be, found herself wishing she was wearing one of the pretty gowns her mother kept buying her, and which were mostly unused, except when she was obliged to show a more conventional façade for her public performances.

She felt Albert's arms tighten around her. She was once so fragile he'd been afraid she would break if he acted this way, but in the last days the colour had returned to her cheeks, and he began to believe the nightmare was truly over.

"If that's what you want, then we'll hear him out," he said, but still somewhat suspicious of this unexpected appearance of their foreign cousin. "I'll close the studio for an hour or so, since there are no appointments until this afternoon."

"Invite him up to the sitting room, and I'll make some tea while we talk," Primmy said.

Mentally, she stood back from herself, feeling a little weird, and as if she was in danger of admitting there could be another side to Primmy Killigrew. It was almost as if there were two people inside her slender body, and the one she didn't know was a vibrant, chaperoned young lady, in

123

the process of inviting a handsome young man to take tea with her and her brother.

The very thought of it shocked her. It was extraordinary that she could even think such a thing! Cresswell Tremayne was nothing to her except through circumstance. And never likely to be.

By the time Cress left the studio it was midway through the afternoon, and Albert's next appointment was imminent. After the first crackling awkwardness between them, the American's frankness and his freely-given apology for the errors of the past, had gradually won them over completely.

When Albert and Primmy were on their own again, they agreed that it was amazing how compatible they had turned out to be. Albie even unbent enough to say that Cress was a Cornishman at heart, if ever he saw one, and nobody could pay him any greater compliment. And Primmy had fallen in love.

While her brother was busy with his next client downstairs in the studio, Primmy went dreamily to her wall closet, fingering the silk gowns her mother had provided so hopefully, and which she rarely saw her daughter wearing. Primmy had had no thoughts of wearing anything other than her usual attire to Justin's party in three days' time, but now, there would be a certain somebody there for whom she wanted to look beautiful. Someone whose blue eyes matched her own, and who spoke in a particularly attractive accent, and who was so intelligent that she knew she had better look to her laurels to keep up with him.

She caught her breath, knowing she was letting her imagination soar away with her, and wondering if being in love was slightly akin to madness. But she'd had no thoughts of falling in love before, and the respect accorded her from her piano playing skills had been fulfilment enough.

But in a few short hours of knowing Cress Tremayne, she knew it wasn't enough. It was never going to be enough again. And for the first time since they'd set up their living and working establishment together, she had a secret she didn't share with Albert.

Cress came again the next day for the first of the preliminary sittings for his portrait. Albert made a series of rough charcoal sketches, so as to become familiar with the shape of Cress's head, the way his hair grew from his forehead, the elegant profile and the broad set of his shoulders. All of which his sister could have described to him in detail, in lyrical terms that were in every way comparable with the most flattering likeness.

"Have you seen the rest of the family yet?" she asked him, in the soft, husky tones that were so like Morwen's.

"I called on Walter and Cathy when I got to St Austell," Cress said cautiously. "Their baby's a fine boy, and I think it was a fairly successful visit."

"I'm glad," Primmy said simply. "And what of Uncle Jack and Aunt Annie? Didn't you visit them while you were in Truro too?"

"I certainly did," Cress said with a smile. "They've surely got two lively daughters now, and I don't even recall seeing young Sammie before."

For the first time in her life Primmy felt the pangs of jealousy as she heard Cress refer to her twin girl cousins. She knew it was stupid, but she didn't want Cress thinking of anyone else but her.

"The girls are going to London soon, to nursing college," she said, glad to be reporting their imminent departure.

"Is that so? I'd say it's pretty progressive of their parents to let them go so far away."

Albert laughed. "Oh, we do have some progressive ideas on this side of the water, Cress," he said. "It's not all left to our colonial cousins."

But the banter was good-natured, and Primmy was warmed by the fact that they were all getting along so well. It was just so frustrating to know that it couldn't last. Cress would only be here for a couple of weeks before his mother took him off to visit the glories of Europe. Primmy had never had any interest in such things herself, but she could see how instructive it would be to see the great museums of Paris, and the statues in Rome, and to hear the music – oh, the wonderful music – in Vienna.

"What are you dreaming about, Primmy?" she heard Albie's voice say teasingly, and she realised she'd been staring into space for the last few minutes.

"Nothing that I intend to share with you!" she said airily.

She dared to glance at Cress, and he was staring at her now, as if he'd seen something special in her face. As if he'd been able to penetrate that dreaming look and know just what lay behind it, with the uncanny sixth sense that was supposedly so Cornish . . . but since his father was Cornish too, there was no reason why he shouldn't have inherited it.

Primmy knew she was discovering a new existence these days. The nightmare days were over, and Albert had been so right in banishing those others from their place. It had been torment for several weeks, but she had seen it through, with her usual determination. And now she was in a very different, bemused state of mind – the far lovelier one of being in love, without having yet fully declared the feeling, either to herself or her beloved, and certainly not to anyone else.

Morwen recognized it at once. She knew it as soon as her son and daughter arrived at Killigrew House for Justin's party, and with the rest of the family, she gaped at the lovely vision Primmy presented. Gone were the shapeless clothes and the tangled hair, and the freakish adornments on the face.

Instead, here was a young lady of quality, with her dark hair stylishly piled into gleaming curls on top of her head, with silver combs to keep it in place, and soft tendrils framing her cheeks. Her gown was the latest exquisite peach silk creation Morwen had had made especially for her, and in which Primmy hadn't seemed in the least interested. She wore it like a princess now, and Morwen knew there was only one reason why she should do so at a family gathering, with her eyes seeking out one particular person.

126

Morwen caught her breath. As Justin had wished, there were few outsiders here. There was Charlotte's young man, Vincent Pollard, in whom she was so besotted; there was the elderly Daniel Gorran, and it certainly couldn't be him for whom Primmy had such doe-eyes! And there was Cress Tremayne.

"You look a real picture, my lamb," Bess exclaimed as soon as she saw Primmy. "Don't she, Hal? Don't she look the most beautiful girl in the county tonight?"

"That's so," Hal agreed, "along wi' Charlotte and Morwen and all the rest on 'em, o' course. You'd best not show favouritism, dar."

Bess looked up guiltily, but no one else had heard her. Besides, what did it matter? She had never seen her granddaughter look so dazzling before, and she was entitled to her opinion in her own home! Then it occurred to her that she wasn't the only one thinking that Primmy looked a picture.

From the far side of the room, young Cress couldn't keep his eyes off her, and didn't Primmy know it! Bess wasn't so old that she couldn't see what Morwen had seen, and as soon as she could, she drew Morwen aside.

"What's going on?" she said bluntly. "What's Primmy playing at?"

"I don't think she's playing at anything, Mammie," Morwen said. "She's not one for games. No matter how she looks, what you see is the real Primmy."

Morwen followed her mother's troubled gaze to where Primmy was by now looking up into Cress's eyes, and where he was leaning down towards her as if to catch every word, and she didn't pretend to misunderstand when Bess continued.

"It can't happen. You know it can't happen. Theym cousins. It has to be stopped."

"How? You tell me that. And why should it?"

Primmy had never shown any interest in a young man before, and Morwen was annoyed that her mother was taking on so. It needn't mean anything . . . although she knew she was burying her head in the sand for thinking so.

Primmy had a creative, passionate temperament, and when she turned that passion onto a young man . . .

For one searing moment then, Morwen envied her so much. She envied her those mind-shattering, wondrous days of learning to love, of longing for the beloved, and speaking his name at every opportunity. Of touching him and glancing at him, and glorying in the kisses that sealed their belonging and promised a golden future . . .

She caught Ran looking her way, and their smiles caught and matched across the room. Oh yes, she had known those glory days, she thought, her throat catching, and they weren't only reserved for the young . . .

"'Tis bad for the future," Bess said delicately, still intent on discussing Primmy and Cress.

"You mean for any future children a related couple might have, I suppose?" Morwen said, less inhibited on such matters than her mother. "It didn't trouble the Queen and Prince Albert, did it? They were cousins, and they produced a fine brood of children between them, Mammie!"

"Maybe 'tis different for royalty," Bess muttered, "but I don't want to talk of such things," she added, just as if she anticipated the comment brimming on her daughter's lips that royalty and peasants were all built the same way, and that there was only one way for producing children.

But there was no point in worrying over something that might never happen. Morwen turned her attention instead to where young Vincent Pollard was offering Charlotte the dish of sweetmeats, and being so heartbreakingly attentive. Now there was a potential love-match, Morwen thought, despite their tender ages. But they were not too young to be in love, and she and Ben had been much the same age when they had first set eyes on one another. Those wonderful, halcyon days . . .

Justin was the star of tonight's party, and rightly so, but Cress too had his share of congratulations and birthday gifts, and the welcome from the Cornish family to the American cousins now was warm and spontaneous. And later on, Primmy was asked to play for them.

To Morwen's surprise, she pinked up at once. She wasn't normally reticent over such a request, and she had performed magnificently in public concert halls in front of influential people. But tonight she would be playing for Cresswell, and that would make all the difference. Morwen saw how nervously she smoothed down her silken skirt, and how a pulse beat noticeably fast in the low neckline of her gown.

Cress moved to her side and said softly that he had no intention of leaving English shores until he'd heard her play. Morwen was just near enough to hear her choked reply.

"I'm not sure I want to play then, if it means I hasten your going away."

"But I'll always come back to you, honey, and that's a promise. You know that, don't you?"

Morwen swallowed. It was an intensely intimate little conversation, said under cover of the general merriment, and she began to wonder just how close they had already become. It was one thing to argue with her mother about the ethics of their relationship. It was quite another to wonder if they were already lovers. But that couldn't be. They had hardly met more than a few times . . .

As Primmy began to play, and the music flowed from her creative fingers, she knew that if it hadn't happened already, it surely would. There was a subtle seduction in the romantic pieces Primmy chose to play, and a less than subtle reaction in the way Cress leaned on the piano facing her, his gaze never leaving that lovely flushed face. Dear God, thought Morwen, everyone must see it soon!

"Let's have something livelier now, Primmy," she said quickly, when the burst of applause from the first selection of pieces had died down. The younger children jumped up and down, calling for their favourites. And Primmy laughed, and played a selection of nursery tunes, then a couple of jigs, and finally her favourite classical piece of Mozart.

"You're so incredibly versatile, Primmy," Cress said, his voice so obviously admiring. "You have a rare talent in those slender fingers."

And in front of everybody, he lifted her hand to his lips and kissed it. The family gave a little cheer, thinking it no more than a gallant gesture in the continental style, but as their eyes met above her fingers, Primmy felt her heart begin to soar. And she wondered now, how she could ever bear to let this beautiful young man go out of her life.

The party went on into the early hours, although the company had thinned out considerably by then. Bess and Hal had retired long ago, and Morwen's two youngest children were asleep in one of the guest rooms, while Bradley tried desperately to stay awake and listen to the grown-up conversations.

Jack and Annie had gone home with their brood, and Justin had decided to stay the night in town at his grandparents' house, rather than go back to New World and return again later in the morning. He would soon be taking up his living accommodation above Daniel Gorran's legal Chambers, and he was patently eager to establish himself as a responsible partner there.

Albert and Primmy lingered as long as they decently could, but once everyone else said they were leaving, they too made their reluctant goodbyes.

"I'll see you both tomorrow," Cress said to them, but his eyes and his words were only for Primmy.

As the brother and sister prepared to leave, Cress turned to his parents, as if it was almost too much for him to have to keep making these platitudes with this wonderful girl and not take her in his arms.

"I'm ready to go whenever the rest of you are," he said, and as he spoke a small whirlwind leapt up from the sofa and threw itself past him and into Freddie's arms.

"I want to go back with you and Aunt Venetia tonight. *Can* I, *please*? I won't be any trouble—"

"Don't be silly, Bradley, you will either go to bed here like the others, or you'll be coming home with us," Ran said shortly.

At once, Morwen saw the mutinous brows on her son's face darken. It would be too awful if this lovely evening ended with Bradley flying into one of his tantrums and shrieking at everyone. It would be shaming for her too, if

130

he showed himself up so badly in front of his American relatives.

She put a hand on her husband's arm before he could say anything more, and pressed it lightly.

"Where's the harm in it if Freddie and Venetia don't mind, Ran? Besides, it'll be a novelty for us to have the entire house to ourselves for once, won't it?"

"You know we don't have any objection, Morwen," Venetia said at once. "We'd love to have Bradley come back with us tonight."

Ran was clearly torn between the delightful thoughts his wife had put into his head, and his need to discipline his unruly son. In the end, Morwen's soft, inviting eyes won.

"Oh, take him then," he said, his ungraciousness coming more from the surfeit of drinks he'd imbibed that evening than from anything else. "For two pins I'd say why don't you take him off to Ireland with you as well! Maybe the schools there can curb his wildness!"

He hadn't meant it seriously, but Morwen's heart pounded at the sudden glorious expression on Bradley's face. It should probably hurt her to see him so excited by the thought of leaving his parents, but it didn't. She loved him, and she understood him, and if his heart was with Freddie and Venetia and their horses, and all that such a life had to offer, then she was prepared to let him go. Letting him go seemed to Morwen the greatest love she could give him.

By tomorrow, she knew Ran wouldn't see it that way, if he ever could. But he'd done the unretractable now. The words had been said, and couldn't be unsaid. Whether or not they were acted upon, was yet to be seen. One thing was for sure, though, Ran wouldn't give in to his own words without putting up a fight.

Chapter Eleven

Their house was all in darkness by the time Ran and Morwen arrived home from St Austell. There was little to disturb the beauty of the night at this hour, no robbers or vagabonds roaming the byways, and no moorland animals wandering abroad. The air was very still; the cobalt blue of the sky was crystal clear; and the full moon lit their way almost as brightly as if it was daylight. All around them were the fragrant, earthy scents of the moors and the hedgerows, enhanced by the cobwebby April mist that covered the ground like delicate baby's breath.

Morwen leaned comfortably against Ran in the carriage. She felt the mellow, expansive glow that told her everything was right with her world. However temporary such a feeling might be in their tempestuous lives, she wasn't one to refute it. While it lasted, it was heaven-blessed.

She would remember this evening for many reasons, not least for the heady memory that Ran had put into words what she herself had not yet dared to say. Letting Bradley go to Ireland with Freddie and Venetia would probably be the making of him, and solve a lot of problems.

And she had seen the dawning of two love matches. Morwen's romantic heart soared because of it. Her girls were in love . . . and while she was filled with the lovely dreaming realization, she intended to ignore the thought of anything standing in their way. Charlotte's position in the Pollard household might be considered by some to be a servile one, and Primmy and Cress were related by blood . . . but love took no account of such difficulties. Love was more powerful than any of them.

She gave a deep sigh as the carriage came to a halt at

the door of New World. Before they alighted to go into the house, Ran took her in his arms.

"That was either a troubled sigh, or one of pure contentment, dar," he said softly.

"I'm sure you know which it was," she said huskily, her lips finding his, and moving softly against them as she spoke. "You know me well enough to sense my moods."

The touch of his mouth on hers deepened to a kiss of barely restrained passion.

"And you know mine," Ran said. "And there are far more comfortable places than this to put my thoughts into deeds."

She could hear the desire in his voice, and knew that it matched her own. The passion for each other they had always known was still there. It was sometimes subdued by the needs and anxieties of everyday living, and by the demands that other people put on them; but it was still there.

They walked into the house still holding each other, as if unable to bear being apart. Ran kissed her every step of the way, and by the time they mounted the stairs and reached their bedroom, his hands were feverishly unfastening buttons and laces on her clothes, and she was returning the actions.

The moonlight shone through the uncurtained windows, throwing patterns of light across carpet and furnishings. To Morwen, it all added to the romantic aura, transforming the room into a place of enchantment. As Ran caressed her, his hands moved over the pearly softness of her skin as if every part of her was new to him, and she caught her breath, all her senses alive and wanting him.

"I may not say I love you often enough these days, Morwen," he said in a voice thick with passion. "But God knows that I do."

"He knows it, and I know it, dar," she said softly. "And if you don't say it in words, you say it in every other way, and I know that too."

He gave a smothered groan of pleasure as her fingers sought and found him, and then he lifted her in his arms and

133

carried her to their bed, and the rest of the night belonged to them.

Because he would be leaving for Europe with his mother quite soon, Cress was perfectly agreeable to sit for his portrait as often as Albert needed him. It would be a great gift to take back to California with him, and he was touched that his aunt and grandmother had thought of it. He visited the studio every day during the next few weeks. But sitting for his portrait wasn't the only reason he went there. There was another, far more important reason now.

Each day when he was due to arrive, Primmy would wait impatiently for his arrival, and Albert would have been blind not to know the reason why. Finally, he had to speak out.

"Primmy, I know you and Cress have become close, but I've got to say this. Once he goes back to America, I doubt that he'll ever come back again. He's got a career ahead of him, and he's not going to change any of his plans. I don't want you having impossible dreams about him, because you'll only end up getting hurt."

She turned her expressive eyes towards him, and then lowered them. Even Albie didn't know just how close she and Cress had become. They weren't lovers in the carnal sense of the word, but in every other respect, she knew they were exactly that. In every look, every touch, every thought, and every gesture, they were lovers.

"I know what I'm doing," she said huskily. "You can't change feelings, Albie. Even if there's no future for us beyond these few months, I wouldn't change that, either."

"Even though you know you'll have to say goodbye to him? In the days when Walter and Cathy met such opposition about marrying, and she had to go to Yorkshire with her parents, they wrote endless letters to one another. Somehow I don't think that would be enough for you, Primmy."

It didn't need a crystal ball to know that Primmy had the same passionate nature as all the Tremaynes, and a long-distance love affair would never be enough.

"Do you think my love wouldn't be strong enough to survive such a separation?" she said.

134

"I know that it would. I just wouldn't want you to have to endure it," he said carefully.

She put her arms around him and kissed him.

"Don't spoil it, Albie. Just be glad for me, and let me enjoy the time I'm having with Cress."

And because he loved her, he knew he would do better to keep silent on the subject, but he also felt more troubled than he cared to admit. True, there was a special glow about her now that he'd never seen before. The heavy-eyed, drug-dazed Primmy of weeks ago might never have been. She sparkled now. Her hair was glossy and well-kept, and her attire was that of a sensual young lady who was in love and knew that love was reciprocated. It was a wonder the whole world didn't know it, Albert thought.

But when Cress arrived that day, and he saw the eagerness with which Primmy threw open the door to him, he gave up worrying. It was none of his business, really. He could only stand by, and be ready if ever she needed him.

Cress wasn't sorry when the day's sitting was finished. He stretched his limbs from the stiffness of sitting in one position for too long, and smiled at his cousins.

"It's far too fine a day for staying indoors. What do you say to shutting up shop for the afternoon and taking a ferryboat ride down the river?"

Albert shrugged. Cress must be well aware by now that once a commission was nearing its final stages, he was always eager to continue with it, and rarely left his studio to go gallivanting. And it wasn't hard to see who was really meant to accept the offer.

"I'd like to, Cress," he said carelessly, "but apart from anything else, I've a client coming in to collect a family portrait in an hour's time. But why don't you and Primmy go? She can do with some fresh air, and I'm sure there'd be no objection to an outing with her cousin."

He didn't bother to analyse whether or not he meant to remind the two of them of their relationship, or if it even mattered to him. The way they both came to life in one another's company was almost painful to watch, thought

Albie. In fact, he'd as soon be absorbed in his work, which was as much an aphrodisiac to him as any female. Not that that couldn't change, he amended. There was nothing unhealthy about Albert Tremayne. The right girl just hadn't come along yet.

"So, will you come for a ferryboat ride with me, Primmy?" Cress asked.

He hardly needed an answer. Within minutes she had fetched her shawl, for although the day was extraordinarily fine and warm for the beginning of May, there was always a fresh breeze on the river.

She and Cress stepped out into the May sunshine, and she saw no reason not to slip her hand in the crook of his arm, when he gallantly offered it. She was filled with excitement at the thought of this unexpected outing, and the sunlight sparkling on the tidal water reflected her sparkling mood.

The Truro River was always busy with water traffic, though of a very different kind from the port at St Austell, where the clay blocks from Killigrew Clay were loaded onto ships and transported to their various destinations. She gave a sudden shiver, for she had never returned to Charleston Port since the terrible day when her father, Ben Killigrew, had had his heart attack at that very place.

"You're not feeling cold, are you, honey?" Cress said at once, feeling the tremor in her arm. "We could always go back if you prefer it. This was only an idea."

"I'm fine," she said. "It was just a dark thought going through my mind, that's all."

"Well, whatever it was, forget it all for today. We're going on a voyage of discovery, aren't we?"

Primmy laughed at his coaxing. "All the way from Worth's Quay downriver and back again! It's hardly a voyage of discovery, is it?"

"It could be," Cress said quietly, and her breathing quickened as she followed his meaning. His arm pressed her hand to his side, and she knew they had already begun a special voyage of discovery that required no oceans of travel to realize.

She didn't meet his eyes as they boarded the ferryboat,

concentrating more on being helped aboard the narrow craft with the help of the ferryman's hand, and then seating herself on one of the planked seats beside Cress for the journey downstream. There was nowhere much to go when they alighted at one of the routed landing-stages, just a village and a wild tangle of shrubby moorland with a view down to the open sea. But the destination hardly mattered. Primmy had the certain feeling that this day was going to be important to them both.

When they left the ferryboat, they climbed the steep grassy slope and left the handful of cottages behind them, and sat down to catch their breaths. It really was a glorious day, and across this relatively fertile stretch of wasteland there was a profusion of wild yellow daffodils in full bloom.

Cress leaned over and picked a handful of them and handed them to her teasingly.

"For my lady," he said solemnly.

Primmy laughed. She buried her nose in them, but there was little scent attached to them. Their pollen dusted her nose, and Cress reached forward to brush the delicate stuff away from her skin. As his fingers touched her, and his face came close to hers, the laughter died away, and she looked at him mutely. The next moment she was in his arms, and the flowers were crushed, unheeded, between them.

"Do you know how many times I've ached to do that?" Cress said quietly, when their first sweet kiss had ended.

"No more times than I've longed for you to do it," she whispered, knowing she should behave with all the modesty such a situation demanded, but hardly knowing how to.

She hadn't ever kissed a young man outside her immediate family before, and they hardly counted . . . Nor had she known this searing excitement flowing through her that was even more exciting than the way the adrenaline flowed through her at a successful recital. She had thought nothing else could match it, but now she realized she knew nothing. And she was so ready to learn . . .

"Dear Lord, Primmy, have you any idea how wild you can drive a man when you look at him like that?" She

137

heard Cress groan, and she looked at him with faint surprise.

"How do I look?" she whispered again, since her voice was stuck somewhere in her throat and wouldn't function properly.

"Like a mixture of innocence and unconscious wantonness," Cress said, almost grimly. "And God knows it's wicked for any man to destroy a girl's innocence."

"But what of the girl's wishes?" Primmy murmured. "Maybe the wantonness is something she wants to discover. Maybe it's time."

She could say no more before his mouth was covering hers again, and she felt the sweet touch of his hand on her breast. A sharp ripple of desire ran through her. He lay half over her, and with the weight of his body pressing on hers, the physical evidence of his desire was very potent.

"I want you so much, but I won't ruin you, Primmy," she heard him say softly. "But there are other ways."

She opened her eyes slowly, unaware that they had been closed. She felt him unlace the bodice of her gown, and her breasts were exposed to the balmy air. She caught her breath as he bent his head and took each rosy peak between his lips, tugging at them gently with his teeth. New, exquisite sensations held her spellbound, so that she could hardly breathe, then she felt Cress's hand slide down the length of her body, to lift her skirts and move softly upwards.

"I want to know your sweetness, my darling girl. But you only have to say the word to stop me now, if it's your will," Cress said, his voice growing hoarser.

With an instinct more primitive than anything she had known before, Primmy felt her limbs relax as his fingers paused in their inching towards their goal.

"I don't want you to stop, Cress," she whispered. "Please don't stop."

For how could anything compare with this glorious feeling of longing, and the certainty that belonging to this man was the only sane thing in her life? The sanest thing she had ever known. How could such a love be ruinous?

By the time they left the daffodil-strewn moors, they

were committed to one another. Whatever scruples Cress had harboured, had been swept aside in the heat of passion and love he felt for this wonderful girl. They existed on a different plane from the rest of the world now, and their need to be together was all-consuming.

Ellis White and his friend had discovered a new waterfront meeting place, where the landlord didn't look askance at the strange attire or habits of some of his clientele. Outwardly the Truro tavern known as The Seaman's Friend was slightly less disreputable than some of the kiddley–winks where the clayworkers gathered in such rowdy numbers, but in other respects it had a sleaziness that few really suspected.

It was a tavern where not even the well-known prostitutes and young girls hoping to make a few pennies by lifting their skirts, dared to show their faces inside, though there were plenty of them crowding the streets nearby. Foreign sailors from the ports and rivers congregated at The Seaman's Friend, as did those characters on the fringes of respectable society. And certain others, grotesque in their women's garb and heavily made-up faces, paraded up and down in the smoke-filled atmosphere.

Ellis and Lawrence watched the parading transvestites with lascivious, yet cautious, eyes as they were still wrapped up in one another. They were a diversion, nothing more. Ellis and Lawrence also scorned the Bohemian set, who only came to the tavern for the drugs they could obtain from the foreign sailors. Lawrence took a long draught of his ale, and pointed out a couple of them.

"Just look at them, my dear, shambling about like vagrants and begging for favours. You wonder where they get the money to pay for their habits."

Ellis was disinterested in the arty set. His interest in a lot of things had waned, not least his enthusiasm for his anonymous letter writing in *The Informer*. It had been exciting to begin with, seeing folk squirm, and filling him with a power he'd never known, but Lawrence had put such a damper on it, saying it was beneath any man to hide behind such anonymity. It had produced a certain amount of bickering between them, and in the end Ellis had simply kept his mouth shut on the subject.

Besides which, there had been nothing of interest to write about lately, and he'd almost forgotten his intention to disgrace the Killigrew sprogs at the studio. Almost . . .

"Just look at those rough fellows," Lawrence murmured as a group of seamen swaggered in. "I think we should get away from here, Ellis dear—"

But Ellis was no longer listening to his friend. His ears had become finely-tuned now to the group of scruffs brooding over their jugs of ale in the corner of the tavern.

"I say we forget all about them," one growled. "The girl's poncing herself up like a lady of fashion now, and Albie don't want to know us no more. The two on 'em have got too big for their boots lately."

"You're right," snarled another. "In any case, if she don't want to sniff the stuff no more, it means there's more for we."

"'Cepting that we don't get their share of payment. Albie were allus generous, and 'tain't cheap."

Ellis felt a new excitement creeping over him. So the Killigrew pair were into more amusements than just sleeping with one another, were they? His vicious brain was already composing the carefully worded letter that would set a right cat among the pigeons.

"Did you hear that?" he hissed to Lawrence. "They're on about the pair I told you about, and there's more to 'em than I suspected. They enjoy the occasional sniff—"

He felt Lawrence's hand grip his arm like a vice.

"You breathe one word of this and you'll have the authorities breathing down everybody's neck, you damn fool."

Ellis felt himself blanch. In recent weeks, Lawrence had subtly introduced him to the twilight world of narcotics, and he could see the sense in what he heard. But it needn't stop him welshing on them about the other.

Incest wasn't the tastiest of subjects in a family . . . but his eyes narrowed, wondering if he was going about this in the wrong way. He had nothing personal against the Killigrews. But where was the real satisfaction in his letter writing? It

140

didn't shame him, for he was a man without shame, but he realized it was a pointless exercise, when there was a far better, and more profitable one, just waiting for him.

"Let's go home, Lawrence. I've got an important letter to write." And at his friend's exasperated look, Ellis gave him a beatific smile. "It's not what you think, lovey. It's something that could prove very profitable to us both."

A few days later, a letter was delivered by hand under cover of darkness to Albert Killigrew's studio. He found it the next morning when he came downstairs to unlock the doors. He picked it up without much curiosity. Enquiries for his services sometimes came from unlikely sources, and folk who were reticent to find out about his charges face to face, frequently used this method.

He tore open the envelope carelessly, and took out the folded piece of paper inside. He stared at the bold, uneven lettering, his mind totally revolting against what his eyes told him, and for a moment wondering if this was some child's trick. And then he re-read the filth, and knew it was no child who had done this.

"Good morning, Albie. Isn't it a beautiful day!"

He heard Primmy's light voice as she came downstairs to join him for breakfast. Her light, so-in-love voice, and surrounded by the aura now that he'd never seen until lately, making him urge to paint her and try to capture that elusive glow on canvas . . .

He was tempted to crush the letter in his hands and destroy it, rather than let her see it. But she couldn't miss the devastated shock on his face. She'd know immediately that there was something wrong. And Primmy being Primmy, she would worm it out of him. Even as he knew it, he saw a look of anxiety shadow her face.

"What's happened, Albie?" she said, without crossing the room.

She stood perfectly still, her sensitive pianist's hands held tightly together. It was as if an invisible strength allowed her to hold herself in check, as if all her senses told her this was too momentous a happening to be resolved by mere platitudes, and all her inner reserves were being gathered up for what was to come.

"Some bastard's sent me an anonymous letter," Albie said, in a voice that didn't sound like his. It was filled with such pain and anguish, and still she couldn't go to him.

"What about?" Primmy said huskily, thinking that there was nothing in the world her dear, sweet brother could do to offend anybody.

"About you and me, Primmy," he said harshly, knowing he couldn't dress it up in any other way. "About you and me."

Primmy stared at him, not comprehending for a moment. Her nightmare days were over, and she wouldn't believe her latterday friends would have betrayed their part in the multi-coloured evenings they had spent here.

So what . . . ? At last her feet seemed to move forward by themselves, and she took the letter from Albie's hands. She instantly knew the meaning from the blatant and carefully-pasted letters cut out from newspaper headlines, and her face flooded with painful colour.

"Oh, how wicked," she whispered, hardly able to look into her brother's face. "How *disgusting*!"

She felt her bile rise, and she clapped a hand over her mouth while her eyes scanned the vicious words again.

INCEST IS AN OFFENCE, KILLIGREW. I KNOW
WHAT YOU AND YOUR SISTER DO IN THAT
COSY LITTLE SETUP. IT'LL COST YOU PLENTY
TO KEEP ME QUIET. THE FIRST INSTALMENT IS
A HUNDRED POUNDS. YOU'LL BE CONTACTED
WHERE TO LEAVE IT. DON'T GO TO THE POLICE
OR *THE INFORMER* WILL GET TO KNOW OF IT.

"It must have taken hours to do all this," Primmy said inanely. "How can somebody hate us so much?"

She looked up, genuine bewilderment mingling with the pain in her voice. As far as she knew, nobody hated them. They were the toast of Truro town, the elite, the successful. And this was all so terrible and so *wrong* . . .

The next moment she was sobbing in Albert's arms, and then she felt him put her gently away from him.

"Not here, Primmy. Let's go into the back room."

Horror filled her eyes. Dear Lord, but he said it as if he thought there might be prying eyes watching them through the windows of the studio frontage. In case he feared that every normal, sibling gesture was to be misconstrued from now on. Whoever this letter writer was, she knew bitterly that he had already destroyed something very precious to both of them.

They spent the next hour in total distress and indecision. Blackmailers should be reported, but if this one did as he threatened and it all came out in the press, it would shame their family and ruin them both. No matter how they denied it, this was the kind of mud that always stuck.

And Cress was coming here today to take possession of the finished portrait to show to Bess and Morwen. Primmy wondered how she could ever face him. How could she tell him? And how could she not? They had become so close that she thought of him as the other half of her. She had been so ecstatically happy with Cress, and now her heart was already breaking for a love that seemed doomed.

When he came to the studio, he was totally unprepared for the reception that awaited him, but one look at his beloved and he knew something unspeakable had happened. It was left to Albie to show him the letter, and Primmy watched his face unblinkingly. If Cress showed by one flicker that he believed it, then all was lost.

In answer to her anxieties, he came to her at once and folded her in his arms. And if Albert had ever doubted their feelings for one another, he could never doubt it now.

"I won't dignify this garbage by asking you what I already know," Cress said. "The thing is, what are we going to do about it?"

Albert shrugged, temperamental and angry now that the first searing shock had worn off.

"Pay up, I suppose. What the hell else can we do?"

143

"That's what blackmailers expect," Cress said, still holding Primmy close. "But if you call their bluff, they'll back off."

"You must be bloody mad if you think I'd risk allowing him to take the story to the newspaper, man," Albie said angrily.

"No. We'll take our own story there instead, and take all the heat out of anything he might think of doing," Cress said. As Primmy gasped, he held her more tightly, and continued steadily.

"You and I will go to the newspaper office, Primmy, with a little piece of information for the social pages. It will state that Miss Primrose Killigrew will shortly be accompanying her aunt and fiancé on a European tour before leaving Cornwall with them for California. What do you say to it, my honey? Will you?"

Chapter Twelve

Now temporarily and comfortably installed at Hocking Hall, Louisa Tremayne had spent a pleasant hour busily assessing her wardrobe, and consulting with her sister-in-law over which clothes should be packed for a European tour, and which could remain. They had quickly become good friends, and now they were ready to go downstairs to where their menfolk were lounging, prior to the early evening meal.

Matt spoke to his wife at once. "Jack and Annie have suggested that you and Cress travel to London with them and their family, honey. They're staying in the city for a couple of weeks now, to see their daughters settled, and to show Sammie some of the sights. It's a good idea for you all to travel together. There's always safety in numbers."

Freddie agreed, but felt bound to add his own comments. "It begins to seem as if all of us are shifting about. I hope it don't all upset Mammie and Daddy too much."

"They must be used to the way the world is changing by now, and all the travelling opportunities there are," Matt said, far more worldly himself than Freddie could ever be. "Times are long gone when folk stayed in the same place from the day they were born until the day they died. Though I daresay your agreeing to take young Bradley off to Ireland was a bit of a shock to them."

Listening to the amicable chitchat, Cress took a deep breath. Things had been quickly settled between himself and Primmy. They had been busy all day, making their plans, and he'd barely been back at the house more than half an hour.

They all knew that Albie would dearly love to go to Europe with them, to see all the wonderful art galleries. But they also recognized that it could be disastrous to their cause of establishing the far healthier relationship between herself and Cress, than the ugly one the blackmailer had fabricated. But something had to be said here and now, and Cress tried to keep his voice steady as he faced his family.

"They're not the only ones on the move," he said. "Mother, I've invited Primmy to accompany us to Europe, and she's accepted, subject to your approval. I'm sorry to spring it on you, but I very much want Primmy along. And I also want her to come to California with us when we return."

There was total silence in the drawing room for a few minutes, and Cress knew he couldn't have sprung more of a surprise on them if he'd dropped a bombshell in their midst. Then Matt's handsome face darkened with suspicion.

"What's been going on in Truro, boy?" he asked.

"Nothing's been going on. Primmy and I have a deep fondness for one another, that's all. She hasn't been too well of late, and needs to get away for a while. This seemed like a very good way of helping her."

"I like Primmy well enough, and I wouldn't object to her company on the trip," Louisa said quickly, seeing tempers beginning to rise. "But you say you've invited her to California as well! Now, Cresswell, we've always given you every leeway in life, but this country is not California. Besides, what on earth do you think her parents will say to such an idea?"

"Primmy's not answerable to anyone. She's a year older than me, for God's sake!" he retorted, raising a hand in apology as he forgot himself in the presence of ladies.

He had a desperate need to protect Primmy from any kind of gossip, and he daren't betray the true reason for their departure. His own father had once been the mildest and dreamiest of men, but he had changed during his years among the Californian gold-miners, and mixing with the toughest of men. He wouldn't stand for the insult of a vicious slander, and Cress knew that all hell would be let loose if he leaked out the urgency of their plans.

Matt would go storming down to Truro to confront Albert

146

and Primmy, and demand that on no account were they to give in to blackmailers, no matter what. And if they all saw the need to have a family council on the problem, there'd be upsets all round, when none of it was necessary. Cress had already seen the way out, and acted on it.

"Are you sure Primmy really wants to travel?" Venetia said in some surprise now. "I always thought she and Albert were like two peas in a pod in their Truro place."

Dear God, thought Cress, but didn't she know she could be innocently turning the knife of suspicion by such a remark? But of course she didn't know. Cress shook his head, and spoke directly to his mother now.

"Primmy's got a touch of wanderlust in her veins, and as this trip is my birthday gift, I didn't think you'd object, Mother. You always said you'd have liked a daughter, so you can look on Primmy as the next best thing."

As his father looked at him with a narrowing of his eyes, Cress went crazily on.

"While I was in Truro, Albert and I met up with one of the reporters on *The Informer*. He was interested in the doings of the American Tremaynes. I told him I'd shortly be leaving on a tour, and he wanted to put a small piece about it in the social column. There must be a shortage of real news these days," he added, trying to sound casual. "I'm afraid I rather recklessly said that my fiancée, Miss Primrose Tremayne, would be accompanying my mother and me."

Matt leapt up and grabbed his son by the shoulders, his fingers digging into him, bellowing into his face in true Tremayne form.

"By God, I think you've gone completely mad! What the devil do you think Morwen and Ran will say to this? And your grandparents? How dare you do such a stupid thing?"

"What is it you're objecting to?" Cress shouted back. "The fact that it's all cut and dried without consulting you, or the fact that Primmy and I love each other?"

He heard his mother give a little cry. "Cresswell, is this really true?" she gasped. "Do you mean to say the engagement is a genuine one and that your affection for Primmy is returned?"

"Of course I do," he retorted. "I wouldn't invent such a story. And is it so very hard to understand?"

Into the general crackle of consternation, Freddie suddenly gave a wry laugh.

"It is that, my young bucko, when 'twas young Primmy who made such a screaming to-do when you first let out the truth about her parents all those years ago!"

Cress grimaced, twisting away from his father's cruel grip. "But as you so rightly say, all that was years ago. We're different people now, and we love each other. I mean to have her, Father, and there's nothing anyone can say or do to make me change my mind."

Matt spoke with a grudging sliver of admiration in his voice. "Christ Almighty, if I ever thought there was any doubt about your being a true Tremayne, I don't doubt it now. I don't know one of 'em yet who didn't go all out for the love of their choice. You've got more guts than I gave you credit for, boy."

"Then don't you think it's time you stopped calling me boy, and recognized that I'm a man?" Cress said crisply.

"Well said, Cress," Venetia said softly. She went to him and kissed his cheek. "You have my congratulations and my approval, but I do think it would be wise to get yourself off to New World as soon as you can, before Morwen and Ran read all about it in the newspaper. You won't be the most popular of young men if that should happen."

"Albert and Primmy will already be at New World now, and I said I'd meet them there after supper," he said quickly. "But as I don't have much appetite, I think I'll go now and have a bite later."

"One more thing, Cress," Matt said sharply. "There's no other need for all this haste, is there? Something you're too shamed to tell us?"

Cress felt his face go hot. Speed to get the information of Primmy's departure in the newspaper was essential, as was news of her engaged status, because it was a sure way of letting the bastard blackmailer see that they weren't giving in to him. But the kind of haste his father was referring to, was farthest from his thoughts right now. If anything, all this incestuous suspicion would be enough to emasculate a lesser man, he thought. But thankfully he was a stronger man than that.

"No, Father. I have not defiled Primmy, and nor would I do so," he said bluntly, disregarding the ladies' scarlet faces. "I love her and I respect her, and I intend to tell her father the same."

He escaped as soon as he decently could, knowing that for all his fine words, he loved Primmy with a fierce and hungry passion that was worthy of any man who had spent his years gouging out the wet clay from the earth. And why he should even think of it in such terms was beyond him, and he tried to forget it as he set out for New World, his heart thudding uncomfortably in his chest.

Albert and Primmy were already there as he had expected. They were with their parents in the drawing room, and the door was firmly closed until he was announced and allowed entry.

He could tell immediately that the parents had been told of Primmy's plans, and his heart sank. He had intended this to be his task, not only to beg Ran to let the girl accompany him and Louisa to Europe, but also to ask for her hand. She might be of an age to please herself, but there were still family rules to follow, and Ran's face was as black as thunder as Primmy moved swiftly to Cress's side and stood with her fingers touching his.

"I don't like this carry-on, young man," Ran said at once. "You've hardly known one another two minutes and yet you profess to love one another, by all accounts – and what does your mother say to your whisking Primmy off to Europe?"

"My mother has agreed, sir, and I apologize for the unorthodox way it's come about. But, as you know, we leave early next week, and so it had to be a hasty decision."

Ran looked at him thoughtfully, and Cress prayed he wouldn't ask the same intimate question that his own father had done. It was a natural question for a concerned parent to ask, but it was excruciatingly embarrassing, all the same, especially when there was no truth in it. The temptation and the desire might be there, but he'd had the strength to restrain himself, and intended to as long as Primmy decreed.

To his surprise, his Aunt Morwen leaned forward and caught her husband's hand. He'd never thought that she might plead his cause, but he saw the way she looked at her husband now, and heard her soft, melodious voice, and he realized he had an unexpected ally here.

"Ran, whether folk have known each other for two minutes or two years, it counts for nothing when they're struck down by love. We both know that, don't we, dar?"

She pleaded with her eyes, willing him to remember the moment they had first set eyes on one another when Randell E Wainwright had come to Cornwall, and called on the family of his cousin Louisa.

Some of Ran's first words to her had been to tell her she was beautiful. She had seen the admiration in his eyes, and known that here was a man of some stature. When he left the house, they had made a formal handshake, and her hand had felt so small and delicate in his. She remembered the absurd feeling of pleasure at knowing they were no longer a bal maiden's hands, but those of a lady. She had wanted him to know the softness of her hands, just as she had known the strength in his . . . and if she hadn't fully recognized it then, she had known the heady excitement of falling in love at first sight. And so had he.

Ran's hard eyes softened as he looked at his wife. Still so beautiful, so fey and mysterious in many ways, and so obviously willing him now into giving into this craziness. And as her calmness penetrated his anger, he hesitated. Why was it so impossible? Grudgingly, his businessman's head propelled him into seeing both sides of the argument. They were young, they were in love, and they had to travel life's journey for themselves. Nobody else could do that for them.

Primmy left Cress's side and moved towards Ran, tentatively putting her arms around him. She smelled of the countryside. She smelled like Morwen. She was soft and sensual, and now that she had discarded those ghastly shapeless garments she used to wear, Ran saw her for the

150

beautiful and highly desirable young woman that she was. And who better to entrust her to than someone she loved, and who obviously adored her?

"Please, Daddy Ran, don't be difficult. I'll never ask you for another thing in the whole world if you'll agree to this," she said in a breathless little voice.

He gave a half-smile, transported back to the past, when Primmy the child had begged for a new toy, and the adolescent Primmy had begged for a new pony, and each time the plea was the same. She would never ask for another thing in the whole world from Daddy Ran if he would agree to it. And he always did, knowing that he was a fool to believe it, but completely smitten by her guile . . .

"I guess if you must have your way as usual, then I must give in to you as usual, honey," he said, his voice as soft as hers. She gave a joyous little cry and hugged him close, and then she whirled around and flew into Cress's arms.

They didn't get the same reaction from Bess. Morwen promised to break the news to her early the next morning, and Bess was openly upset. Her face creased into a frown of some proportions, and Morwen knew she had a battle on her hands.

"'Tain't right," she said forcefully. "I said it before, and I'll say it again, Morwen. What will folks think at the two on 'em going off to foreign parts together?"

"Mammie, what is it you don't like? If 'tis the fact that they're cousins travelling together, then there's nothing to fret about, since Aunt Louisa will be accompanying them!" Morwen said, just as heated. "And if you're worried about the two of them wanting to be together for other reasons, well, you might as well try to stop the tide as stop that!"

"So you approve on it, do 'ee?" Bess said, her country ways becoming more obvious at every bit of this obstinacy from her strong-willed daughter.

"I approve of two people who love one another being allowed to show it, and not having to hide away in corners because of it," Morwen said bluntly, knowing this degree of intimate talk would stop Bess in her tracks.

151

"As for what folk will say," she swept on, "when did that ever stop a Tremayne doing whatever he wanted to do? It didn't stop our Matt going to America, and it didn't stop Daddy moving on from being Works Manager to bein' a clay boss. It didn't stop me marryin' Ben Killigrew, neither, and that was enough to make folk raise their eyebrows to the skies at the time."

Bess's lips were clamped tight together now, but her eyes were steely blue, and then she lashed out something that Morwen had never expected to hear.

"It didn't stop 'ee lusting after Ran Wainwright, even afore your husband was cold, neither, did it, my girl? And don't pretend it didn't happen, because I know it did."

Morwen couldn't have been more shocked if her mother had said outright that she'd seen her and Ran in the little London hotel where they'd pledged their love, no matter how long it took for them to be together. No matter how long it took for Ben Killigrew to die . . .

She felt her face flame, and she snapped at Bess, in a way that was quite unlike her.

"I was a grown woman then, Mammie, and capable of making my own decisions. And Primmy's a grown woman too, and I won't stand in her way."

"And you'm both still daughters, and there's no changing that, neither," Bess snapped back, with what Morwen thought was a quite illogical statement.

But she was inflexible, and Morwen left her with nothing resolved between them. She hated falling out with her mother, and it rarely happened, but Primmy had her whole life ahead of her, and she wasn't going to spoil things for her.

She wasn't ready to go home yet, and since she was in town, she decided to call on Justin at the lawyer's chambers. Despite his surprise at seeing her, his greeting was like a breath of fresh air. Daniel Gorran had taken one of his frequent days off, and Justin said there was nothing to do here that couldn't be left in his assistant's hands.

"I usually take my midday meal at The Anchor Hotel,

Mother, so why don't you let me treat you, and you can tell me what's troubling you," he said with a grin.

"Why should anything be troubling me? Why can't I just call on my son for a change?"

Justin laughed. "Because I'll be seeing you this evening, and because I know you too well. Something's ruffled your feathers, and you're needing a sympathetic ear. Am I right?"

"And you're becoming too astute a counsellor," she said drily. "But of course you're right, and thank you. It's a while since I've been to The Anchor."

She smiled naturally for the first time that day, her heart lifting at his thoughtfulness, and the ease with which he proposed the outing. The Anchor was a very pleasant, genteel hotel, and there had been a time, long ago, when she had gazed in wonder at the rich folk alighting from their carriages and entering the establishment in their finery and taking an indulgent meal in the middle of the day. Justin hadn't known those penny-pinching days, but she had.

They didn't need a carriage to take them the short distance to the hotel. They walked along the cobbled streets in the warm May sunshine, and she thought how tall and elegant this son of hers was, and how she wished he too could find a love of his own. But he seemed in no hurry.

"There's that shadow passing over your face again, Mother," he said, as they were seated at an alcove table by the dining room window. "Do you want to tell me now, or should it wait until we've eaten?"

At her small sigh, he put up his hand.

"No, let me guess. It won't be Bradley up to his nonsense again, since the little brat has turned into a cherub at the thought of going to Ireland, though the Lord knows how long that state will last!"

Morwen smiled faintly, and let him ramble on, content to look through the hotel windows at the panorama of folk passing by in the street below.

"So it'll be one of the girls," Justin guessed.

"Why should it be?"

"Girls give parents more trouble, that's why," Justin

153

grinned. "So which one is it? Not Emma, that's for sure. And Charlotte's so high in love, she's on cloud nine. So it must be Primmy. That's my considered opinion, Ma'am, and I'll send you my consultation fee in the morning."

Morwen felt her mouth twitch at his nonsense. He had a lawyer's sharp way of deduction, and he'd quickly come to the right conclusion. She felt his hand cover hers, and as his expression changed to one of concern, she looked into Ben Killigrew's eyes.

She drew in her breath, knowing that in times of family troubles, her senses were always heightened, and then it seemed as if past days were the best of all days. It wasn't always so, and of course she knew it. But she couldn't help but wish that the joys and burdens of an expanding family didn't weigh quite so heavily.

She blurted out the situation quickly and concisely, and Justin sat back with a faint smile on his face.

"Is that all? I thought it was something terrible!"

"Your grandmother thinks it is!" Morwen said passionately. "Please don't make light of it, Justin. She's very upset, and it is Primmy's whole future."

"Exactly," he said. "It's Primmy's life, and good luck to her. If she's made up her mind, then don't start putting doubts in her head. Anyway, we all know that Grandma Bess sees it as her role in life to make objections. She's living in another age, Mother, and I bet she had plenty to say when you wanted to marry Father. Did you care what other folk thought?"

"I cared about what my children thought!" Morwen said, remembering the family discussions.

And remembering too, how the children had been the ones to provide the solution so simply. Walter, Albert and Primmy, would live at Killigrew House with their grandparents; while Justin and Charlotte would live at New World with her and Ran. The children hadn't been in the least put out that their mother wanted to marry again, and to a kind of cousin too.

"Your children wanted the best for you," Justin said quietly. "And that seemed to be Ran Wainwright. From

154

what I've seen of Cress and Primmy in these past weeks, I'd say he was the best for her. Let them sort out their own lives, Mammie."

She smiled at him through eyes that suddenly prickled.

"Do you know how long it is since you've called me by that name?" she said softly.

He raised her hand to his lips and kissed it without self-consciousness.

"Maybe I should say it more often. But perhaps not for all the world to hear," he said, his eyes twinkling as he nodded to an influential business client at the next table.

He was right, of course. Due entirely to his own efforts, Justin was well respected in the town, and being heard to use a childish pet name for his mother in public, was hardly the best advertisement for an up-and-coming lawyer.

Morwen gave up worrying, and concentrated instead on the succulent fish dishes that the hotel provided, straight from their own Cornish waters, poached to perfection in a creamy sauce, and surrounded with tiny carrots and potatoes.

They had almost finished their meal when there was a sudden rustle at the door of the hotel dining room, and out of the corner of her eye, Morwen saw the head waiter talking rapidly to someone and looking in their direction. Her heart gave an uncomfortable lurch, praying that it wasn't bad news about one or other of her family. She hated unpleasant surprises, but as long as it didn't involve illness, she vowed that she could always cope . . .

The head waiter wove his way between the tables and approached them. Morwen's knife and fork clattered onto her plate, regardless of etiquette. It must be bad news, she thought desperately, her mind flitting through the list of family members like a litany.

"Mr Killigrew, there's a message for you," the man said quietly to Justin. "A runner has come from Doctor Vestey, to say that Mr Gorran has collapsed and been taken to Truro hospital, and that you are summoned there immediately."

Justin leapt up at once, flinging down his table napkin. Daniel Gorran had been his mentor and his friend for many years, and had taught him so much more than the mere rudiments of the legal profession. He was a longtime family friend and lawyer too, and Morwen's eyes were anxious, even while she sent up guilty thanks that it wasn't one of her own that was in trouble.

"I'll come with you, Justin," she murmured. "You may be glad of my support."

She heard herself speaking as if he was about to attend a wake, and wondered if that was truly to be the case. Daniel Gorran was a frail old man now. He had been very tottery at Justin's party, and she had always had a sixth sense about these things . . .

They called a hire cab to take them to the hospital, and were quickly taken to Doctor Vestey's office. He knew them both well, and greeted them gravely.

"He's been asking for you, Justin, and it's a good thing you got here quickly, for I don't think he'll last out the day," he said, without bothering to dress up the facts. "You'd best stay here, Mrs Wainwright, and I'll ask my nurse to bring you some tea."

"Thank you," Morwen said woodenly as Justin departed, his face white. Children shouldn't be subjected to seeing folk die, she thought inanely, forgetting that Justin was a man, and used to seeing much of life's darker side through his profession. The nurse brought the tea, and she drank it without tasting it, trying not to let herself imagine the hospital room where Daniel Gorran was dying.

An hour later, she wondered if she should go home, but it seemed wrong to leave Justin here by himself. No one had invited her out of the doctor's office, and she wouldn't have wanted to sit with Daniel Gorran, anyway. A man deserved dignity and privacy in dying, no matter how sympathetic the onlookers. But he'd asked for Justin, and that was different.

She was gazing out of the window when the door opened, and her son entered, looking stricken. His voice was young and bewildered, and very vulnerable.

"He's gone, Mother. It was horrible, like a light going out. One minute he was talking to me, still instructing me, and then his head lolled, and he was gone."

The doctor came into the room and handed Justin a glass of brandy.

"Drink it straight down," he ordered. "You've had a shock, and this will help to settle your nerves. And then I suggest you go home with your mother."

Justin obeyed, swallowing the drink and coughing at the bitter taste. Then, to Morwen's horror, he began to laugh.

"Do you know what that kind, gentle old man wanted to see me for, Mother? He's left me everything, and he wanted to tell me in person so that it wouldn't be too much of a shock when his will is read. He's left me the practice and goodwill, and his entire estate and investments. I'm rich, Mother, and you know what? It doesn't mean a damn thing, because I've just lost the best friend I ever had."

And then the laughter turned to tears, and he was weeping in Morwen's arms.

Chapter Thirteen

Whenever Bess Tremayne was troubled, she resorted to her needle and thread, stabbing at the homely household linen repairs, even though there was no longer any need for her to take on such tasks. But she was more than troubled now.

She had never been as fey as Morwen, but she was a true Cornishwoman, and she didn't dismiss signs and portents either. Even young Bradley had read out that spooky old tale and made them all shiver . . . though why she should remember that now, a month on . . .

But things were changing far too quickly for Bess's peace of mind. Nothing stayed the same for ever, but she didn't like the way her family seemed to be going in all different directions. Times were best when a family stayed together, and didn't start moving about to foreign parts of the globe, so that you hardly knew who was where. To Bess's mind, they should stay in the place where they belonged.

Now Freddie and Venetia had taken Bradley off to Ireland, a decision she thought was an outrage on Morwen's part, and Jack and his family had gone up to London, which she privately thought of as a hotbed of sin. Primmy had gone to Europe with her American cousin and his mother, leaving Matt comfortably installed at Hocking Hall, and Justin had moved out of the family home as quick as lightning when he'd come into his inheritance.

Bess liked things to happen far more slowly. It was all too much for her, and none of it sat comfortably on her mind. And there was young Charlotte too, living the life of a lady in that Pollard mansion, and she could be heading for trouble by going all soft-eyed over the Pollard boy.

In the end, it probably wouldn't come to anything, Bess

158

thought, and she wasn't at all keen that it should. The Pollards weren't their kind. But then, she'd never thought the Killigrews were their kind either, and it hadn't stopped her daughter from marrying one of them. Nothing stopped the young ones from doing whatever they pleased, and they took little notice of the wisdom of their elders these days . . .

Hal caught his wife sitting tight-lipped in their vast drawing room with her stitching. He was about to leave for the clayworks with Walter and Ran that morning, and knew at once that she wasn't best pleased.

"Now then, dar, what's all this glum face about?" he said. "I thought it was your day for seeing Morwen at the Tea Rooms, and you're usually in a better-looking humour."

"Well, I'm not goin' today and I sent Morwen a message to tell her so," Bess said tartly. "Me and the young folks seem to have too many different ideas from one another these days, and I'd as soon keep away as start an argument."

Hal looked at her, frowning. "But you never miss the chance to gossip with our Morwen."

Bess glared at him. "There's enough gossip about us in the town, with all them newspaper accounts."

He didn't like this kind of talk, and he didn't want to acknowledge the truth in it, neither. He pressed her shoulder as he stood beside her. He hadn't left the house yet that day, but he still managed to smell of the outdoors. He was a simple man with simple tastes, not given to flowery speeches or gestures, but his voice was full of unease as he looked into her face.

"What's brought all this on, then? You ain't still scratchy wi' Morwen over this Primmy business, are you? It's been over a week now since you last saw her."

Bess gave an impatient sigh, wondering how it was that men could be so dense at times, and then put their finger on the itchiest spot just when you wanted to keep it to yourself. And she wasn't one for putting thoughts into words easily, any more than Hal himself. But she was obliged to answer now, and she did so grudgingly.

"Oh, well, I know they all have their own lives to lead, but I feel left out of it all nowadays. 'Tis as if I'm on a back shelf in the larder, and nobody thinks my opinion's worth listening to any more."

"Well, that's about the daftest thing I ever heard," Hal said forcefully.

"No, it's not," Bess snapped. "I knew you wouldn't see it my way, but I can do without you standing there and patronizing me, Hal Tremayne. You'd best get off to the clayworks and see what's to do, if you're so all-fired up about these rumours about that woman clay boss."

"Aye, that I had."

He moved back with some relief, glad of her lead, and never easy with what he called women's tantrums. And Bess knew where his thoughts really lay. He'd been steeped in clay business for too many years to give more than lip service to domestic doings, when real troubles were looming.

And this new outrage that that bastard Askhew had blazoned across *The Informer* this week, had stirred up a hornets' nest among the clayers. Some ferret of a reporter had got an interview with Harriet Pendragon, and she had confirmed that she had already bought up several small clayworks in the area to add to her grasping little empire.

Now she had her sights set on the big boys, according to Tom Askhew's paper, and was going round them all with tempting offers. She had already approached several in the area nearest to Killigrew Clay, and it didn't need a genius to see that it was surely their turn next.

It had prompted a hasty meeting between himself and Walter and Ran, resulting in the three of them deciding to present a solid front at Killigrew Clay today, assuring the workers that they'd do what was right by them – providing the clayers were loyal in return.

"It has to be a two-way commitment," Ran had said to him shortly. "They have to see that we're always ready to listen to them if they do right by us."

"All that sounds fine and dandy, Ran, but I ain't so damn sure of their loyalty. They'll be full of good intentions, but

I know these folk better'n you. All theym interested in is a guaranteed wage and food in their bellies, and if the Pendragon woman was to offer substantially more—"

As he remembered the arguments between himself and Ran, he heard Bess draw in her breath as the needle jabbed into her finger, and drew blood. She brushed aside his sympathy, saying it wasn't the first time she'd seen blood and it wouldn't be the last. And both of them were secretly hoping that the tartly said words wouldn't prove to be prophetic.

But by the time he met up with his son-in-law and grandson, Hal had forgotten the small incident. There was more important work ahead of them than sympathizing over a pricked finger.

The three men travelled on horseback, despite the fact that Hal found the exertion of it uncomfortable, stiffening his joints and tightening his chest by the end of the ride. But not for worlds would he admit it to the others. He knew there was a psychological advantage in the three tall, well-setup bosses arriving on horseback to overlook their clayworks. It presented a far more powerful sight than arriving in a carriage, however grand. Hal wasn't a particularly imaginative man, but even he could see that.

"Something's wrong," Walter said suddenly, long before they arrived at Clay One.

They reined in their horses and held them perfectly still. The moors were particularly abundant with gorse and heather now, and bursting into summer bloom. Ahead of them, the sky-tips sparkled in the sunlight as always, almost dazzling the eyes with their glittering whiteness.

But the sound of silence was what penetrated their minds most of all now. There was no rumbling of trucks, no throbbing of beam engines, no clatter of machinery . . .

"The bitch has got here before us," Hal said harshly. "I'll wager she's rounded 'em all up now, and is wheedling her way into their confidence at this very minute."

"Then what the hell are we doing, wasting time talking?"

161

Ran said, digging his heels into his nag's side so fiercely that the animal whinnied in protest.

Walter said nothing, but his jaw was set tight. He wanted no troubles to cloud his horizon right now, and certainly no clashes between himself and Tom Askhew. The Yorkshireman had long been his least favourite person, but he was Cathy's father, and he felt obliged to allow the man a grudging smidgeon of respect on her account.

And he had no doubt that wherever Harriet Pendragon went, one or more of Tom Askhew's minions would be sure to follow, with their usual muckraking. Newspapermen were like vultures, he thought scathingly. Bad news was always preferable to them than good, and they fed on other folk's miseries.

"The bastards got wind of it before we did, Grandad," Walter said, as they neared Clay One and the great dip in the ground towards the area around the clay pool. He swore beneath his breath as he saw Tom himself, together with a thin, ferrety-faced man he vaguely remembered seeing somewhere before. The man brandished a notepad as importantly as if it was a badge of office, and was clearly one of *The Informer*'s reporters.

The unusual silence among the men was broken by the sound of a woman's voice. With one accord the three newcomers moved closer, reining in their horses at the back of the huge crowd assembled there. Pit captains, clayers, bal maidens, kiddley-boys skirmishing and being clouted by their elders to keep quiet, and the newspaper reporters busily worming their way to the front to hear better. But there was hardly any need. The woman's voice carried clearly, and she commanded attention.

"By God, but the bitch knows how to pull a crowd," Hal growled, trying not to betray the merest touch of admiration in his voice at the sight of Harriet Pendragon.

The other two said nothing, but Ran too was mightily struck by the picture the woman made. She knew damn well the effect her appearance would have on these folk, he thought angrily. She too, had arrived on horseback, elegantly side-saddled, her gleaming sapphire satin gown draped in glowing folds over her figure, as if it had been moulded there. She held the reins with long satin gloves that caressed her slender arms, and her bonnet was of the same colour as the rest of her ensemble.

It was an outrageous outfit to wear among these simple folk, in their tattered working clobber, and streaked with clay dust. As if the gown itself wasn't enough, her horse was a contrasting light grey. It was obviously a purebred, and no doubt chosen to complement her silvery-grey eyes and that extraordinary silvery hair. She was bloody magnificent, Ran thought furiously, and hated himself for acknowledging it.

He pressed his knees into his horse's flanks and urged it forward, scattering the outer groups of clayers and ignoring their howls of protest. Hal and Walter followed through the path he had made until they were almost level with Harriet Pendragon. Ran's voice was short and sharp.

"You're trespassing, Ma'am, and if you don't leave this place immediately, I shall have you forcibly removed."

The clayers had begun muttering at their bosses' approach, but now they had fallen silent again, and all eyes turned towards the Pendragon woman to see her reaction. She was completely unimpressed, and gave an amused laugh.

"And who's going to remove me, Mr Wainwright? Not any of these fine folk, who know a good thing when they hear it."

Ran didn't miss the rumbles of assent among the workers, and knew that Hal had a shrewder knowledge of these people than he did. But he didn't give up easily. Dammit, he thought, he wasn't giving up at all!

"Then I shall remove you myself," he said contemptuously. "But I hardly think you'd care for the indignity of it, Ma'am."

Out of the corner of his eye he could see the reporter busily scribbling down, word for word, all that was said.

"Oh, but perhaps I would!" Harriet Pendragon said, and to his fury, he realized she was teasing him, her eyes provocative and gleaming as if she was enjoying the chase. "Why don't you come and try it, Mr Wainwright, because I surely don't intend leaving by myself."

163

"Leave it, Ran. I'll deal with this," Hal said angrily, seeing his fury.

"No. It's me she wants," Ran said, brushing his restraining hand aside. "It's me she wants to bring down, for some Goddamn reason of her own."

"Why don't our fine Works Manager have summat to say about it all, or is he too afeared of what his father-in-law might say about un in his newspaper?"

The catcalls began from the middle of the crowd, but were quickly taken up by the rest. They were like bloody sheep, Walter thought, his face reddening as the jeering was directed towards him. He knew that few of them would attack Hal. He'd been one of them for too long, and was too well-respected.

But Ran was a foreigner, which was even more damning than being a "grockle" from upcountry. And to many of those who'd had the clay in their blood for generations, Walter was still wet behind the ears, despite his fine status at Killigrew Clay. It made no difference that Walter had clay in his blood too, he thought angrily, and that concern for the prosperity of them all was in his soul.

But he was too much of a man to let the jibes go by unheeded, especially regarding himself and Tom Askhew.

"You all know me, you scum," he yelled out above the din, in language they would understand. "I worked here as a kiddley-boy, same as the likes of your own, and there's nothing we'd like more than to give you all a handsome bonus. But when times are bad, you can't squeeze money out of a stone, so you've got to be patient, same as the rest of us—"

"Oh ah, we know all about you and your family bein' patient in your fine houses, while the rest on us scratch a living—"

"Shut up a minute, you shit-bags," Hal bellowed out. "If Walter has a decent house to live in, it's because he's bloody-well worked for it—"

"And because he's got a wife wi' money," somebody jeered out.

164

"I don't live on my wife's money," Walter snapped coldly. "And neither does anyone else in my family."

Ran shifted in his saddle, knowing that the situation was getting out of hand. It was dwelling too much on personalities, instead of on the state of the business as a whole. And Harriet Pendragon was content to sit on that damn great horse of hers and let the wrangling go on. It angered him to know that she was witnessing it, and he was doubly angry at allowing himself to be humiliated by the woman.

He cracked his whip in the air, in an effort to call for silence. The cat calls dwindled away as his horse reared protestingly at the sudden noise, and he swiftly brought it under control.

"We all seem to have forgotten why we're here, and I've yet to hear exactly what Mrs Pendragon is doing here. Please explain yourself in a few sentences, Ma'am, which is all I will allow you before I see you off this land."

"Really?" Harriet said, still with that infuriating amusement in her voice, so that Ran began to wonder if anything ever really irked her. Or was the power she'd inherited from her husband's death enough to give her this vast confidence that overcame all else?

"Your time is running out, Ma'am," he said coldly, as the crowd waited expectantly for her to speak.

"Answer the man, Mrs Pendragon, and let's all get back to our business," Tom Askhew called out now in his sharp nasal tones, clearly getting tired of all this fencing. "If you want my reporter to give a good account of what's to do here today, you'd best get on with it."

At his words, Walter remembered where he'd seen the ferrety-faced man. He'd been at the men's meeting in the St Austell meeting house, when Harriet Pendragon had first swept into their midst. Walter had dismissed the man as of no account then, and he'd like to dismiss him and his master now.

But he was too well aware of Askhew's contempt for the clayworkers, and of himself in particular. Tom had never forgiven him for marrying Cathy, and baby Theo

165

was half Tremayne, which was condemnation enough. His brother and sister had taken the Killigrew name, but Walter never had. He was a Tremayne, and would always be a Tremayne . . .

He blinked, realizing he'd let his attention wander, and that the Pendragon woman had slid down from her horse with all the grace of a queen. He watched as the clayworkers moved aside like the parting of the Red Sea as she approached the bosses with her sensuous walk, and he scowled again, wishing these damnable attributes didn't keep coming into his mind.

He wondered briefly how the others were assessing her. His Grandad Hal wouldn't be moved by a woman's teasing and taunting, but Ran . . . he wasn't so sure about Ran. Harriet Pendragon presented a powerful attraction for any man, but more especially one of similar dynamic power, and for the first time in his life he felt an anxiety on Morwen's behalf.

He tried to shrug off the feeling as the woman came right up to the three of them, tipping back her head and looking up at Ran as he remained mounted on his horse. With any other woman, it might have looked subordinate. With her, it merely looked provocative. She bloody well knew it too, Walter thought savagely, and so did Ran.

"Well, Ma'am?" he snapped. "We don't have all day to waste, so get to the point."

"Very well, Mr Wainwright," she said in her clear, carrying voice. "I'll tell you what I've told these clayworkers. I'm willing to offer sixpence an hour more for them to work for me at any of the small pits I've recently acquired. Unless, of course, you're willing to sell out to me. I admit that I've a hankering to own Killigrew Clay, and rid it of a name that lost any meaning when Ben Killigrew died. When that day comes, the workers will get a handsome bonus into the bargain."

There was uproar as she finished speaking, and the bosses didn't miss the cheers from many of the listeners.

"By God, but she's a clever bitch," Hal said under his

166

breath. "She'll turn 'em her way, Ran, and God knows what we can do about it."

"Shut up and listen to me, all of you." Ran ignored him, and bellowed out into the crowd. They fell silent as his horse reared up in protest, and Harriet Pendragon stepped back hastily from the flailing hooves.

"You've heard Mrs Pendragon's terms," he said loudly. "She's offering a bonus if we sell out, which I can assure you we don't aim to do now, nor at any time in the future—" he was obliged to pause as the uproar began again, and he cracked his whip for the second time, "and she's also offering you sixpence an hour more if you leave Killigrew Clay. But stop and listen for a minute before you go hot-headed into thinking this is such a good deal. This is a woman who's ruthless enough to try to undermine the good name of an established firm, and to cold-bloodedly steal away loyal workers. Is this the boss you'd choose to work for, instead of those who have always treated you fairly, and shared the good times with the bad?"

"That sort of talk don't put food in the babbies' bellies, Mr Wainwright," the pit captain, George Dodds, spoke up, "and you ain't never guaranteed that we won't have to face a cut in wages if the autumn orders be no better than the spring's."

"Then I'll guarantee it now," Ran said swiftly. "And we'll match the extra sixpence an hour that Mrs Pendragon has offered. In fact, I'll do more. There are promises of new orders coming in, so to show our good faith in you, I'll guarantee a bonus payment next Christmas for every man, woman and child who remains loyal to Killigrew Clay and its rightful owners until that day."

"What the bloody hell do you think you'm playing at, Ran?" Hal muttered angrily beneath his breath. "We've never risked putting such forward guarantees into their heads—"

"Then maybe it's time we did," Ran said, through the burst of noise as the clayworkers digested this new move.

"Ran's right, Grandad," Walter said quickly. "We've got to offer 'em something definite, or we'll have lost 'em for good. The woman's offers are too tempting for us to be wishy-washy now."

The woman in question was eyeing up these three now, and wondering just which of them was worth her while tempting in other directions. She dismissed the old man at once, and the young one was too besotted with his wife and new child – besides, there was a newspaper tie there, and that was an apple-cart she wouldn't care to upset. But the other one . . . the handsome American with the wife who was once a bal maiden here, and had then married the boss . . . she turned her startling silvery-grey eyes towards Ran Wainwright, and gave him a beatific smile.

"All right. You've had your say, and your workers seem to approve of it. I'm tired of all this arguing, so for the moment we'll call a truce, Ran Wainwright," she said, her voice softer than the strident tones she normally used in business dealings with men. "I'll concede that you've played a trump card, though you'll have to be seen to carry it through. And you and I haven't done with one another yet."

She turned swiftly, and was helped onto her horse with willing hands. She dug her heels into its sides and cantered away from Clay One with her back straight and her head held high. Even in defeat, she still looked magnificent, Ran thought grudgingly. She was as ruthless as any man, and twice as deadly, because it was obvious that half the earthy men here lusted after her, however unattainable she would be to the likes of them.

But not to the likes of himself. The thought was in his head before he could push it away, and his face darkened with the unwanted idea. He'd as soon bed a rat as the Pendragon woman . . . and again, his own thoughts conjured up a subconscious imagery that was abhorrent to him. He turned his attention to the crowds of clayers, still gabbling in groups about this new turn of events.

"Well, now that all the excitement's over, how about you shit-bagging buggers getting back to work?" he bellowed into the crowd of gabbling clayers, in words that would have done justice to Hal in his heyday. "If you think we're

168

going to pay you dung beetles extra dues for standing about like spare parts at a wedding, then you can think again. Get to it, all of you!"

The horses of the three riders stamped restlessly at the angry tones, and the clayers began to move back to their appointed tasks. George Dodds lingered a moment, his gnarled hand on Ran's reins. Ran would have flicked him off as impatiently as if he swotted a fly, but the man had something to say and wouldn't be put off.

"This new rate of sixpence an hour extra comes into force right away, I take it, Sir," he said, unconsciously putting an insult into the final word. "It 'ouldn't do for 'em to have to wait now, 'specially wi' the lady sniffing at their heels so prettily."

"Are you threatening me, George Dodds?" Ran said coldly, hating the man more with every second.

"No, Sir. I'm only speakin' up for the rest on 'em, as they'd want me to do. Ain't that the right way for a pit captain to act, Mr Tremayne?" He ignored Walter altogether and looked directly at Hal.

"It's right, and you know it, but you'd best keep a civil tongue in your head. Pit captains can be replaced, and you know that too," Hal said, and twisted away from the leering man to ride away from the pit.

He needed fresh air. He'd done with all this wrangling and sniping a long time ago, and he wanted no more of it. He shouldn't have come up here today. His chest was tight, and he felt ill. He should do as Bess wanted and lead a more leisurely life, reaping in the profits from his stake in Killigrew Clay when they were due, and learning to be a gentleman. Hal scowled, knowing it was something he could never be, not in the way that society dictated.

Walter caught up with him.

"Are you all right, Grandad? You looked quite sickly a while back, and I was afraid—"

"There's nothing wrong wi' me, boy, that can't be cured by fresh air and a quiet life," he grunted.

And Walter knew at once that there was definitely something wrong with a man who'd once exalted in the

169

cut and thrust of dealing with these scumbags, and who suddenly seemed too weary to care any more. But he pushed down the fear he felt on Hal's behalf, and thought instead that it was more likely that he was just growing old. It was high time Hal had a going-over from the doctor, though Walter knew how he'd hate the suggestion. In his own mind, Hal was still as strong as he ever was, and didn't give in to old age gracefully.

"I'm staying on here now, Grandad, to see that production is going ahead. Ran's in discussion with Tom Askhew and his reporter fellow at present, to see that they don't distort our side of it, so will you wait for him?" Walter said, keeping his face poker-straight as he mentioned the men from *The Informer*.

"I might, and then again I might not," Hal said, as contrary as ever. "If I've a mind to get on home, I'll do so, and if not, he'll soon catch up wi' me. You go on back to Clay One, boy, and be the fine Works Manager I know you to be."

It was rare for Hal to pay such a compliment, and Walter found himself blinking. Impulsively, he reached out and pressed the old man's arm in a rough gesture of affection.

"Those words mean a lot to me, Grandad," he said. "I'll go back then, and don't worry. Ran will handle things."

Ran had got them out of trouble once before. So had Matt. So, unknowingly to many, had Hal himself, offering all his dividends from his share of Killigrew Clay that were carefully salted away in a Bodmin bank, since such accumulated wealth was unnecessary in the life of a simple man.

Families such as theirs were all the richer for the way they helped and supported one another, Walter thought, as he turned to retrace his way to the clayworks he loved. And it would take more than the likes of a woman with silvery eyes and hair to fracture that closeness.

Hal rode slowly down over the hillside, wanting to put all the noise of the clayworks behind him. He'd loved it, once.

He had been its throb and its heartbeat, like the young uns were now, especially Walter, but it was a part of his life that was gone. The past could never come again, and he was gradually realizing that he was more than ready to let his life wind down, like the winding down of an old clock that had seen its day, and was contentedly ticking slower and slower.

The sun was warm on his back, and his nag was content to meander slowly, taking its time, as if to savour this lovely day to the fullest. Hal glanced back for a moment, to where the sky-tips looked so magnificent now, like moon mountains in their glinting whiteness.

He looked beyond the clayworks, where he could just see the roof-tops of the old cottages, and remembered how one particular cottage had been so filled with love. He remembered how his daughter Morwen had come bursting into the cottage on her seventeenth birthday, and told them all that they'd been invited to old Charles Killigrew's house that evening. And he'd known, even before she knew it herself, that his girl had fallen in love with the boss's son.

Hal turned and gazed ahead of him, down towards St Austell and the shimmering sea. Alongside where he paused were Ben Killigrew's rail tracks, that were such an important part of the business now, taking the clayblocks to the port and the waiting ships. But his heart tugged as always at the sight of them, for it was here that the subsidence had occurred. Ben's little train had been taking the cheerful crowd of clayers and their children on a joy ride to the sea. And the terrible accident had plunged the carriage into the depths of a disused tin mine, killing his first-born. Killing his strong young son, Sam, whom he would never see again . . .

Hal's eyes blurred, and he dashed away the unmanly rush of emotion. And then he turned his head sharply as a whispering voice seemed to fill his head to bursting.

"Daddy, don't be afraid. 'Tis me, come to guide you. Take my hand, for we're to travel the road together."

Hal was awestruck as Sam's voice suddenly filled his

head and his heart, and Sam's image was beautiful and ageless in his vision. Gladly, so gladly and confidently, he reached out his hand to take the one that invited him on the journey, and felt its grasp, as warm as summer.

Chapter Fourteen

A pair of truant kiddley-boys came upon the wandering horse a while later. They crouched down in the bracken, hearts trembling, and fearing an ear-cuffing from the old boss when they were discovered. And then, since there was no sign of Hal Tremayne breathing fire and brimstone on them, the braver of the two became curious and started dancing about the moor in a frenzy of release from the morning chores.

He stumbled over the old man with a yelp of fright, and the second boy rushed to see what had happened. For a moment neither of them spoke as they stared down at Hal Tremayne's inert body.

"Be 'e hurt?" the boy said in a scared voice. "Looks like 'e fell off his horse. What ought we to do about un, Davey?"

"I think 'e's snuffed it," the other one croaked. "He ain't movin', and as far as I can tell he sure as hellfire ain't breathin'."

As soon as the fear was put into words, the two of them sprang away from Hal Tremayne as if all the demons in hell were after them.

"We'd best go and tell t'other bosses while theym still there," Davey said quickly, grabbing the other's hand.

They turned and raced away, thankful to be doing anything, rather than stare down at the lifeless body in the bracken where it had fallen. They were barely eight-years-old, and the sight of Hal Tremayne with that strange, soft, welcoming smile on his lips when he'd been so angry a little while ago, was more unnerving than if they'd found him bleeding to death with a knife stuck through his heart.

They raced back to Clay One where Walter was re-organizing work shifts with George Dodds now, and the American boss was still talking and arguing with the reporters a little distance away from the rest. With one accord the boys split up and babbled out their findings to each man.

Walter's face went white as he grabbed the frightened child by the shoulders and shook him until his teeth rattled and his eyes bulged.

"Are you telling me the truth, you young whelp? You're not inventing the story to save yourself from a hiding?"

But even while he spoke in a desperate way as if to shield himself from the truth just a little longer, he knew in his soul that it wasn't likely. Hadn't he himself been aware of a strange kind of acceptance in Hal when he'd last spoken to him? Hadn't he felt a compulsion to touch him, one last time, and to thank him for acknowledging his own worth so unexpectedly?

He glanced across at Ran, who obviously had no such reluctance to accept the news, as young Davey Stithian babbled it out to him. Ran leapt onto his horse at once, scattering the newspapermen, and knocking the notepads out of the younger man's hand as he galloped away from the pit.

Walter was less able to move. His legs seemed to have turned to lead, and it was only when his father-in-law came stalking over to him, followed by his insufferable minion, that he felt the first real stab of pain at what he had heard.

"This is a turn up then, lad," Tom Askhew said in his hated nasal voice. "Ain't you off to see if 'tis true as well, same as me and young White here? 'Twill be a twist of fortunes if the old man's popped his clogs just now, but mebbe you young uns will be coming' into a useful bit o' brass—"

He said no more before Walter's fist caught him fair and square on the jaw, and he went sprawling to the ground, taking Ellis White with him in the process. Before Tom could catch his breath and bellow out abuse at being manhandled by his son-in-law, Walter had grasped him by the throat and was hauling him to his feet.

"You keep your bloody nose out of my family business, you Yorkshire toe-rag, and if my Grandad really is dead, you'd just better show some proper respect—"

Walter stopped speaking, as the horror of his own words sank into his brain. He dropped Tom Askhew again, ignoring his avowed howls that he'd pay for this insult to his wife's father. He went running over the moors in the direction that Hal would have taken, without waiting to untether his own horse. Above his own panting breaths, he could hear the two newspapermen running and cursing behind him, and he was also aware that the news would have spread like wildfire, and that a great crowd of clayers was starting to follow on behind.

Ahead of him he saw the two riderless horses, and then he saw Ran Wainwright kneeling beside something lying in the bracken. And Walter knew, with all the certainty in his soul, what he was going to find when he reached him. Hal Tremayne was dead, and nothing was ever going to be the same again.

The crowd behind him fell silent, circling at a respectful distance as Walter reached his stepfather. Ran looked up at the white-faced young man and spoke rapidly.

"He must have gone quickly. There's no sign of a struggle, and no anguish on his face. The doctor will no doubt have the proper words for it, but I reckon his heart just gave out. There was nothing anybody could have done, Walter."

He heard the words, but they meant nothing. The only thing he could absorb was that his beloved grandfather was dead. He was consumed by sorrow, and yet, even in the midst of that sorrow, Walter felt a vitriolic anger that was suddenly impossible to contain. He had to blame somebody. He had to hit out, to release the surge of emotions inside him. He found himself shouting.

"His heart didn't just give out. It was wrenched out of him by all the upset going on at Killigrew Clay. He gave

175

his life to it, and now it's killed him." He turned round to the hushed crowd and the busily writing reporters, angry tears streaming unheeded down his face. "Do you hear me, you bastards? This is what's left of Hal Tremayne, who always did right by you, and who you were ready to betray by listening to the voice of a harlot."

There were gasps in the crowd, and Ran pulled at his arm, his voice harsh. He mourned the loss of this good man as much as anybody, and in particular he dreaded the thought of having to tell Bess and Morwen, but he was able to be less emotional than Walter.

"Be careful what you say, boy. Every word of it is being recorded—"

"Do you think I give a damn about that? Hal Tremayne never minced his words, and I'm Hal Tremayne's grandson and proud of it. And nobody tells me what to say and what not to say," he snapped, shaking off Ran's arm.

George Dodds stepped forward, for once having the sense to tactfully intervene, before their young Works Manager made even more reckless remarks in the hearing of the muckraking reporters. He spoke loudly, addressing them all.

"I'm sure folk always say things they don't mean on occasions like this, and 'tis best for all on us to overlook it and forget it. But right now, I reckon we'd all like to see Hal Tremayne taken home. If you wish it, Mr Wainwright, I'll see that a cart is brought down from the works, and me and some of the men 'ould be proud to accompany him home."

Ran agreed at once, and there were mutters of sympathetic assent from the clayers, before George Dodds turned to Tom Askhew.

"And if you put Walter's damning remark about the Pendragon woman in the newspaper, the lot of us will deny it was ever said. Ain't that right, folks?"

As the clayers became more vocal in defence of their Works Manager, Tom Askhew suddenly found himself being pilloried and heckled on all sides from the more aggressive of them. Ran thought grimly that if ever he

176

needed a show of loyalty, it was being given him now. Hal himself would have relished it. Ran spoke quickly to George Dodds.

"Do as you suggest, George, and we'll stay here with Hal until you return." He spoke coldly to Tom Askhew. "You heard what my Pit Captain said, and you've heard the opinions of the clayworkers. I'd advise you to heed it well. And we have no further need of you today."

The look Tom gave him was one of pure hatred, but Ran was not a man to flinch from the likes of that one, and after a moment Tom shrugged and moved on with his assistant. Ran turned to Walter at once.

"You were a bloody fool to slander the woman in public, boy, but I trust the loyalty of the men will see that no real harm's been done," Ran said crisply.

Walter didn't answer. His limbs had felt so heavy before, and now they felt as if they were turning to water, and he sank down in the bracken beside Hal. He stared into his face, as if trying desperately to see what final thoughts had been going through his mind to bring that strange, glad smile to his lips. If Walter had been a more fanciful man, he'd have said it was as if Hal was truly happy to be going to the better place that pious folk said was beyond the grave.

Walter wasn't a religious man, and such talk always made him uneasy. But when you saw such a wondrous expression on a man's face, it was hard to dispute the thought that he had glimpsed something not of this life, just before he slipped out of it.

Ran produced a hip flask from his pocket, and thrust it under Walter's nose.

"Take a stiff drink," he ordered. "You need it, and it will give you strength to face your grandmother."

The flask was already at Walter's lips, but he spilt some of the bitter spirit as he flinched at Ran's words.

"Dear God, how am I going to tell her? I can't do it, Ran. I can't tell my mother either. I *can't*—"

"Pull yourself together and stop behaving like a snivelling idiot," Ran said harshly, knowing it was the only way to deal with this. "Would you have some stranger tell them?

177

Don't you think they'd prefer some loving member of their family to break the news? When the time comes, you'll find the words. We both will," he added, lest Walter thought he had to deal with this burden alone.

But, dear Lord, there were so many of them to tell, Ran thought in a momentary panic of his own. And some of them couldn't be contacted soon enough to attend the funeral, either . . . they'd get word to Jack and Annie in London right enough . . . but Matt's wife and son – and Primmy – were God knows where in Europe. Freddie would want to come home, and somebody must go to Ireland to tell him in person. That would have to be arranged quickly.

As for the rest of them – well, they'd just have to inform them all as quickly as they possibly could. There was so much to do after a death, but Ran knew that in many ways the business side of death relieved the initial grief and shock. He remembered that now, and he looked more compassionately at Walter as the boy's colour began to return.

He felt a swift sympathy for him. Walter had been devoted to Hal, even more than the rest of the grandchildren. There had been a special kindredship between them that grew out of their inborn love for the clay. Walter had also been on the crest of a wave with the arrival of his new baby. Everything in his world had been rainbow hued, and now he simply looked crushed.

Ran became practical. "Do you think Justin would go to Ireland to tell your Uncle Freddie? He'll be the best one, I think, having no ties, providing he'll leave his beloved practice in his clerk's hands for a few days."

Walter looked as if he didn't understand what was being said to him, and then he nodded slowly. It was as if he mentally braced himself, and somehow managed to shake off the awful inertia that had held him in its grip.

"I know he will. I'll ask him," he said. "And once George brings down the cart for Grandad Hal, I'll suggest that the rest of them get back to work. It's what Grandad would expect. He'll not want production to stop because of a'dying."

Unconsciously, he used Hal's own phrase, but Ran could see that his back was straighter, and his eyes were clearer. There would be many times when Walter would feel Hal's passing keenly, but right now he was shouldering the mantle Hal had left him, and Ran felt touched and proud.

"I think you're right," he said, more gently. "It might be a good time to talk to them now, if you feel able, before they take Hal home. They want direction, Walter, and you're the one to give it."

Walter looked at him, his eyes and his heart still full. He was twenty-five years old, and he wasn't ready for this. He'd been proud of the responsibility that had come his way, through his own love and efforts, yet there were times when he felt as helpless as one of the young kiddley-boys.

He knew he could no longer indulge in such feelings. Through all his grief, common sense told him that as far as his work and as far as Killigrew Clay itself was concerned, nothing had changed. The clay was still there to be brought out of the earth. Men passed on, but the clay remained, and if the essence of all that it stood for was to survive, the work must go on.

He stood up, brushing down the fronds of bracken from his clothes, and dashing the tears from his eyes. Except for the clayers who had gone back with George Dodds, and those who couldn't bear to stay, many more still remained, crouching silently in a kind of ghostly vigil, uncertain what to do. Walter saw that Ran was right. They needed direction, and he was their Works Manager. He walked slowly across to them.

"You all know what's happened," he said, trying to be as efficient as it was possible to be. "And I know that you all share my sorrow and that of my family."

The mutters of agreement heartened him, though several groups of bal maidens who were openly sobbing unnerved him. He turned away from them, unable to stand much more of this.

"You all heard Hal Tremayne earlier this morning. You know that he dearly wanted us all to get on with the work we're paid for. I'm obliged to leave that work in your hands

179

today, but I know I can trust you not to shirk it. I know, and you know, that Hal Tremayne will always be with us in spirit. He was one of us. We'll all miss him, but the best thing we can do to honour his memory is to carry on in the way he'd have wished it."

He hadn't meant to say as much, but if ever there was a time for honest speaking, it was now. And it was obvious that the clayers appreciated this fine young man who wasn't ashamed to say what was in his heart. In their eyes, it made him more of a man, not less.

One by one, the groups began to disperse and to return to Clay One. By now the news would have got around to the other Killigrew pits, and Walter knew he needn't do any more.

"Well done," Ran said quietly. "That was a fine speech, Walter."

"Was it? It wasn't intended to be. I'm no speech-maker and never have been. Grandad always said—"

He stopped abruptly. Hal always used to say that Walter would find the right words for speechifying when the time came, and until then it didn't matter a tuppenny toss whether he spoke up or not. And he'd been proved right, this very day. The sad thing was that Walter couldn't tell him so. Or maybe he could. He knelt down beside Hal, and touched his cold face for the first time.

"I'll not let you down, Grandad, and I promise 'ee they'll always remember the name of Hal Tremayne and all that he stood for."

He stood up, straighter than before, and Ran knew the first searing shock was receding from his mind. There were other ordeals to come, but thankfully, this one was over.

Bess paused, her stitching stilled, as she heard the mournful sound of Penwithick church bell tolling in the distance. Tolling for some poor lost soul, she thought. Some clayer, perhaps, with the misfortune of falling into one of the clay pools, like that young friend of Morwen's had done, all those years ago.

She hadn't thought about Celia Penny in years, but the

180

sound of that tolling bell could always remind her, and always chill her bones. You couldn't always hear it from the house here, but when the wind was in the right direction, the sound was blown clear over the moors and down into St Austell town.

She turned her head as the door opened, and felt a surge of gladness as her daughter came into the room. She hadn't expected to see Morwen today, since she'd sent the message to say she wouldn't be jawing with her at the Tea Rooms. But she'd regretted sending the hasty note ever since, knowing the day would stretch endlessly in front of her, and missing their weekly gossip.

But now Morwen was here, and with an anxious look on her face. She came across the drawing room and knelt beside her, taking Bess's cold hands in her own.

"I was worried about you, Mammie. It's not like you to miss our day in town. Is everything all right? You're not feeling ill, are you?"

Bess smiled. "I'm not ill, dar, I just didn't feel like going out, that's all. But we'll have some tea here instead, and you can tell me all that's been happening, and I'll try not to let off too much steam about the young uns."

"All right. And I'll try not to say too much to provoke you," Morwen said with a laugh, thankful that after their recent scratchiness, all was well between them again.

Bess rang the bell for tea to be brought in, and told Morwen she might as well stay for a bite to eat since it was nearing midday.

"I doubt that the men will be back until later," she commented. "Your Daddy won't miss the chance to spend a day up at the clayworks, whatever Ran does. And Walter will be tickled pink to be showing 'em both around."

"You make them sound like visitors," Morwen said.

"So they be, compared wi' Walter. Not that your Daddy 'ould like to hear me say it. But 'tis good for a man to know when to take a back seat, and that boy took to the clayin' like a duck to water," Bess said, with such satisfaction and pride in her voice that Morwen laughed out loud.

"You and Daddy always did have a soft spot for Walter,

181

didn't you, Mammie?" she said, without any jealousy on account of the rest of her brood.

"Ah well," Bess said, "it was hard not to dote on un a bit after we lost Sam, and he were allus more of a clayer's son than any of t'others."

"I know," Morwen said softly.

They turned their heads simultaneously as the amicable quiet of the day was broken by sounds outside.

"What is it?" Morwen said curiously.

"I don't rightly know," Bess said, frowning. "But I've had a fearful knot in my stomach ever since I heard that bell tolling earlier."

"I'm sure it's nothing to do with us, unless it's somebody come to reassure us there's been no awful happening at one of the pits," Morwen went on, more to cover her mother's sudden hand twisting than anything else.

She hadn't missed the tolling of Penwithick bell on her way here, and her own stomach had felt tied up in knots for a while. She'd been so keen to get here, to put things right between her mother and herself, that she hadn't even questioned the feeling as a portent of disaster.

The door of the drawing room suddenly burst open, and Mrs Horn rushed in, holding her apron to her streaming eyes. The women half-rose to their feet, automatically reaching for each other's hand. But before the housekeeper could get out her gasping words, they had seen Ran behind her. And behind him, stood the Pit Captain from Clay One, and some of the clayers, reverently carrying something between them. Something that looked very like a long stretcher of the kind that was kept at the works in case of injury, or worse . . .

Bess gave a great cry and rushed forward. Ran tried to restrain Mrs Horn, but she wouldn't be stopped. She clung to Bess, as distraught as if Hal had been one of her own.

"Oh Mrs Tremayne, your poor man is dead, but you'd do best to let Mr Wainwright tell you what happened, and you and Miss Morwen should wait in here until they find a proper place to put the poor body," Mrs Horn sobbed, beside herself with grief, and saying everything in the wrong order.

182

"Is it Hal?" Bess screamed. "Have you brought my Hal home to me?"

Ran brushed Mrs Horn aside and held on tight to his mother-in-law's shoulders, cursing the men for bringing in Hal's body like this, and not waiting until he'd been able to tell her more gently. But he'd reckoned without the flustering of the housekeeper. He spoke gently, close to Bess's ear.

"He's gone, Mother, and the only comfort I can offer you is that I'm sure he never suffered. He was even smiling when we found him, so I don't believe there could have been any pain at all."

Bess pushed past him, leaning over the stretcher where Hal lay, weeping and keening in a way none of them had ever heard the stoical Bess Tremayne do before. And the men could only stand dumbly, their heads bowed at this violent explosion of grief.

While her mother mentally collapsed, Morwen stood quite still. It was as if she were encased in ice, as if the sight and sound of one woman's grief was enough to expend at one time. But just as suddenly the ice cracked, and she leapt forward with an anguished cry, her arms around her mother, and weeping with her.

"Will you direct the men where to take your husband, Ma'am?" Ran said in a quiet voice, when the worst of the sobbing had subsided. The clayers were hard put to it to hold on to the poles of the stretcher, with Hal's considerable weight on it, and the two women leaning heavily over it now. But it wasn't decent to hurry them, and he distanced himself from any familiarity at this time by his formal words.

Bess raised her head, her eyes swollen with pain.

"Where else would 'ee take un, except to his own bed?" she said thickly. "'Tis where he allus slept, and where 'e'll sleep now."

"Mrs Tremayne, I'm sot sure that's wise," George Dodds said urgently. Bess's eyes flashed at him.

"Who are you to tell me what's wise and what ain't, George Dodds?" she snapped. "I mind the day my Hal took you on, when you were no more than a snivelling little kiddley-boy with a runny nose and boils on your bum, so don't you go ordering my Hal's whereabouts in his own house."

"Mammie, Mr Dodds is only thinking that there'll be a layin'out to do," Morwen said gently, hating the very words, but knowing they had to be said, and that Bess looked incapable of thinking of such things. "It might be best for Daddy to rest in one of the guest rooms for the time bein'—"

"I know what's to be done," Bess snapped again, as if she couldn't abide these nonsensical instructions of which she was quite well aware. "But he'll sleep in his own bed until the buryin', and I'll take the couch beside un. We'll not be parted until we have to be."

Morwen straightened, and nodded helplessly to Ran.

"Take Mr Tremayne to his own room," Ran ordered. "Mrs Tremayne will show you the way."

He spoke quietly to Morwen. "We'll deal with what has to be done in due course, when she's calmer. For now, it's best that she has her way."

The small cortège obeyed instructions, led by Bess and Mrs Horn, and while it was being organized, Morwen was at last able to cling to her husband. Ran folded her in his arms, and held her close while she sobbed out her own pent-up grief.

"Oh Ran, she'll miss him so much, and so will I. He was always our rock, and I can't believe he's gone."

Ran's voice was gentle. "He'll never be truly gone while there's you and Matt and Freddie and Jack. And certainly not while there's Walter to carry on."

It was no more than a crumb of comfort to hear Ran's words, but Morwen knew they were kindly meant. And she knew too, that it was to his credit that he forbore to mention the other grandchildren at that moment. Walter was the one nearest to Hal's heart, and they all knew it. Ben Killigrew had sneered at Walter for wanting to work at the clayworks and start from the bottom, thinking that his stepson should aspire to better things. And Hal had been

184

the one to support Walter. Hal had always been Walter's champion.

"I'll be all right now," she whispered after a few moments. "But I can't help thinking how eerie it is how quickly a day can change from happiness to tragedy. One minute Mammie and I were gossiping together, and then—" she shuddered. "I should go to Mammie, Ran, and I know there are things we must do. People to inform."

She brushed a hand across her heated forehead as a million things seemed to jostle for importance in her mind, and he held her tighter.

"We all have certain tasks to perform to give your father a good sendoff," he said, and she gave a thin smile.

"He'd have liked the way you said that, dar. He liked the honest, simple approach to things. And he'll want a simple sendoff too. Nothing fancy. Maybe a long walk to Penwithick Church, starting out from the clayworks, and passing our old cottage would please him. The clayers can join in the procession and show their respects. Daddy would like that, if Mammie thinks it fitting."

"I'm sure she will," Ran said steadily, thankful enough that Morwen was already thinking ahead to the practicalities that had to be faced. And if finer folk than themselves raised their eyebrows at a man of Hal Tremayne's stature being buried in such a way, so be it. It was his funeral, not theirs.

Chapter Fifteen

Morwen didn't want to leave her mother alone in the days leading up to the funeral, so she moved into Killigrew House that same evening, leaving Luke and Emma in the capable hands of Mrs Enders and the live-in tutor Ran had recently engaged for them. There was no question of the whole family leaving New World, and the children needed the security of having one parent still on hand.

And Ran had much to think about concerning the clayworks and the promises he'd made. Life had to go on, despite everything. At present the clayworkers were paid two shillings and sixpence a day for seven and a half hours work. By putting their wages up to three shillings a day, he knew he could be risking trouble with the Unions, but Killigrew Clay was still a privately-owned company, and he considered it worth the risk – providing the payments could be met.

He also knew damn well that since Harriet Pendragon had been ready to offer the same amount, she'd already have sounded out the Unions on that score. And he hadn't been entirely reckless in stating that there were new avenues to follow regarding outlets for the clay.

Clay from the Killigrew pits had been transported to the Midlands potteries for some years now, and there were family connections between one of their old-established outlets and a newly-formed medicinal manufacturing firm. Ran had had approaches from them, showing interest in obtaining large supplies of the raw material for medicinal purposes, and he was exchanging letters with the owners keenly.

It was well known that the china clay properties had

proved beneficial in many instances. Not least in the way that the clayers themselves habitually scooped up some of the untreated stuff, swearing that it cured all stomach ailments from dyspepsia to cramps. Though since the Lord only knew what other impurities there were in their self-treatments, it was a wonder they didn't kill themselves in the process sometimes, Ran thought, with a grin.

He was still smiling, and taking a moment's relief from the mass of paperwork in his study, when Mrs Enders tapped more sharply than usual on the door. When he invited her in, he could see at once that she was annoyed.

"It's that other clay person, Sir," she said sharply. "She's come calling on you, and refuses to go away until she's seen 'ee, no matter how often I tell 'er this is a house o' mourning, and any respectable body knows that casual visitors aren't welcome at this time. And as for the sight of 'er – well, words fail me!"

They obviously didn't, and Ran's eyes narrowed as she paused to draw breath. He knew very well there could only be one female clay person to bring this spark of defensive anger to his housekeeper's face.

"Slow down a minute, Mrs Enders, and tell me who it is. I presume there was a visiting card?"

She handed him the card without speaking, her lips tightly pursed, and Ran saw the expected name on it.

"You won't want to let her in, will you, Sir? And 'specially not in here, in your private business quarters," she said scathingly.

Ran kept his face straight at her quaint turn of phrase. God dammit, the woman knew very well that this was his study. There was no need to dress it up with fancy words . . . but she was right, all the same. There was no way he wanted Harriet Pendragon anywhere near his private domain. Morwen joined him here when it was necessary to discuss business affairs, but basically this was a man's room, and he wanted no temptress of a woman inside it.

"Show Mrs Pendragon into the drawing room," he said shortly, irked that he'd inadvertently thought of her that way. "I'll see her briefly, since she's come all this way."

Mrs Enders sniffed. "It just shows the kind of person she is, having no more respect for the dead than to come bothering folk afore the dear man's properly cold."

"Just leave it, Mrs Enders," Ran soothed her. "This isn't Hal Tremayne's own house, so we can at least be charitable about that. And if I ring the drawing room bell, you can bring us some tea. But not unless I do so," he added quickly, seeing her indignation rise again.

He didn't see why he should practically apologize for offering tea to a visitor in his own house, but they both knew that this was no ordinary visitor. Mrs Enders read the newspapers and heard the gossip, and she would be well aware that the Pendragon woman still had her sights set squarely on Killigrew Clay.

Ran knew that Hal Tremayne's death would only prove to be a slight hitch to her proceedings. But he'd hardly expected her to come calling before the man was even buried. He agreed with Mrs Enders totally on that score.

He got a shock when he entered the drawing room. Instead of her usual garish attire, Harriet was dressed in shimmering black, and it complemented her colouring so spectacularly that for a moment he was stunned. She gave a half-smile as if registering his thoughts exactly, and then she stepped forward, her hand outstretched.

Without thinking, Ran took the elegantly gloved fingers in his, and felt their warmth inside the soft silk fabric. Just as quickly, he pulled his hand away, and managed to resist wiping his hand down his jacket, as repulsed as if he had just held a slimy object in it.

He was furious at his own reaction, but he mistrusted this woman completely, and he wanted nothing to do with her. Before she could speak, he spoke coldly.

"This is an unhappy time for my family, Ma'am, as I'm sure you're very well aware, and since there is nothing that you and I have to say to one another, I'll ask you to be quick in explaining your reason for being here. I can give you five minutes only."

He was being ungracious, and he knew it. But now that he had recovered from the first shock of seeing her, he was outraged by her appearance. If it was a pretence at mourning, it was cruel and mocking, and he was only thankful that Morwen wasn't here to see it. If it was unintentional, then he could only wonder at the woman's bad taste and lack of sensitivity.

"I came to offer my condolences," she said sweetly. "I know what a shock your father-in-law's death must have been, and I'm prepared to suspend all our negotiations for the time being, Mr Wainwright."

The gall of the woman took his breath away.

"We do not have any negotiations, Madam," he snapped. "Please understand that Killigrew Clay is not for sale, and never will be as long as I draw breath."

"I daresay Hal Tremayne said much the same," Harriet said coolly, "but the worry of it all killed him in the end, and it would be a pity to see a strong and virile man go the same way as these old ones. I saw it happen to my late husband, and I would hate to see it happen to you."

He didn't miss the way her pale eyes flicked over him now, as keenly and insolently as a rake assessed a streetwoman. Ran had never met a woman like this before, but he'd be damned if he'd let himself be unnerved by this blatantly obvious approach.

"I think you forget yourself, Madam," he snapped. "I would also suggest it was yourself who killed off your late husband, not the worry of the business—"

Harriet threw back her head and laughed, not in the least put out by his insult. Her eyes sparkled with the thrill of the chase, and her cheeks were flushed with a heat that had nothing to do with embarrassment.

"You do me credit, Mr Wainwright, and I take that as a compliment," she said, as provocative as ever.

"It wasn't meant to be any such thing, and you know it. Your five minutes are now up, and please don't come back here again. We have nothing more to say to one another."

Before he guessed what she was about, she came to stand close beside him in a cloud of perfume. The scent of her seemed to envelop him for a moment. He hadn't asked her to sit down, but such lack of gentility didn't seem to

189

bother her. She was nothing but a she-devil, Ran thought furiously.

"Oh, but we have, Sir," she said sensually. "I have many more things I want to say to you, but they can wait, since this is obviously not the time. But make no mistake about it. Our time will come, and we will definitely meet again."

"I begin to think you have a hearing problem," Ran snapped. "Killigrew Clay is not for sale. I cannot make it any clearer than that."

She turned away from him with a rustle of skirts. She moved towards the door, a seductive smile on her lips. She caressed the handle for a moment with those silk-clad fingers, and her voice oozed sexuality.

"Nor you can, my dear Mr Wainwright, but perhaps it's not Killigrew Clay that I want the most."

Ran stared at the door for a good few minutes after she had gone, still enveloped in heady perfume. She couldn't have made it plainer that she wanted him. She was as blatant as a whore, but far more dangerous. For this was no streetwoman, this was a highly intelligent, highly desirable, rich bitch . . .

His feet suddenly moved as if they were on springs. He marched towards the door that Harriet Pendragon had so quietly closed behind her, and wrenched it open. He left it open, hoping the air would dispel the smell of her, and went roaring along the passageway, uncaring who heard him.

"Mrs Enders, if that woman ever comes near this house again, you are not to let her in, is that clear?"

The housekeeper came out of another room, startled by this display of anger.

"I never wanted to let her in in the first place, Mr Wainwright," she said indignantly.

He was still bellowing, as if he needed the twanging sound of his own voice to clear the air. "I know, and I'm sorry I told you different. But in future, she is not to be admitted here. I do not want my wife to be bothered by her, and neither of us will be at home to Mrs Pendragon in future. Is that quite clear?"

"It surely is, Sir," Mrs Enders said with alacrity.

Ran went striding back to his study, slamming the door behind him, and wondering just why the devil he was so out of sorts, when he sure as hell meant every word he said. And he was glad that he'd never offered her any tea. The last thing he wanted was to remember that he'd ever shared a kind of tête-à-tête with the Pendragon woman.

A week after Hal Tremayne's death, in a sad drizzle of warm rain, a cortège of carriages left Killigrew House to wind its way up the hills towards the clayworks on the high moors. From there, only one black-ribboned, horse-drawn carriage would continue towards Penwithick Church with its burden, while the walkers followed behind. Hal Tremayne would travel in style on his last journey. By then, his family had all made their personal goodbyes, and his wife, looking smaller than ever in her black mourning, had shed all her tears in private.

"I still can't believe I'm here, like this, when a week ago Daddy was alive and well," Morwen mumbled, in an attack of nervous panic as she walked with her husband behind her mother and her three tall brothers.

Thank God Matt had been here, Morwen thought fervently, knowing how doubly cruel it would have been for Bess had he been far away in California at this time.

She herself was flanked by Ran and Walter, and behind them came Albert, Justin and Charlotte, with Annie and the twin girls, and Cathy Askhew Tremayne. Venetia had stayed in Ireland with Bradley, and Freddie had come home alone, so soon after he had left. None of the smaller grandchildren were attending the burial, and Walter and Cathy's baby was being cared for by Jane Askhew.

Even now, on such a day, Morwen couldn't escape the intervention of Miss "finelady" Jane, she thought, even while she despised herself for thinking it.

But at least it took her mind off the finality of this walk, skirting Hal's beloved clayworks that were closed for the afternoon, and where so many clayers fell into step behind them; past the little cottage where the Tremaynes had once lived; through the churchyard where Celia Penry and Ben

191

Killigrew were buried; and Sam and Dora too; to pause at last, while the oak coffin carrying Hal Tremayne was carried reverently into the church, and the family and close friends followed it inside.

The rain had stopped before the burying was over, and by then there was an undeniable sense of relief among them all. They had done the right and proper thing by Hal Tremayne, and for those that were left, lives had to go forward. One of his own favourite sayings was that the past was a distant country.

The family and friends, and a few of the older clayers who had worked so long with Hal, gathered at Killigrew House. Bess presided over the eats and beverages with Mrs Horn, and took umbrage at anyone too afraid to mention Hal's name.

"I don't want sad faces around me," Bess declared. "Hal wouldn't have wanted it, and I prefer to think of today as a celebration of his life, not a wake. Mourning's best done in private, and that's what I aim to do, so you'll all oblige me by remembering the good times you all had with un."

"She's a perishing marvel," Jack muttered to anyone who would listen. "I never thought she'd be so strong."

Both he and Freddie seemed to have been knocked sideways by the news, Morwen thought. But then, neither of them had been close enough at hand to hear the news on the day, and both were feeling unnecessarily guilty because of it.

Walter was handing round sandwiches, doing women's work and looking no less of a man for it. He obviously needed to do something with his hands, Morwen thought, and one look at Charlotte's blotchy face and trembling hands proved that she'd have been little use at the task. Morwen tucked her hand through her daughter's arm, feeling how tense it was.

"Try not to take it so hard, love," she said softly. "I know you're feeling sad, but Grandad Hal wouldn't want to see a gloomy face, and we must try to keep smiling for Grandma Bess's sake."

"How can she be so cheerful?" Charlotte said in a choked voice. "If I'd just lost my husband, I wouldn't be able to laugh and joke with those awful clayworker fellows."

Morwen sighed. "We all deal with grief in our own ways, darling, and this is Grandma Bess's way. Believe me, it's no lack of feeling for your Grandad. Those two – well, they were like—" she searched for the right words and couldn't find them – "like twin souls," she finished lamely. "And there will be times enough when Mammie will miss him dreadfully. She needs this breathing space from all the loneliness ahead of her, Charlotte, so don't be disapproving."

Charlotte went even redder and blotchier, and she looked shamefaced.

"I didn't mean to," she said in a small voice. "I just didn't understand. Will she have noticed, do you think?"

"I'm sure she won't. But why don't you go and have a few words with her?"

"I can't!" Charlotte said in a panic. "I wouldn't know what to say!"

"But she'll know," Morwen said, giving the girl a gentle nudge in Bess's direction. "Just be there, Charlotte, and leave the rest to her."

She stood near the open windows of the drawing room, watching her girl move purposefully towards her grandmother, and saw at once how Bess turned and hugged her and put her at her ease. Morwen couldn't see what was said from here. But Bess, who was frequently tongue-tied in making conversation with folk, had obviously found a strength and a dignity today that was all the more remarkable because of the occasion.

It was just as if Hal was still with her, guiding her, helping her, as he'd always done. As if she was drawing on some unknown strength . . . the curtains blew inwards with a little whispering sound at that moment, but the breeze that blew them was a warm one, and Morwen's eyes momentarily glazed as thoughts of her brother Sam unexpectedly entered her head.

She didn't consciously think of him a lot nowadays, but

193

she had felt a sliver of comfort at knowing that Hal was with him now, somewhere in that great beyond. And the feeling was very strong in her soul at that moment.

"Dreaming, dar?" she heard Ran's quiet voice beside her, and she turned to him gladly. There was a limit to how much time a person wanted to spend in speculating about that misty other world, and Ran was her solid, flesh and blood husband. She clung to his arm.

"I was, but I'm back now," she said. "Daddy always said it was foolish to live in the past, when there's so much future ahead of us."

"He was right," her brother Freddie said alongside them. "Trouble is, our Morwen, none on us knows how much future we have, do we?"

"Oh, why did you have to say that?" she said crossly. "I don't want to think like that today, when we're all trying to keep up one another's spirits for Mammie's sake!"

"Mammie's fine right now. But 'tis tonight that she'll be fretting, and all the other nights that she's alone."

"You're staying on here a couple of days more, aren't you, Freddie?" Morwen said quickly. "You won't go back to Hocking Hall? I know Matt feels the need to be there alone."

Suddenly, Morwen knew how desperately she wanted to return to her own home with her husband and their young children. From the day of her father's death, she had stayed with her mother at Killigrew House, but she had found it more emotional than she had expected to be in the house where she'd spent so much of her married life with Ben Killigrew.

She was thankful when Freddie came home, but Matt hadn't wanted to move out of his temporary home at all. After all these years in America, he was oddly apart from the rest of them now, Morwen thought sadly.

"Don't fret, our Morwen," Freddie said. "I'll see that Mammie's not left brooding for the next week."

And after that? How would Bess feel then? Especially when two of her sons left her for foreign parts again.

But Morwen wouldn't think so far ahead. It did nobody any good.

"And I'll be glad to have my wife home again," Ran said. It seemed ages since he'd said anything half so warming to her. Things had been much calmer though, and he'd stopped his heavy drinking. But he'd been oddly restrained on the days he'd come to Killigrew House during the last week, as if wanting to tell her something, then deciding against it. She didn't know what it was, but she knew it was there.

And although some might think this an odd occasion for Ran to make such a loving comment, she knew her daddy wouldn't have objected. The belief in an honest love between a man and his wife was one of Hal Tremayne's best qualities. Morwen felt as if her mouth was able to smile for the first time on this sad day, and she knew Hal would never begrudge her this special glow in her heart.

She saw Justin move towards Bess and kiss her cheek. He was evidently about to leave, though he had a few words to say to his grandmother first. Bess nodded, her face crumpling a little. Dear God, surely Justin knew better than to squash her buoyant mood with a few ill chosen words? Morwen thought, with a stab of anger. But then she saw that Bess was smiling again, and hugging Justin tightly.

It took quite a while for him to make his farewells to members of the family and old friends, but as soon as he reached her side, she tackled him.

"What did you say to Mammie earlier? You didn't upset her, did you?" she said bluntly.

"Give me more credit than that, Mother," he said, reverting to his formal name for her. "I reminded her that Grandad's will is in a safety deposit box at my chambers. It was drawn up long ago when Richard Carrick was his lawyer, and then put in Daniel Gorran's chambers. I've told her I'm ready to bring it here for the reading whenever it's convenient for everyone to be together again."

Morwen felt her heart lurch. No matter what the thought of an inheritance might be, she hated this reminder of a person's dying. When old Charles Killigrew had died, leaving a bequest to her, it had caused such an uproar

. . . though she couldn't think that her daddy would cause any ructions. It would all be straightforward, and if she had ever given it any thought, she had simply assumed that everything was left to Bess, and rightly so. But Justin's words made her uneasy.

"So when did Mammie say?" she said quickly.

"Tomorrow afternoon," Justin said. "I think Jack and Annie are planning to stay the night, so it will save them another trip over from Truro."

"That's a sensible idea. Justin—" she hesitated, wondering if she dare ask the question brimming on her lips. But there was no need. He leaned forward to kiss her before leaving, and answered it for her.

"No, I wouldn't tell you what's in the will, even if I could, and the simple fact is, I don't know. Richard Carrick always considered a will to be a private document between himself and his client, and Daniel respected that. I don't even know if he was aware of what's in it. I certainly don't. But now I have the key to the safety deposit box, and I'll open it in the morning to read through before bringing it here. Until then, you'll just have to contain your curiosity."

He spoke lightly to take the sting out of his words, but a shadow passed over Morwen's face as he left the house. She couldn't imagine why her daddy's will should be kept a secret from Justin of all people. He'd been an employee in the accountancy and legal firm for so long, then Daniel's trusted partner, and now its head. Though, Ben had once told her that Richard Carrick was a strictly old-fashioned lawyer, guarding his clients' wishes as if they were the Crown Jewels, which probably explained things, she thought vaguely.

It also gave her a disagreeable reminder of how much the lives of a narrow community were intertwined, since Carrick was Jane Askhew's father . . . Miss "finelady" Jane, whom she had imagined Ben to be so much in love with at one time. She pushed the thought aside, knowing it had no place in her life now, but the secrecy of the will didn't rest easy on her mind, and it put an air of mystery into its reading. And she fervently hoped there would be no shocks forthcoming.

*　　*　　*

But tonight, she was going home to New World with Ran. She was longing to see the children again, to be free of gloomy thoughts and the oppressive atmosphere of Killigrew House, despite the false cheerfulness of her mother. Even that was starting to get on her nerves now. She wanted normality. She wanted children's chatter and laughter. She wanted love.

She felt her face grow hot, knowing it was the wrong time to be having such thoughts. But it had happened in her life before, and it hadn't seemed wrong. To be able to briefly dispel the bad times by the warmth of loving arms around her, and the caress of a loved one's hands, was surely to be heaven blessed. It had never seemed wrong before, and it didn't seem wrong now.

Folk who were far more sophisticated than herself might think so, Morwen conceded. Folk who felt the need to go about with long, black faces, and brood upon the passing of friend or relative as if the end of the world had come. So it had, for a time. But Morwen knew in her soul that those who were parted would meet again, and it was surely not an affront to God to rejoice in a person's lifetime span, instead of incessantly grieving.

She gave a small shiver, hugging her husband's arm as they rode home in their carriage towards New World. The sun was dying into the horizon now, turning the sea to a sheet of flame, and spreading its reddish glow across the early evening sky and the moors, with the promise of a good day tomorrow. The summer rain that had fallen so softly that morning had put vigorous new life into the dry moors, and tomorrow there would be new blossom bursting forth.

To Morwen, it seemed oddly symbolic, and she never questioned her reasons for feeling that way. For didn't she know that no God worthy of His salt would put such a promise into a day, unless He wanted his people to be happy.

"Are you sad, dar?" Ran said gently, mistaking her soft sigh. She leaned her head against him as the sight of their house came into view, solid and welcoming.

197

"I'm only sad for the times that I won't see Daddy any more," she said honestly. "But I'm not sad at remembering the life that he had, and I'll always be grateful for the love that he and Mammie gave to us all. I know he wouldn't want me to grieve for him unduly, and so I won't. He always wanted to see me smile, because he said it made his day shine brighter."

Ran leaned across and kissed her mouth. "I know he did, and who could wonder at it, with such a smile as yours, my dear Mrs Wainwright."

"Are you flirting with me, sir?" she whispered, after a moments' hesitation.

"I don't know. Am I? Is it permitted?" he asked cautiously, unsure of her mood.

"Oh, I think it is," she said, as breathless as a young girl. "I think Daddy would be pleased to know that we still love one another so much, even after all this time. And we do, don't we, Ran?"

"We do," he said, as solemnly as if it was a marriage vow. "And we always will, my honey."

Chapter Sixteen

All except Cathy and the youngest children were gathered together in the large drawing room of Killigrew House the following afternoon. Jack and Annie's girls were returning to London to their nursing college the next day, but were here for the reading of the will. Justin was very formal and correct as he stood in front of the fireplace with the documents ready to open, while the others sat and waited expectantly, murmuring quietly amongst themselves. It was more like a wake, Morwen thought irritably, knowing Hal would never have wanted that. He'd never liked sad faces around him.

She caught Ran's glance, and gave him a half-smile that tinged her cheeks with colour. Last night . . . oh, last night had become so tender and loving, and Ran had swept her into his arms with all the gentleness and finesse of their first tremulous lovemaking, and the glow of it all was still with her . . . but she remembered where she was, and why they were all here, and she looked away quickly, lest the glances they shared should be understood too well.

But she knew that no one was really bothering about anyone else. They were all intent on trying to be solemn. Trying not to look too eager, or too interested, or too avaricious. Morwen played a little trick of detachment, trying to see the occasion through their eyes, instead of her own . . .

It was no longer strange to think that Hal Tremayne, one-time clayworker who had risen to such dizzy heights through his own hard work and his daughter's marriage connections, was a wealthy man. And his wife would naturally and rightly inherit everything, Morwen thought.

Though she would almost certainly hand over the future business dealings to Ran, or maybe Justin, as the family lawyer and accountant. Bess had no head for business, and the very thought of it would unnerve her.

Her brothers . . . well, Hal would certainly have provided something for them, and for herself, she supposed . . . at this point, Morwen abruptly stopped speculating. It suddenly seemed all too grasping and sad, and besides, Justin was starting to shuffle his papers about, and looking surprisingly uneasy.

Her heart missed a beat. Justin would have opened the safety deposit box that morning, and read her daddy's will, but there could surely have been nothing unusual in it, she thought . . .

"If we're all ready, I'll begin," Justin said, and Morwen readjusted her thoughts thankfully as his voice became formal and businesslike.

"This is the original last Will and Testament of Hal Tremayne, as signed and witnessed in the presence of Richard Carrick of Truro—"

"Original?" Jack echoed sharply. "Did you say the original will, Justin?"

"I did. The first part is the original will, but a codicil was added and witnessed three years ago. The instructions are for the original will to be read out, and then the codicil, in explanation of Hal Tremayne's wishes. Everything's in order, Uncle Jack, and I'd be obliged if I can get on with it."

Jack glanced at his wife, and for the first time Morwen wondered just how anxious Annie Tremayne was to get her greedy little hands on some of her daddy's money. Not that she needed it. Her own family was well-heeled, and Jack's boat-building business was a thriving success. Annie had been sweetness itself when Jack married her, but over the years she had proved to be quite a shrewd one, always wanting more.

Morwen ignored such unpleasant thoughts, and listened quietly while Justin went through the bequests in the original document. The house and all its contents, and all Hal's personal assets were left to Bess, as expected. And then Morwen's eyes filled with tears at the next words. The will had been expressed in Hal's own turn of phrase, with none of the pomposity of a lawyer's hand in it. She blessed Richard Carrick for that, even while it stirred up such memories.

"To all my natural-born grandchildren, however many scallywags there may be at the time of my death, I leave the sum of three hundred pounds each, to be used for their own enjoyment with no interference from their elders, unless they be too young to know what they're doing. This is my wish, that they use the money for pleasure, or whatever purpose they choose, and that they spare a kind thought to their grandaddy while doing it."

Charlotte was openly sniffing now, and Morwen had to swallow hard as she saw Bess's slight smile. Bess would probably have known all about this, Morwen thought, so it would be no surprise to her. But it must stir up many memories as the ghost of Hal's voice came through his wishes.

"To my beloved daughter Morwen," Justin's voice went on, "I leave the sum of two thousand pounds, providing the coffers in the bank say 'tis there to be had." He paused, hearing the communal gasps, before stating quickly that of course the bequest would be honoured, while Morwen sat in amazement, not expecting this fortune.

She felt Ran's hand reach for hers and squeeze it, but she hardly knew how she felt. What did you do at such a time? You could hardly say thank you very much, and it didn't seem right to express great delight. She simply kept her eyes lowered and said nothing at all.

"To my sons, Jack, Matthew and Freddie, I leave my shares in the land and clayworks known as Killigrew Clay, making them equal partners in my portion of the business."

"That was a fine and thoughtful thing for Daddy to do," Freddie said at once, his voice choked.

Justin went on reading Hal's words. "I have left my daughter Morwen out of this bequest for the following

201

reasons. She is already a partner in her own right as the widow of Ben Killigrew, and will eventually inherit her present husband's shares also. And I don't want to burden her with too much responsibility in a man's world."

Morwen blinked. She had never thought things out like this before, and she knew that Richard Carrick must have been guiding her Daddy's words at that point. But even though she knew that as long as Killigrew Clay flourished, she would never be poor again, she had no wish to be a controlling woman clay boss like that other awful creature.

In the buzz of excited conversation Jack moved across to Freddie and shook him by the hand, cautious smiles on both handsome faces now. Matt nodded more gravely as they turned to him in the same spirit. The other two were obviously thinking they had something to celebrate, but the wealth from a china clayworks clearly didn't mean so much to a man who had found vast riches in the gold fields of California.

But then Morwen saw her mother bite her lip and shake her head slightly, and she wondered if there was too much exuberance being shown. Or whether this codicil Justin had mentioned was going to put a sting in the tail.

She heard her son clear his throat, and the chatter in the room settled down again.

"I said there was a codicil to the will. It's legal, and it's watertight," Justin said, and Morwen knew him well enough to know that his deliberate choice of words was a warning. She held her breath, wondering just what her Daddy could have done to change things, or why he would have wanted to do so, when everyone seemed more than content with their lot. Hal would have known that . . .

"The codicil is signed by Grandad, and witnessed by two outside lawyers from Bodmin. Like most of the will, it's written in Grandad's own words. But this is in the form of a letter, and it was dictated to Daniel Gorran, who declared its authenticity in the presence of these witnesses."

"Get on with it, for pity's sake," Freddie snapped, with

202

a rare loss of patience at this time-wasting. "If Daddy's ousted us from his will, then let's hear it."

"He wouldn't do that," Jack said quickly. "There must be summat else to come."

He looked expectantly at Justin, who had gone decidedly paler, thought Morwen. Dear heaven, but she too wished he'd get on with it. He cleared his throat again, and began to read in an expressionless voice.

"My dear family," he read.

"Being of sound mind, and knowing I'll probably be throwing an almighty cat among the pigeons, I intend reviewing my earlier will. Everything stands as stated afore, regarding the bequests to my wife, Bess Tremayne, my daughter Morwen Killigrew Wainwright, and my natural-born grandchildren.

"But I've seen my three sons prosper and grow rich by their own achievements, and no man could be prouder of them for that. None of them needs my Killigrew Clay shares, and what's more, none of them has the heart for the claying."

Amid the gasps of shock and outrage in the room, Justin held up his hand and carried on reading doggedly.

"I attach no blame or censure to my sons for that. A man can only follow his own heart, and there's only one among you all who has the true heart of a claying man."

Morwen heard Walter give a strangled gasp, and she didn't dare look anywhere but at the floor.

"If my first-born son had lived, and in the natural way of things, he would have been the rightful inheritor of all that was mine to give, and in time it would have passed to his own eldest son. Over the years I've seen Walter grow in stature, and his love for the clay has never diminished. I see in him the essence of myself and of Sam. Because of all these considerations, I hereby revoke all the bequests to my three surviving sons, namely Jack, Matthew and Freddie Tremayne, and leave the shares of my third portion in Killigrew Clay, in total, to my eldest grandson, Walter Tremayne."

"No! It's not right! He can't do this to us!" Annie leapt

203

to her feet, red-faced and angry. "The original will should stand. Jack, tell them! Don't let this happen!"

Tight-lipped, Jack brushed her clinging hands aside, and growled that he was sure Justin knew what he was doing in saying the codicil was watertight. He glanced at his mother, and saw by her face that she had been very well aware of what was to happen. He hesitated a moment, his face as red as his wife's, but obviously thought better of a similar outburst. Matt said nothing for the moment, but Freddie spoke up loudly above the mutterings in the room.

"If 'twas Daddy's wish to leave it all to Walter, then we must abide by it and good luck to the boy, I say."

He strode across to Walter, grabbing his hand and shaking it. "And 'tis quite true what Daddy said. The three on us don't need the shares, and you were always the one wi' the clay in your blood, same as Sam. So good luck to you, Walter."

"Well done, Freddie," Matt said forcefully now. "That goes for me too. As for you and your wretched womenfolk, Jack, I'd have thought you were comfortable enough if you can send your daughters to London for expensive training."

"That's not the point," Jack said angrily. "And I'd thank you not to slander my family. Anyway, Annie's perfectly right. Why shouldn't we expect summat from Daddy's money?"

"Because he had every right to do as he liked with it," Matt said, just as coldly. "Just listen to yourself, man, and stop behaving like a skinflint, for God's sake."

By now, Jack's girls were grizzling noisily, and being comforted by their mother. Morwen had never thought Annie would be quite so outspoken, nor that the twins were so much like her. She hadn't thought that a man's dying could bring out the worst in folk, either, and it was only when the man concerned had money and possessions that it happened.

If Hal Tremayne had died as modestly as he'd lived in his early years, he'd have had nothing to leave behind, and there wouldn't be all this upset and wrangling. But, thank

God, Matt had managed to calm the storm that had seemed so imminent moments ago.

And not everyone was upset. Although Walter himself was still white-faced and stunned by the turn of events, she saw that he was being hugged by Albert and Charlotte now. They were both openly pleased for him, and begrudged him nothing. Morwen was quite sure Primmy would react in the same way. The other children in Hal's large family were too young to have their heads bothered by it all, and as for Justin . . .

With a huge shock, she suddenly noticed how grim and gaunt her clever son looked now, as he gathered up the papers, inviting anyone who cared to scrutinize them to come and do so before he left for his chambers.

And she didn't need any sixth sense or fey Cornish intuition to know that it was Justin who was most put out by what he had heard. Despite having had prior knowledge of it when he'd opened the safety deposit box that morning, it was Justin who was eaten up with jealousy that his stepbrother had got the lion's share of her daddy's estate, and who was finding it devilishly hard to hide it.

Ran was deep in conversation with Freddie and Matt now, and she walked swiftly across to where her mother sat a little apart from the rest of them, letting the flow of conversation wash over her. Morwen sat down beside her, taking her cold hand in her own.

"You'll have known all about this, Mammie," she said quietly. "You and Daddy would have discussed it between you."

She tried not to sound accusing, but surely, *surely*, Hal must have known of the upset it would cause. She was so very glad for Walter, but so desperately sorry for Justin.

Albie wouldn't care a jot, but Justin . . . she remembered with a searing jolt the time when Cresswell had so innocently blurted out the truth of the children's parentage. And how Justin had turned against Walter, when he discovered that he was the rightful first-born son of Ben Killigrew, and the three older ones were only his adopted brothers and sister. It had shadowed their relationship for quite a while.

205

And yet Morwen could hardly believe that Justin had been harbouring resentment against Walter all these years. In her heart she knew it wasn't so, but the very thought of a bitter family feud made her so fearful that she clutched at Bess's hand even more tightly.

"I knew of it, and when it was certain that our own three boys were secure and well set-up, I agreed with Hal that it was the way to do things," Bess said. "As our eldest, it was Sam who would rightly have inherited the shares, and it was Sam's eldest that was due for them in the end. 'Tis the way 'tis done in the best circles. You know that better'n me, our Morwen."

Oh, but they didn't belong in the best circles, Morwen wanted to cry out. They were humble folk, despite their fine clobber, and the way they'd come up in the world. They weren't kings and princes who handed down riches to the eldest son and to blazes with the rest of them. But her daddy had acted in just that way, grander in death than he'd ever been in life, and Justin was the one who was suffering for it now.

It could be the makings of a great gulf between brothers. She felt it in her soul. And as if to underline her thoughts, Walter, her best-beloved, who could rant and curse with the best of the clayers when it came to a verbal fight, seemed totally unable to know what to say to his brother now.

"We're leaving now, Mother," Jack said, hovering near with his family. "The girls have to get packed again, and we're taking them back to London early tomorrow morning."

The goodbyes were swift and awkward, and Morwen wondered how it was that moments ago they had been such a united family, and now it all seemed to be splitting apart. Annie would hardly look at her, knowing she'd been too outspoken, and still flushed and embarrassed because of it.

"I'll come with you, Uncle Jack," Albie said at once. "I've got a client coming for a portrait tomorrow, and I need to put the finishing touches to it tonight."

His words were enough to set the twin girls giggling

slightly, and Morwen saw that the thought of their handsome artist cousin joining them in the family carriage was enough to brighten their day.

"What about you, Charlotte?" Jack said, thankful for a lighter moment. "Are you in need of a ride back to that posh mansion of yours?"

"It's hardly mine. I just work there," she grinned. "But no, thank you. I'll wait for Justin. We're having a meal together tonight, and I think he intends going to the newspaper offices with brief details of the bequests to publish on the local affairs page. I understand Mr Askhew suggested it, so that people wouldn't speculate and get the wrong end of the stick."

Freddie snorted. "Oh, Tom Askhew were always clever in ferreting out the news he wanted to print, and I daresay he'll be glad to hear his son-in-law's being so well set-up."

"I thought you said you held no grudges, Uncle Freddie," came Walter's troubled voice behind him.

Freddie turned at once. "I don't, Walter, but I never had any love for your father-in-law, and neither did you, and I know he'll make the most of this news."

"Well, I don't know that I want it published for all to see," Walter said at once.

"It's the way things are done," Justin said coldly, over-hearing the conversation. "All notables in the area have the main bequests in their wills published, and since Grandad Hal came into that category, you've got no choice."

"I damn well have," Walter said belligerently, at which Morwen put her hand on his arm at once, pleading with her eyes for him not to make a scene here and now.

If it came to a fist fight between them at some later stage, well, her daddy always said a heated exchange of blows between men was a healthy enough way to clear the air. But not now. And not here.

"Go home, Walter. Go home and tell Cathy your news. Enjoy your little Theo, and have a private celebration. I'm so pleased for you, my darling, but don't create any extra upsets for Grandma Bess today," she said quietly. "There'll be time enough for other things later."

He put his arms around her and hugged her tightly. His voice in her ear was young and unsure, and so dear to her that it almost broke her heart.

"You don't resent me for it, do you, Mother?"

"Of course not. You know how very special you are to me, Walter, and nothing will ever change that," she said softly, for his ears alone.

He nodded, and turned to kiss his grandmother before leaving the house to go home to his own little family. Cathy would put the spring back into his step, Morwen thought, watching him go.

Cathy Askhew had been the love of his young life, and still was, and they had proved that a love as sweet and fresh as springtime didn't have to wither when autumn came. Not that they were anywhere near that time of their lives, of course, but she had no time for those folk who said that young love inevitably faded. Hers for Ben Killigrew hadn't . . . her fine thoughts faltered, knowing that Ben himself had strained her feelings to the limit, with his drinking and gambling . . . but through it all, she had loved him, she thought fervently.

"Are you going to sit here dreaming all day, honey?" Ran's voice said quietly beside her. "The others are leaving, and I need to do the same. There's much to do, before the news becomes public knowledge through *The Informer*."

"Is there?" she said vaguely, finding it hard to adjust to what he was saying, but Ran didn't elaborate.

She frowned, wondering what he had in mind, but then Charlotte came to hug her swiftly, and she breathed in her fragrant scent. No matter what happened, Charlotte was young and in love, and nothing could dim her starry eyes. Rather than annoy her on such a day, Morwen was uplifted by it. Life went on, and they all had to go on with it.

By the time she and Ran were on their way back to New World, she had begun to relax. Her daddy's wishes would be strictly adhered to, and once Walter had become accustomed to his new-found status, he would revel in his ownership of the second love of his life, Killigrew Clay. The first was Cathy . . . but his two loves were so intertwined, and so much a part of his whole life, she guessed there was hardly any separating them.

"Are you quite happy with the way things turned out, Ran?" she said suddenly, when he seemed unusually quiet.

"I think it's the best thing that could have happened. Though I'm mighty sure Justin didn't felt the same."

Morwen shook her head slowly. "I hope it won't cause any trouble between them, and I don't know why it should. Justin's got what he always wanted, after all."

"But he's Ben Killigrew's son, and Walter isn't," Ran pointed out, "so maybe he feels done out of what should be rightfully his."

"I know," Morwen said uneasily. "But there's nothing we can do about it now. Daddy had his reasons for doing what he did, and they were sound enough. Justin will have to learn to accept it, and I'm sure he'll do so quickly enough."

She had so rarely disagreed with anything her father did, but she wondered now if he had been altogether wise in his bequest. But even as the thought passed through her head, she knew it had been the right thing to do. Walter and Killigrew Clay were like the finely-stitched seams on one of her mammie's garments. They blended together so smoothly, you could hardly see the joins.

"What is it you have to do now, dar?" she said, not wanting to think about it any more. "I thought we could have an early tea with the children, and take a stroll afterwards, as it promises to be such a fine evening."

"Not possible, honey," he said firmly. "As soon as I've changed my clothes, I'm riding up to Killigrew Clay, to acquaint the pit captains and the workers with the news."

"What? But surely that can wait? Won't Walter want to do it himself?"

"It can't wait, and nor do I think it best for Walter to go there and announce his new status. Think about it sensibly, Morwen. There are sure to be some who'll resent it, and Walter's nerves are probably on a knife edge already over the news. No, I want to prepare the way for him, and when it's done, I'll call on him and Cathy to tell them what I've done."

She couldn't argue with his logic, but she thought he might have discussed it with her first. After all, she was a partner in the clayworks too . . . with a leap of her heart, she adjusted her thoughts to the new order of things. Ran and herself, and Walter . . . it was no wonder that Justin felt momentarily shut out. As company lawyer and accountant, he was still on the fringe of things, despite being well aware of every detail of the fluctuating fortunes of the business.

Her head was beginning to ache with thinking of it all, and she decided that if Ran was too busy to stroll with herself and the children, then she would continue with her plans. Some fresh air was what she needed, and the children would have been cooped up at their lessons all day, and needing an outlet for their energies.

"I think I shall take the children to the beach," she said. "Gillings can take us in the trap, and a run on the sands will do them good. It will also help to dispel any gloomy thoughts Miss Pinner may have been putting in their heads about funerals and wills and the like."

The new governess was a sound woman, but given to detailed and graphic descriptions of current events to educate the children in worldly or domestic affairs. In Morwen's opinion, it wasn't altogether best for their peace of mind.

But she was greeted so enthusiastically by the two of them when she went to the nursery that she assumed that all was well.

"I thought we'd have an early tea and go to the beach," she said as Emma ran to her for a hug.

"And I shall find some new shells for my collection," Emma said at once, clapping her hands.

"I shall look for fossils," Luke said importantly. "Mammie, will Grandad Hal be turned into a fossil by now? Miss Pinner didn't seem to know."

Morwen mumbled something beneath her breath in answer. Then she hugged her daughter a little closer, hiding her face in the burnished dark hair, as her glimmer of laughter at such an audacious question threatened to spill over into tears.

Chapter Seventeen

Gillings drove them to the nearby little bay beneath the rocks, where the beach was golden, and the sea stretched endlessly towards America. To where Matt would shortly be returning with his family, Morwen thought with a pang, and taking Primmy with him . . . but she wouldn't think of that now.

"I'll be back for 'ee in an hour or so, then, Ma'am," Gillings said, respectfully touching his cap.

"That will be just right. The sun will be going down by then, and I don't want the children to be chilled," Morwen told him. It was warm now, and the bay was sheltered, but there was always a cool wind from the sea. Emma was susceptible to minor ailments, and coughs and colds, and a summer cold could be just as debilitating as any other kind.

Besides which, there had been several cases of measles reported in the area, and the very thought of one of the children catching such an infection was enough to freeze Morwen's bones. Dora, Walter's natural mother, had died of the measles, and an epidemic could sweep through a close-knit community as quick as lightning.

"So what do you think, Mammie?" Luke said, when their driver had gone clattering away with the trap and left them to their poking about between rocks and into pools.

"What do I think about what?" she said, thankful to drag her thoughts back to the present from the uneasy place where they had gone.

"Will Grandad Hal be a fossil by now, or does he have to moulder away in the grave for years and years before it happens?" Luke said, ghoulishly anticipating the thought.

At his graphic words, Emma gave a little scream, and Morwen snapped at her wretch of a son. So much for moving away from gruesome thoughts.

"Don't be ridiculous, Luke, and stop putting such ideas into Emma's head. The two of you will be having nightmares tonight, and I shall speak seriously to Miss Pinner if she's been teaching you such things."

Luke scowled, and Morwen sighed, seeing the echo of his brother Bradley in his dark glower.

"Well, Miss Pinner said that all dead things turned into fossils, so why is it so daft to ask if Grandad Hal will turn into one?" he said defensively.

Morwen had no argument with the logic of it, though she could have wished the correct Miss Pinner to Kingdom Come at that moment. And, seeing that Emma was still shivering, she tried to lighten the moment.

"Because Grandad Hal is my daddy, and I don't like to think of him in any way except how I last saw him, laughing and talking and being happy with his family," she retorted, and then had to swallow the sudden lump in her throat at the sweet imagery of it all.

"I don't want to talk about Grandad Hal," Emma said shrilly. "I'm going to look for shells."

She went scampering along the beach, scuffing her shoes into the sand to dig up the flotsam left by the tide. If she could, Emma would bury her head in it, rather than have to hear about unpleasant happenings, Morwen thought. Young as she was, she had the ability to shut herself off from reality when she chose, and Morwen wasn't too sure that it was such a clever achievement.

Her brother Matt had once been considered a dreamer, but his feet had remained fairly firmly on the ground. But this aura that she sometimes felt surrounded her beautiful little daughter was different. This was almost an escape from the everyday world, as if Emma wasn't truly meant for it, or that she was mentally being prepared for another. As if . . . dear Lord, where were her thoughts going? Morwen thought, as a great shudder ran through her.

"Emma, don't go too far away," she said, her voice suddenly husky.

"I'm only just here, Mammie!" the girl said, totally unaware of her mother's momentary compulsion to snatch her to her breast and feel her heartbeat next to her own.

"Look what I've found!" Luke shouted, brushing the sand away from something in his hand. He rushed across to Morwen excitedly, holding out a large ridged object in his hand. It was beautifully intact, the fossilized crustacean silvery and brittle.

"What is it, Mammie?"

"I've no idea. A mollusc of some sort, I suppose—"

"It's got a face," Emma said. "Look, there's a face, and there's hair as well—"

"Don't be so dippy, Emma," Luke hooted. "Fossils don't have faces."

"Well, I can see one!" she said crossly. "And the hair's all pale-coloured, like the lady that came to the house that day."

A cloud passed over the sun at that moment, sending a shadow across the bay.

"What lady?" Morwen said, though there was only one that she knew who could fit that description. And she was more than irritated to know that her heart was beating sickly.

Luke was more interested in his fossil than remembering the incident, but Emma spoke up at once.

"We were looking out of the nursery window, until Miss Pinner said we weren't to be nosy. But the lady was so pretty in her black dress, and her hair shone like silver."

"When was this, Emma?"

"When you were staying at Grandma's house. But we weren't really being nosy, Mammie. We just wanted to look, that was all—"

"*I* didn't," Luke said.

"Yes, you did, the same as me!"

As Luke began to taunt her, Morwen could see the angry red flush appearing on Emma's face now, and guessed that she also feared a telling-off for staring at a visitor.

213

"Never mind that now. Do either of you know who the visitor was?"

They didn't, and they were obviously getting bored by the questioning, and Morwen gave up quizzing them. But it had to be Harriet Pendragon, of course. No one else in the district was striking enough to be remembered so clearly.

Morwen was torn by a mixture of emotions at that moment. It was insulting and outrageous enough that the woman had come calling at a time of mourning. But the thing that gnawed away at her most was that Ran had never mentioned it.

When they returned to the house and the children had gone upstairs to get ready for bed, she spoke to Mrs Enders.

"Did my husband have any callers while I was staying at Killigrew House?" she demanded to know.

"Oh yes, Ma'am. We had quite a number of 'em after your father's death, enquiring after your family's health, and offering condolences. Mr Wainwright would have had all the visiting cards—" the housekeeper said.

"But was there anyone in particular?"

Mrs Enders stared at her, clearly not understanding the oblique remark. Fuming, Morwen knew she would have to be more precise, though she had no doubt in her mind who the pale-haired woman would be. Hadn't she already tangled with her herself? But she still couldn't believe that Harriet Pendragon had had the audacity to come here again, and she needed this confirmation.

"Did Mrs Pendragon call on my husband, Mrs Enders?"

She saw the housekeeper go a dull red, and knew instantly that Ran had forbidden her to say so. That in itself was a shock, and she remembered vividly how the Pendragon woman had intimated that it wasn't only Killigrew Clay that she wanted, but the virile man who was part-owner. She couldn't have made it more obvious . . .

"I don't know what I should rightly say, Ma'am," Mrs Enders said unhappily. She began to wring her hands, and Morwen found herself thinking in a kind of detached amazement that it was true what was said in the penny-dreadfuls. People did wring their hands when they were in distress . . .

"Your loyalty does you credit, Mrs Enders, but this is my house as well as my husband's, and I've a right to know who enters it. Especially when it's someone I've no wish to see."

"Oh, you've no need to fret yourself on that score, Ma'am! Mr Wainwright showed her the door good and proper, and gave orders that she's never to be admitted here again!"

She clapped her hands to her mouth, knowing she'd given herself away now. Morwen's mouth quirked slightly, knowing that if this was a cheap melodrama, then Mrs Enders was making all the right moves. For some reason, she couldn't rid herself of the theatricality of the situation, and it made her even more angry.

"Thank you for not lying to me, Mrs Enders. And providing you do as you were told, we'll not mention it again. Please return to your duties."

The woman gave a small bob and scurried out of the drawing room. And Morwen wilted onto the sofa, wondering what devil was possessing her to make her treat a respected member of the household staff as if she were no more than a skivvy.

But she knew the devil, of course. She knew its name and recognized its evil. It was jealousy, raw and searing.

She was still sitting on the sofa in the darkening dusk when Ran returned home. By then the children had come to say their good-nights and Morwen had promised to go and tuck them in. But she hadn't stirred, and they would probably be asleep by now. Mrs Enders had come and lit the fire to cheer the room, glancing at Morwen's marbled expression in a troubled way, and tiptoed out again, saying nothing and closing the door tightly behind her.

And Morwen continued to stare blankly into the leaping flames, seeing nothing but the gloating, sensual face of

215

Harriet Pendragon. As she made a small, involuntary movement, she heard her husband's startled voice.

"Morwen! Good God, you made me jump. What the devil are you doing, sitting here in the gloom like that?" he exclaimed. "I'll light the lamps—"

"No, don't. Leave them," she said sharply.

He came to sit by her side and took one of her hands in his own. The fire warmed the room, and it was midsummer, but her hands were still as cold as ice, and mistakenly, he thought he knew the reason for her apparent misery.

"Darling girl, you know your father wouldn't want you to spend your life in mourning. Didn't he always say that life is for the living?"

She turned towards him, her eyes dark and luminous in the firelight. "And is that what you think, Ran?"

She saw him frown. "Well, of course it is. It's a fact of life that we all have to die, honey. We all lose people who are dear to us. You know it more than most."

"Oh yes, I know it. I've just lost my daddy. And a long time ago I lost my best friend, and then I lost my brother Sam, and Sam's wife. And I lost my husband. You make it sound as if I've carelessly put them all down somewhere, and they'll turn up again at any minute." She stopped abruptly, as misery swept over her.

He didn't speak for a moment, and then he leaned forward and kissed her cold cheek.

"You lost your husband, but you found another," he said gently. "Or have you forgotten?"

She felt his hand move softly to caress her breast, and she flinched as if she had been stung. He was so unused to this reaction that he paused.

"Maybe I'm not the one who's forgotten whose husband you are," she muttered.

His hand dropped away from her at once, and from the stiff set of her shoulders he knew she wasn't sitting here in the dark out of any sense of grief.

"What the hell is that supposed to mean?"

"You had a visitor while I was staying with my mother," she stated.

"I had plenty. Some days the house seemed crammed with them. So what? It's the natural thing after a death. It shows respect. You've seen the visiting cards—"

"Not all of them."

"What?"

"I said I haven't seen all of them. I was never shown Harriet Pendragon's. Why was that, I wonder?"

She turned her head slowly to face him, and in the flickering firelight she imagined she saw guilt, embarrassment and shame written all over it. In return, Ran read the silent accusation in hers, and his eyes flashed angrily.

"Since you seem to have decided the reason for yourself, there seems no point in my saying anything more about it," he said shortly.

"Oh, but there is," Morwen said, hot with anger. "I want to know what that woman was doing here in my absence, and why you were so underhand as to keep the visit from me."

"Dear God, Morwen, you surely don't think—" Ran said in exasperation.

"I don't know what to think. But I've seen her for myself, and I know that she – she—"

"She what?" he said, yielding nothing as she floundered.

Her head lifted and her chin was tilted high. Ran had seen the movement many times before, when all seemed lost, and the survival instinct in Morwen Tremayne was strong enough to overcome it all. He hardly realized that in his mind at that moment, he'd thought of her as Morwen Tremayne, when he'd never known her as such. Nor why she should think she had anything here to overcome . . .

"I don't trust her," she said passionately. "And I don't want her to have anything to do with my family."

Ran didn't speak, but her ragged breathing told him all he needed to know. Ignoring her stiffness, he gathered her into his arms, and smoothed her tangled dark hair as he would have done Emma's.

"By your family, I presume you mean me. And since I guess you've discussed all this with Mrs Enders—"

"She didn't want to tell me. I got it out of her—"

"I can imagine," Ran said, with a hint of a smile in his voice that he quickly smothered. "Well then, you'll know that the woman was sent packing on my orders. I don't trust her any more than you do. But how about me?"

"What's that supposed to mean?" Morwen said, her voice muffled against his chest.

"Do you trust me, honey? Or do you think I'm weak enough to be swayed by the first woman who looks invitingly in my direction?"

She lifted her head away from his chest and looked into his eyes. Typically, she responded to the only words of importance, and ignored the rest.

"Then you admit that she looked invitingly at you, as you so quaintly put it?"

The closeness Ran had been striving to re-establish between them was instantly shattered. She felt his hands grip her shoulders as he glared stonily down at her.

"My God, you don't have any faith in me at all, do you? As for *admitting* anything, there's nothing to admit. And I'll tell you this, Morwen. There's more than one man who's been driven into the arms of another woman by being so falsely accused, so you might think about that!"

"Are you threatening me?" she said, her voice shrill.

"No. Just making an observation," Ran said coldly.

Morwen knew she was practically screaming at him now, but she couldn't seem to stop. "Then I'll make one as well. I'd remind you that I know full well what the Pendragon woman was here for. She wants Killigrew Clay, and she wants you, but as long as there's breath in my body, I swear to you that she'll get neither of them. Do you hear me?"

"I should think the whole bloody house can hear you," he snapped. "Stop behaving like a demented fool and get to bed. You've had a bad day, even though you came out of it better than your brothers, but I'm sure everything will look clearer in the morning."

She stared at him in shock as he strode across the room, poured himself a glass of brandy from the decanter, and downed it in one angry swallow before pouring himself another. Her head was throbbing, and on top of all the emotion generated by the reading of her father's will, her husband was turning to the demon drink again, she thought savagely.

She moved quietly to the door, and paused beside it. Unknowingly, she reminded Ran of the way Harriet Pendragon's silk-clad fingers had so sensuously caressed the doorhandle, and he gave a smothered oath, and swallowed the second glass of brandy in one gulp.

"Aren't you coming to bed?" she said woodenly, unaware of his anger.

He took refuge in sarcasm. "Oh, I think not, my dear. No, I intend to stay here and drink myself into a stupor, and when I think I've had enough, I doubt that I shall disturb your slumbers by my crassness. One Ben Killigrew in your life was undoubtedly enough. If I make my way up the stairs at all, I shall spend what's left of the night in a guest bedroom."

He turned his back on her, and she heard the clink of glass against glass as he replenished his drink. Morwen bit her lips until she was in danger of splitting them with her teeth, and then she turned swiftly and left him, slamming the door behind her and shaking from head to toe.

Tonight, of all nights, she needed his strength and the familiar comfort of his body beside her in their large bed. Tonight, of all nights, she needed their quiet, habitual bedtime discussions in the soft darkness of their private sanctuary. And tonight, of all nights, as she undressed and crept shiveringly into bed, she felt bereft and alone, and willed this traumatic and hurtful day to come to an end.

When she went downstairs to breakfast the next morning, her head feeling as though a thousand bees still buzzed inside it, she discovered he had gone. The children were already there, their breakfasts nearly finished, and chattering loudly enough to make her wince with their exuberance. When she had greeted them, she spoke quietly to Mrs Enders as she refused all but the strongest coffee and toast.

"Did my husband leave a message for me?" she asked,

knowing that a wife who was so unaware of her husband's movements was as good as admitting that there was a rift between them.

"He said nothing to me, Ma'am," the housekeeper said, still stuffy with her. Morwen sighed. Sometimes it seemed as if the whole world was against you, she thought wanly. She gave a nod as if she had just remembered, even while she hated the subterfuge.

"Oh, I recall it now. He was meeting up with Walter and going to the clayworks with him."

Her head was too muddled to know if he had really mentioned the fact, or if it was merely guesswork. She knew Ran had already gone to prepare the way yesterday. But it was a fair bet that today the two of them would show a united front to the clayworkers. The two present partners, solidly standing together . . . and she was the third.

"You children hurry along now and go to the nursery," she said. She felt as if she spoke quickly, but in reality she heard how her words dragged. She had spent such a miserable and wretched night. And if Ran had drunk himself stupid, then God only knew what his head would be like this morning, she thought. Her own was still aching and woolly, and she needed to breathe some fresh air into her lungs.

Luke and Emma needed little persuading. They were still full of importance from the things they'd collected on the sea-shore yesterday, and eager to win Miss Pinner's praises. Each of them kissed her dutifully, and went off, still chattering like magpies.

"They'm good children, Mrs Wainwright," Mrs Enders said for no reason at all. "They were no trouble at all while you were staying at Killigrew House."

"I'm sure they weren't, Mrs Enders, and I never doubted that they would be well cared for in my absence," she said, lest the woman thought otherwise.

"That's all right then. Just so long as you know."

As she went out of the dining room, Morwen resisted the urge to salute her stiffly retreating back. She stifled an unexpected giggle, which was something of a relief after feeling as if she were slowly being constricted, when the old Morwen had so revelled in being a wild child of nature.

But even as the thought struck her, it sobered her. She was no longer a child, and a responsible woman in her forties should have more sense than to yearn for such youthful recklessness. She left the dining room, and went upstairs to change into a suitable garb for riding. What she needed now was fresh air, and to feel the strength of a horse's galloping gait beneath her. And she too, would put in an appearance at Killigrew Clay, to explain the new order of things to any who wanted to hear it. It was her right, every bit as much as the men's.

The air was as clear and sharp as wine on the moors today. It was the kind of morning her daddy always said was spruced up and polished to a green and golden lustre, with the glittering, silvery clay mounds the jewels in the crown.

She reined in her horse when she had ridden him hard across the moors, keeping away from the clayworks until her head had cleared. Until that happened, she wasn't ready for the undoubted curiosity from those who wouldn't be backward in asking Hal Tremayne's daughter what was what.

She steadied the horse to a trot, and squinted her eyes against the bright June sunlight. Nearly July now, she remembered, thinking how quickly the weeks were moving forward. Matt and his family would be going back to California very soon, and taking Primmy with them. She pushed down the sadness at the thought, knowing it was what her girl wanted so much. Knowing that she wanted to be with Cresswell.

Her heart suddenly jolted. She had come farther than she realized, and ahead of her was an old standing stone with a great hole in the centre, as if some gigantic mystical hand had forced its way through. Such a pagan memento of a long-forgotten past was a familiar feature on these moors. But this stone was special. It was their stone, hers and Celia's.

Morwen shivered. She hadn't been this way for years,

and it was probably a mistake to be here now. Ghosts of the past were opening up old memories, and she didn't want them. She didn't want to remember how she and Celia had danced so wantonly around this stone, chanting the words the old witchwoman had suggested to them, each hoping to see the face of their true love through the stone.

But she couldn't deny the warm and pleasurable feelings stealing through her now, remembering how she had seen the face of Ben Killigrew. She could still remember how her heart had leapt with such unbridled joy at the magic of it all. And she had known, even then, that he was the only one for her, no matter how unlikely it might seem for a bal maiden to wed the boss's son.

And Celia had seen the leering face of Jude Pascoe, Ben's cousin, who had been the cause of her bitter downfall, and so much agony.

"Be 'ee seein' ghosts, me dear?" came a shrill, cackling voice close behind her, and Morwen jumped so much that she almost stumbled and fell. She felt the snatch of a claw-like hand reach out to save her, and she twisted away fearfully as she turned and faced the old woman.

"Zillah," she whispered hoarsely, her face white. "I thought you were dead."

The cackling laugh rang out again, chilling Morwen through. Dear God, she wasn't really seeing a ghost, was she? And especially not this old hag of a woman, with her wispy grey threads of hair and her wizened old face. If she was still alive, she must be nearing a hundred years old by now . . .

"There's many a fool thought that, after my cottage burned down, dearie. But you can't kill couch-grass, no more'n you can kill a body who ain't finished wi' the world yet."

Morwen licked her dry lips. "I must go—"

"Why must 'ee? Be 'ee too fine now to spare the time o' day wi' a body that was once of help to 'ee?"

Morwen fumbled in her skirt pocket for a few coins.

"Maybe this will help to repay you, Zillah. I've got no more with me at the moment—"

222

"What do I want wi' your money?" the old crone wheezed. "No. 'Tain't me who's wanting summat, be it, girl?"

"What do you mean?"

"Well, 'tweren't just chance that brought you here today. You came for a purpose, and you'd best say what it is, afore old Zillah can help 'ee."

Morwen gave a forced laugh. "I certainly did come here by chance. I was out for a ride to clear my head—"

"Oh ah. And is it cleared now?"

Morwen realized that it was. It had cleared from the moment she'd seen the standing stone. Dear God, had she really been in the grip of this old woman's magic these last minutes? She tried to dismiss the idea, but Zillah had proved herself in many ways before now. She'd concocted the love potion that had produced the images of hers and Celia's future lovers . . . and she had brewed the bitter mixture that induced Celia's miscarriage, and instructed them what to do with what she had so poignantly called "the waste".

"And I see that you ain't forgetting old Zillah's help," the old woman wheezed again. "So say your piece, my fine lady, and let me get back to my cats."

Morwen dragged her thoughts together, pushing this madness out of her head with a great effort.

"I want nothing from you," she said forcefully. "I just want to live in peace."

The old hag's eyes seemed to look into her very soul at that moment, and the throbbing headache was instantly back again. But Morwen stared her out, trying desperately not to show how very afraid she felt. She was Cornish-bred, and she knew that there were more things born of mystery than could ever be explained.

But, finally, Zillah seemed satisfied by what she saw in Morwen's face. She nodded, pursing her thin lips together until they were all but absorbed into her leathery cheeks.

"Peace, is it? It'll come to 'ee in due course, me dear, but I'd say you've a way to go yet afore you reach it. Your daddy's found it, but not you—"

"My daddy's dead!" Morwen said, her heart lurching

223

with fright. "I'm not asking to die, nor for anyone else in my family to die!"

"I know all about yon Hal Tremayne," Zillah said, turning to hobble away across the moor in her ancient boots. "And you ain't fit for joinin' 'im yet, girl. Peace will come to you in other ways, you mark my words."

Her voice faded as she disappeared into a dip in the hillside, seeming to vanish into thin air. And Morwen almost fell over the back of her horse, as she urged him on. She was suddenly frantic to get away from this place as fast as she could, feeling as young and vulnerable as the two young girls who had once ventured here at midnight with such eager, ill-advised, romantic hopes.

Chapter Eighteen

Tom Askhew stalked purposefully through his newspaper offices with a vitriolic expression on his face and a sheaf of papers in his hands. His staff fell silent, wondering who was to get the brunt of his wrath this morning. Most of them breathed a sigh of relief as he stopped at Ellis White's desk, since few of them cared for the fellow. Ellis himself visibly paled as Tom flung down the papers on his desk and leaned on it, palms flattened, and his face puce with barely-contained rage.

"So, my fine treacherous bastard, 'tis you who's been filtering in these anonymous letters to my paper, is it?"

"I don't know what you mean—" Ellis blustered, glancing around for support and finding none.

"Yes, you bloody well do! I've suspected for a long time that it had to be an insider. The wording was too slick by half to have come from a peasant, and the pet phrases were becoming just too familiar, my fine laddo. So what d'you mean by it, eh?"

Ellis capitulated at once, as he always did under pressure. "I meant no harm, Mr Askhew, sir. It just seemed a good way to get my point across—"

"To get at my family, you mean!" Askhew roared.

"I never did that—"

"Oh no? Then what's this?"

Slowly, like a cat playing with a mouse, Askhew drew out a crumpled piece of paper from his trouser pocket, and Ellis's face blanched even more as he saw it. He felt physically sick. He wished Leonard was here to help him, but Leonard had never really approved of the letter writing, and they were out of sorts with one another lately.

225

Leonard had tired of the quiet life and was preparing to move to London. He'd said Ellis could come with him, but it had been said so carelessly that Ellis had dithered, and he didn't even know if the offer was genuine or not. But it was the last thing on his mind as he gaped at the crumpled paper that Tom Askhew was slowly unfolding in front of his eyes.

He wanted to die at that moment. He'd merely been playing with the idea of a taunting letter about how the fortunes of Walter Tremayne had changed. He hadn't intended publishing it. He'd just set it out for his own amusement, to see how the words looked on paper, and then got rid of it . . .

"You should be more careful of the things you throw in your wastepaper basket, you scumbag," Askhew raged. "This is my daughter's husband you're sneering at here, and however little love I've got for the Tremaynes and the rest of them, I'll not have my Cathy upset by your measly-minded slander. So clear your desk and get out."

"*What?*"

"Are you deaf as well as an imbecile? You've got ten minutes to get out of my office before I send for the constables and have you forcibly thrown out."

"You can't do that! You have to give me notice, and there's wages owing to me—"

"Don't push me, White," Tom said, his eyes glinting dangerously. "Ten minutes, and no more. Collect any money that's due to you from the wages clerk, and if I get wind of any more letters appearing in any other newspaper, make no mistake about it, I'll make bloody sure that your private life is made public. Do I make myself clear?"

Ellis's white face changed instantly. It was scarlet with humiliation now. He'd always been so careful in the office, but from the sniggers from one or two others, it was obvious he hadn't been careful enough.

"You can't do this—" he spluttered.

"I've already done it. And you can take this with you as well."

As he flung a battered notebook on the desk, Ellis's

226

bowels felt dangerously near to opening at that moment. He recognized his own notebook at once. It was the one in which he'd kept a record of all the letters he'd sent to the newspaper, and he'd revelled in recording all his shady doings in a barely disguised code of his own devising. It wouldn't have been hard for someone of Askhew's ability to break.

"You had no business prying in my notebook—" he began shrilly, and then wilted at Askhew's look.

"Don't come the pious martyr with me, lad. I've had my say, and your ten minutes is already down to six."

He marched away, and Ellis knew there was nothing left for him to do but to go. He hurled his belongings into a box within minutes, and scurried out of the office, head bent. He didn't even bother to collect his wages. He knew Leonard would take care of him. Right now all he wanted was to go home and be soothed by Leonard, and to start a new life in London with him.

Ironic as it seemed, he could even thank Tom Askhew in a way, for making up his mind for him. Now, he felt a growing excitement inside him, imagining the freedom of the new, Bohemian city life ahead.

Morwen felt far too unsettled to go to the clayworks after her confrontation with old Zillah. She was troubled and upset, and she couldn't face a clamour of voices, some sympathizing over the death of her father, some more than curious to know how she felt about the new order of things. She couldn't answer any of their questions today. And if Ran or Walter were there, they'd know at once that something was wrong. They'd see it in her face and hear it in her voice.

She turned her horse away from the moors and the sky-tips and began the descent towards St Austell. She would visit her mother, and try not to feel guilty because it had only just occurred to her that Bess would be glad of her company. Freddie would be leaving for Ireland any day now, and she could hardly expect Matt to dance attendance on her mother. Besides, he'd be preparing for his family's return from Europe, and then they would all be leaving for America.

Morwen sighed, wishing things didn't ever have to change. Wishing she could hold everything in a state of perfect serenity, the way a chrysalis remained so still and safe inside its protective covering until it was forced into the real world. And knowing she was being utterly ridiculous to feel that way.

"You're a fool, Morwen Wainwright," she said aloud, since there was only the breeze and the gorse to hear her. A fool to be so unsettled when she had fulfilled all the dreams a bal maiden could ever hope to attain. She had everything . . . yet right at that moment she felt as if she had nothing.

She rode past the little house that old Charles Killigrew had insisted that her parents should move into, after her marriage to his son, despite her daddy's resentment of so-called charity. But when Charles had rightly pointed out that it wasn't seemly for his daughter-in-law's parents, and a man of Hal's new status at that, to continue living in a little clayworker's cottage on the moors, he had given in.

It was such a nice, cosy sort of house, Morwen thought now, and for all the splendour of New World that Ran had built especially for her, there had always been so much love in the Tremayne family in the meanest of dwellings. She gave a sigh, knowing she was fast descending into melancholy, and it was the last thing her mother would want to see. She had to perk up by the time she reached Killigrew House, for Bess's sake.

When she arrived, she discovered she wasn't the only visitor that day. She had been prepared to sit quietly with her mother, knowing she'd be missing Hal keenly now that all the initial fuss and sorrow over his dying were past. But she stopped in amazement outside the drawing room as she heard Bess chuckling in quite an animated way, and she opened the door quickly.

The two women in the room glanced round, both faces flushed with pleasure as they leaned over something lying

228

on the sofa. Something that kicked energetically and gurgled loudly. Walter and Cathy's baby.

"Well, this is another surprise," Bess said, almost gaily. "Come you in, lamb, and see how this little charmer's growing so fast. I swear his grandaddy Hal wouldn't even know him now."

She said it so naturally, so determinedly bringing Hal's name into the conversation, that Morwen swallowed hard. She nodded to her pretty daughter-in-law, thinking that this visit was exactly what her mother needed. And Cathy had been so thoughtful to have come here with the baby today. She had inherited her mother's thoughtfulness all right . . . Morwen bent over baby Theo and clucked at him, tickling him under the chin and seeing a windy grimace that might just pass for a smile.

"Oh, I'm sure Daddy would know one of his own anywhere," she said, just as determined. "Look at those blue eyes, Mammie. There's not been a Tremayne yet who didn't follow Daddy there."

"My father says just the same," Cathy put in, and then looked a little awkward. Morwen patted her hand, imagining the sarcastic way Tom Askhew would have put it.

"After all these years, there's no need to be embarrassed about the lack of feeling between your family and mine, Cathy," she said drily.

"Not on my mother's account, though," the girl said quickly. "My mother admires you so much, and always has done."

It was the most ludicrous statement Morwen had ever heard, and the thought that Miss "finelady" Jane had ever admired her sent her own colour rising.

"You're surely mistaken, my love, but I thank you for your tact."

"But I mean it, truly I do!"

Theo gave an obliging belch at that moment, and the attention of all three women was drawn towards him. The tortuous smiles the baby had been making turned to twists of pain, and the next second he was roaring his head off.

"He's got a good pair of lungs on un, I'll say that,"

Bess remarked, and Cathy picked him up at once and tried winding him.

"I haven't mastered the knack of this yet," she apologized. "He always seems to fight me, and we both end up tearful."

She looked so hot and bothered at appearing inadequate in front of the older woman that Morwen held out her arms for the baby.

"It's no disgrace to admit it, Cathy. We all have to learn how to be mothers, and you're still new at it. Just try to be as calm as you can when you soothe him, and the feeling will get through to him, won't it, precious boy?"

Tiny though he was, she could feel the strength in Theo's stiffened little body as he wrestled with the colic. He looked up at her with a puzzled expression in his eyes, and she felt an extraordinary rush of love for him. Yet it wasn't just for the baby himself, she thought. It was for all that he represented, for Sam, and Walter, and Hal. It was for the continuity that shone through Theo Tremayne's blue eyes.

Morwen smoothed the baby's furrowed forehead as she murmured softly to him, and after a few more rewarding belches, the angry little body relaxed against her, and she smelled the baby sweetness of him as his eyelids drooped.

"You see?" she said softly, trying not to let Cathy think she was cleverer than the child's own mother. "It only needs a bit of practice, Cathy, and it helps to think happy thoughts at the same time."

"Oh, I think it's more than that," Cathy said, grateful that this tranquil afternoon for Walter's grandmother hadn't been spoiled. "My mother used to tell me how you had the gift of healing hands, Mrs Wainwright, and from the nights I've sat up with Theo while he battled with the colic, I only wish I had them too. I'm sure that nobody but you could have calmed him so quickly."

"And I'm sure it's due more to experience than any old gift," Morwen said lightly, wondering just why she seemed to be hearing so many indirect compliments from Jane Askhew today. She didn't want them now, any more

230

than she ever had, but nor could she deny the connection between them. Of all the girls in the world that Walter could have chosen to love, it had to be the daughter of her old rival.

She dismissed such thoughts quickly, knowing that she wouldn't begrudge Walter one moment of the happiness he had found with this lovely young girl. Cathy was a joy, and their happiness was complete with their first-born. As she handed Theo over to her eager arms, Morwen felt a real pang for days like these that were gone. Days when her own first-born baby had looked up at her with that same far-seeing blue gaze, and she'd laughed into Ben Killigrew's eyes and declared Justin to be the most beautiful baby on earth.

Her heart jolted. Justin. Not Walter. Despite her love for him, and the way her brother Sam's children had been so lovingly assimilated into her family, Walter was not her flesh and blood, and she shouldn't forget how Justin must be feeling now. They hadn't spoken since the day of the will reading, and she hated to think he might still be smarting at what he considered an injustice. She had to see him.

"I just wanted to see how you are, before I go and call on Justin, Mammie," she said now. "But I'm glad to see you smiling, and you already have the best tonic to raise your spirits."

"How is Justin?" Bess said at once.

"I'm sure he's well," she said cautiously, knowing it wasn't what Bess meant at all, but not wanting to be drawn into any awkward discussion. But she should have known her mother wouldn't leave things there. She had always been direct in her manner, and had no patience with shilly-shallying. If something needed to be aired, then out in the open was the place to air it.

"I hope he ain't still feeling put out then, and if he is, you tell un to come and see me. The last thing your daddy would want is for his boys to be squabbling over his wishes."

"I'm sure they won't, Mammie," Morwen said swiftly, seeing how Cathy's head was bent over the baby now, and that her cheeks were flushed. She shot a warning glance at

231

her mother, for Cathy would be sure to pass on all this conversation to Walter, and Bess could be as sharp as a butcher's blade when she chose.

She moved across the room and took her mother's cold hands in her own. They were always cold now, and she wondered if they had ever been warmed since the day Hal died.

"Let them sort out their own troubles, Mammie," she whispered in her ear as she bent to kiss her. "'Tis not for us to be concerned about."

But she avoided Bess's candid blue eyes as she spoke, knowing it was exactly what she herself intended doing.

She turned to kiss Cathy and the baby, promising to come and see them in their own little house very soon. And mentally crossing her fingers, that Jane Askhew wouldn't be there at the same time.

She banished the thought from her mind as best she could, willing the sudden rapid beat of her heart to slow down. She then thought of her new rival, Harriet Pendragon, for the clayworks, maybe, but never for Ran . . . but she remembered that avaricious look in the woman's eyes, and knew that any woman who ever had to fight for her man would have a formidable adversary in Harriet Pendragon.

Morwen shivered, even though the day was very hot. The sun had climbed high in the sky by now and the summer was as beautiful as only a Cornish summer could be. The scent of blossom was carried on the breeze between St Austell and Truro, even among the houses and business properties of the towns. It was a day to make the heart sing, and to ease all troubles away.

Which was a fair contradiction of the way Morwen Wainwright was feeling as she reached Truro. She had left her own horse at her Mammie's house and borrowed the little trap, feeling it was a more dignified way to be visiting her lawyer son, and once at the Chambers, she handed over the reins of the horse to a groom to be stabled and watered. She climbed the stairs to the offices of the late Daniel Gorran, and saw the surprise in the clerk's eyes as she asked if it was convenient for her to see Mr Justin Tremayne.

She shouldn't have come unannounced. She knew it at once. The clerk was a pompous little man, fastidious in his work, and clearly seeing this visit as an intrusion in the day's business. He knew her identity, of course, but that didn't make his guardianship of his master any the less keen.

"If it's convenient," she said pointedly again, when the man Briggs didn't seem at all eager to move towards Justin's inner sanctum. He went a slightly darker red than his normally florid colour.

"Of course, Mrs Wainwright," he blustered. "If you would please take a seat, I'll just enquire if Mr Justin can see you. He had a client earlier, but I believe we have the rest of the afternoon free."

Morwen wondered fleetingly what had happened to the morning. She had missed a meal, and hadn't noticed it. The meeting with Zillah had unsettled her far more than she should have allowed it to, and she had lingered at Killigrew House to play with the baby. It was mid-afternoon already, and the pangs of hunger were beginning to gnaw at her stomach. Or perhaps it was simply her disturbed state of mind that was doing that.

The door opened and Justin appeared, a cautious smile on his face as he welcomed her into his splendid office. He was so grand now, she thought, so much the man in charge, and deservedly so. He had the brains, and knew how to use them.

"Is anything wrong, Mother? It's not Grandma Bess, is it?" he said at once, motioning her to a chair.

"Nothing's wrong with Grandma Bess," she reassured him, "though it's strange that you should mention her, since I've just come from Killigrew House."

"Why should it be strange for a daughter to visit her recently-widowed mother?" Justin said, always so correct in his pronouncement of relationships.

"Cathy and the baby were there," Morwen said.

"Oh? And am I supposed to find something significant in that statement?"

If she had been looking for some underlying bitterness

233

in Justin's manner, she didn't need to look any further. His eyes flashed with sudden vigour. "Or was my brother's wife there to assess the situation in case Grandma Bess followed her husband to the grave? Calculating the worth of the Killigrew silver, perhaps?"

Morwen's mouth dropped open with shock as he went to a cabinet and poured two small glasses of port and handed one to her. She took a large swallow without thinking, and the red liquid trickled down her throat, making her cough.

"I think that was totally uncalled-for, Justin," she said, when she had breath enough to speak.

"Do you?" he said, quite unrepentant. "Well, I don't. All these years I've had to suffer the knowledge that you loved Walter better than me – oh, please don't bother to deny it," he said, as she gasped in protest, "but I didn't think Grandad Hal could have been so damned thoughtless as to make his own preference obvious for all the world to see."

"I won't sit here and hear you criticizing your grandfather," Morwen said angrily. "What he did, he did for the good of Killigrew Clay, and I don't need to tell you how he gave his heart and soul to it. You never wanted it, Justin, so don't pretend that you did. It was always Walter who was desperate to work with the clay, from the time he was a small boy. He was like my daddy's shadow in that respect."

"Really? I always thought I was the one to walk in the shadows, as far as this family is concerned."

Morwen became exasperated. "You're talking like a child, Justin. Just listen to yourself! You have everything you ever wanted, so why should you begrudge Walter the same?"

"Because he's not a Killigrew, and I am," Justin said deliberately.

She spoke slowly into the small silence between them. "And you're never going to forgive him for that, are you?"

"I can't. You can't change facts, Mother."

Morwen stood up. "I obviously made a mistake in coming

234

here today. I hoped to see some generosity of spirit in you, Justin, but there is none. I'm sure your attitude is hurting Walter, and that he'd give the world to have you shake his hand and wish him well."

As her son gave an angry snort of derision, she felt her heart sink. The hurt in Justin's mind was far more acute than she had believed, and his final taunt cut her deeply.

"I'll see the moon turn blue before that happens!"

"Then you're no son of mine," Morwen said, and turned and walked out of the office on shaking legs.

She simply couldn't go home yet. She was so out of sorts, she hardly knew what to do with herself. She couldn't call on Jack and Annie, because they were off to London again with their girls, and even if they'd been at home, she couldn't have borne listening to Annie's barbed tongue today. She could talk to Matt . . . she'd always been able to talk to Matt . . . but she was nowhere near Hocking Hall. She was in Truro now, and there was someone else here who would always be glad to see her and to welcome her with open arms. Albert.

She climbed into the little trap, and egged the horse onwards, wondering how such a lovely day could turn so sour. But all of it was forgotten as she arrived at the artist's studio and pushed open the door. A set of Bohemian door chimes heralded her presence in the outer area, and the next minute Albert came hurrying through from the back room, wiping his hands on a piece of rag, and exuding a strong smell of oils and turpentine. His delight at seeing her was clear.

"Mother! By all that's wonderful. I was just thinking about you!"

She couldn't speak for a moment. Such a warm and spontaneous welcome after the horrendous day she had just spent was almost too sweet to bear.

"Oh, Albie! *Albie!*"

She felt the weak tears running down her cheeks, and couldn't stop them. It was so feeble of her to cry, but as she held out her arms to him, he came towards her at once, with never an ounce of inhibition at being hugged and kissed, nor even any concern about marking her travelling dress. Not that she cared a hoot about that! It was just so good to be held in a pair of uncomplicated arms, and welcomed so readily.

"Now then, come through to the back and take some tea, and then we'll talk. But tell me one thing first. You don't bring bad news, do you?"

"No," Morwen said, shaking her head. "I just wanted to see you, Albie."

"That's all right then, because there's somebody here I want you to meet."

She drew back at once. "Oh, but this isn't a good time for meeting people. I'm so out of sorts, and if you've an important client—"

Albert laughed. "She's not a client, though she's a very important lady to me, Mother, and it's time you met."

Morwen looked at him in astonishment. He sounded so full of assurance, not wallowing in unhappiness now that Primmy had gone off with Cresswell and Louisa, when Morwen really thought it should be Albert who had the chance to see the great art galleries and museums of Europe. But obviously there was something more important keeping him here.

He took her hand and led her through to the cosy back room where he and Primmy used to entertain their odd friends. And as she appeared, a young lady rose to her feet and smiled shyly at the newcomer.

"Mother, this is Miss Rose Slater." He spoke the name as lovingly as if he caressed it, and Morwen recognized all the signs, from the girl's soft blush that matched her name, to the adoring way she looked at Albert.

"How do you do, Miss Slater?" Morwen said gravely, at which Albie burst out laughing, and said for goodness' sake why didn't she call her Rose, since he hoped she was going to become one of the family one of these fine days!

"Don't go rushing in so, Albie," Rose said, her awkwardness diverted for the moment. "I haven't said yes yet!"

"But you will," Albert grinned, and from her answering laugh, Morwen knew that she would.

"So how did you two meet?" she said a while later, when they were all replete from jam scones and afternoon tea, and her stomach felt more settled.

"Rose's father owns an artists' supply store in town, and Rose helps out in the shop sometimes."

"I see. It must have been fate then, you being an artist and all."

Albie laughed out loud. "And now you're wondering how I come to be entertaining a young lady without a chaperone, aren't you, Mother?"

"It did occur to me," she said mildly, wondering if she was just being an old fuddy-duddy in thinking it.

Albert picked up his lady-love's hand and pressed it to his lips. It was such an innocent, artless movement that Morwen felt moved by the gesture.

"Her father trusts me, and Rose trusts me, and I know that you trust me too, Mother," he said simply. "So what does the rest of the world matter?"

Chapter Nineteen

Rose's father came to collect her some while later, and Morwen found him to be a jolly, pleasant man, who obviously adored his daughter, and admired Albert tremendously. Her heart glowed at seeing how happy he was, and when it was just the two of them, she told him so.

"I was afraid you'd be missing Primmy badly," she said, when they had retired upstairs to his sitting room overlooking the river. "The two of you were always so inseparable before Cresswell came to stay."

She saw him hesitate, and knew there was something he wanted to say. Whatever it was, she was prepared to wait, although she realized with a little shock that the day was ending, and that long shadows were already darkening and rippling the surface of the river as the sun dropped lower in the reddening sky.

"Mother, can I tell you something in strictest confidence?" Albie finally said.

"Of course you can. The Tremaynes have a reputation for being clamlike when it comes to keeping secrets. You know that, darling," she said lightly, though he looked so grave now that her heart began to flutter uneasily.

"It's a secret concerning Primmy and me," he said.

Morwen stared at him, unable to imagine what it could possibly be that was so deadly serious. Her heart beat faster.

Dear God, there wasn't some fatal illness that one or other was suffering from that they had been keeping from her all this time, was it?

"I'm sure it can't be such a terrible secret, Albie," she spoke gently, mutely encouraging him to go on, when he couldn't say any more. He wasn't helping her peace of mind at all, she thought, and old Zillah's predictions were very strong in her head as he slowly shook his head.

He got up suddenly and went to a desk at the side of the room. He unlocked a small drawer and drew out a small sheaf of papers. He didn't unfold them at first, and when he came to sit down again, his hands were clenched around them, and his knuckles were white.

"Primmy thinks I've burned these, but something made me hold onto them, Mammie," he said, unconsciously using his old childhood name for her. "I know Primmy and Cress are right for one another, and you've seen how happy Rose Slater makes me. We've nothing to fear from slanderous bits of paper, and I swear to you that we never did. But we couldn't take the risk of such terrible rumours starting a family scandal, you see."

He seemed to be rambling now, and Morwen couldn't really make sense of any of it. She put her hand over his, where it held onto the papers so tightly.

"Whatever it is, why don't you show me, darling, if that's what you want? Is this the secret that you want to share with me?" She spoke quietly, and as many had discovered before, her touch had a strangely calming effect.

Gradually, Albie's hands unfolded the incriminating pieces of paper with their evil messages. As Morwen looked down at them and took in all that they implied, her face blanched, and her heart went out to her two children at having to be faced with this filth. Especially Primmy, her lovely, ethereal Primmy . . .

"Tell me you don't believe any of it, Mammie."

She heard Albert's voice, deep and scratchy, as if the words were being dragged out of him, and she let the papers slide to the floor as she took him in her arms.

"My sweet, darling, boy, of course I don't! How could anybody who ever knew you, think it of either of you?"

She felt his body shudder against her, and knew what a burden it must have been for him all this time, guarding such a wicked secret. She didn't believe it for a moment, and never would. But what of Cresswell . . . and Rose? If

they ever discovered that these vicious lies had been said
. . . As if in answer to her thoughts, Albie began speaking
again, muffled in her shoulder.

"We felt obliged to confide in Cress, and he was an
absolute brick. He saw the way out for Primmy, and she
adored him for it – not that she didn't adore him already.
But it was Cress who insisted on the piece being put in
The Informer about their engagement, Mammie, before that
black devil could make his allegations public knowledge.
So that was why it all seemed to be done in such haste."

"I see," Morwen said, knowing she must tread carefully.
"And was Cress quite happy about the situation?"

Albie moved away from his mother now, looking her
straight in the eyes. "If you mean, did he ever doubt us,
the answer is no, not once. As for Rose – well, this is where
I feel so confused. All this business is a pack of evil lies,
and none of my making, but the fact that it happened at
all is on my conscience, Mammie. So should I tell her?"

Morwen didn't need to think twice.

"Never in a million years, darling. If you want my advice,
you'll put this rubbish straight into the fire, and when it
burns, so will the secret. According to the words of an
old wisewoman I once knew, there's magic and cleansing
involved in the burning."

Oh, Zillah, Morwen thought, you come to my aid more
times than you know . . .

"Come on now," she said briskly. "There's no fire in the
grate, so we'll light one with this trash, put on a few twigs
and logs, and make some dripping toast."

"I thought we'd just had tea," Albert said vaguely, but
she could see the way his face was starting to relax.

"That was ages ago, and there's nothing like a bit of
magic to sharpen the appetite," she said, with a half-smile.
In all respects . . .

It was dusk by the time they'd finished discussing the
kind of twisted person who could try to blacken the names of
two innocent people. And by then Morwen's calm manner
had made Albert resolve to put it all behind him for ever.
It was the only way, she assured him.

240

"You're such a good person, Mother," he said quietly. "You hold us all together, in the same way that Grandma Bess must have held you and the family together in the old days."

"Dear Lord, you make me feel like Methuselah!" she said, laughing, but her eyes were damp, because it was the greatest compliment he could have paid her.

"Well, maybe we'd best get those old bones moving," he said, grinning more like the old Albie, "or Ran will wonder what's happened to you. I'm not letting you go all that way alone, either. I'll come with you in the trap, then return it to Grandma Bess's, and stay the night there."

"Oh, she'll like that," Morwen said softly.

"I know she will," Albie said.

By the time they were within sight of New World, Morwen was feeling apprehensive. She had been away from the house all day, without one word of explanation as to where she was going. If Ran had bothered to send Gillings to Killigrew House to see if she'd gone to see her mother, he'd have known she'd been there, and that she was going to see Justin. But apart from that, nobody would have had any idea where she'd been for the entire day.

As she alighted from the trap near the front door, she gave Albert a quick hug.

"Don't come in unless you've a mind to," she said, but he shook his head.

"I'll get back to see Grandma Bess before she goes to bed. I'll enjoy having a jaw with Uncle Freddie as well, and maybe a game of backgammon."

It all sounded so blessedly normal, and the only sadness in Morwen's mind was the thought of how Hal would have enjoyed a jaw with his boys as well. But she was glad Albie wasn't lingering on here. She was already anticipating the uproar when she got inside the house.

The wheels of the trap had hardly rumbled away before the front door was wrenched open and Ran stood there, toweringly tall against the lighted interior. Her heart faltered for a moment, and she forced a smile to her lips and began to stumble out an apology for her absence. But before she could get more than a few words out, Ran had grabbed at her arm and pulled her cruelly inside, shaking the living daylights out of her.

"Where the devil have you been all day, woman?" he bellowed. "You've worried us all sick, and frightened your children half to death, thinking that some terrible accident had befallen you. Emma's refusing to go to sleep until she's seen you, and Mrs Enders is having a wretched time with her, trying to stop her wailing and weeping. I daresay the woman will give notice in the morning, and I won't blame her!"

"For God's sake, will you stop shaking me!" Morwen screamed. "How can I explain anything to you, when you're treating me like a rag doll?"

"I'd treat a rag doll with more respect, since it wouldn't go off and leave its children all day long without a bloody word," Ran swore.

"Well, it could hardly do that, could it?" Morwen said with a burst of sarcasm, and was rewarded by a swift cuff about the head. She gaped at Ran in total shock, but it had been a purely involuntary reaction, and he was too incensed to realize what he'd done. She smothered a sob of impotent rage, and rushed past him. He grabbed her by the arm again, and she knew she'd be black and blue by the morning.

"Not so fast, my lady—"

"You said my children need me, and I'm going to them," Morwen said shrilly. "I want to see Emma, and I want to see her *now*."

"So where have you been?" Ran thundered.

"Oh, dallying with my *lover*, of course," she screamed. "That's what you're expecting me to say, isn't it? Maybe it's what you want, to give you the right to do something of the same. What's sauce for the goose is sauce for the gander too, I daresay, or should it be the other way around?"

She wrenched away from him and fled towards the stairs, sobbing in bitter frustration. Since they had been yelling at the tops of their voices, the servants must have heard all that was going on, but she didn't care. Her marriage was

242

in tatters, and all she had was her children. There had been very few bright spots in this terrible day, and she began to wonder just how much more one person was expected to bear.

Outside Emma's bedroom, she controlled herself as best she could. Thank God the door was closed, and since she could hear Emma wailing noisily inside, she doubted that the child could have heard any of the furore downstairs. She could be thankful for that. She opened the door and went inside, and found Mrs Enders in a right old state of distress as she tried to comfort Emma.

"Oh, Mrs Wainwright, thank goodness," the woman gasped. "We were that worried, and this poor little mite was convinced you were dead and buried, same as her grandaddy."

If ever anything was needed to fill her with guilt and remorse, that was it. She'd never given a single thought to such a thing. In fact, she guiltily knew that she'd hardly considered Emma and Luke's feelings since her daddy had died, being so concerned with the older ones, and her mammie. She'd simply overlooked the way a child's imagination could turn the simplest slip from a normal day into a disaster of monstrous proportions. And remembering their tutor's relish for telling them ghoulish stories, she knew how badly she had neglected her children.

"Emma, darling," she croaked. "Mammie's here now."

She hardly knew how she crossed the room. She felt as though she flew across to Emma's bed, and the child leapt out of it and met her halfway, to be swept up in Morwen's arms and kissed and hugged and wept over.

"I was afraid you'd gone to be with Grandad Hal and the angels," Emma sobbed.

"What nonsense," Morwen whispered against her hot little cheek, her eyes damp. "Just as if I'd leave my darlings!"

"Well, Grandad Hal did," Emma said with a child's accusing logic. "And so did my Uncle Sam and Aunt Dora."

Morwen's heart skipped a beat. She held Emma slightly away from her now, looking searchingly into her swollen eyes.

243

"Who told you that?" she said huskily.

"Miss Pinner told me and Luke in a lesson about fam'ly history. She said everybody should know about the folk in their own fam'ly, and I never even knew I had an Uncle Sam and an Aunt Dora, Mammie!"

"Well, you did, darling—"

"And are they with Grandad Hal now?"

"Yes, they are."

And, dear God, at some stage in this little one's life, there would be more explanations to be made, about the tangled relationships between all the children. And Morwen vowed at that moment that it must come about properly, and not in the disastrous way that Cress had blurted out the truth to Walter and Primmy and Albert all those years ago. It was something that needed to be done calmly, and soon.

She kissed her daughter's cheek, and smoothed back her dishevelled hair as she tucked her up in bed once more.

"We'll talk about it tomorrow, darling, and we'll make a big chart of all our family for you to put on the wall of the nursery."

"Miss Pinner will want to help," Emma said miserably.

"No, she won't, Emma. Miss Pinner will be leaving."

She was rewarded by a strangling hug around her neck, and she realized anew how the woman had frightened the sensitive child by her ghoulish tales. The woman definitely had to go.

She stayed in the bedroom until Emma had fallen asleep, and then she tiptoed out to look in on Luke. He was sprawled out in his bed, surrounded by his toy soldiers and snoring gently. And she gave a half-smile, knowing that nothing would have disturbed him.

When she went back downstairs to face Ran again, she felt calmer, knowing she had made the resolution to get rid of Miss Pinner. He too, looked less black than previously, and she took the bull by the horns before she lost her nerve.

"May I please say something, Ran?"

"Of course," he said, his voice giving nothing away.

"Firstly, I apologize for my thoughtlessness in staying away all day, and of course I'll tell you exactly where I've been. But there's something more important that we have to deal with."

"Oh?"

"The tutor has been frightening Emma, and I won't have it. Luke's not bothered by her tales, but Emma's very disturbed. I want the woman out of the house tomorrow, Ran."

She couldn't even say her name. She had never liked her, despite her credentials and Ran's respect for her, and she prepared to tussle with him over this. To her wild relief, she saw the semblance of a smile on his face now.

"Is that all? I thought there was another trauma in the offing."

"There will be, if that woman doesn't go," she said quietly, unable to be so jocular over Emma's distress. "Do you agree to it, Ran?"

"Of course, if you think it necessary."

"I do. And tomorrow, please."

"Tomorrow it is," he said, almost carelessly.

She swallowed. His carelessness seemed to extend to herself and her children, she thought, in her heightened state of nerves. He no longer cared for any of them in the way he once had, and she mourned the fact as if she mourned the passing of someone very dear. She felt instant shame at the thought, because at least they were still here, still alive . . . she walked swiftly over to him, and put her hand on his arm, looking up pleadingly into his eyes. There was a time for pride, and a time for swallowing it, and this was it.

"Ran, I truly am sorry about today. I intended going to the clayworks—"

"What the devil for? Checking up on me, were you, to see if I was keeping Walter in order?"

She felt her face flush with annoyance. She turned away and went to the fireplace, to stand with her hand on the mantel, as if suddenly needing its support.

"I did not. I wanted to be where I felt I belonged, where

245

all the Tremaynes had once belonged," she said with quiet dignity, and daring him to deny her the right to the name. He said nothing at first, and then he shrugged.

"So what made you change your mind? You didn't turn up at the clayworks, so where the hell were you?"

He was so hard and unforgiving, and she knew at once that she could never, *never* share Albert's secret with him, or anyone. It had been burned to ashes, and must remain that way.

"I went to visit a very old friend on the moors," she said truthfully, for old Zillah had surely been a kind of friend to herself and Celia. "Then I went to see my mother. I thought she'd be in need of company in these early days after Daddy's death. Cathy and the baby were there, and—"

She stopped suddenly, and looked down, biting her lips in sharp remembrance of the way they had looked when she had arrived. So cheerful and bright, enjoying baby Theo, not needing her . . .

"Go on," Ran said, more gently.

"I stayed awhile," Morwen said in a choked voice, "but I didn't feel like coming home yet. I felt so unsettled. I went to Truro to see how Justin was, hoping he'd calmed down after the will reading, but he's still feeling bitter towards Walter, and it breaks my heart. We – we didn't have a very easy time."

Ran came slowly towards her, and took her trembling hands in his.

"My poor baby. It's turned out to be one hell of a day for you, hasn't it?"

She couldn't bear this sudden tenderness. She swallowed back the lump in her throat and looked at him with eyes that were diamond-bright with threatening tears.

"Not entirely. I decided to go and see Albert at the studio, and he has a lovely lady-friend, Ran. They were so sweet together, and I was so glad for Albie, knowing how much he'll be missing Primmy—"

She stopped abruptly, knowing she had to keep the awful secret that was none of their making, knowing she must keep it from Ran, from whom she had never kept anything before.

246

Their love had always been so open and so honest, and now there was this . . . she felt his arms go around her, and she leaned against him with a little sigh, feeling his strength.

"So you stayed with Albie for a while, did you? And were this girl's parents there too?"

"I met her father at the studio," she said, with a faint bending of the true circumstances. "He's a widower, and a dealer in artists' materials in Truro, and clearly very impressed with Albie."

"So he should be," Ran said generously.

"So then Albie and I had tea together, and I was appalled to realize how late it had got, truly I was. Albie brought me back here, and he's staying tonight at Killigrew House with Mammie, and hoping for a game of backgammon with Freddie. And that's all."

It was very quiet when she had finished speaking. She was still in the circle of Ran's arms, and she couldn't tell what he was thinking. She could feel the steady beat of his heart, and it was nothing like as erratic as her own. She felt his lips brush her forehead and her eyes stung, because it seemed to her as if all the passion they had once known had somehow drained out of their lives. It was sad, and terrible, the way that time and circumstances could change people.

"I've got something to tell you too," he said quietly.

He released her then, and Morwen felt an uneasy, sinking feeling in the pit of her stomach as she recognized the seriousness in his voice. Not more trouble, she thought. Not at Killigrew Clay . . .

She watched as Ran walked across to a side table and poured himself a large brandy. She made no comment on the quantity, nor the fact that she'd already gleaned that it wasn't the first drink he'd had that evening. When he turned to face her, she saw he was gripping the glass tightly.

"Walter and I had a long consultation this afternoon," he said.

"Oh? A successful one, I hope," she said, not betraying for a moment the fear that they might have begun wrangling already.

"More than successful." He took a long drink now, but

247

he didn't move to sit down. The brandy wasn't impairing his faculties at all, she thought fleetingly. He was very much in control, and he knew the unconscious power of a man standing tall. "It seems that Walter and I are more in accord over the fortunes of Killigrew Clay than I believed."

"Well, I could have told you that!" Morwen sat down abruptly on one of the silk-covered sofas, wondering just what he was about to tell her.

Walter had always had the good of Killigrew Clay first and foremost in his heart. Surely Ran hadn't somehow managed to persuade him into doing anything rash? Guiltily, she knew she was suspecting her husband's motives in thinking that way, but for all Ran's buying into the clayworks and dealing with the monetary side of it so skilfully, the clay wasn't in his blood, the way it was in Walter's. He hadn't been born a clayworker's son, he hadn't worked with the clay and known the feel and the smell and the taste of it, almost as soon as he drew breath, like her Mammie and Daddy, and all her brothers and herself. And Walter.

"Well, since you're so all-fired clever, perhaps you've also worked out how we're meant to pay the clayworkers the dues and deals we've offered them, honey?"

There was an edge to his voice, but she didn't heed it. She leapt to her feet, her face flooding with angry colour, her hands tight by her sides in total shock.

"You wouldn't dare to welsh on your offer, Ran! You'd have outright mutiny in a minute, and worse. The men would be ready to do bloody murder if they thought you weren't going to honour your words—"

"Did I say that? By Christ, Morwen, but you get your dander up quicker than any woman I ever knew," he said, in an infuriatingly scathing voice.

She stood her ground, her blue eyes flashing dangerously.

"Don't play with me, Ran Wainwright. If you've got something to say, let's have it. I suppose all that talk about new contracts with some medical manufacturing firm was all pie in the sky, was it?" she ended bitterly.

"It most certainly was not, and to put your suspicious

248

mind at ease, I've got someone coming to see me on that score in a week's time, but obviously we can't expect any proceeds from there until after the autumn depatches, and then it will depend on the quantities they purchase."

"It looks likely to go ahead then, does it?"

"Yes, my doubting little Thomasina, it certainly does. But that wasn't what I wanted to tell you about, and nor was it the most important thing that Walter and I discussed."

"You surprise me then. The fortunes of the clayworks are always uppermost in Walter's mind."

Except for Cathy, and now baby Theo, of course. Walter was a family man now, and had other commitments as well as business ones. As a man grew, his commitments grew with him, Morwen thought; widening and spreading, like the ripples in a pool . . . as she brought her dreaming thoughts sharply back to what Ran was saying, she gasped.

"*What* did you say?"

"I said I discussed the proposition thoroughly with Walter, and he heartily approved of it, and that all three of us should go together—"

"To *Harriet Pendragon's*? *That* woman!"

She felt as if she could hardly draw breath. However illogical it was, she felt as if every evil thing that had ever threatened her life was taking shape and form, and emerging as the triumphant and sensuous Harriet Pendragon.

"Listen to me, sweetheart—"

"I won't listen! I don't want to listen to any suggestion of negotiations with her. My daddy and my brother Sam would turn in their graves if they knew, and so would old Charles Killigrew, and Ben – my poor Ben—"

She choked on the final name. The clayworks had been their lives, and this – this colonial upstart was threatening to throw it all away. And she was too incensed to realize how her words and her thoughts were wounding the man who was her husband now.

"Morwen, will you stop!" Ran bellowed.

He pulled her to the sofa again, sitting beside her and grasping her hands in his own. He held her captive and glared into her burning face.

249

"You haven't listened properly to a word I've been saying. All you can see is your own misplaced and absurd jealousy."

"Misplaced? Absurd?" she echoed witheringly.

"Totally," he snapped. "And if you'd just keep quiet for one minute, you'd know that my proposition will rid us of Harriet Pendragon's greed for good."

She subsided, hearing the anger in him, and knowing she had simply gone off half-cocked, as her daddy used to say.

"I'll listen," she muttered.

"And don't interrupt," he snapped again, not ready to forgive her yet.

"Can't I even offer an opinion?"

After a brief silence, when the ticking of the grandfather clock was the only sound in the room, Ran put his fingers gently across her mouth.

"Not one word, woman. Do I make myself clear?" he repeated, but his voice was calmer now, and Morwen merely nodded, prepared to submit. At least, for the moment.

Chapter Twenty

A short while later, she stared at him, her eyes luminous now, where they had been so angry before.

"Oh, Ran. Are you quite sure about this?" she said. "Prosper Barrows meant so much to you."

He shrugged. "It's a business, that's all. And when I bought it, it was no more than to give me a legitimate reason for staying in Cornwall when I found the joy of my life. You know that."

She had the grace to blush. "I haven't been much of a joy to you lately, have I?"

His arms went around her, holding her tightly.

"You'll always be a joy to me, Morwen, honey, even when you're being your most irritating, difficult, cantankerous, beautiful self—"

She gasped, ready to hit out at him, and then the anger turned to laughter when she saw how his eyes were teasing her. She leaned against him.

"I'm sorry for being so – so – irritating, difficult, cantankerous—"

"And beautiful," he reminded her. "Always beautiful."

She nestled against him for a few glorious seconds, revelling in the closeness that seemed to be miraculously restored to them – for however long it lasted. It was so rare a commodity now, that it seemed cruel to spoil these moments by speaking of mundane matters. But they had to be discussed properly.

"And you really intend to offer the Pendragon woman Prosper Barrows to give you all the extra capital you need between now and the autumn despatches?" she said dubiously. "China stone has always been your mainstay,

Ran, and never such an up-and-down business as the clay."

"That's why I'm damn sure she won't be able to refuse it. But it's not just to provide the capital we need. We could no doubt find other ways to raise the money. But this has an added advantage. We're dealing with a shrewd and avaricious woman, Morwen, who will know a good proposition when she hears one. And we'll insist that when she buys me out, she'll sign a cast-iron document to say that she refutes any further interest in Killigrew Clay, and that this statement is to be legal and binding in perpetuity."

"My Lord, how impressive that sounds!" Morwen said. "Have you been swallowing a dictionary?"

"You forget that I had legal leanings myself at one time, and I'm quite familiar with the terms," he said with a smile. "Walter and I have discussed it all in great detail, and once the woman accepts the deal, we shall bring Justin into it to draw up the document."

She was instantly charmed at the thought of bringing Walter and Justin together in this way.

"Shouldn't Justin be in on the meeting between you and Walter and the Pendragon woman, Ran?" she went on. For the life of her, she couldn't bring herself to speak of her more charitably.

"No, love." He caressed her hands in his now, and spoke gently. "There are three partners in Killigrew Clay, and they are the ones who must face the dragon."

She drew in her breath as the meaning became clear, and bit her lip at the unconscious comparison with the woman's name. It fitted her so well. But she didn't want to do this . . .

"Justin's part in it all comes later, as the legal representative of the business," Ran went on. "This is how it must be. Are you brave enough?"

He deliberately challenged her, and she knew she couldn't back down. She knew what he was giving up for Killigrew Clay. For all that he dismissed it so carelessly, he'd been so proud of his ownership of Prosper Barrows, and it would be a wrench for him to see it go. It hadn't turned her wild colonial upstart into a home-bred Cornish landowner, but at the time it had been the next best thing.

Despite her hatred of the woman clay boss, and her wish never to see her again, Morwen Tremayne told herself stoically that she had never been afraid of anything, and she wasn't afraid now.

"We'll go whenever you say, dar."

His answer was to fold her in his arms and to press his mouth on hers in the sweetest kiss.

"Tomorrow afternoon then. Once Walter and I had come to the decision, I sent a messenger to tell her to expect us all at three o'clock."

"Tomorrow! But I need time to get used to the idea—" she said, in a sudden panic.

"If you'd been here earlier today, you'd have had plenty of time," Ran said drily. "I came home especially early to tell you."

"I'm sorry. I had no way of knowing."

He gave her another squeeze. "Let's just forget it and go to bed. You must be tired after all your jaunting about."

She looked at him with loving eyes. "I'm not in the least tired," she said.

"Good. Let's go to bed anyway."

Morwen didn't feel quite so brave the following afternoon when the time came for the meeting with Harriet Pendragon. Walter arrived in time for an early lunch, and the three of them set out together in the Wainwright carriage. By then Miss Pinner had gone, sourly protesting that children needed to learn the facts of life and not be treated like paper dolls . . . and Morwen had told her in no uncertain terms that ghoulish and frightening tales were hardly the best facts of life to teach them.

She felt much better when she'd put the stupid woman in her place and sent her packing. But now the nerves were back, and they became much worse when they came in sight of the Pendragon mansion overlooking Bodmin. She had never seen it before, and the aura of wealth it exuded was almost tangible.

"Saints preserve us," she muttered. "Anyone who lives here must be worth a fortune."

And well able to pull the purse strings of lesser folk, she thought. No wonder so many of the smaller clayworks had gone under when this woman bought them out with her handsome offers.

"So she might be," Ran said. "But don't forget that she still wants more, and that's what we're here to stop."

"I still think there should be some other way than by offering her your own business, Ran," Walter said, shaking his head, and Morwen could see he was no happier about the situation than she was.

"The decision's been made, so let's hear no more arguments," Ran said shortly. "We need to show a united front this afternoon, so we're all agreed that this is the way to do it, aren't we?"

Morwen put her hand in his. "You know we're both behind you, Ran," she said quietly. But to her surprise, he shook his head.

"That's not where I want you to be. I want you both at my side. We're equals in this, and that's the only way we'll be strong. The woman musn't see one flicker of doubt from any of us, no matter how much she offers for Killigrew Clay."

"Ran's right," Walter said now. "We owe it to those who've gone before, and to those who'll come after us."

He sounded as noble as if it was Justin speaking then, Morwen thought, loving him. Sometimes they were so alike. It was a pity they were the only ones who couldn't see it.

Gillings drove the carriage to the imposing frontage of the Pendragon mansion, and a starched and uniformed flunkey came outside to take the horses' reins and to inform him where he could stable the carriage while the lady and gentlemen were in consultation with Mrs Pendragon. The man sounded grander than they did themselves, Morwen thought in some amusement.

A butler opened the great door of the house, and bowed stiffly. It was the grandest of entrance halls, and Morwen tried not to gape or be too overawed. The floors were of palest patterned marble, enlivened by glowing scatter rugs. There were costly paintings on the walls, and huge floral arrangements in jardinières. And this was only the entrance hall.

"Madam will be ready to receive you in ten minutes," the butler said sniffily, as if they were so far beneath him.

But Morwen forgot about the stiff-necked butler as they were shown into a vast drawing room. Several of the best rooms at New World could be swallowed up in this one room. It all reeked of money and indulgence, from the thick Persian carpets to the heavily ornate Chinese lacquered furniture.

The wall over the mantel was dominated by a life-size portrait of Harriet Pendragon, dressed in shimmering white silk, against a deep red background. Having seen the woman for herself, and hearing her described as normally wearing garish colours, the contrast with her silvery hair and eyes was stunningly beautiful. Morwen would have been less than gracious not to see it.

But her graciousness quickly evaporated. She wasn't here to see any good in the Pendragon woman. She was here to support her menfolk, and Ran in particular. She glanced at him, and saw that his eyes were drawn to the portrait as well.

"A good likeness, isn't it?" she said, annoyed by the fact that the three of them seemed momentarily mesmerized by the portrait.

"Amazingly so," said Ran. "It would do credit to Albie."

Morwen felt her flesh tingle. God forbid that this woman would ever sit for Albie, she thought, fully aware of the seductive invitation in those silvery eyes. And then she heard Ran laugh softly.

"Don't show your claws too obviously, honey," he said. "I think it's an amazing likeness, because I didn't think any man could turn a she-devil into a goddess, even on canvas."

"Well said, Mr Wainwright," came Harriet Pendragon's voice right behind them. They all started, and Morwen thought Ran would be chagrined at having his words overheard. But instead, he merely laughed, his eyes challenging this elegant woman in the black satin gown with splashes of scarlet silk at the ruched neck and hemline.

With all these different outfits, she must personally keep the garment world in funds, Morwen thought. But there was a great vulgarity about this need to flaunt her wealth, and as she invited the visitors to sit down, she spread the folds of the satin gown around her, caressing them as if she caressed a lover. And in a single moment, Morwen was intuitively aware of the loneliness in this woman, with no husband and no family. All the wealth in the world couldn't make up for that.

But it didn't soften one snippet of Morwen's feelings towards her, either. This she-devil could ruin them all, and she hardened her heart against any tiny thought of sympathy. In any case, Harriet Pendragon would probably spit in her face if she even suspected Morwen had ever thought such a thing.

"If I guarantee that it's not poisoned, will you take some tea with me?" Harriet asked pleasantly, her eyes shining like diamonds.

She looked only at Ran. She was really enjoying the sparks that flew between them, and Morwen knew how dangerous that could be. When a man and a woman sparked off one another so viciously, that feeling could so easily change to something else. The line between love and hate was very fragile. And the damnable thoughts wouldn't go out of Morwen's mind, no matter how much she tried to rid herself of them.

"Thank you, no," Ran said coldly. "We've come to see you on a business matter, Mrs Pendragon, and we don't want to take up any more of your time than is necessary."

"My, how grand you sound today, Sir," she said, teasing him. "Well then, what is it you want to see me about that necessitates bringing your whole family with you? Were you so afraid of having a private tête-à-tête with me, Mr Wainwright?"

Morwen gasped in fury at the sheer gall of the woman.

She was baiting them all, and she felt Walter put his hand over hers as if to stem her hot-tempered reaction. But she heard Ran laugh again, as if the woman really amused him.

"My dear lady, a private tête-à-tête with you is the last thing in the world I would wish. As for bringing my family with me, you are mistaken. Family doesn't come into this. We're the three business partners in Killigrew Clay, and the future of Killigrew Clay concerns us all."

"I see." As she spoke, Harriet's smile didn't slip.

In fact, Morwen was sure that the lights in her eyes danced even more, and she wondered again if this meeting, however it continued, was a bright spot in an otherwise dull and dreary day. It was a startling thought, but it was a well-known fact that the woman had no friends. Everyone hereabouts was afraid of her money and her ruthless need for power, and it was rumoured that she received no invitations into society, since she had been ostracized by all. For any normal woman, it would make for a lonely existence.

And then, as if she could read Morwen's mind, and didn't like what she saw there, she spoke more sharply.

"All right, Mr Wainwright. Cards on the table, if you please. What is it that you want?"

"I'm here to ask that you refute all interest in Killigrew Clay, now and in perpetuity, and that you sign a legally drawn up document to that effect."

It was clear that he couldn't have staggered her more if he'd dropped a thunderbolt into the room. For a moment, she said nothing at all, and then she burst into noisy laughter, moving to a sideboard and pouring herself a large drink from a whisky decanter without any attempt to offer the others any refreshment. They had refused tea, so it was obviously assumed that they wouldn't imbibe alcohol in the middle of the day. And nor they would, not in the way this woman was swilling it down like a man, Morwen thought in some disgust.

"Are you completely mad, Randall Wainwright?" she said at last. "I've heard that our colonial cousins are somewhat thick in the head when it comes to business, and go into things like the proverbial bull at a gate, but—"

"You had best hear me out, Ma'am, before you start throwing insults about," Ran said coldly.

Harriet shrugged, seating herself again, and glaring at him insolently.

"Personally, I don't see that I have to give you the time of day, man, when you come here with your ridiculous demands. If I want your petty clayworks, I'll damn well have them—"

"Not while I have breath left in my body, you won't," Morwen said loudly, and Walter jumped to his feet, his hands clenched by his sides.

"That goes for me too," he said harshly. "I promise you a fight before we let one clay block from Killigrew Clay fall into your greedy hands."

"Well!" Harriet said, looking at the two of them. "It seems you've stirred up quite a bit of family support, Mr Wainwright."

"You still don't understand, do you? There was no need for me to stir up anything. The family business has always supported itself, and will continue to do so. It's as strong as it ever was when it belonged to the Killigrews. Nothing's changed in that respect, and we intend to keep it that way."

"Oh? And what makes you think I'll agree to your absurd demand?" Harriet drained her glass and challenged him with those fine eyes of hers.

"Because I have a better proposition for you," Ran said deliberately, motioning to Walter to sit down again.

"Really? And are you sure that this is something we should be discussing in front of your wife?"

The innuendo in her voice and her smile was blatantly obvious to Morwen now, but she gritted her teeth and said nothing. Let the woman think what she liked. Ran would soon make it clear that the only communication between them would be a business one.

"Perfectly sure. My wife has my full support in what I intend to do, as does Walter Tremayne."

Harriet suddenly looked bored with the whole meeting. She shrugged and stared distantly out of the window.

"Get on with it then, for I'm tired of your visit. Say whatever you came to say and then I shall be more than glad to show you the door."

"I'm offering to sell out Prosper Barrows to you."

Morwen had wondered why he hadn't said this right away, but she could see his strategy now. He used the legal kind of tactics that dangled the bait in front of her and allowed her brain to begin working out the pros and cons for herself. Truth to tell, Harriet didn't really care whether or not she bought out their miserable clayworks, despite its size. It was the challenge of it, more than the business itself, that had grabbed her attention.

And she had already sensed that she had met her match in Randall Wainwright. Having already laughed at his audacity in telling her to refute all interest in Killigrew Clay, and that he would never sell out, Harriet now saw that he was offering her a going concern. It was a bargaining deal, and she was at her best with business deals of this kind. It was one for one. She could take the china stone works, and leave the china clay well alone. She knew the score in such deals. And this classy wheeler-dealer would want a cast-iron declaration that she wouldn't be able to welsh on her word. She could respect him for that.

"What's in it for me?" she said at last, and Ran knew they were halfway there.

From his document case he drew out stock-sheets and lists of business contacts, together with outline details of the latest accounting figures from Prosper Barrows. The china stone works had never wavered in productivity or prosperity, and Harriet would be able to appreciate that.

"I would naturally ask you to inspect these documents thoroughly, Mrs Pendragon," he said evenly. "And I would also request a speedy reply."

She took the papers out of his hands without a word, and took her time in running her manicured fingers down the columns. Morwen hadn't expected her to study them so minutely at this stage, and nor had Walter. She felt him

259

shift irritably beside her, and knew he was tiring of this cat and mouse game.

Even the time spent in enjoying the comfort of this lovely house, would be considered wasted time in Walter's eyes. Walter would far rather be back on the moors with his beloved clay, or at home with his wife and baby, than listening to Ran arguing the toss with this woman. Finally, Walter could stand it no longer.

"Why don't we call it a day, Ran?" he said angrily. "'Tis obvious we're getting nowhere here. She's just playing wi' us, and I for one am tired of all this shillyshallying."

Harriet didn't even look up from the documents.

"I'm sure we can do without your presence, Mr Tremayne. If you want to leave, you know the way out."

"Stay where you are, Walter," Ran said shortly. "I believe the lady is astute enough to know a good thing when she sees it, and I prefer not to leave these documents with her unless I have to."

Harriet raised her eyes now, her voice faintly patronizing. "You surely don't expect me to agree to this sale without letting my financial advisor look over these papers? You know business ethics better than that, and since you're probably acquainted with Mr David Meadows of Bodmin, you can be assured there'll be no skulduggery. And I'm quite sure you have duplicate copies of everything here."

Ran permitted himself the ghost of a smile at her shrewd remark. "Of course. Then I suggest that you submit them to Mr Meadows as soon as possible, and that we meet again once he's seen what a sound proposition I'm making. Meanwhile, I shall advise Mr Justin Tremayne to draw up the legal document we require—"

"Hold your horses, if you please, Sir! I haven't said I agree to buying out Prosper Barrows yet, nor to your preposterous terms."

"You haven't said you don't, neither," Ran retorted. "And I prefer to have the documents ready the moment you do so. It's good business practice, wouldn't you agree?"

Morwen sat silent all this time, listening to them fencing with one another. Ran was clever, but so was Harriet

Pendragon. The woman was far cleverer than Morwen Tremayne, clayworker's daughter, and more perceptive in business matters than Walter, clayworker's son. She despised herself for the thoughts that seethed through her mind right then, but she couldn't deny them, either.

"Then we'll leave things there for the moment, and Meadows will be in touch with you," Harriet said lightly, and the Killigrew Clay partners stood up to leave.

Morwen was still annoyed at letting Harriet make her feel so inadequate in business matters, but then she glanced back and saw the almost envious way the woman's eyes were following the three of them. And for all that she had such wealth and power, and this rattling great mansion to live in, Morwen imagined again just how empty her life must be without a family around her, and she knew how strong the three of them must appear together.

"How do you really think it went, Ran? At first I didn't think she was going to budge at all," Walter said, as soon as they were back in the carriage and away from the house.

"I did," Ran said. "I knew it in my bones. It was too tempting an offer for her to refuse. She'll do well out of Prosper Barrows, and David Meadows will assure her of that."

"But to relinquish all interest in Killigrew Clay for all time – or whatever it was you said," Morwen said. "I was sure she'd argue about that."

"Well, she didn't, and the two of you can ponder about it from now until doomsday if you like, but I'd advise you just to take it at face value and thank your stars that it looks as if we'll come out of this smiling after all."

"It's just as well she didn't know about your new northern contacts, isn't it, Ran?" Morwen said suddenly. "If she'd got wind of new clients putting big orders our way, it might have changed things."

"It might. Which is why I've kept very quiet about it. No, I think we can safely start to think hopefully about the future now. With the new medical clients being so enthusiastic about taking large deliveries of china clay,

261

and David Meadows is sure to advise the woman to buy out Prosper Barrows, I'd say our worries could well be over."

"Well, I just hope you're crossing your fingers when you say so!" Morwen said, keeping hers well crossed for good measure as she spoke.

Walter laughed. "You always did believe in such little tricks, and good and bad omens, didn't you, Mother?"

"And why not? They don't usually fail me."

As the carriage neared the clayworks, where they would deposit Walter for what remained of the day, Ran put his hand over Morwen's.

"And what does your superstitious little head make of today's outing, honey?" he teased. "Do you have good or bad thoughts about it?"

She examined her thoughts quickly. She had a natural feeling of caution and suspicion about anything to do with the Pendragon woman, but she undoubtedly felt an uplift of her spirits, if only on account of Ran's own cheerfulness. And there was no way she wanted to dash that now.

"Good," she said promptly. "Only good thoughts, dar."

He laughed and leaned forward to kiss her cheek, and wondered why it couldn't always be as sunny as this between them. There was no reason why it couldn't, but somehow things didn't always turn out as simply as you expected.

"I'm leaving you two lovebirds before you start twittering to one another," they heard Walter say with a grin in his voice as the carriage slowed at Clay One. He leapt down and smiled up at them.

"You'll let me know of any developments, of course. And I presume you'll beard Justin in his den, Ran?"

Using such archness wasn't Walter's usual way, and it told Morwen how awkward he still felt about seeing Justin. She sighed, wishing it wasn't so, but understanding, all the same.

"I'll see to it," Ran said. "But at some time we'll all need to sign the document in the presence of witnesses."

But not now. Not today. And as the carriage trundled away, Walter turned his back on all such complications, and went to his Manager's hut, to change out of his fine clothes into more workaday ones, and become once again the clayworker he'd always been.

The horses drew the carriage towards St Austell, before turning away towards New World. And Morwen thought, as always, how beautiful it all was.

Morwen glanced back at the panorama of the open moors and the sky-tips behind her. She could hear the regular throb of the machinery that had long replaced the old laborious handwork methods now, and helped to keep Killigrew Clay alive. She imagined too that she could hear the constant hum of chatter from the clayworkers and bal maidens who were its heartbeat. And she felt a swelling of pride mixed with humility that she and her family had always been so much a part of this land.

"You love it all, don't you, Morwen?" Ran said softly.

"I always have. I should miss it so much, if ever it was taken away from us. Is that so absurd, when I'm little more than a figurehead here now?" she asked, feeling an unexpected nostalgia for the days when she had grubbed among the slurry with the bal maidens, carefree and young.

"It's not absurd, honey. It's just you," he said. "And I wouldn't have you any other way."

Chapter Twenty-One

Domestic matters took up all Morwen's attention in the next few days, and she was glad to put aside all thoughts of business dealings, whether good or bad; confrontations between stepbrothers; and the unsavoury knowledge that she wasn't yet rid of Harriet Pendragon. But for now, all that could wait, because this weekend Matt was travelling to London to meet Louisa and Cress and Primmy, and bringing them home to Cornwall from their European tour.

There was great anticipation about the homecoming in the Tremayne and Wainwright households now, trying to imagine all the places the little group had seen and the things they had done, and knowing it was impossible to remotely imagine any of it. The homecoming would also be marked with a certain sadness, because once the family departed for America, it was unlikely that they would meet again for years, if ever.

There would be another sadness in their minds too. Louisa and Cresswell would naturally have been sobered at hearing of Hal Tremayne's passing, but it wouldn't have affected them as deeply as it did Primmy. They hadn't known and loved him as she had. But Morwen had no doubt that Cress would have comforted Primmy when the letters had reached them.

For Bess's benefit, Freddie had stayed on at Killigrew House far longer than he had intended, supported by Venetia's letters that generously encouraged him to stay for as long as his family needed him. But Freddie would be looking forward to returning to Ireland very soon too. And Hocking Hall would be put in the hands of the land agents for renting once Matt and his family went home.

Matt had already told them that it would happen at the beginning of August, and they were already halfway through July. His family had been away from their own home a considerable while now, and the visit had been filled with both joy and sadness. But by their very nature, all visits were temporary, and had to end sometime.

Cresswell would be returning to America with far more than memories, thought Morwen, if all went well for him and Primmy. And she would know, by one look at her girl's face, if it were so. In a few days from now, she would know if Primmy was gloriously happy, or if that delirious, tingling first love had faded. In her heart, Morwen was sure it wasn't so, and prayed it was the same for them both.

"I wonder if it would be in order to have a farewell get-together here for Matt," Morwen said dubiously over breakfast one morning, and the children whooped with excitement as she spoke. When they had quietened, she went on.

"It would be too much for Mammie to do, and I'm also wondering how she'd feel about it, Ran, having a party so soon after Daddy's death, even if we didn't call it a proper party. But we can't let Matt go without a decent sendoff, either, and I know Daddy wouldn't want that. What do you think?"

"Whatever you say, honey," he said, only half-paying attention to her, and more concerned with reading an official looking letter that had arrived that morning. Morwen hadn't given a thought to what it might be, but now she felt her heart leap. She moved quickly to his side in the dining room and put her hand on his arm.

"It's not bad news, is it, dar?" she said.

"Not at all. It's from David Meadows in Bodmin. Harriet Pendragon obviously wasted no time in passing on the Prosper Barrows papers for him to see. He says he's giving it serious consideration and that Mrs Pendragon will be advised by his findings. He suggests that we meet in a month's time, to discuss matters further."

"He'll not be hurried then," Morwen said, having hoped it would be all over in days.

265

"Financial advisors never are," Ran said drily, folding up the letter and replacing it in the long envelope. "But I do believe this will go through, Morwen, and since we can do no more than we've already done, there's no use worrying about it, is there?"

"That's what Daddy used to say."

"I know. I thought you'd see the sense in it."

She couldn't argue with that, and nor did she want to. She could remove Harriet Pendragon a little further away from her thoughts, at least for the time being.

"But what about your northern contacts? When are they arriving? And maybe if they make a good offer for the clay you could withdraw the sale of Prosper Barrows—"

Ran stopped her. "There's no turning back now, honey. We've decided what's to be done, and the wheels are very much in motion. My guess is that the Pendragon woman will already be casting her eyes over the china stone works, and seeing what a good bargain she'll be getting. My first meeting with Bradley Stokes of Stokes and Keighley Medical Manufacturers, takes place the week after next."

"But if they place a big order for clay blocks, maybe all this wouldn't have been necessary—" she persisted.

"Morwen, please leave it."

She could see that he was getting tetchy now, and the children were fidgeting as Mrs Horn whisked them away to the nursery. She promised to come and see them later and read to them, but her mind was only half on the little ones, as she resumed her seat and drank her morning coffee.

"I'm sorry. I'm only trying to save things for you."

"Did it ever occur to you that I don't want things saved, as you call it? A man can have too many interests, and Killigrew Clay is enough for me, especially if we expand as I hope with the medical supplies. I'm ready to let Prosper Barrows go, Morwen, and concentrate on what I have here."

If she allowed herself, she could almost think he spoke with a double meaning. But he didn't, of course. He had no interest in Harriet Pendragon, other than settling this

266

matter with her. She had to believe that, and she did. Their lovemaking of last night had proved beyond doubt that Ran's love for her was as strong as ever. No woman had ever been more loved or felt more cherished . . .

"So can I begin thinking about this farewell evening for Matt then?" she said, determinedly switching the conversation. "I don't know the exact date they're leaving, so it doesn't give us much time for planning."

"Arrange it for as soon as you like," he said. "Why not for the end of next week? They'll have settled in here again by then. It's a pity it's well past midsummer's day, or I'm sure your romantic little heart would have found something appealing in that."

"Of course!"

As romantic as taking a witch's potion and chanting around the Larnie Stone at midnight and seeing your lover's face through the hole in the stone . . . the thought was in her head before she could push it away, and she drew in her breath at the sweet, poignant memory of it.

"Right," she said, quickly dragging her thoughts back to the present. "I'll inform Mrs Enders at once what we're planning."

"Can we make streamers to decorate the house?" Emma piped up eagerly.

"I'm not sure whether that will be a good idea, my love—" Morwen began, wondering if that would be just too much frivolity for Bess.

But with the practical minds of moorland folk, they weren't a family for plunging into deepest mourning once the burying was over. And to blazes with what polite society thought about that! Morwen thought in a spurt of defiance. But still, Bess's feelings had to be considered.

"But if it's a party, Mammie, we have to have decorations!" Emma howled at once, not understanding.

"I doubt that a few trimmings will be out of the way," Ran commented. "Let them do it, honey. It will be good to give them something pleasant to look forward to."

"All right. If you say so." And as long as she mentioned the decorations to Bess in advance.

"Hadn't you also better check with Matt that he wants a party?" Ran enquired.

"Oh, he'll want it! I know my brother. Any excuse to bring all the family together again. I want us all to give Cress and Primmy our blessing too, Ran, for whatever the future holds for them."

He came around the table and kissed her.

"Did anyone ever tell you you're a good woman, Morwen Wainwright?" he said.

She pulled a face. "I'm not sure I want to be described in such terms, thank you very much. It makes me sound so deadly dull and matronly!"

Ran laughed, squeezing her shoulder, his eyes dancing with mischief now.

"I think I can safely say that isn't the case, my wanton hussy," he said meaningly, reminding her of their glorious lovemaking of the previous night. "But I must go now, honey, delightful though this conversation is becoming. You organize whatever you like, and I'll fall in with it."

He was a very satisfactory husband at times, Morwen thought, when he'd left the house for the clayworks. And she grinned at the mundane word, which sounded as sane and sensible as calling her a good woman. And both descriptions were so incongruous when applied to last night's passionately abandoned lovers . . .

"Were you wanting me, Ma'am?" she heard Mrs Enders say, as she still sat dreamy-eyed at the dining table. "Afore he left, Mr Wainwright said there was summat of importance you'd be needin' to discuss wi' me."

"Oh yes, there is," Morwen said quickly, becoming suitably businesslike, and hoping that her cheeks weren't too fiery. She smiled at the housekeeper. "We have a farewell party to arrange, Mrs Enders."

She couldn't deny the pleasure that the thought of a family party was giving to the children. They had been somewhat in the doldrums since Miss Pinner had left, and as yet, no other tutor had been employed. Morwen had spent part of every day teaching them herself, but she knew it wasn't a situation that could continue indefinitely. And very soon now, Luke would have to go to a proper school.

Guiltily, she knew how she had been pushing the thought of it aside, wanting to keep her little ones around her as long as possible. And it had been Freddie and Venetia who had now got Bradley into a good Irish school, where, amazingly, he seemed to be flourishing, and behaving himself.

But she knew she didn't have the knowledge to instruct Randall Wainwright's children in the way they should be taught. She could teach them about nature and good manners, and about the intricate family history, and where all the family members fitted into it. She could help them with their reading and writing, but she couldn't teach them clever, intellectual things, and she knew her own capabilities.

But for today, such things were farthest from her mind. She had set them to their learning tasks that morning, promising that they could help her make the paper decorations and streamers for the party.

While they were occupied in the nursery schoolroom, she wrote brief notes to all the family members, telling them what she and Ran were planning, and inviting them all to a family get-together for Matt's farewell, providing her Mammie didn't object. She was careful not to call it a party, since the word might seem too carefree. Gillings was to deliver the notes tomorrow, and wait for the replies.

It was right and proper, she thought, that her brother Matt and his wife, Ran's cousin Louisa, should have their sendoff here. Despite the way brothers could wrangle, and upsets could split families, there was a strength and charm in the ties of their intricate family relationships.

But today, while the children were occupied in their lessons under the watchful eyes of a trusted servant, she was going to call at Killigrew House. Her mother needed to be consulted before anyone else, and Bess's eyes were soft as she looked at her anxious daughter.

"Of course our Matt must have a farewell sendoff, Morwen. It's the right and proper thing for un, and you can be sure your daddy will be there wi' us all in spirit, my lamb."

It was exactly the way she should have known her mother would react, strong and forward-looking. But her simple acceptance of it all brought a lump to Morwen's throat, just the same. And the two women shared a rare and spontaneous hug that spoke of their affection more than words ever could.

Later that afternoon, Morwen and Luke and Emma spent a happy couple of hours in the nursery making paper decorations and streamers. And when they began to tire of that, Morwen had another surprise for them. She took them up to the rarely-opened little turret room where Walter and Cathy had once hidden from prying eyes after running away from their objecting parents. They had been so desperately in love, and so wanting to be together.

Morwen opened up a dusty trunk in the turret room, full of the most exciting and amazing things for children's eyes to see. Old clothes, broken toys, and letters tied with ribbons, were all there for the finding, and Emma was instantly enchanted with a yellowing white bonnet and apron that she tied around herself. The small girl was totally lost in the voluminous folds and creases of the coarse cotton that had once been starched, and was now softened with age.

"Am I a nurse or a kitchen maid, Mammie?" she giggled.

"Neither," Morwen said, sitting back on her heels and laughing at the comical picture her daughter made. "You're a bal maiden, my lovely."

"What's that?" Emma echoed, and Luke spoke up at once, important with his knowledge.

"I know what a bal maiden is. It's a lady who works for Daddy and Uncle Walter at the clayworks. I've seen 'em wearing bonnets like that."

"That's right, Luke," Morwen said, quite calmly. "And a long time ago, I used to wear this one myself. Grandma Bess once wore a bonnet and apron just like this one too."

Luke looked at her in astonishment, his knowledge not

270

having stretched this far. "Did you both work at Killigrew Clay like the clayworkers, Mammie?"

She nodded, praying she wouldn't see the same derision she had seen years ago in Primmy's young eyes, when the truth had dawned on her. How superior Primmy had been in those days, and how bitterly she had hated Cresswell when he'd blurted out the truth about her background that Morwen should have told her long ago. And how ironically the tide had turned for those two. Now, today, seemed the perfect time to tell these two little ones, so that they absorbed it naturally.

She told them quickly how deeply all her family had been involved in the clayworks, before they themselves had become the bosses. To her relief, the children were fascinated by the picture of it all.

"I'm going to be a bal maiden when I grow up," Emma declared, twirling around in the voluminous apron. "I'm going to be just like you, Mammie."

"And I'm going to work with Daddy and Uncle Walter," Luke said swiftly, and Morwen felt a great lump in her throat.

Afterwards, she could only liken her feelings to one of those elating and illuminating moments that didn't come along every day. To hear her children speak so simply and unaffectedly of their futures – even if it would never happen as they envisaged – certainly not for Emma – was both humbling and wonderful.

She hugged them both, her heart full, and said that they'd better delve into the trunk and see what other treasures they could find, or they'd be sitting here daydreaming all day and Daddy would be coming home soon and wouldn't want to find them all dusty.

There were old bits of jewellery that had somehow found their way to the trunk. They were worthless, but great fun for the children to wear, and Emma was soon draped in rows of beads and ribbons. As well as clothes and jewellery there were Chinese lanterns that thrilled both children, and which Morwen said they could hang in the gardens among the paper streamers on the night of the party.

They could rely on the lush Cornish summer evening to be warm and balmy, and they could all spill outside and enjoy the rich bounties of this wonderful county that was their heritage. They all became more excited by the minute, and Morwen was carried along by their enthusiasm.

As they foraged still deeper in the trunk among the old-fashioned clothes that had the children shrieking with laughter, Morwen picked up a small worn box containing a piece of gentleman's jewellery that made her catch her breath.

"What's that, Mammie? Can I have it?" Emma said at once, seeing how her mother stared at the piece.

"No, darling. Not this one," Morwen said softly. "The pin is too sharp, and it could scratch you."

The children lost interest. There were too many other exciting things in the trunk, and Morwen let them scrabble on among the treasures, while she was lost in the past. She hadn't been to this turret room for years, nor had she needed to. It was simply a place where forgotten mementoes and memories gathered dust. Everything that was no longer wanted was stored up here, some things too precious to throw away, others that they simply didn't know what to do with.

By now, Emma had discarded the bonnet and apron, and was enveloped in a white muslin dress that had blue and mauve silk ribbons swathed and crossed over the bodice, and looped around the hemline. Morwen remembered how lovingly Bess had decorated the dress for her, and how she had felt when she wore it at Charles Killigrew's party. She remembered too, how she had caressed the silk ribbons, given to Bess Tremayne by a lady for whom she did dressmaking, feeling their sensuous softness, and wondered how it must feel to wear gowns made of silk . . .

And this pin that she held in her hand now . . . this gentleman's neckcloth pin . . . brought back such a store of memories that she almost gasped at the sharpness of it. As sharp as the pin itself, scratching her cheek when Ben Killigrew had automatically put out his arms in a steep St Austell street to stop her from falling.

This was Ben Killigrew's pin, warm in her hand, forgotten and saved for all these years, and she could hear his voice in her head as clearly as if he stood right beside her. His lovely, tidied and educated Cornish voice, so different from her natural moorland one. So different, and yet so much the same, with the same deep roots.

"My name is Ben. We have no need to be so formal, especially when I have your blood on my shirt, if only a tiny spot. Surely that fact is of some significance."

She closed her eyes, breathing him in, wanting him, aching for days that were gone . . . conjuring up the words they had exchanged in the midst of a Killigrew party of fine folk, when it had seemed, magically and briefly, that only the two of them existed in the world.

"I apologize for branding you, Morwen. I don't normally treat young ladies so—"

"It's nothing. It will soon fade. It was my fault for not looking where I was going."

Branded . . . it was the way she had felt from the moment she fell into his arms. And she'd had the ridiculous feeling, that if he dared, he would have leaned over and kissed the tiny mark on her cheek, then and later. Kissing a bal maiden, here on sufferance in his father's fine house, just because old Charles Killigrew had taken a whim to invite the whole crazy Tremayne clayworking clan to his gathering . . .

Morwen felt as shivery now, all these years later, as she had felt then. Knowing that as surely as the sun rose and set, hers and Ben Killigrew's paths had been destined to cross. She moved her fingers gently over the pin, and her eyes were clouded with memories.

A movement behind her made her jerk up her head, and her heart stopped for a moment. Surely . . . surely, she hadn't done the impossible . . . conjured up Ben's image so completely that he had come to her at last . . .

"Morwen. What the hell are you doing up here?" she heard Ran's angry voice say.

None of them had heard him open the door and step into the room. But as Morwen blinked and started, she knew he must have seen the way she held the pin, and the lost, longing expression in her eyes. And she felt the most enormous guilt for putting this defensive note in her husband's voice. She scrambled to her feet, but before she could get her feelings in working order again, the children had rushed at him.

"Daddy! Daddy! Look what we've found!" Emma shrieked. "All these things for dressing up were here all the time, and we didn't know!"

"Did you know our Mammie was a bal maiden?" Luke shouted, trying to outdo his sister in noise and information. "And Grandma Bess was a bal maiden as well. Emma says she's going to be one when she grows up."

"She most certainly is not!" Ran snapped, diverted.

"And I'm going to work with you and Uncle Walter," Luke babbled on, neither hearing nor heeding his father's words in his excitement. Ran grabbed his arm and shook him.

"You will not work at Killigrew Clay, Luke. And Emma will most certainly not have anything to do with those uncouth women. She will learn how to become a lady, and you will have a proper education and learn how to be a gentleman, and I'll hear no more about such nonsense."

He let him go just as quickly, and Luke staggered a little, his eyes frightened at such an unexpected and violent reaction. There was a sudden palpable silence in the turret room. The children stared with wide, uneasy eyes at their father, while Morwen's face went scarlet, and her heart pounded with rage.

"Are you saying that my mother and I are not worthy to be called ladies? Or that all my menfolk are less than gentlemen?" she said in a shrill voice, vibrant with fury.

Ran cursed forcefully and loudly, using words that he rarely did in front of the children. Luke sniggered, and Morwen pulled him to her, as if afraid that Ran would strike him for his insolence. Emma was already clinging in fright to her skirt and starting to whimper.

"You know bloody well I'm not saying that, woman," Ran stormed on. "I've always held you and your family in the highest esteem—"

"Oh, really? It didn't sound like that a few minutes ago. And when you sneer at those hard-working folk who put money in your pockets by long hours of work in appalling conditions, up to their necks in slurry and muck in the winter, and choking with the clay dust in the summer, then you also sneer at Mammie and me, and Daddy, and Sam, and all my brothers, and Walter—"

She had no breath to go on. Besides which, her throat was so tight with pain, and her eyes so full of tears that she couldn't see straight, and she couldn't think straight.

"For God's sake, get things in perspective, Morwen. I'm not sneering at anybody, but just listen to yourself, will you? You've described a clayworker's life quite graphically enough, and I hardly think you can condemn me for wanting a better future for my children."

Emma was snivelling loudly now, where minutes before she had been so happy. Luke said nothing, but his young mind was clearly absorbing everything that was going on between his parents, and both children looked utterly bewildered at the way their parents were hurling insults at one another. Hurt though she was at what she still saw as Ran's sneering, Morwen knew she must swallow her pride for the moment, if only for the sake of these little ones.

"I can't argue with that last statement," she said stiffly. "And in any case, I think we've had enough arguing for today. We came up here to see what we could find for the party, and we thought it would be cheerful and bright if we hung these Chinese lanterns in the garden. What do you think?"

She threw the question at him, bringing him into their day. And begging him with her eyes to let the quarrel lie alongside the dusty memories in this turret room. As if to underline her words, she replaced Ben's neckcloth pin back in its box, and closed the lid. Ran didn't speak for several long moments, and then he shrugged.

"Just as you wish," he said curtly, "and if you've finished up here, I suggest that you make yourselves presentable and come down to the drawing room. I've got some news for you, and the children might as well hear it too."

He went out of the turret room, and Morwen wilted for a moment. But not for long. The children were looking to her for a lead, worried and wondering what was to happen next. She forced a smile to her lips.

"Well, that was a bit of a storm in a teacup, wasn't it, my lambs? Daddy has obviously had a bad day, and wondered where we'd all got to. I daresay it gave him a fright to find us all hidden away up here."

It didn't exactly pacify them, and Luke, especially, wasn't fooled by her forced brightness.

"But we didn't do anything to give him a bad day, did we, Mammie?" he said belligerently, more perceptive than Morwen had expected. "He shouldn't come home and blame us for things we haven't done."

She gave him a hug. "Unfortunately, that's the way grown-up people sometimes behave, Luke," she said sadly. "When they have something worrying them, they often act badly to those who are closest to them. That's why we musn't be too worried about it. It just proves that we're the closest ones to Daddy, do you see?"

It was just about the most appalling piece of logic she'd ever tried to explain, and it didn't come out at all in the way she wanted it. But such clumsiness seemed to be enough for the children, and Emma wriggled away from her, climbing out of the muslin dress and letting it drop to the floor.

"Can we go down now then, Mammie? My nose is all dusty and tingling," she complained.

"Yes, I think we should. Let's go and wash ourselves and put on clean clothes, and go and see what Daddy has to say. It's nearly time for tea, anyway," she said in relief.

She bundled the Chinese lanterns into a box to take down to one of the nursery closets in readiness for the party. And when she had seen the children safely down the narrow, winding stairs leading from the turret room, she glanced back, just once, and then closed the door on the memories.

Chapter Twenty-Two

By the time the family met in the drawing room, freshened and tidied and wearing clean clothes, Mrs Enders had brought in a tea trolley with buttered buns and drinks for the children, and a steaming pot of tea for the adults. Ran looked slightly less huffy now, and was pleasant enough to the housekeeper, though still cool towards his family. Always quick to sense any atmosphere, Morwen was pained by it.

How could he be so jealous of a past love?, she mourned. And yet, how could he not, when she herself had been so swept up in the memories of Ben Killigrew that she felt as though she could have reached out and touched him at any moment? She pushed away the thought, and poured the tea for them both, glad of this civilized little ritual.

"What did you have to tell us?" she prompted. So far he had confided nothing, and after his outburst the children had become momentarily too tongue-tied to speak.

"The Pendragon woman came to Killigrew Clay this afternoon," he said, without expression.

"*What!*" Morwen's cup clattered on her saucer, the tea spilling onto it. Emma ran to her mother, clearly expecting another quarrel to erupt between her parents.

"It's nothing to get excited about," he went on irritably. "She came to see Walter and me at the clayworks, informing us grandly that she assumed she wouldn't be welcome if she called on us here."

"I hope you told her she wasn't welcome at any place to do with Killigrew Clay," Morwen snapped, wondering if this was going to be suitable for the children's ears.

"I did. Though you won't object to her being in Justin's

277

office with us, I presume, to sign the documents in the presence of witnesses," he said sarcastically.

Morwen said nothing for a moment.

"You're not telling me she's agreed to it just like that, are you?" she said at last. "I thought David Meadows told you in his letter that it would be a month before anything was decided."

"So he did, but apparently the lady doesn't work that way. A financial advisor is just another skivvy at her beck and call, as far as Harriet Pendragon is concerned. She makes her own decisions, and once her mind is made up, she doesn't believe in wasting time."

"Nor in rough riding over anyone who stands in her way," Morwen couldn't help saying.

He shrugged. "She asked to see Walter and myself today, and I gather from what she said that Meadows is none too pleased at the way she counterminds all his suggestions," he went on, confirming Morwen's opinion. "But she's decided she wants Prosper Barrows as soon as the sale can be legally arranged, and she's agreed to my conditions that she'll have no further interest in Killigrew Clay."

Morwen's eyes stung as the relief and surprise of it all hit her in equal measure. She realized her hands were trembling, and fought to keep them still. But to be rid of the threat of *that woman*, in all departments, was as good as a doctor's tonic . . .

"Are we rich now, Daddy?" Luke said, his brows puckering at the business dealings he didn't really understand, but which sounded so grand and important. And Ran laughed shortly for the first time since coming home that day.

"Let's say we're more than solvent, boy, which is just as good," he said. Luke didn't understand that, either, but seeing that it was something that apparently pleased his father, he spoke hopefully.

"So if we're solv – whatever you said, can I have a pony of my own sometime?"

"Perhaps. We'll think about it."

Although Ran sounded congenial enough for the moment,

Morwen didn't find it a totally convincing sound. Always perceptive to atmosphere, she knew Ran hadn't forgiven her yet for the misdemeanour of still wanting Ben Killigrew. It was ridiculous and untrue. And it was heartbreaking and unbelievable that the ghost of a past marriage could threaten the love they had shared all these years.

But with the half-promise of a pony for Luke in the vague future, the bad moments in the turret room were forgotten as far as the children were concerned. As if to make further amends, their father deigned to romp and play with them until bedtime. But it was obvious to Morwen that his smiles and laughter weren't for her.

When the two of them were alone, and the silences lengthened between them, she commented on the fact that he had spoken of business matters in front of the children. He didn't normally discuss business in their earshot, and she knew she had to think of something to say, if only in some desperation at how distant he seemed.

He didn't answer at first. He poured himself a large brandy, drinking it down in one swallow. Then he poured himself another, just as large, and drank it just as fast. She had no doubt that he fully intended to drink himself into a stupor tonight.

"There seemed little point in keeping it secret from them, since they seem to know so much already about the goings on at the clayworks."

"Well, why shouldn't they? It's part of their heritage. They have a right to know their family history," she said, defensive at once.

"Including the fact that their mother and grandmother were once bal maidens. It's a fine credential for Luke to take to his school and university, isn't it?"

Morwen jumped to her feet, stormy-faced and humiliated by his sarcasm.

"So you *are* ashamed of me. You would have preferred it if I pushed it all under the carpet, like you've hidden your distaste all these years, I suppose! Well, you can't hide it now! You're more of a snob than Cresswell ever was when Matt first brought him to Cornwall. At least he came out and said what he thought. He didn't disguise his true feelings under the pretence of love!"

"I've never pretended that I loved you—"

"What?" she whispered, and he gave a smothered oath.

"That didn't came out the way I intended. You know I've loved you from the day I saw you, and there's never been any pretence about my feelings for you. I can't make it any plainer than that."

Nor he could, except that he said it as curtly and unemotionally as if he was giving an instruction to one of his minions. It wounded her more than if he'd said he'd never loved her at all . . . but she knew that wasn't true. In the end, seeing the stranger he had suddenly become, the love they had once had was all she had to cling on to.

"So what happens now?" she asked.

"I'll see Justin tomorrow and get all the documents drawn up, and we'll meet at his chambers next week for the formalities."

Morwen stared ahead blankly. He spoke of business matters, while her heart was breaking for want of a soft word from him. They had always been able to talk freely on any subject under the sun, and their sweet-talk had been as uninhibited as business-talk. But that special closeness and empathy had dissipated like so much will o' the wisp.

"I take it your mother had no objection to Matt and Louisa's farewell evening then?" he said, as if just remembering why his wife and children had been in the turret room to look out old decorations and trimmings.

"No. She'll want him to have a proper send off."

It was the way the clayfolk spoke of buryings, and Morwen couldn't help knowing the symbolism and sadness of the words. Earlier that day, they had all felt so joyful, and now, for her, everything had changed. And into the midst of everything else, came the certain knowledge that once Matt left for America, she would never see him again.

"Ran—" she put out a tremulous hand, not knowing what to say, but knowing she had to say something, to try to put things right between them.

He moved away from her hand, as if he couldn't bear to feel her touch, and she flinched as if she was stung.

"I've a great deal of work to do, so I shall be in my study for the rest of the evening," he said coldly. "Have Mrs Enders send a tray of food in for me later, and please see that I'm not disturbed for any other reason."

He strode out of the room without another word or another glance. And he took the brandy bottle with him.

Hours later, Morwen was lying dry-eyed in bed when he came upstairs, stumbling across the room and falling into bed beside her with only half his clothes removed. He was asleep at once, snoring loudly and disgustingly, and stinking of spirits. And at last the stinging, helpless tears flowed from her eyes, wondering if things would ever be the same between them again. And wondering how something so innocuous as finding a pearl neckcloth pin could have been the trigger for stirring up such violent emotions.

No one in the New World household could miss the fact that there was a brittle coolness between the Wainwright parents. On the surface they were polite to one another, exaggeratedly so at times, but from the very next morning after his drinking rampage, Ran ordered everything belonging to him in their bedroom, to be removed to one of the guest bedrooms.

If there was anything more humiliating for Morwen, than to see the wide-eyed maids scurrying to do his bidding, she couldn't think of it. Maids were notorious gossips, and not only within their own households, either.

Soon everyone in the county would know that Ran Wainwright no longer slept in his wife's bed, she raged irrationally, but knowing that rage was the only way she could keep her heartbreak in check. They might just as well announce it in Tom Askhew's wretched newspaper, and really give him something to crow about.

To help release some of the pent-up anger and the energy it evoked, Morwen threw herself into the plans for Matt's farewell party. And also in trying to prepare herself for

281

comforting Primmy, which she fully expected she would have to do.

Primmy would feel awkward and embarrassed, not quite knowing what to say to the family, and probably feeling a sense of guilt that she wasn't here when her grandfather died. Morwen knew so well how guilt assailed a person at such times, unnecessary though it was. Primmy would need reassurance that Hal would have been more than glad that her future was settled.

All these things weighed on Morwen's mind, but they took her thoughts away from the appalling one that Ran seemed simply to have turned his back on her. It was ludicrous that he thought she was still pining for Ben after all these years, but it was a vulnerability in Ran that she had seen before, and one that he had to work out for himself.

The fact that he was drinking heavily again did nothing to ease her nerves, and didn't seem to be doing much for him either. Anyone with half an eye could see that it was doing his temper no good at all, but she was shocked to get unexpected reports of his behaviour from her mother.

The afternoon before Matt was meeting his family home from Europe, Morwen and Bess met at Fieldings' Tea Rooms. It seemed such a rare occasion to do this now, when it had once been such a happy, habitual event for the Tremayne women. Annie had promised to join them on this day, but Bess had something to say to Morwen before she arrived.

"From what I hear, your husband seems to be stirring up a hornets' nest at the clayworks," she said bluntly, never one to waste words.

"Is he?"

Bess looked at her keenly. "So young Cathy told me yesterday, and all in a fluster she was too. Your husband gave Walter a dressing down for summat or other, in front of the clayworkers, and that ain't a fair and right thing to do, Morwen. You know as well as I do that your Daddy would never have done such a thing. Nor Sam neither."

It was a long while since she had said her eldest son's name, and it brought a lump to Morwen's throat. Nor did she miss the fact, that to Bess, Ran was referred to as "your husband" at this time, which spoke volumes about her strong disapproval of his methods.

"I can't answer for what Ran does, Mammie," she said stiffly. "I daresay 'tis the sale of Prosper Barrows that's got him riled up. He was determined to sell, but I'm sure he has a certain amount of regrets about it."

She prayed that the explanation would satisfy her mother. But she should have known that it wouldn't.

"That don't explain the dark shadows under your eyes, nor your woebegone face, my girl. There's summat troubling 'ee, and troubles don't improve by letting 'em fester."

"Well, if we've got troubles, they belong to us, and we'll sort them out ourselves."

"Mind you do, then. And 'twouldn't be a bad thing to warn your husband about his drinking, neither. It killed one of 'em, and 'twould be more than careless of 'ee to let t'other un go the same way."

She wasn't trying to be comical, because that wasn't Bess's nature, and in any case, Morwen was in no mood to see it that way. She was thankful to turn away from her mother as her sister-in-law Annie came into the Tea Rooms and joined them at the corner table.

Bess was too knowing by half, thought Morwen, but as a family, they'd never indulged in baring their feelings to one another, and she didn't want to start now. If Bess thought it was merely the drinking that brought on Ran's bad humour, so be it. Besides, how could she possibly say that the trouble was all in her husband's mind – that he was jealous of her first love, who'd been dead and buried for more than a decade!

"You look well, Morwen," Annie said brightly, defying all that her mother had just said, and Morwen smiled faintly. Annie had only ever seen what she wanted to see, but her temperament was much improved lately, now that her girls were happily settled in London. Morwen quickly asked after them, and Jack, and their boy.

"They're all well. And we're looking forward to Matt's party. It will be good to be all together again."

She stopped abruptly, remembering that the last time was for the reading of Hal's will, when she had made such an exhibition of herself, and she had the grace to blush. But Bess had obviously put such shows of temper into the past where they belonged.

"Have you let all the others know about it, Morwen?" Bess asked calmly.

"Oh yes. It will be just the family, of course, but since Charlotte has asked if she can bring Vincent Pollard, and Albie is desperate to show off Rose Slater to us all, I couldn't say no, Mammie."

Since neither of the others had ever heard of Rose Slater, they were diverted from more personal matters, as Morwen described the girl to them, thinking how life moved on. All her older children had friends who seemed destined to be more than friends now, and she prayed and believed that each of them had found the right match. It was the order of things. And the family had had enough sadness in the past. Maybe in the not too distant future, there would be weddings to plan . . .

"'Twill be a fine sendoff for Matt, for us all to be together," Bess said, nodding, and not letting her eyelids flicker for a moment, even though Morwen knew there had been one place missing at family gatherings for many years. Sam . . . and now Hal. And Ben.

With a feeling of horror, Morwen realized she hadn't instantly counted Ben in her thoughts. Ben, who had once meant everything to her – and in the mind of her hot-headed, darling, short-sighted Ran, still did.

"You'll have to face the fact of losing him again, Mother," Annie reminded her gently.

"I lost Matt many years ago, Annie. He's as dear to me as any of my sons, but he's made a good new life for himself, and 'tis right for un to go."

And taking Primmy with him . . . Morwen felt a pang in her heart that she couldn't share with anyone. Especially not Ran, and that was enough to give her the sharpest pang of all.

But once they had done their talking, Bess reminded them

284

that she didn't like to be away from home for too long now. Apart from the long hours she had once worked as a bal maiden in all winds and weathers, she had always been a home-body, and cherished the moment when she could be inside her own four walls.

For all•the grandeur of Killigrew House, where Bess had never thought she'd live in a million years, she still thought of it as no more than having her own private place when she closed the door on the rest of the world, and that was the way she liked it.

"I'm going to see Justin before I go home, Mammie. Do you want to come with me?" she asked when they had finished their tea and scones.

"No, dar. I said I'd visit Cathy today, to make sure young Theo's still thriving," she answered.

"I'll come with you," Annie said, to Morwen's surprise. "I haven't seen much of the little scamp. And then I'll see you home, Mother."

For some reason, the small, satisfying conversation between them made Morwen feel oddly redundant. But she had shaken off the feeling by the time she reached Justin's chambers, having previously sent a message that she would call on him. The clerk showed no surprise in seeing her this time, and showed her straight into Justin's office. Her tall, handsome son greeted her warily, not too sure exactly what this visit was all about, and the clerk brought more tea without being asked, until she began to feel that she was awash with it.

"I wanted to see you, to have your word that you and Walter won't be getting up to any tricks at Matt's party," she said at once, as blunt as her mother ever was.

She saw him redden slightly. It was hardly the way an up-and-coming lawyer cared to be addressed in his own chambers, despite the fact that they were alone. But however old he was, and whatever his status, he was still the child, and she was the parent. It was a remark her daddy had frequently made to his own brood in their growing up years, whenever he felt a reprimand was needed.

285

"What tricks?" Justin said. "I've no intention of doing anything, Mother!"

"All I ask is that you're sociable for the few hours you'll be spending together. And if you can't manage that, then please keep away from him."

"And have you instructed Walter to keep away from me?"

"Not yet. But I will. I won't have anything spoiling this farewell party for Matt, do you hear?"

Lord knew that she and Ran would have to mask their own feelings, she thought. No one must know or guess how estranged they had become in these last days. It terrified her to know how cold the atmosphere between them was now. It was like a barrier of ice that neither of them could break through. Or apparently even wanted to.

"Don't worry," Justin said, seeing her drawn face now, and assuming it was on account of himself and Walter. "I'm sure we can call a truce for one evening."

"One evening? Oh Justin, don't you know how I hate all this?" she said, with a burst of her old passion. "You're *brothers*, for pity's sake—"

"No, we're not. You keep forgetting that, Mother," he said, with the infuriating calm of a lawyer's logic.

"Well then, just try to behave like the brothers you were brought up to be, can't you? I love you both, but you'd try the patience of a dozen saints with your stupid pride!"

"I know," Justin's face suddenly broke into a grin. "But that's something we all have to live with, Mammie."

She managed a smile then, knowing it was true. He changed the subject quickly, telling her Ran's business document was almost ready, and that there'd be no problems or delays with the sale of Prosper Barrows. Since she knew the dealings with Killigrew Clay were so involved with this sale, there was no breach of confidentiality in telling her.

"Good. Ran will be pleased to hear it."

"So cheer up. You've got a party to look forward to, and money in the coffers. And there'll be no more angst from the Pendragon woman, once the deed is done."

And that was the most important of all. There would be

286

only one more meeting with her, here in this office to sign all the papers, and then they would be rid of her for ever. She crossed her fingers for good measure at the thought, but praying that such a superstition wasn't necessary. She just did it out of habit, to be on the safe side. And because she guessed how peeved David Meadows must be at the way Harriet Pendragon carried on in her own sweet way, no matter what his advice, or the effect on other people.

But there was no use worrying over any of them. At least Ran had got what he wanted, though he seemed to spend far more of his time in a bad humour than appearing to be pleased that the deal had gone through so easily.

If *only* he hadn't caught her being so soft-eyed over Ben's old pin, Morwen thought miserably. She knew very well that was the cause of his unpredictable tempers, with her and the children. And it was all so foolish, and so unnecessary . . .

"I saw Justin today," she told him over dinner that evening.

He had allowed himself to join her and the children for the evening meal. More often than not, he'd continued eating alone in his study, under the pretext of a heavy workload, until Morwen had complained angrily, saying that if he wanted to stir up more gossip he was going the right way about it.

"Why?" he asked.

She seethed at the way he answered her as briefly as possible, as if he couldn't bear to exchange a few civil words with her.

"I asked him not to make any scenes with Walter at the party," she said coolly. "And it might be something for other folk to remember as well. I don't want anything to spoil this occasion."

His eyes flashed at her, taking her meaning at once, but the children were watching them closely, and he poured himself a large glass of table wine instead, and from the way he swallowed it, he might have been parched, Morwen thought in some disgust.

But she was also becoming alarmed. She had seen the

effects of heavy drinking on Ben, and she couldn't bear to see Ran going the same way. Suddenly, her Mammie's unintentional burst of humour didn't seem so funny any more. Nor so unlikely.

"There'll be no disharmony on my account," he retorted. "You forget it's my family as well as yours. I knew my cousin Louisa long before your brother ran off to America and married her."

Morwen flinched at the words, and she shot a warning look at him as Luke showed a new interest in these visiting relatives. As far as he knew, Matt had always lived there, and he was too young to question the reasons for him being there. But he remembered at once now, how his mother had said that all her brothers had once worked for Killigrew Clay, and his young mind began to put things together.

"Did Uncle Matt run off to America?" he said, clearly charmed by the thought.

"He didn't run. He left on a ship, Luke," Morwen said shortly. "He and a – a friend went to seek their fortunes. After they parted company, your Uncle Matt got rich by finding gold. He met Aunt Louisa in America and they got married. Aunt Louisa is your daddy's cousin, and when your daddy visited Cornwall, he decided to look up his new Cornish relatives."

The children were both gaping at her now, having heard nothing of all this until this moment. She hadn't meant to say so much, but once she'd started, it all came spilling out. All the charm, and the sweet irony that had brought Ran Wainwright to these shores, a stranger looking to make acquaintance with the family of his cousin's husband. And when he found Morwen, he told her he'd found his destiny.

She looked at him now, and her heart was mirrored in her eyes, willing him to remember it too. But he seemed only interested in drinking more red wine, while the children clamoured to hear more.

"What happened to his friend, Mammie?" Emma said, and Morwen's heart jolted, wondering why she had been so foolish as to mention a friend at all. It would have been

288

just as easy to say that Matt went to America to seek his fortune, without ever having to remember the hated name of Jude Pascoe.

"I don't know," she said quickly. "It doesn't matter, anyway."

"Did he find gold, like Uncle Matt?" Luke persisted.

"I tell you I don't know! I never heard of him again."

But she had. There had been that terrible moment at Truro Fair, when they had come face to face, and she knew he was back. And then the knowledge that he was blackmailing her after he'd seen her with Ran; so in love, but still married to Ben Killigrew, Jude's own cousin.

And the way she had refused to give in to his blackmail and got rid of him for good, by threatening to tell the authorities what he'd done all those years ago. Of how he'd impregnated her dearest friend, Celia, causing her to have an agonizing abortion that had turned her brain, and sent her walking into the milky slime of the clay pool to drown.

"I'll be in the study for an hour or two," Ran's voice penetrated her tormented mind, having no idea of the turmoil she was going through now.

"Ran, please don't work this evening," she said, her voice desperate. For once the children had gone to bed, there would be nothing to do but think. And she couldn't bear to have to think, and remember . . .

"Oh, I'm sure you can do without me for an hour or two, honey," he said sarcastically, and left the room without even saying good-night to his children.

Chapter Twenty-Three

Later, Morwen reflected that at least a few of her anxieties had been groundless. Matt had brought his family home, and taken them to see see Bess straight away, and she learned that Primmy had spent a long private time with her grandmother.

Whatever had been said about Hal was between the two of them, but Bess's common-sense approach to life and death had left Primmy clearer-eyed than Morwen had expected. And, of course, much of her resilience was due to her happiness with Cresswell. One look at them both, and Morwen had no doubts where her daughter's future lay.

The excitement of the wanderers' return was added to when they heard of the party that was planned. As she'd told Ran, she knew her brother, and that he would welcome this family get-together. It had proved just as she had said. And her brother knew her, too.

Before Matt left for London to meet his family, he'd held her hands in his and as he looked searchingly into her face, the colour of his eyes was a match for hers.

"I hope all will soon be well with you, our Morwen," he said.

"I don't know what you mean," she began, but she should have known it was no use trying to hide things from Matt. They had always been the closest in the family when they were children. He was always her dearest, dreamy-eyed brother, and she had been so amazed and so proud of him when he'd turned out to be a businessman after all.

"I mean that you and Ran are at loggerheads, and trying to hide it from the rest of us, and it don't suit you, dar," he said simply.

"We'll work things out between us," she said. "I don't want you worrying about us, Matt. It's nothing that can't be resolved."

"Do it soon, then. I don't want to leave for home until I know you're happy."

America was home to him now, of course . . . after all these years, it still gave her a little shock to hear him refer to it that way. And America would soon be Primmy's home too. Her girl would no longer think of Cornwall as home . . .

As she looked at her across the room at New World on the night when the farewell party was in full swing, and saw how Primmy positively sparkled, she thought of it again, and felt a sharp pang. She would miss her so much. It didn't matter a jot that Primmy had lived these last years in Truro. She was still near, still a part of them all, and soon she would be gone.

"Mammie," she felt a touch on her shoulder, and turned with a bright smile as she saw Charlotte standing there, looking so pretty in her flounced blue frock. She still had Charlotte. And Emma. There were other daughters, other sons. But somehow – and folk could say what they liked about the rights and wrongs of it – the first was always special. The first daughter and the first son, Primmy, and Walter. She thought of them as this – even though she knew they weren't really her own.

Her heart gave an uncomfortable leap, as she looked through the long, open French windows and saw Walter and Justin arguing and gesticulating furiously in the garden. But even as she watched the little cameo scene, she saw Ran go to them. She couldn't hear the words above the noise, but it was clearly enough to pacify them for the moment, and she was mightily relieved when the two young men separated. But she also knew it wasn't over yet . . .

"Mammie, I've been trying to tell you something!" came Charlotte's impatient young voice again.

"I'm sorry, lamb, my mind was wandering, like it always does on these occasions. It's advancing age, or so they tell me," she said, with an attempt at a joke.

291

Charlotte hugged her arm as they both strolled out into the garden. The night was so warm, the indigo sky dotted with a million stars, the air as fragrant with blossom as only a Cornish summer night could be.

"You'll never be old, Mammie. You'll always be young and you look so beautiful tonight. That colour is wonderful for you," Charlotte said, so unexpectedly that it brought tears to Morwen's eyes.

Justin was the one who was easy with the compliments, with his lawyer's ease with words, and it didn't often come from her daughter. But the glorious russet-coloured silk gown had brought compliments from many sources tonight, except from the one she would most like to hear it from.

"Anyway," she went on, before Morwen could think how to answer her. "I wanted to ask you something very private, and before I do, I want you to promise me you won't say anything to anybody about it."

They were strolling in the shrubbery now, where the scent of roses was overpowering, and Morwen suddenly felt faint. She knew she shouldn't anticipate the worst, but right now, Charlotte sounded more anxious than happy. If she was about to hear something bad, she wasn't sure she could bear it. If her girl had got herself into trouble, it would disgrace the family name . . .

"Of course I promise, darling," she said quickly, because Charlotte was waiting intently for her answer, and there was no other that she could give.

"Well, it's to do with Vincent and me," Charlotte said.

Morwen stared stonily ahead, trying to keep her heart-beats steady, and failing miserably.

"I know you've been seeing a lot of one another, but it was with his family's approval, wasn't it?" Morwen questioned.

"Oh yes." Charlotte dismissed such a formality with the impatience of youth. Even if it hadn't been with the Pollards' approval, the two of them would have found a way to be together, Morwen thought, with a glimmer of humour, and a lot of love.

"Hadn't you better tell me what it is that's bothering

292

you, then?" she asked, as they reached a garden seat and sat down together. "I'll help you, Charlotte. You know that – whatever it is."

She couldn't be more outspoken than that at this stage, but to her surprise Charlotte burst out laughing.

"Oh Mammie, I can see what you're thinking! Oh, it's nothing like that! Vincent and I – well, he respects me, truly he does, but he loves me as well. And I love him." Her voice sobered at once. "And – well, this is what I wanted to ask you about. We want to be married, to be together always, and I know Daddy will say we're too young. Vincent will do the proper thing and ask his permission, but I'm so afraid that with Daddy like he is just now, he'll refuse and get in a temper and spoil everything."

She ran out of breath, and in the moonlight and the lights streaming out from the house, Morwen could see the glint of tears in her eyes. She hugged the girl's hands tightly, her heart going out to her. And feeling an enormous anger at Ran, that Charlotte could think his recent moods far-reaching enough to threaten her happiness.

"Your father wants the best for you, same as I do, and I know that you and Vincent will be happy. But you are very young, my darling, and this is not the best of times—"

"But why should we be made to pay for his black drinking moods?" Charlotte said passionately, and Morwen was sick at heart to hear her speak so.

Charlotte didn't even live at home any more, but the news of Ran Wainwright's drinking bouts had spread far and wide. Even to the extent of an outrageous cartoon appearing in *The Informer*. No names were mentioned in the caption, but the sketchy sky-tips in the background of the cartoon, and the furious, angry face of a man slating his inferiors with a bottle in each hand, made it more than obvious. The thought that the whole district would have seen it, had mortified Morwen for days.

"Will you do something for me, Charlotte?" she said evenly now. The girl nodded dubiously.

"Wait until after the autumn clay despatches. It's not that far away now, and you know how everyone gets tetchy around that time. And with all the business deals still to be settled, it's not a good time to suggest anything else. But after that I promise you I'll smooth the path for you and Vincent, darling."

Charlotte threw her arms around her neck and hugged her. And Morwen's own eyes were moist, knowing only too well how desperately time apart dragged for two people in love, when all you wanted was to be together.

"Let's go inside. And not a word of what we've been saying," she went on. "It will be our secret, Charlotte."

And as long as Vincent Pollard respected her . . . the two of them walked into the house with linked arms, and Charlotte could never have guessed the way Morwen was remembering another secret that had happened so long ago. Remembering how desperately she and Ran had made love in that little London hotel while her husband, Ben, lay in hospital. It had been wrong . . . and yet nothing had seemed more right, because their love for each other had been all-consuming.

She looked at Ran in the drawing room now, fiercely discussing something with her brothers. If only Ran hadn't become so aggressive. If only they could all be happy . . .

"Freddie's taking me home now, Morwen," she heard her mother's voice say. "I've a need to be in my own bed, and I've made my goodbyes, so we'll be leaving. Jack and Annie and young Sam will be coming with us too."

"But it's still early, Mammie!"

"Not for an old un, my lamb," Bess said with a smile. And when Morwen could see how this arrangement suited them all, she bade them all good-night.

The party went on until the early hours. Justin had left for Truro long ago, clearly wanting to get away from this place, where he had to see how Walter Tremayne and his wife and child were so adulated. And the Wain-wright children had been put reluctantly to bed, while the rest of them lingered as long as they felt able. Albie and Rose Slater had gone, and Albie was clearly elated to see how everyone had adored Rose from the out-set.

Before they left, Morwen needed to have a quiet word with Freddie.

"Are you sure Bradley's all right?" she said, anxious and guilty, because she'd hardly had time to worry about him lately. "You would tell me if all wasn't well, wouldn't you, Freddie? And I do miss him—"

"Oh ah! Like a thorn in your side!" he said, with a teasing laugh. "Don't you fret none about that young man, our Morwen. He's well and happy, and I'll persuade un to write to you to tell you so."

"That'll be the day," she said, smiling back. "But I'll write to him, Freddie, and that's a promise. And Ran and me are so grateful to you and Venetia for everything."

"That's enough now, or you'll have us both slobbering, and I'm too old for such nonsense," he said briskly, as her eyes began to fill. He gave her a quick hug, and went to collect his mother.

Matt and his family were the last to leave. He put his arms around his sister quite uninhibitedly and without any hurry to release her. He was her dearest brother, and had always been so. He spoke softly in her ear, so that only she could hear.

"I don't always find the words to say what I feel, my honey girl, but if I don't say it now, I probably never will. I just want you to know that no matter how far apart we are, you'll always be in my heart."

"And you'll be in mine," she whispered.

It was a sweet, private, poignant moment, and when she let him go and saw him turn to his family, she felt as possessive of him as if he had been a lover. The feeling passed just as quickly, and thankfully so. She loved him so much, and always would, but he was her brother and nothing more. And he belonged to Louisa.

Finally, she and Ran were alone, and she felt an awkwardness she couldn't explain at first. And then she knew the reason for it. They had had many family parties over the years, and the evening had always ended with the two of them dissecting the success of it all, talking about how

295

the rest of them fared, and amicably or forcefully putting the family problems to rights.

Tonight, none of that happened. Morwen was too emotional over the thought of Matt leaving for America next week, and she couldn't confide in Ran over what Charlotte had told her. As for Ran . . . the need to talk seemed to be overtaken by the need to drink. He must have consumed plenty all evening, she thought in some alarm, but he still had the capacity to take more and remain standing.

"It's time for bed," he slurred, speaking very slowly and measuring every word.

"I'm sure you can find your own way upstairs," she said coolly.

She rose from the sofa and made to swish past him, but he caught at her hand. His palm felt sweaty, and she felt a sliver of fear, as an instant flash of memory reminded her of how it had been with Ben. He too had been drinking heavily, his skin sweaty and ill at ease in the days before the heart attack. She brushed aside the feeling. Ben had been a fit man in his youth, but had never been as full of vigour as Ran, and it was ridiculous to make such a comparison.

"But I want you to come with me," Ran said now, his voice soft and full of meaning.

She felt a little shock. He had stayed in the guest bedroom ever since they had hurled insults at one another. He hadn't wanted to be in her bed then, and she hadn't expected it now. From the look and the smell of him, all he needed was to fall into bed and sleep the clock round.

"Ran, you've had too much to drink. What you need now is sleep—"

"I need my *wife*," he shouted, his mood instantly changing with the ease of the very drunk. "It's been too long since I've felt your charms, my honey, and I want to feel them *now*."

He pulled her to him so fiercely that she gasped for breath. He stunk of spirits, and his eyes were wild. But there was a primitive hunger about him that excited her despite her revulsion. She felt his hands on her breasts, and the way his tongue forced itself into her mouth.

Her revulsion won, and she wrestled with him silently, hating this.

"No, Ran. Not here. Not like this!" she gasped. Because she knew it wouldn't be love that made him take her, but lust, and a need to possess her.

"You're right," he mumbled, his hands going to her hair now, unpinning it roughly, so that the pins flew everywhere, and his fingers raked through the tumbling blue-black hair. "We'll go upstairs, before the need for you drives me mad."

She went with him dumbly, half-supporting his stumbling form now, and knowing that if she didn't, he would carry out his lovemaking right here in the drawing room. Once, such lovemaking had been erotic and beautiful. But she couldn't bear it now. It wouldn't even be lovemaking. It would be rape. And such an outrage would be a humiliating end to a wonderful, emotional evening.

Upstairs, he flung the door of their bedroom shut behind him, and began tearing off his clothes. She undressed as quickly as she could, her fingers shaking so much she could hardly unfasten the buttons on her gown. Her beautiful, vibrant, russet-coloured silk gown, bought specially for this evening, that Ran had hardly noticed.

She was inside the bedcovers while he was still fumbling irritably with his clothes, his haste and foul temper doing nothing to help him. But at last he was beside her, quickly covering her body with his own, and pressing kisses on her mouth.

"I need to know you belong to me, Morwen," he said against her lips, in an odd voice that she couldn't fathom for the moment. She struggled to speak, although she was pinned down by the unrelenting weight of him.

"You know I do! I always have—"

"Not always," he slurred, his hands roaming urgently over her body as if he had never seen or felt it before. "I wasn't the first, was I?"

"Ran, for goodness' sake," she said, with a mixture of nervousness and alarm. "You can hardly condemn me for having been married before I even knew you existed!"

"Every man has the right to expect a pure bride on his wedding night—"

"Well, that could hardly have troubled you, since you didn't even wait for our wedding night," she said, bitterly defensive.

Appalled, she listened to their own accusations, and she could have wept at the way they were destroying the sweetness of that long ago night in London, when they had first made such tremulous, forbidden love. When she had belonged in marriage to Ben Killigrew, and not to him.

"I don't recall that you objected too strongly," he said, insultingly.

"That's not fair," she said, choked. "You know how I battled with my conscience, Ran."

It was unbelievable how he could continue his sensual arousal of her body, while his words degraded her. It was as if he had become two different people. The Ran she adored, and the one she hated.

"But not for long. And you seem to have forgotten the rudiments of lovemaking, honey."

He grasped her hand and thrust it downwards to where his half-hearted erection was attempting to thrust into her, and not succeeding. It was the fault of the drink, of course. He should have known all along that he wouldn't be able to perform tonight, but he was starting to curse savagely now, as her own efforts to arouse him produced nothing. She ached with embarrassment for him, knowing how the rare occasions when he'd failed had angered and embittered him, but he must surely see that it was no good . . .

"Ran, why don't we leave it until another time?" she said gently, trying not to sound upset or let down. In truth, she wasn't at all, for it wasn't the right time for loving, but she didn't dare let him see that either.

"What other time? A time when this useless piece of flesh decides to perk up for a change?" he said in frustrated anger. Sorrow for him fluttered in her heart then.

"Don't say such daft things, dar. It hasn't happened often before, and I doubt that it will happen again, once you give up the drinking," she said, very quietly.

He gave a bitter laugh close to her ear. "Not happened often before? That's all you know, my sweet, loving wife! And you should know there are more ways to emasculate a man than by drowning himself in a bottle."

He rolled away from her, breathing heavily and raggedly. She wished the drink would render him insensible, but it seemed to be having the opposite effect on him now, and he was belligerent and restless.

"It will pass, I'm sure," she murmured, not knowing what else to say, and bewildered by his words. "We're both very tired, Ran. Let's try to sleep—"

"Sleep? There's time enough for bloody sleep when I'm six feet under. That's the only time I'll find any real peace, like your Killigrew."

Morwen's heart jolted. "I don't know why you keep bringing Ben's name into it. My marriage to him was a long time ago, and you and I have had a good life together—"

"*Had?*" He picked up on the past tense at once, and she sighed, knowing she would have to choose her words with eggshell care now.

"We still have a good life, if only you'd relax and not dwell on the past so much. It's not healthy, Ran—"

"Maybe *I'm* not healthy—"

She sat up in bed, staring down at him. He lay like a statue, his ruggedly good-looking face carved and angular in the light from the window. Visions of Ben trying to deal with the prospect of being ill flashed in front of her eyes, and her Mammie's words seemed oddly prophetic at that moment.

"What do you mean? You're not ill, are you? Don't frighten me like that, please!"

He didn't even turn to look at her. If it had been any normal time she might have expected him to gather her in his arms and reassure her. But nothing seemed normal between them any more, and his voice was brittle with sarcasm.

"I'm sorry to disappoint you, honey, but I'm not ill, nor proposing to drop dead like your number one husband. I've no intention of making room for number three."

He turned his back on her then, and the shocked tears ran down Morwen's cheeks. How *could* he be so insensitive, she raged? And it was a long while later before her crying was done, and by then he lay sleeping noisily beside her.

But she had made her resolve. If there was nothing else between them now, they had the children and they had the clayworks. There was nothing for it now, but to make the best of things. She was strong, and she would prove it.

That strength was put to the test when Morwen came face to face with Harriet Pendragon in Justin's office at the appointed time for the document signing. The other woman was as flamboyant as ever, in a peacock-green silk gown and matching hat and parasol. Beside her, Morwen refused to feel dowdy, but no one could avoid seeing the contrast between the two women. Morwen wore dark blue, and although her clothes were expensive and elegant, she immediately felt inadequate. Even so, she held her head high, and didn't bother to acknowledge the woman.

The office was crowded that afternoon. Justin held court, and the three Killigrew partners sat on one side of the room with their witnesses, while Harriet, the disapproving David Meadows, and her two witnesses, sat on the other.

"Let's get this over quickly, Justin," Ran said, as he began to read out the lengthy document. "We're all agreed on the sale price of Prosper Barrows, and the terms of it, so let's just get on with it."

Justin looked at his stepfather coldly. "I'm sorry, but you know this has to be done legally, and I'm bound to read it out to all concerned, and to give the parties the choice of signing or making another decision."

"There's not going to be any other decision," Ran snapped. "It's already been made."

"But we should hear Mr Killigrew out, my dear Sir," Harriet Pendragon said prettily, obviously enjoying this wrangle between kinsmen.

"We certainly should," David Meadows put in at once. "I've already advised Mrs Pendragon not to act too hastily—"

"I think the lady can make up her own mind," Walter said. "She made no bones about her decision when she came to see us at the clayworks."

"Against my wishes and better judgement," the man snapped, his face red with annoyance.

By now, the witnesses were beginning to enjoy it too. What had seemed to be a foregone conclusion to their mundane task that afternoon, now promised to be a bit of verbal rough and tumble.

"Don't you have anything to add, Mrs Wainwright?" Harriet said insultingly. "You're a sort of partner, I do believe. Or is your role merely to keep the children out of the way and let the men deal with men's business?"

Morwen felt Walter's hand cover hers. Walter's, not Ran's. She removed her hand from his at once, and stared icily at the other woman.

"And do you believe you're the first woman clay boss in the county, Madam?" she asked.

Harriet's eyes narrowed for a moment, and then she shrugged. "Oh, I believe there have been one or two attempts at it by those who should stick to their domestic chores."

"Not only those," Morwen went on, ignoring Justin's attempt to bring the room to order.

But Morwen was incensed now, and had no intention of letting this woman get the better of her. "And if you think I'm merely a sleeping partner in Killigrew Clay, then you underestimate me, and you underestimate my family. I didn't marry the first man who asked me for the power it gave me. I married a man I loved, and who loved me for what I was then – a clayworker's daughter, who loved and understood the clay—"

"Morwen, will you *stop* this!" Ran thundered at her now, wrenching her arm as she leapt to her feet. She shook him off, while the others in the room sat open-mouthed and transfixed at the extraordinary sight of two well-dressed ladies glowering at one another. By now Harriet was on her feet too, her face scarlet with rage.

"You bitch!" she screamed. "If you think I'm buying your

301

husband's poxy little china stone works now, you can just think again. You can rot in hell, the lot of you!"

She swept out of the room like a ship in full sail, with her financial advisor and all the witnesses scurrying after her, while Morwen almost staggered at the speed of it all. Ran whipped round on her, shaking her like a rag doll.

"Do you know what you've just done?" he bellowed. "You've buggered up the best deal I could have got on Prosper Barrows. You're a bloody menace in business, and in future you can keep your hands out of my affairs."

She wrenched away from him.

"*Your* affairs? Whatever concerns Killigrew Clay concerns me, and don't you ever forget it," she screamed. "It was mine before you ever came on the scene—"

"Mother, for God's sake—" Walter sprang between the two of them as they looked fit to do bloody murder. Justin ran round the front of his desk at the same time, and each brother pulled one of the warring partners away from the other.

"She didn't mean it, Ran," Justin said quickly. "She didn't know what she was saying."

"And if she did, it was a spur of the moment reaction, because she's so passionate about Killigrew Clay and will protect it to the death, as we all will."

Justin nodded. "He's right, Ran. Now you sit tight while I get some brandy to calm you both down," he said quickly. "And you keep him away from her, Walter."

"I think I'd better, before they kill each other," Walter said grimly, seeing the murderous looks that passed between them.

Even as she knew that this was undoubtedly the end of her marriage, Morwen found the hysterical thought running through her mind, that now that she'd said the unforgivable to Ran, her sons seemed to be both on the same side at last.

Chapter Twenty-Four

She hardly knew how they got out of Justin's chambers, nor could she properly comprehend that a minor miracle must have taken place as she saw Walter and Justin talking quietly and sensibly together as they left. It was the one good thing to come out of this terrible day. But uppermost in her mind was what she had done to the one she loved most in all the world.

He held her arm so tightly she knew she'd be bruised as he strode to the stables where they'd left the gig. She had a job to keep up with him, but she was too proud to complain. Once they had reclaimed their vehicle, they travelled home in total silence, which gave Morwen far too much time to think. Such a silence was ominous, and she knew how tightly Ran's anger was bottled up inside him. If it once spilled over, she didn't dare think what he might do or say.

She couldn't stop shaking. All those carefully planned negotiations for the good of Killigrew Clay had come to nothing, and she had been the one to ruin them by her stupidity and her reckless tongue. She wanted to weep, but she was too shocked to weep. It was one of the worst days of her life, and the future looked as bleak as on the day Ben died.

She stifled a sob in her throat then, knowing that this was the wrong thought to come into her mind at that moment. For the first time in her life she cursed the fact that her thoughts always reverted to the past when she least wanted them to. But when they had travelled several miles, the aggressive silence began to unnerve her.

"Look, Ran, we can't go on like this, and you know I'm

sorry," she managed to say, as well as she could through her tightly clenched teeth. "You must know I never meant to hurt you! Please tell me you know that, at least!"

His voice was as sharp as steel. "I don't know anything any more. I don't know this bloody family, or the clay business, or the contrariness of women, including my own wife. I wish to God I'd never come here."

"You don't mean that!" she said through shaking lips.

"Why wouldn't I mean it?" he snarled, and she was thankful they were on a lonely stretch of road now, where no one could hear the influential Ran Wainwright shouting like a common docker at his wife. "I wish I'd never set foot in this godforsaken country, and never set eyes on the Tremaynes or Killigrews, and that's a fact. It's caused me nothing but trouble ever since I got here."

She gasped, wondering how he could say such things. As if he truly felt that all the years they had been together counted for nothing.

"If that's the way you feel, perhaps you'd best go back where you came from then, when Matt leaves next week," she said shrilly, her voice harsh with pain.

"Don't think I haven't thought about it," he snapped.

Morwen stared straight ahead, unable to see the track for the tears blurring her eyes now. Had he really said those words? That he'd contemplated leaving her, and their children, and all that he'd built up here over the years? But she had virtually destroyed all that success today. She had taken away his power, which, in effect had emasculated him, and guilt rushed over her again.

"Ran, you *know* how much I regret what happened back there. You *know* I never meant it to happen. Do I have to grovel on my knees before you'll believe it?"

He glanced towards her then, and she was heartsick at the unyielding look in his eyes.

"Oh, I believe it. But you're just like the rest of your blundering family, Morwen. You rush in before you stop to think. And if I'm to stay here at all, I'm seriously wondering if it mightn't be the best thing for me to buy you out of Killigrew Clay, if that's the only way to stop your meddling."

Her mouth dropped open at the sheer bloody gall of the man. She might have taken a crumb of comfort from the fact that he was as good as saying he didn't intend leaving her, and it was only an idle threat . . . but she was more outraged by the very idea that he thought he could buy her out of Killigrew Clay. It was hers and Ben's, and in the heart and soul of her, it always would be . . .

"How dare you!" she screamed. "I'll never sell out to you or anyone else. You'd have to kill me before I let you have my shares—"

She stopped abruptly. They had reached an even lonelier stretch of road, and a faint summer drizzle had begun to turn the tracks to mud. There was a descending mist over the moors, and far below the cliffs alongside them, the sea was already blotted out by the greyness of the late afternoon.

And Morwen felt real fear, knowing her words had a ring of truth about them. He would have to kill her to gain two-thirds control of the clayworks, and he was angry enough to do it. He was strong and powerful . . . and what better place to do it than here and now, where no one would ever know . . .? It would only take a moment to push the flimsy gig over the cliffs, with her still inside it . . .

The full horror of her imaginative thoughts were too much for her, and without warning, she slid from her seat in a dead faint. As she did so, Ran reined in the horse furiously.

She had no idea how long she had been unconscious, but she came around to find herself in her husband's arms, with her face being slapped. And at once her worst fears were uppermost in her mind again.

"Don't kill me, you devil! Please don't kill me," she shrieked. "You can have whatever you want—"

The slaps became sharper, stilling her frantic words, and bringing her glazed eyes back into focus.

"For God's sake, Morwen, nobody's going to kill you. You fainted, that's all. Pull yourself together, unless you're planning to frighten the wits out of any passers-by. We're nearly home."

He wasn't tender with her, but he didn't seem quite so angry any more, either. His voice was rough, and as he held

305

her tightly to try and stop her shaking, she sobbed silently against him.

"Oh Ran, please don't hate me for what I've done."

She could tell he was making an effort to stay calm and in control. "I don't hate you. But who's this devil that you thought was going to kill you?"

She said nothing, and his voice became incredulous.

"Dear God, Morwen, you surely didn't think *I'd* do such a thing? What sort of a bloody maniac do you take me for?"

She couldn't speak for a moment, and when she did her voice was husky with remorse. "One who had every right to take revenge on a stupid woman."

"Revenge isn't a word that belongs between us, honey," he said. "The fact is that I still own Prosper Barrows and its income, and providing we get as good a deal as I hope from the northern folk, we shan't need any of Harriet Pendragon's bloodsucking money. We probably never did."

"What? Then why—"

"It was more a way of getting her to sign away any interest in Killigrew Clay than anything else. Anyway, what's done is done, and there's no use fretting over it."

She was still too shaky to feel real relief at his words. No matter what he said, she knew she'd publicly shamed him. It just proved to her how big a man he really was, to be so magnanimous. She wanted to tell him so, and to say how much she loved him, but for once the words wouldn't come.

"Let's go home," she whispered instead.

There was an uneasy peace between them during the next days. Each made an effort to be sociable in company, especially when Freddie came to say goodbye on his return to Ireland, taking with him a long and newsy letter to Bradley from his mother.

But the time was fast approaching when Matt, Louisa, Cresswell and Primmy would leave for America, and Morwen viewed the day with dread. She had lost Matt to that far-off land many years ago, but she had never thought to lose her darling Primmy in the same way, and the thought of never seeing her again had suddenly begun to overwhelm her.

Matt was firmly entrenched in his new life now; her brother Sam had died so long ago his face didn't even come to her clearly any more; her Daddy had gone; the young ones all had their own lives and their independence; and Primmy was leaving her.

It seemed as if all her family was disintegrating, as if the gods or fate were decreeing that Morwen Tremayne had had enough good fortune in her life, and now she had to pay.

She tried desperately to put the uneasy thought out of her mind, and to hug Primmy tightly as they finally stood on the Falmouth quayside where the ship awaited its final passengers.

"Promise me you'll write often, my darling, and tell me everything," she said to her girl, trying not to betray how unhappy she felt.

"I promise, Mammie," Primmy said, and Morwen could see she was near to breaking down too. They held one another mutely, and then Primmy whispered in her ear the sweetest words Morwen could wish to hear.

"I do love you, Mammie, and I wanted to tell you that you've been the best mother in the world to me."

The ship's hooter sounded, and the time for farewells was over. They had all come to see the family depart, and Morwen linked arms with her mother now, knowing this would be a bad time for her. She and the children were to spend the rest of the day with Bess, to soften the blow. And she didn't admit to herself that it served two purposes, for she and Ran wouldn't have to spend more time in false politeness with one another.

She discovered that Cathy had the same idea of taking little Theo to his great-grandmother's house, while Ran and Walter went back to the clayworks together. It irked Morwen a little, to know that Cathy had had the same idea, even though it was a kindly and loving thing to do, but she pushed aside any antagonism when Cathy confided in her how glad she was that Walter and Justin had forgotten their differences now.

"Walter was so unhappy about it, Granny Morwen," Cathy said shyly, using the new name she called her on Theo's behalf now. "But the other night Justin came to the house and we had a long talk and a meal together, and it was so good to see them being brothers again."

It was the best news Morwen could have heard, and in acknowledging it, she silently forgave Cathy everything. Guiltily, she knew her only antagonism towards this lovely girl was because she was the daughter of Jane and Tom Askhew.

Everyone in her family had disliked the brash Yorkshire newspaperman when he first came to Cornwall . . . but Morwen's feelings went deeper than that, and it was not on account of Tom that they were disturbed.

It was that ridiculous long ago name she had bestowed on Jane, when she had been so convinced that she and Ben Killigrew were attracted to one another. Miss "finelady" Jane . . . and it was high time she put such adolescent nonsense behind her. They were both grandmothers now, for heaven's sake, and both of them had a stake in this bouncing baby boy with the blue Tremayne eyes and the engaging smile.

And his cousins simply adored him. When they were all safely back at her mother's house, Bess had dried her eyes and resumed her usual stoical manner, ordering tea for the women and lemonade for the children. And Luke and Emma played with Theo, delighting in his chuckles as they tickled him and encouraged his vigorous kicking on his play-rug.

"Was I ever as small as this, Mammie?" Emma said once, flushed with pleasure at the baby's antics.

"You were, my lamb," Morwen smiled. "And so were Luke and Bradley, believe it or not!"

"Can we have a baby of our own one day, Mammie?" she said next, her eyes full of hope, and Morwen felt her cheeks flood with colour to match her daughter's.

It wasn't so much for the unlikelihood and undesirability of it happening, it was because she and Ran were no longer on intimate terms to produce it. Nobody knew it but themselves, and the servants could make what they would of separate rooms. But Morwen knew it, and it hurt her beyond words to know that their politeness didn't yet extend to the marriage bed.

"I think I've had enough babbies of my own, darling," she said lightly. "You just enjoy sharing little Theo."

"She can share him any time she likes, Granny Morwen. She's a proper little mother," Cathy said, laughing, and the awkward moment passed.

But she was obviously in her husband's confidence, because while the children were all occupied, she spoke quietly to Morwen.

"When does Ran expect his northern visitors?"

Morwen's heart jolted. In the sadness of the American family's departure, which was how she was steeling herself to think of them now, she had virtually forgotten all about Ran's important meeting. She thought quickly.

"The day after tomorrow. They're staying in Bodmin, but they'll be making an extensive visit to the clayworks, and if all is well they'll come to New World to go through the details of supplies and transport with Ran."

She mentally crossed her fingers as she spoke. This deal was very important to her husband, especially after all the other bad business with Harriet Pendragon. And presumably the representative of the medical manufacturers, would expect to be offered an evening's hospitality by Randall Wainwright and his wife. But this arrangement left out the third partner.

"Cathy, will you and Walter come to dine with us while they're here? Ran will arrange the time and date. Will your mother sit with Theo for the evening?"

God, what was wrong with her, that she still couldn't be comfortable with the woman's name!

"I'm sure she will. And thank you. That will please Walter. Will you ask Justin as well, seeing that he handles the legal side of things?"

"Of course."

But to her chagrin, Morwen knew that it had been left to

this golden girl to remind her of her obligations, whether it was tactful or merely taking an interest. And when the moment came to suggest it all to Ran, she unashamedly took the credit for thinking of it, and was rewarded by his thanks. She knew it was pathetic to be so grateful for a warm word from him, however grudgingly given, but that was the way it was. She also took an absurdly superstitious grain of hope from the fact that Mr Bradley Stokes had the same name as one of their own sons.

On the appointed day of the visit from Stokes & Keighley to the clayworks, Morwen was decidedly nervous. Ran was short and snappy, and she couldn't honestly blame him. It was a matter of pride and prestige to him to secure this large order for the china clay. The autumn despatches were approaching, and if they could secure an important new client, it would do so much for the security of everyone who worked at Killigrew Clay. She prayed that it would all go well. And even more than the good of the clayworks, she prayed for Ran's own self-respect to be restored in the process.

The representatives were already housed in an hotel in Bodmin, and had sent word that they would meet Ran and Walter this morning. There were three of them, and Morwen had already adjusted her dining invitation to accommodate them all. They would be quite a large party in the end, but perhaps that was no bad thing, she thought. Temperaments would surely be held in check in such company.

As Ran was about to leave the house, she deliberately kissed him in front of the housekeeper and the children, knowing he could hardly make some snide comment about this show of affection. But she thought sadly that they had come to a sorry state if she could even think such a thing.

She spoke softly to him, her eyes large and unblinking.

"I'll be thinking of you all day, dar, and wishing you all the luck in the world."

"I hope I shan't need your Cornish luck," he said briefly.

"I hope the quality of the clay alone will swing the tide in our direction."

She bit her lips. Couldn't he even be soft with her now, when she knew how anxious he was, despite his brave words? But it seemed he could not, and he disentangled her arms from around his neck, and kissed his children with more warmth than he spared for his wife.

That afternoon, when their lessons were over, she decided they would go to the beach again. It was too glorious a summer's day for staying indoors, and time spent with her children was a kind of panacea these days. Besides, watching the rippling, silvery-tipped waves, she could imagine that Primmy's ship wasn't so far away after all.

By now, she could only think of it as Primmy's ship . . . and as if Emma followed her train of thoughts with uncanny accuracy, she felt her small daughter's hand creep into hers as they sat idly on a rock, while Luke skimmed pebbles into the sea.

"Will we ever see Primmy again, Mammie?" she said sorrowfully.

Morwen didn't like lying to her children, and she had always been innately honest, sometimes regrettably so, when it stirred up too many unpleasant thoughts. But seeing the trusting, anxious look in Emma's blue eyes, she found herself prevaricating from the absolute truth as she saw it.

"Who can tell, my lamb? America is a very long way over the ocean, and Primmy's a young lady now, and has her own life to lead, so as long as she's happy—"

She tailed off lamely, knowing how badly she wished Primmy hadn't been so compelled to make this endless journey to the other side of the world. Knowing how she missed her already. Just being in Cornwall, just a few miles away in the studio she'd once shared with Albie, was being home, and no more than a carriage ride away. But home to Primmy now, would always be where Cresswell was.

"Anyway," Luke said boisterously, his ears attuned to all that was going on around him as usual, "Uncle Matt came back more than once, didn't he? If he did it, Primmy will probably come back as well."

Seeing the way Emma cheered up at this, Morwen blessed him at that moment. He wasn't normally sensitive to female moods and emotions, but there were times when a common sense male perspective was useful, even one of such tender years.

"Perhaps I'll go to visit her when I'm grown up, Mammie," Emma said hopefully.

"Perhaps you will, darling," Morwen said, giving her a hug. But the hug was mainly to hide the tell-tale dismay in her eyes at such innocent words. She couldn't bear it if she lost Emma too . . . not her sweet, ethereal darling . . .

A cloud passed over the sun at that moment, making her shiver. How many times had that happened – or was it no more than her over-active Cornish imagination that produced such feelings of presentiments she wondered.

"Mammie, can we go to Truro Fair?" Emma said now, her quicksilver mind having already moved on from thoughts of Primmy, while Morwen's was still there.

"Truro Fair?" she said blankly, as if she'd never heard of it before.

Luke began dancing up and down on the sand, scattering it in all directions, and blinding the others with it, until they shouted in protest.

"Daddy promised that we could, and we want to go! There's stalls and horse rides and sales, and Daddy might see a pony there that he can buy for me—"

"I want a pony as well!" Emma piped up at once.

"You're too young to own a pony of your own," Morwen said automatically. "But if we go, I daresay you can have a ride on one—"

Luke howled at once, hearing the doubt in her words.

"We're going! We *are*. Daddy said it, so there!"

At that moment, he looked and sounded so like Bradley in one of his black moods that it gave Morwen a shock. Luke had never been much trouble, but without his older brother's leading influence, he was beginning to assert himself, and it had almost gone unnoticed until now. They were all growing up, and when they grew up, they grew away from her.

She snapped back, because she was so irritated with herself for such a thought. It made her sound like a clinging vine, and she never wanted to be that.

"Well, if Daddy said so, I suppose it must be right. Now, let's get back to the house. It's getting chilly, and I'm ready for my tea."

She had to listen to their whoops and cheers all the way back to New World, as they discussed how exciting it was going to be to go to Truro Fair. Emma hadn't been allowed to go before, because of the crush of people who flocked to its stalls and pleasures. Luke had been once, with Ran and Bradley, and hadn't cared for the noise and bustle last time, but he was older now, and seemingly bolder too.

At the time, Morwen had been glad of an excuse to stay away. She had conflicting memories of Truro Fair, and was never anxious to revive them. But it was obvious she wasn't going to avoid it this year, unless she wanted a riot in the house to rival that of a bunch of warring clayworkers.

"Will the bal maidens come down from the moors again, Mammie?" Luke said eagerly.

"Of course! It's always a big day for them, when they have a day away from work," she said, putting as much enthusiasm into her voice as she could.

For oh, couldn't she remember so well how the fine townsfolk of St Austell and Truro lined the streets to watch the unruly procession of these women, accompanied by their menfolk, all filled with excitement at spending a few dizzy hours among the hurdy-gurdy men with their little monkeys, and the horse traders, and the stalls selling sweetdrink and Cornish pasties and baked potatoes?

She remembered it all so well . . . how Jude Pascoe had tempted Celia with the sweetdrink and turned her willing head so easily. And didn't she remember how she'd seen him there so many years later, still the same, still as hated, and filling her heart with black thoughts of revenge?

"I think your clothes are lovely now, Mammie," Emma

said, just as if she knew how the pangs of so many mixed emotions were milling through her mother's head.

"Thank you, darling," she said swiftly, thankful that they had reached the road and were only a short distance from the house now. "Now you listen to me for a minute. I don't want any fuss at home tonight. You know your father's had important business dealings today, and he'll not want to be bombarded with questions about Truro Fair."

She mentally crossed her fingers as she spoke. She presumed Bradley Stokes and his colleagues would have been at the clayworks for much of the day, inspecting every part of it, and finding out every last detail for their products. They were keen to acquire the raw material for the manufacture of dyspepsia mixtures and the like, and Morwen could have told them of the benefit of Killigrew clay for that.

Times without number she had seen one or other of the clayworkers, her daddy included, scoop up a handful of the white slurry and drink it down to cure all manner of ills. It was cheaper than going to the doctor and she wondered if it would work any better miracles than some of the so-called magic elixirs that appeared at Truro Fair with the travelling quacks.

The thought flitted through her mind that she'd put more trust in old Zillah's potions than some of the dark, evil-looking mixtures they sold. And with that thought came another one. Maybe Zillah could have done something to help Killigrew Clay's fluctuating fortunes. Maybe she could have provided a love potion to make Ran love her again, the way he once did. Maybe she could have mixed up a potion to rid the county of Harriet Pendragon . . .

Horrified, Morwen brought her thoughts up short. Dark thoughts like that led to nothing but evil. Zillah always said Morwen had the sight, and her hands had been called healing hands by some . . . but she had no wish to dabble in any kind of witchcraft that would bring harm to others. Not even to one she thought of as her declared enemy . . .

"Mammie, why has your face gone all funny?" Luke demanded to know, as she apparently gazed into space. But what she was seeing was a kaleidoscope of past and present, where the future was still no more than a misty mirage. She blinked the images away and laughed at her son.

"I'm not sure I care to have my face called 'all funny', you imp!"

"But it is, Mammie," Emma said, with the relentlessness of childhood. "It looks like you're not here any more, and I want you to come back!"

There was a sudden note of real distress in the child's voice, and Morwen moved swiftly to her and gathered her up in her arms.

"I'm not going anywhere, sweetheart. We'll always be together," she said softly.

But she remembered her earlier morbid thoughts, when she had listed all the family members who had departed in one way and another, and a little chill, like a passing breeze, seemed to clutch at her heart.

She forgot all such presentiments when Ran came back to the house late that afternoon, his face more animated than she had seen in weeks. He caught at her hands and swung her around the drawing room where she and the children were drawing pictures together.

"It's good news! There's little doubt that Stokes and Keighley will place a large order with us, and I'm going to press them to sign with us for the next five years."

"That's wonderful, Ran. You must be so relieved!"

And glad, and happy, and looking so much more like the dynamic man she had loved and married. The children were caught up in the general delight in the room. They danced around their father, pushing their advantage and begging to be taken to Truro Fair, to which he laughingly agreed. His eyes met Morwen's over their chattering heads, and her heart leapt at the warmth she saw in his eyes.

That night, he returned to their room, and he made love to her with all the need of a man long starved of it. He told her passionately how much he needed her and had missed her. He held her and kissed her, and when it was over, he didn't rush to move away from her, and in the

315

moonlight from the window she watched his face, relaxed in sleep.

But she couldn't stop the glimmer of tears on her lashes, knowing that something of the old, sweet ritual of their lovemaking had been lacking. His need for her had been unquestioning, and she had gloried in it, but she knew he still hadn't quite forgiven her, because he never said he loved her.

Chapter Twenty-Five

The dinner party was a great success. The children had been introduced to the visitors before bedtime, and the adults were to enjoy the evening meal before the gentlemen retired to Ran's study for the business part of the evening.

Bradley Stokes and his colleagues were clearly enchanted by Cathy, and to Morwen's relief, Walter and Justin were at their most affable. They had all accepted how very important it was to their future that this meeting was concluded well. As for Ran, his confidence in the outcome put him at his most charming. They were all in sparkling mood that evening, and Morwen was proud of her family, almost forgetting herself in the process.

So it came as a shock when the man Stokes, large and red-faced, and correctly-spoken with only a slight northern accent, leaned across the dinner table to smile approvingly into her eyes.

"I've been looking forward very much to meeting you, Mrs Wainwright, since I've heard so much about your beauty. Even in the short time I've been here, I've learned that it's quite legendary in these parts. And if you don't think it an impertinence, I'd like to compliment your husband on his good fortune in being wed to such a beautiful lady."

"Aye, an' that goes for the rest of us an' all," said one of the other men, a thin, earnest-looking Yorkshireman. The other hardly spoke at all, and was seemingly dumbstruck by the occasion.

"It's very kind of you," Morwen murmured, somewhat flustered, for it had seemed that Cathy was getting most of the attention, and she hoped the girl wasn't upset by this accolade to herself.

When they were alone in the drawing room, and the men had departed to crowd into Ran's study, she tactfully mentioned it. Cathy shook her head at once.

"Of course I wasn't upset, Granny Morwen! And what Mr Stokes said was quite right. You *are* something of a legend—"

"My Lord, I'm not sure I like the sound of that," Morwen said with a laugh. "It makes me sound so ancient!"

"Oh no, you'll never be that," Cathy said softly. "Yours is the kind of beauty that lasts a lifetime. It comes from inside the soul as much as in the face. And now I'm embarrassing you, and myself too. I'm sorry. I don't normally say such silly things."

Morwen leaned towards her and kissed her cheek, immeasurably touched by the awkward words.

"It was the sweetest thing anyone has said to me for a long time," she said. "And I thank you for it, my love."

They spoke of other things then; of young Theo and of the Wainwright children, and how Bess was coping without Hal, and how grateful Morwen was to Cathy for seeing much of Bess, which she realized was the truth.

"We seem to have found a deal of communication between us," Cathy said. She hesitated. "I wondered if you resented it, or thought I was trying to take your place, and I would never be able to do that, nor try to—"

"I never thought that," Morwen said, ignoring the sliver of jealousy she had once felt.

She liked this lovely girl more and more, which rather amazed her, since she was the daughter of the two people she had always held at arms' length. And there was something else too, she thought, as they smiled into each others' eyes in perfect accord. Morwen was missing Primmy badly, and Charlotte was so involved with her own life now, and while this girl would never take Primmy's place in her heart, she was the next best thing. She was almost a daughter.

It was more than an hour later when the gentlemen returned, full of satisfaction and *bonhomie*, and the deals had been struck. Justin had brought the necessary papers with him,

318

in the hope of a signing there and then, and there had been no dissent on that. There was just one more signature to add to the rest, in the presence of so many witnesses, and that was Morwen's.

The rest of the evening was taken up with plans for the future of the china clay, and the assurance of an acknowledgement on all bottles of dyspepsia mixture and the like, that the Cornish clayworks of Killigrew Clay had been the only source of supply for the raw ingredients.

Stokes and Keighley had requested that they would send their own wagons and drivers south to transport the clay-blocks direct from the clayworks, which was another little point for rejoicing. They would be taking a substantial amount of the autumn despatches, and the rest would be loaded onto Ben Killigrew's rail trucks for transport to the port of St Austell and to the usual local outlets. The deal was struck for the next five years. The contract was signed, witnessed and sealed, and nothing that Harriet Pendragon could do now, would alter that.

But the lady didn't give up that easily. The next day Ran and Walter called a meeting of their pit captains and clayworkers, and announced the new business deals. All should be plain sailing, and wages would be assured. But then George Dodds, always the most outspoken and aggressive of the pit captains, spoke up loudly.

"Can we take it that there'll be bonuses at Christmas time and quarter-days then, boss?"

"I daresay we'll think about it—" Ran said with a smile, not realizing the seriousness of the question. He knew it the next minute, as a babble broke out among the clayworkers. And some of the bal maidens, never backward in coming forward, began screeching in support of their menfolk.

"You'd best put your money where your mouth is, Ran Wainwright! We'm good workers, and deserve good wages. And if we don't get it, then we'll tak' yon Pendragon woman's offer, and where will your autumn despatches be then!"

"What the devil are they talking about?" Walter said, as

319

the babble became a roar. George Dodds held up his hand
for silence, and the rioting died down to mutterings.

"Are you telling me the woman's been here again
recently?" Ran snapped out.

But, God almighty, he thought savagely, surely it wasn't
all going to go sour on them now? Neither he nor Walter
could be at all four pits at once, and it would be easy
enough for an unscrupulous person to flit from one to
another and undermine all the good work they'd done in
keeping Killigrew Clay afloat. And there was none more
unscrupulous than Harriet Pendragon, especially now that
they'd failed to extract her promise to leave well alone.
They would survive, and survive well, but only if they
had the workers to do so. And if the bitch was persuasive
enough to make them see what an advantage it would be
to work for her . . .

He could see a number of shuffling feet as he glowered
at them all, and it was one of the older bal maidens who
spoke up now. Some of these old harridans were tougher
than their men, Ran thought grimly.

"We ain't averse to listening to what's on offer, boss, but
that don't mean to say we'm agreein' to it. Not unless we'm
given more dues than we'd ever dreamed about, o' course.
So you'd best look to your coffers, Yankee-man, or you'll
still be losing half your workers."

She cackled like an old witchwoman, and those around
her yelled their agreement.

"What in hell's the matter with you all?" Ran yelled
back at them, when he could make himself heard. "If you
haven't been listening to a word I've been telling you about
the good times coming, then haven't you buggers ever heard
of loyalty?"

As George Dodds tried in vain to restrain the eruption
of noise at this, Walter cracked his whip sharply. He'd got
into the habit of carrying it with him, even when he wasn't
riding, and it had the required effect at once.

"Give us a chance, you scum-bags," he roared out, as
strong-voiced as Hal Tremayne ever was. "You've heard
what Ran Wainwright had to say, and no doubt the rumours are

already flying about that he's not selling Prosper Barrows. He's staying put, like we all are, if we've got any sense in our noddles. He's one of us, you buggers, and the sooner you believe it, the better."

"Oh ah. So what about the bonuses?" jeered one and another, until they were all taking up the chorus.

"You'll get whatever bloody bonuses you deserve," Ran shouted. "If we flourish, then you'll all benefit, and that's a promise. But I'll make you another promise, here and now. I'll see hell freeze over before I sell this business to the Pendragon woman, or anybody else. And even if every last rat leaves here at the bitch's beck and call, I'll work the bloody clay with my bare hands if I have to."

He listened to himself, startled by his own fervour. He spoke like a true clayer, he thought, in amazement, and whatever conviction there was in his voice, the rest of them were aware of it too. George Dodds cleared his throat.

"There's none that can say fairer than that, and I say we stand by the bosses. He may not be named Killigrew nor Tremayne, but by God, he's got the guts of a Cornishman."

"We've got them, Ran," Walter muttered by his side as the murmurs of agreement rippled through the crowd. "But that devil-woman nearly did for us again."

"That she did," he said grimly. He called for order again, and when he had commanded silence, he spoke briefly.

"I'll say one last thing to you. Show faith in us, and we'll show faith in you, and to prove it, there'll be a fat bonus for every man, woman and child who sees that the autumn despatches get away on time and in good order."

He could afford to say it now. Bradley Stokes had given him an advance banker's order on account of the clay-blocks they'd be sending north, and this gesture of generosity to the clayworkers wouldn't do his cause any harm at all. His thoughts were instantly proved right by the cheers and shouts all around him.

"Get to it, then!" he shouted again. "I'm not paying you buggers to stand around gossiping like fishwives! The first idle slackers I see will be out on their backsides."

It wasn't his normal way of speaking to them. It was

321

usually left to Walter and the pit captains to treat the workers to tongue pie, but by talking to them at their level he was gaining an unexpected amount of respect. And it felt good. In all the years he had been here, he realized he'd never felt one of them, as much as he did right now.

It was a feeling he wanted to share with Morwen. She'd be warmed and gladdened by the knowledge . . . but even as he thought it, he remembered the barrier between them, and he doubted now that he could express these private, innermost feelings to her. Not yet. If ever.

As he and Walter left the workers to their tasks, and George Dodds and the other pit captains assured them there'd be no slacking from now on, the two men decided to call it a day. They rode companionably across the moors to where it began to slope steeply towards the town of St Austell. And as always, the sight of the blue sea beyond the crowded houses of the town, never failed to stir Ran's imagination.

No wonder few people ever wanted to leave it, he thought. Only something momentous, and stronger than himself, would make a true Cornishman leave these lovely and mysterious shores . . . like a man's fear of being accused of a crime he didn't commit, that had driven Matt from these shores with his wicked companion all those years ago. And like Primmy's love for Cresswell . . .

"Are you listening to me, Ran?" he heard Walter say now, and his subconscious registered that the young man had been speaking to him for some minutes.

"I'm sorry, I was far away," he said quickly.

"So I noticed. But I was asking for your opinion. Me and Cathy have thought it over at some length, and we hesitantly approached Uncle Freddie about it before he left. Do you think it's a good idea?"

Ran looked at him blankly, having no idea what the devil he was talking about. At the look, Walter laughed, relaxed now the trouble at the clayworks was behind them.

"We're thinking of renting Hocking Hall – maybe even buying it if ever Freddie and Venetia want to sell, though I'm not sure we'd be able to afford it. But Freddie seemed quite keen to let us have it at a reasonable rent to keep it in the family, and Cathy loves it there. It's a grand place, as you know, but it still feels like a family home. Theo would love it too, and when we have more babbies there'd be plenty of space for them to grow."

He was more talkative than usual, and Ran could see that he was totally taken up with the idea. He felt a pang of envy for the light in Walter Tremayne's eyes as he spoke of his adored wife and son, and the family unit they represented. Oh yes, they were destined to have a brood of healthy babies, and they would continue the Tremayne dynasty in true fashion. As if Ran was blessed with Morwen's second sight at that moment, he'd stake his life on it.

"It's a great idea, Walter. So what's stopping you?"

"Well, nothing!" he said laughingly, as if wondering the same thing himself. "I'll go and see the land agent about it tomorrow before somebody else steps in."

Morwen thought it was a wonderful idea too. It always charmed her when the threads of continuity in the family interwove so effortlessly. She visualized young Theo growing up in that lovely old mansion, with its deer park and stables, and no doubt one day having a pony of his own and learning to ride with his father . . . At the thought, she was reminded of something else.

"Ran, you did say we'd take the children to Truro Fair next week, didn't you? It will break Luke's heart if we don't go. And he's desperate for you to buy him a pony as well."

"I haven't forgotten," he said with a grimace, since spending time at such rural events wasn't his favourite pastime. "And what does Emma want?"

"Emma never wants anything except to be happy," Morwen said. She blinked, not having meant to say any such thing. But when she thought about it, it was true. Her youngest daughter asked for nothing, and was just happy to be. She was a child of nature, Morwen thought, with a rush of love for her, and remembered it was the way she herself had been described when she was Emma's age. They were so

323

alike, and all she would wish for her daughter was happiness and love. They were the two most important things anyone could bestow on a child.

"She's bound to want something," Ran said practically, not following her winsome train of thought in the slightest. "Children always do."

"We'll see," Morwen murmured, wishing they could have been on the same wavelength at that moment. Wishing she could have said: *let's give her a star to call her own*, and known that Ran would have understood.

Brilliant sunshine greeted them on the day of Truro Fair. The air was hot and still, and heavy with the hum of bees and the scent of pollen and wild blossom. It was the perfect summer's day, and it would be made even hotter by the crush of folk streaming into the outskirts of the town from all directions for the fun and festivities.

For a moment, Morwen stood apart from herself, imagining herself and Celia Penry in the midst of them, young and alive, and so wildly excited to be among the motley collections of folk. And never realizing how they themselves, flocking down from the moors above St Austell town and taking no heed of the miles of walking to Truro, whether booted or barefoot, were considered the most motley of all.

"When are we going, Mammie?" Emma's impatient voice broke through her thoughts, and she smiled at her eager young daughter. So pretty today, in her fine lawn dress and matching bonnet, and her dainty shoes. And she gave her an unexpected hug, because Emma would never know those heady but uncertain days, and her future was so much more assured.

"Right now, my love," she said gaily, and had to quieten down Emma and Luke's boisterous shrieking as Ran announced that the carriage had arrived at the front of the house. She smothered a moment's guilt at the thought that they would arrive in such style, able to leave their carriage and horses stabled at Justin's chambers, while the clayfolk they'd be passing would all have sore feet by the time they arrived at Truro Fair. And yet they'd hardly notice them. She knew that too, and gave up the pointless feelings of guilt.

Cornwall had many fairs throughout the county, and Truro had its share. But the summer pleasure fair always followed the same pattern and had become a kind of ritual for folk from near and far. The smells, the noise, the sights and sounds of it all, were always the same. The streets of Truro were blocked by people and horses, and vehicles trying vainly to make a passageway. Almost before daybreak, the streets became miraculously lined with stalls, selling goods of every description, cheap toys and amusements, gingerbread and pasties, toffee apples on sticks, and sweetdrink, the heady potion that could turn a gullible young girl's head at the slightest bit of flattery from an ardent young man.

The bal maidens were out in force today, and the young clayers were clearly enjoying the delicious sense of freedom that the fair always evoked, in more ways than one. Morwen smiled as she saw one pretty girl's scarlet face as a clayworker whispered something in her ear. She couldn't hear the words, but she could imagine the daring remark. In the midst of such a crush, it would be no more than a sweet, innocent, flirtatious moment . . .

Ran was not so nostalgically taken. He was more concerned with fighting a way through the crowds for his children so that they wouldn't be trampled underfoot. But the children had their own ideas.

"Mammie, can we see the horses?" Luke shouted. "Daddy said he'd buy me a pony—"

"I said I might," Ran corrected. Emma jumped up and down, emphasizing her brother's words.

"You said you would, Daddy. I heard you," she said. "You've got to do it now, or God will punish you."

Ran sighed. Truth was, he couldn't remember what he'd said. Too many other things had clouded his mind these past weeks to give due consideration to Luke's demands. He felt Morwen's hand slide into his.

"It wouldn't hurt to look at the ponies, would it, dar?"

she said softly. "Leave it until the end of the day, and 'twill give Luke something to look forward to."

"All right," he agreed. "Providing you behave yourself, young man, we'll take a look at the pony sales later this afternoon."

"Can we watch the boxing then?" Luke said doggedly.

Morwen groaned. In the squares there would be wrestling arenas and bare-knuckle fighting, and she disliked all of it. But her brother Jack was coming towards them, in time to overhear Luke's remark. He was taking his own son to watch the wrestling, so Luke could go with them.

"Just as long as I don't have to watch," Morwen said. "Where's Annie today?"

"She's not feeling up to it, so I've left her at home. I'm glad Mammie didn't want to come. This crowd would be too much for her now."

Morwen nodded. She'd been only too thankful when Bess said she wouldn't go to the fair. Apart from the fact that she was becoming quite frail now, it would have stirred up too many memories of past times with Hal and all the family.

"Can we go and see the gypsies, Mammie?" Emma said, when Ran said he'd accompany Luke and the others. "Can we buy something from the stall? They say it brings you luck."

"Who says so?"

"Everybody! It's good luck if you buy something, and it's bad luck if you don't," she recited. "They say the gypsies can tell your fortune as well, just by looking at you, or reading your hand."

"Well, we don't need any fortune-telling," Morwen said swiftly. "But we'll buy a posy from a gypsy if it will keep you quiet."

And also because she herself believed in the old superstition only too well. Buy something for good luck, refuse it for bad.

In the distance she could see Albie and Rose Slater, and she waved to them as they became lost in the crowd. Justin was too important now to deign to come to the fair, and Walter was staying away with Cathy and the baby. It was somewhat different from the way all the young and lusty Tremaynes had once flocked down to the town, Morwen thought, but time changed everything.

She felt a shiver at the thought, and hugged Emma closer to her side as a flamboyant seller of quack medicines came swaggering through, shouting his skills and announcing that he had obtained a quantity of a miracle tonic to cure all ills at an amazing bargain price.

"That man must be very clever," Emma said in some awe.

Morwen smiled at her innocence. "So he must," she agreed, though not with the same meaning as her daughter.

"Mammie, can we go and see the horses now?" Emma said later, when they had tired of watching the tinselled ladies perform on a makeshift stage to the tune of a hurdy-gurdy.

"I didn't think you were all that interested—"

"Oh, please! I want to guess which pony Daddy will buy for Luke."

"Well, all right then. But I daresay the races are on now, so you be sure and stay close to me, Emma."

It was a feature of the Truro summer fair for the young bucks to hire the gypsy horses and race among themselves, with their followers putting wagers on the outcome, and also tipping the gypsies handsomely. Some said it was also to bribe the gypsies to give their rivals the slowest horses, but no one had ever proved as much.

And no one really cared. It was all part of the fun of the day, and if the gypsies went away with their pockets jingling, then the daredevil young men who raced their horses went away quite satisfied with showing off their prowess and the exhilaration of it all.

There was no sign of Ran and Luke just now, and Morwen guessed they would be absorbed in the fisticuffs of the boxing matches or the sweaty tortures of the wrestling arenas. She held Emma's hand tightly and took her to where the roped off short section of road alongside the river was habitually designated for the horse races. There was already a large crowd there, and the races had been going on at intervals all day. The scent of horse manure and heaving bodies was pungent in the air, but it all added to the excitement and atmosphere.

Morwen recognized a number of acquaintances in the onlookers, smiling and nodding to various ones, and then she glimpsed a scarlet silk gown and bonnet among the crowd. For a moment, she wondered at the vulgarity of such a garb for the daytime, but the wonder lasted no more than a moment before she knew instantly who the person would be. For so long now, she had been able to put the thought of Harriet Pendragon to the back of her mind, and her heart gave a sickening, uncomfortable lurch, just because she was breathing the same air as the woman she despised so much.

"We'll go along to where the horses line up," she said quickly to Emma. "There aren't quite so many people there, and you can see the winning line quite easily."

After a few minutes of jostling through the mêlée, she realized too late that it was also where Harriet was heading. But by then, Emma's excitement was at fever pitch at being close to the horses, and to the bright-waistcoated men with the swarthy skins and gleaming earrings, who controlled them.

"Stay close to me, Emma," she said again. "Some of these horses are really wild, and you must stay well back when the race begins."

She saw Harriet move near to one of the young men and hand him a scarlet ribbon. It was so blatant that Morwen couldn't even feel derision for her. Since her husband had died, there had been faint rumours of her attentions to young men, but nothing so pathetically obvious as this.

Maybe it was because she was preoccupied with the woman that she saw what no one else saw at that precise moment. Or maybe it was because her fey Cornish instinct told her when something bad was about to happen. Or maybe it was just the rolling whites of the horse's eyes that told her . . .

Whatever it was, she seemed to leap forward at the same

328

time as the horse reared on its back legs and struck out
viciously with its front hooves. If she hadn't done so, and
if she hadn't given Harriet Pendragon an almighty push
at the same time that sent her flying into the arms of
the nearest small crowd of male onlookers, Harriet would
certainly have been badly hurt.

Emma screamed as Morwen lost her balance and went
sprawling, but by then there had been a piercing warning
whistle, and the start of the race had been halted until the
trouble was sorted out.

"I'm all right, really I am," she almost snapped at the
many enquiries. "I'm not hurt, just winded, that's all."

Willing hands had hauled her to her feet, and she dusted
herself down, mortified by the indignity of falling to the
ground, and even more so, at being the unwitting saviour of
a woman she actively hated.

She glanced around. If Harriet Pendragon had the gall
to thank her, she wasn't sure how she would react. She
wanted no thanks – and she soon saw that she wasn't likely
to get any. Harriet was being escorted away by the solicitous
young man who had by now abandoned the horse race for
apparently more agreeable pleasures, while the crowd spoke
loudly and indignantly of the lady's ingratitude.

Morwen didn't care. All she wanted was to get away.
She was more shaken than she had thought, and when Ran
and Luke came looking for them, suggesting a sojourn to
the tea rooms, she escaped her admirers thankfully, and had
to listen to Emma's excited telling of the encounter.

Chapter Twenty-Six

Morwen had always been able to close her mind to the things she didn't want to think about. There had been a small report in *The Informer* about the incident at Truro summer fair, when Mrs Morwen Wainwright had so gallantly come to the rescue of Mrs Harriet Pendragon and saved her from a trampling under the vicious hooves of a gypsy horse. It had been a small report, recorded with verve, and Morwen had screwed up the paper and thrown it on the fire. There had been no word of thanks from the lady herself. If there had, Morwen would have scorned it.

Besides, a week or so later, she had far more distressing things on her mind than the whims of a woman clay boss. She had Emma to worry about. By now, all Luke's spare time was taken up in being taught to ride the small pony Ran had finally bought him. And Emma had fallen sick.

She had looked like a little waif for a few days, and with what appeared to be no more than a heavy cold. Then the angry red spots had begun to appear, covering the whole of her body so rapidly that she seemed to change overnight from pale to red. Morwen discovered it when she went to waken her one morning, and Emma's small puffy face had peered from the bedclothes, her eyes almost closed and complaining that the light was hurting them.

"Mammie—" the child croaked.

Morwen rushed to her bedside and put her hand on her brow. It was burning, and Emma seemed to have difficulty in breathing. Her throat was sore, and a harsh, dry cough punctuated her words. Thoughts of diptheria or chickenpox swept through Morwen's mind, but she dismissed them instantly. She knew what this was. She had seen it before, and she knew how deadly it could be.

Frantically, she rang the bell pull by the side of Emma's bed, and Mrs Enders came hurrying into the room.

"Call my husband straight away," she said. "And send Gillings for the doctor. Tell him it's urgent, and that I believe Emma has a severe attack of measles."

"Dear Lord," she heard the woman breathe, and Morwen snapped at her, not wanting to see fear on the housekeeper's face, in case it reflected her own. Measles could be a killer. It had killed so many in the past, including her brother Sam's wife, the mother of Walter, Albert and Primmy . . .

"Please don't waste time, Mrs Enders, and see that someone brings me a bowl of tepid water and some cloths to bathe Emma. See to it that Luke keeps away from the bedroom. And there are to be no visitors admitted to the house."

Luke was so sturdy that he may not even catch it, and in any case they had suspected a mild attack when he was younger. But Emma . . . Emma had always seemed so frail and ethereal, and Morwen had always been aware of that strange sixth sense that she was only loaned to them by the grace of God . . . she smothered a sob, for if ever she cursed the insight she was born with, it was now.

Dear Lord, she prayed frantically, *don't take this lovely child from me; from us. Don't tear our family apart still more . . .*

Ran came hurrying into the room, going straight to Emma's bedside and cradling her small hot hand in his.

"Have you had the measles, Ran?" Morwen said swiftly.

"I don't know. I think so," he said irritably. "What the hell does it matter—?"

"It matters, because it can so quickly become an epidemic. If you were to catch it you could take it to the clayworks—" she swallowed, not wanting to remember the small cottage on the moors where Dora had died, leaving three orphaned children. "Years ago the doctor said I was probably immune to it because of all the times I'd helped with other sick children."

She spoke jerkily, too concerned with her own child to rightly recall just who it was she had nursed and comforted with her healing hands. Some folk were just too frightened to do it, but Morwen Tremayne had never been afraid of anything. Until now.

"Then I'll not go to the clayworks," Ran retorted. "And why should you think I would, when Emma's so poorly? Do you think I have so little concern for my own daughter?"

She looked at him dumbly, not understanding how their mutual concern should be making them act like enemies. But fear did that, she thought. Fear enclosed each person in their own little self-contained world, just when they most needed to reach out and help one another.

One of the maids came into the room, her eyes like saucers, a bundle of towels and washing cloths over her arm. She set down the jug of tepid water on the washstand and gave a quick bob, backing towards the door.

"I ain't had the measles, Mrs Wainwright, Ma'am," she said nervously.

"It's all right, Clara, I shan't ask you to do anything more. But you musn't leave the house until the doctor says it's all right to do so, do you hear? Everyone must stay here until Emma's properly well again."

"Can't I even see me ma? She'll be that bothered—"

"We'll see that she's informed, but no one must go into the towns until we're clear of infection here," Morwen said clearly, feeling a mite of her own strength return at taking charge. "I know the doctor will say the same thing."

"Just so long as I don't have to do no nursin' then," Clara whimpered. "I ain't no good wi' sickness."

She fled from the room as Mrs Enders came back.

"The doctor's sent for, and will be here directly. Will the little maid be wanting breakfast?"

"I just want Mammie," croaked Emma.

Morwen knelt by her bedside, stroking the fevered brow. "I want you to drink lots of water to help cool you down. And I promise I won't leave you, sweetheart.

"Nor will I," Ran said gruffly. All this time he had watched and listened silently, as if he was the onlooker in a play, and Morwen knew instantly how helpless he must feel. While she had always been so adept at dealing with illness, he was not. She looked anxiously at her daughter now, but her words were for Ran.

"We'll both be here, my darling. We'll sit each side of your bed. When I've bathed you to make you more comfortable, I'll hold one of your hands and Daddy will hold the other, so that we're linked together."

As if obeying orders, Ran brought two chairs to the bedside, and Morwen squeezed out a soft cloth in the tepid water and began sponging down Emma's feverish body. She was horrified to discover how densely the spots covered her, and how pathetically small Emma looked. Without her usual bright spirit, she seemed to have shrunk overnight, and Morwen willed away the thought. When the comforting sponging was done, she lay a damp soothing cloth on Emma's forehead, and the mother held one of the child's hands, while the father held the other, as she had promised.

Ran seemed to have run out of words to say. Morwen ached for him, knowing he was suffering as much as herself, but at such a time he had always seemed emotionally constricted from putting feelings into words. They sat in virtual silence for an hour, broken only by the harsh dry coughs from the child in the bed, and then at last the doctor came, and confirmed what Morwen already knew. He was a new man that she hadn't seen before, but nonetheless thorough.

He gently peered inside Emma's mouth, where the telltale bluish-white raised spots on the inside of the mouth and cheeks, further confirmed the diagnosis. Emma looked at him dully for a few moments, and then simply closed her eyes and lay still. The doctor looked grave.

"You've obviously done all the right things, Ma'am," he said. "And I'd advise you to keep the curtains drawn across, so that the light doesn't hurt the child's eyes. There's little more I can suggest, except to keep her warm and comfortable until the fever breaks. And see that she has plenty of fluids."

It was like reliving her own thoughts. She knew all that; she had done all that; and she felt an impotent anger raging through her. Why couldn't someone invent some miracle cure, to rid them of this childhood scourge?

"I'll send a nurse—" the doctor said.

"There's no need. I'll nurse her myself."

"But you'll need your rest, dear lady, and this could go on for some days. You need professional help—" and his unspoken message was that they could obviously afford such luxuries. Morwen looked at him coldly, her eyes large and penetratingly blue.

"I shall nurse my daughter myself, Doctor Daker," she said again. "But I would be grateful if you would continue to visit her as often as necessary."

Their gazes locked, and the doctor's was the first to fall away. He spoke shortly, but this lady's reputation had already reached his ears, and he gave a small shrug.

"Naturally I shall call on you daily, Ma'am."

"Thank you."

Ran had been standing by while the doctor examined Emma, but now he prepared to see the man out.

"I intend to stay at home until my daughter recovers," he said shortly. Morwen knew at once that he didn't like the man, but it mattered little to her which doctor attended any of the family, as long as they got well again.

"A wise decision, my dear sir," she heard Doctor Daker gush, and she knew Ran wouldn't like that either. She turned to her daughter as Emma's cough started up again, and instantly forgot such trivial concerns.

"Will you bathe my face again, Mammie?" Emma whispered. "I'm so hot."

She did as she was bidden, and when Ran returned he informed them he'd sent word to all the family to keep away until the infection was over. It simply wasn't worth the risk, and it isolated them in a world of their own. New World.

By the end of the day, Morwen realized she had eaten nothing, and that hunger pangs were gnawing at her. She agreed to go downstairs for some food when Emma fell into a fitful sleep, and Ran continued the vigil. When Morwen came back, Emma was sleeping more deeply, and her throat filled at the anguished look on her husband's face. She returned swiftly to her chair on the far side of the bed, linking them all together again.

Although it was still light outside, the bedroom was darkened to soothe Emma's eyes, and the tension in the room was palpable. They spent the next hours in uncomfortable silence, hearing only the intermittent coughing and scratchy breathing, and it was long into the night before Ran finally found the words he'd been unable to say.

"If we lost her, I couldn't bear it," he said in a low, tight voice. "She's everything to me, just as you are, Morwen. You're one and the same in my heart. I find it hard to display my emotions in words, but it doesn't mean that I don't have any."

"I know, dar," Morwen said softly. "But we won't lose her. God wouldn't be so cruel."

She closed her eyes as she said it. But she had to believe it. If you lost faith and you lost hope, then you lost everything. She felt Ran's hand reach for hers across the bedcovers, and now the link was truly complete, she thought, an unbreakable circle.

"I love her so much, Morwen," Ran said. "And I love you too. Nothing ever changes that, and nothing ever will."

"I know. It's one of the wonderful things about love. If it's real, it's eternal."

And if you take that to mean that my love for Ben Killigrew is as constant as my love for you, then so be it. Love never changes, but there's room in my heart for more than one love. It was so simple a fact of life, she wondered why everyone couldn't see it.

Was she becoming light-headed?, she wondered. She had hardly moved from Emma's side for hours, and she was stiff and aching. Ran must be the same, and neither of them would do Emma any good if they collapsed from exhaustion.

"Ran, why don't you go and sleep for an hour or so, and then come back?" she said numbly.

"Only if you promise to do the same later. We'll take it in turns."

"We'll see," she said, knowing that she had no intention of doing any such thing. Her healing hands were needed. Almost feverishly, she repeated the words to herself like a litany.

The next day, and the one after that, Mrs Enders brought various food trays to the bedroom at intervals, though Emma still refused to eat, and Morwen only picked at the fare. Both she and Ran were red-eyed from lack of sleep now, and Morwen knew that being banished from the bedroom on several occasions hadn't helped Ran at all. She caught herself up with a little shock. She hadn't *banished* him . . . but something occurred later that day that made her examine her own feelings still more.

Mrs Enders came bustling into the room, all of a fluster, her face red and indignant.

"I told 'er you weren't seein' visitors, Mrs Wainwright, but she insisted and 'ouldn't take no for an answer. 'Tain't right, I told 'her, when the little maid's near to death's door, and the parents' feelings should be respected—"

"Who is it, Mrs Enders?" Morwen said sharply, shutting off the woman's invective.

There was a rustle of skirts behind her, and Morwen blinked in the shadowed room as Jane Askhew came towards the bed and knelt down beside Morwen's chair, taking her cold hand in hers.

"Morwen, darling, I had to come, to see if I could help. You look so exhausted—"

"You shouldn't be here," Morwen said jerkily. "You can't risk taking the infection back to Cathy and little Theo. You should have known better—"

The hand that held hers gripped it even tighter.

"Morwen, why will you never let anyone help you, when you've always helped others so much?" Jane said, her voice as soft as ever. "Have you forgotten all those years ago when Cathy was so ill with the measles, and I felt so useless? You were so wonderful, and I went to pieces. Let me help you in return, my dear, in whatever way I can."

Morwen looked at her dumbly. Yes, she had forgotten.

336

Because of her insane jealousy over Ben's fondness for Jane, the woman had been a thorn in her flesh all these years, and she had always been the one to hold off any attempt at friendship between them. Yet time and again, Jane had offered friendship, only to have it spurned.

"I'll fetch Mrs Askhew a chair," Ran said, and then, as if to make Morwen feel even more ashamed of her feelings, he said: "everyone needs friends at a time like this, even though my wife believes she can hold the entire world together by herself."

Morwen looked at him in astonishment.

"I do not!" she said. "What a stupid thing to say!"

"No, it isn't, honey. You shut everyone out, even me, and you give yourself the luxury of retreating into your own little world where no one can reach you."

Whatever she might have said to that was halted as they realized Emma had woken, and immediately it seemed terrible to Morwen that they'd been on the verge of a row while Emma was so ill.

"Mammie," the child said feebly. "Can Mrs Askhew stay with me? I like her, 'cos she smells like the rose garden."

Jane smiled gently, accepting the child's compliment without comment, and ignoring the adults. "I'll stay as long as you want me to, precious."

As Morwen went to fetch more cooling cloths to place on Emma's brow, she saw Jane take her place near her daughter, and fought to smother the pang it gave her. It was like an unwelcome little cameo picture. Jane, and Ran, sitting opposite one another, with *her* daughter between them . . . dear God, she thought furiously, would this jealous madness never leave her? But at least it told her she was still alive, still capable of loving and wanting her husband . . .

Emma was rambling a little now, asking for a story, and Jane began telling her about a ball she had attended, at which there were lords and ladies and even royalty, and Emma absorbed it all through those poor sore eyes. And memory instantly took Morwen back to when the tiny Cathy Askhew had rambled in her measles delirium, asking for stories about the clayworkers' boots.

Morwen hadn't thought of the incident for years, but she remembered now how Cathy had adored hearing how the clayworkers' long boots were especially made for each man by the local cobbler, so that each man could be identified by his own footprint. She had even made up a tale about the fearless clayworker who had led a group of lost children to safety over the mist laden moors. Cathy had been calmed and charmed by the tale, just as Emma was now, at hearing about lords and ladies and royalty.

Morwen swallowed, and moved to the bed, putting her hand on Jane's shoulder as she saw Emma's eyes droop.

"Thank you," she said. "You're a true friend, Jane."

"So take a friend's advice, both of you, and take a rest together," Jane said quietly. "I'll sit with Emma, and if you'll permit me, I'll be happy to stay for a night or two."

Her eyes didn't falter as she looked at Morwen for her approval, and finally it came. For the first time ever, Morwen leaned forward and kissed Jane Askhew's soft cheek.

"I'd be honoured to have you stay," she said, and she moved quickly away before she could burst into unrelenting tears. "I'll let Mrs Enders know – but you'll be sure to call me the minute you think I'm needed?"

"Of course."

Ran assisted her out of the room. Part of her wanted desperately to stay, but she knew how exhausted she was, and by now she'd lost count of the days and nights she'd sat up with Emma. Even though Doctor Daker was quite satisfied with her progress, Morwen still couldn't rid herself of the fear that was like a sickness inside herself.

Was this a punishment for all the sins of the past? The ultimate wickedness in what she and Celia Penry had done in ridding Celia of an unborn child? The jealousy and hatred she had felt for Miss "finelady" Jane Askhew over the years, and who shamed her now by showing such generosity of spirit towards her? The passion she and Ran had shared while her husband Ben was under the threat of death? The love they had acknowledged, even while Ben was still alive, and couldn't ignore . . .

Had these sins come back to haunt her by threatening to

338

take another, sweet daughter from her, the way they had taken Primmy to the other side of the world, and removed Charlotte from her care . . . ? Her imagination had taken her down this road before. But with Emma, this was the cruellest way.

She tried to smother her rising panic. She needed sleep, but she doubted that sleep would come, even when she was held in Ran's arms. But he couldn't understand how she felt. How could he understand, when she couldn't tell him . . .?

As she tossed and turned, her body felt so fiery that she even wondered if she herself was succumbing to the measles . . . in her mood of self-condemnation, she knew it would be a just punishment . . .

She suddenly realized that Ran's shoulders were shaking, and, aware that she was awake, that he was speaking in muffled tones. She couldn't hear him at first, but then she felt a great and extraordinary calmness of spirit as she realized what he was saying.

"Why won't you let me into your thoughts, Morwen? Why must you always try to bear everything alone, always shutting me out, when Emma's as much mine as she is yours? I grieve for her too. Do you think a woman has the monopoloy on grief?"

He had said something of the kind before, but never with such passion, such pain. And it didn't lessen him in her eyes to know that he was weeping. She held him close, kissing his face where the tears were damp on his cheeks.

"I know she does not, my darling, and I know I've been selfish," she whispered. "Will you forgive me?"

"Don't I always?" he said roughly. "But you always seem so strong, when sometimes I just want you to lean on me—"

"Oh, my love, I'm not strong. I'm just a woman who foolishly wants the whole world to be always sunny, when I know it can't be. And I'm filled with so much fear now—"

His arms tightened around her slender body. "We have to have faith that Emma will get well, my love."

"Then – you don't think it's a punishment?"

He held her away from him for a few seconds, not understanding. And she knew it had to be told: all the foolish fears and superstitions that made her what she was, and tormented her so. When she had finished, Ran didn't scoff at her fears, but spoke quietly and logically, as only he could. And if she didn't feel cleansed, at least she felt as though all the shadows were lifting at last. She felt closer to him than she had in many months, and at last she slept.

She awoke with a start, to find someone tapping her shoulder, and her thoughts leapt to Emma at once. But it was to find Ran, already fully dressed, smiling down at her.

"She's come through it," he said. "The fever's down and her eyes are brighter, and she's asking for food."

"Oh, thank God," Morwen said weakly.

"I think you should thank Jane as well," he said. "She's been awake half the night, sponging Emma down, and telling her stories. She's been a good friend, Morwen."

His eyes challenged her, but there was no need. Donning a dressing gown, Morwen went quickly into her daughter's room, to see the healthier looking child and the exhausted woman. She squeezed Jane's hand tightly.

"Thank you," she said. "I won't forget your kindness."

Jane nodded tiredly. "I was glad to do it. We've travelled a long way together, Morwen, however distant we may have seemed at times. But now the corner's turned, and I must go home."

"Won't you at least stay and have some breakfast?" Morwen said, but Jane declined. Then Emma spoke.

"Will you come and see me again, Mrs Askhew?"

Jane looked at Morwen, who responded quickly.

"Mrs Askhew is welcome here any time," she said.

Once the doctor had pronounced Emma well and free of infection, one by one the family came to visit, and she was petted and spoiled with so many presents that Luke howled that he wished he'd had the measles too.

His Grandma Bess told him not to be so wicked, and

340

Morwen knew she'd be remembering Sam's wife, but it was said with good humour, knowing the boy hadn't meant anything by the remark. And Ran reminded him that it was all due to Emma being so ill and their normal lessons being suspended, that he'd had all the extra tuition on his pony, so that he already had the makings of a fine young rider.

But by now Morwen could see that Ran was becoming restless at being at home all this time, and she told him it was time he went up to Killigrew Clay. The autumn orders would soon be ready for despatch, some to go to the port, and more stacked in readiness for the all-important long journey north by wagonload.

It seemed odd to think that road wagons were to be used for transporting the clay blocks again, when Ben Killigrew had been so proud of his little railway that took them from the works to the port. And yet it was also right. The northern contact had been Ran's achievement. Morwen felt her heart gladden as she saw his face lighten. He was as much a part of the clay now as she ever was, and how could she ever have doubted that?

She put her arms around him and kissed him, and as he breathed in her sensual, musky scent, it was as if her inborn optimism was transmitted to him.

"I need to talk with Walter and the pit captains, anyway," he said. "I want nothing to go wrong at this stage."

"Nothing will," she said softly, and he smiled at her.

"Is that more Cornish intuition?"

She shook her head. "Just faith," she said.

It was good to see his enthusiasm return, Morwen thought thankfully, but he stayed to entertain Emma for the rest of that day after all, deciding to return to the clayworks the following morning. He was up and away early, even before Charlotte came bursting into the house. Like the rest of the family, she had quite rightly stayed away until all risk of infection was passed, since she had her own small charges to care for at the Pollard mansion. But she was eager now to see her small sister, and had brought her toys and sweets. But first of all she wanted to see Morwen.

341

It was an unusually early hour for her to have come all this way, and Morwen felt a brief anxiety until she saw the glow on her daughter's face as she rushed into the drawing room where Morwen was writing letters to the more distant family members, assuring them Emma was well on the way to recovery now, and that all danger was over. It would be a tussle to persuade her to stay in bed until later in the day, but the doctor had insisted on it until she recovered her strength. And now here was Charlotte, her eyes glowing, and her supple young body practically quivering with excitement.

"Have you seen the newspaper, Mammie? Oh, please say you haven't! I wanted so much to be the first to show it to you!" she said, almost squealing in her excitement.

"Of course I haven't! I've hardly had time for such frivolous things lately!"

Nor to care about whatever scandal it might be that Tom Askhew was delving into now, she thought. But Charlotte gave a triumphant whoop as she drew out a copy of *The Informer* from her bag. It was folded so that one of the inner pages was prominent, and a large item had been heavily ringed around.

"Read it, Mammie," Charlotte said, almost choking with excitement now. "I know how much this will mean to you, and if I have to read it aloud myself I shall simply burst out crying, I know I will!"

Mystified and urged on by her agitation, Morwen quickly read the several paragraphs inside the ringed item. And then she read them again, trying not to let the words dance crazily in front of her, or to wonder if it were really true, or if she was dreaming. And maybe Charlotte couldn't read it aloud, but she had to do so, just to make herself believe it.

"To all whom it may concern," she read, "Notice is hereby given that Harriet Pendragon refutes any and all interest in the property and clayworks known as Killigrew Clay, now and in all perpetuity. This declaration is legally binding, and has been made and witnessed before Messrs Showering and Ball, solicitors of Bodmin, and may be inspected by any interested parties. The said Harriet Pendragon is currently putting her property on the market, together with all the Pendragon clay holdings, such sale which is also in the hands of Messrs Showering and Ball. All communications shall be made through them, as Mrs Pendragon will be removing to London immediately, and is unavailable for comment."

Morwen felt her eyes prickle with shock and relief. They were rid of that woman for good, and with no logical reason that she could think of. Except that there was a certain familiarity in the wording of the announcement, ". . . refuting all interest in Killigrew Clay in all perpetuity . . ." surely it was the way Ran had worded it . . .

She felt Charlotte shaking her, impatient to get a reaction from this apparently stunned silence.

"Aren't you going to say anything, Mammie? It's all because of you, of course. It's because of what you did at Truro Fair, and this is her way of thanking you."

The girl's face came into focus. "Do you think so?"

"Of course! Everybody's saying so."

"Everybody doesn't know yet! Ran doesn't know!"

She suddenly came alive again. "Charlotte, can you stay a while with Luke and Emma? I have to tell Ran myself. I have to go to Killigrew Clay—"

"Of course. But I've something else to ask you, Mammie. Vincent wants to come here tonight to speak with him. Will it be all right, do you think?"

She looked so anxious, just as if Morwen couldn't guess exactly what it was that Vincent wanted to ask. And it would be more than all right. It would be perfect. A wedding in the family was just what was needed to restore all their spirits. Life went on . . .

But there would be time enough for that later. Once the children were settled with Charlotte, and Gillings had saddled her horse, she rode like the wind with the precious newspaper item. Just as Charlotte had been bursting to show it to her, so she was bursting to show it to Ran, and she prayed that no one else had got there first. It was unlikely. Walter was in the habit of buying a copy on the way home in the evenings, and Ran didn't always bother with the scandal rag.

She rode the horse hard, and both of them were breathing fast by the time they had slithered over the grassy slopes of the moors, fragrant and beautiful with its carpet of late summer foliage now. The white clay tips were ahead of her. They glinted in the sunlight as brightly as if they were diamond studded, symbols of all that the Killigrews had been, and all that they were, whether or not they had been born Tremaynes or Wainwrights.

Morwen felt a sudden choking in her throat, because their fortunes had never been stable, but for now, at least, they were safe. And she couldn't wait to tell Ran as much.

She saw him before he saw her, tall and virile, and so very dear to her, striding towards the linhays where the clay blocks were drying in the sun, ready for despatching. She called his name, but her voice was choked with emotion and carried away by the summer breeze. He couldn't have heard it from that distance, but he turned instinctively.

She saw his face change, and he dropped the sheaf of papers he was carrying and ran towards her as she slid from her horse. He grasped her hands, and spoke swiftly.

"What is it, dar? Is it Emma? Dear God, don't tell me she's worse—"

"It's not Emma," Morwen stuttered, speechless for once, now that the moment was here. "She's improving by the minute. I've got some good news to tell you—"

He grabbed her around the waist and pulled her towards Walter's little hut. Walter was nowhere around, but in any case, Morwen didn't want him now. This was too stupendous a moment, too private, too intimate, to be shared, even with her beloved Walter. Inside the hut, Ran kicked the door shut behind them, and she blinked to accustom her eyes to the dimness after the brightness outside.

"So tell me your news," he demanded. "After giving me that little scare, it had better be really good!"

He was masculine and arrogant in his relief, but she didn't care. Nothing mattered but that they were free of all worries. But, just like Charlotte, she was unable to speak, and she held out the newspaper mutely, letting him read it for himself. Joy almost exploded out of him when he'd finished, and he swept his wife into his arms.

"This is all your doing, honey. Your instincts did this, in pushing that woman out of harm's way."

"Charlotte said as much, but my instincts are not always to be trusted," she said shakily. "They almost scared me to death when I thought fate was going to rob us of all our daughters."

"Sometimes you can be a crazy woman," he said, with a small indulgent shake of his head.

But his arms were around her now, and love flowed between them like a tide. His hands were in her tangled hair, and to him she was as spectacularly beautiful as the day he'd first seen her, so many years ago, when she belonged to someone else, and he'd wanted her so much.

"I'm sorry—" she mumbled.

"It doesn't matter now," he said. "Nothing matters except that we have each other."

She leaned into him, drawing on his strength, and so glad to relinquish her own.

"Oh Ran, I do love you, and no matter where else my wild imagination takes me, I can't imagine life without you."

His kiss was gentle on her lips, but with all the passion she knew was hers for the taking.

"You don't have to," he said softly.